T5-AGM-611

Elisabeth Shackelford

www.DontSitHere.com

First Edition, Houselights Publishing, December 2012

Published in the United States by Houselights Publishing, Ltd.
Originally contracted for publication by EP Dutton/Viking Penguin, New York, 1989.
Chapters from this work were also published in slightly different form in
The Greensboro Review.
Other chapters have been accepted by
Raritan, Confrontation, and *Boulevard.*

Library of Congress Cataloging-in-Publication Data
Shackelford, Elisabeth

Don't Sit Here / Novel by Elisabeth Shackelford - Houselights Publishing, Ltd.
cm – Houselights Publishing

ISBN 978-0-615-70146-2

Designers for book cover, script cover, collateral material:
Harry Hartofelis of Harry Hartofelis Graphics and April LaJune of April LaJune Designs,
And
BA Albert and Alissa Davis of Big Table Agency, Cyndi Horn-Petryakov of Night Owl Design, and Joyce Kelly of Joyce Kelly Designs

Front-of-jacket photograph: *Snow-Covered Park Bench in Central Park*
by Lou99, Central Park, New York City
Interior photograph: *Snow-Lovers* by Alan Chaniewski
Author's photo by Foster Soules, 2012, Atlanta

Manufactured in the United States of America
I

This book is dedicated to my sons,
Matthew and Fletcher "Shack"
With the two of you, I hit the Best-Sons-On-Earth lotto.

And to
Elaine, Foster, Katrina
You are my sisters. And you are smart and brave and good and steadfast and wise and true.
And I am blessed.

And to
FCJ, and SDC, and FRS, and JSY, and MDB, and ALF, and EEA, and WDA, and GAH
The proud, hard-working Godmothers and Godfathers of this book.

And to
Gwen Cleghorn, and Rawson, and my beloved Dad
Whose encouragement and love made all the difference.

And to
AQ and JBM
Mentors like you come around only once or twice in a lifetime.

Be patient toward all that is unsolved in your heart,
and try to love the *questions* themselves...

— Rainer Maria Rilke

DON'T SIT HERE

PART I

Here and Now

CHAPTER 1

Here and Now
Pope's Crossing, Connecticut

The other day, the wooden curtain bracket finally came unmoored from the stucco wall where it hung, just barely, by its bottom anchor screw. To fix it, Francis Taylor simply took down a long dowel floating atop another window and used it to prop up the bracket from underneath. This was as good as it was going to get. Drilling, anchors, screws—forget it. Maybe Scotch tape. Or possibly duct tape lopped over the entire bracket and pressed against the wall.

From my vantage point in the kitchen, I'd watched him go about his business in the usual manner. He was always deadly serious when he was jerry-building. I'd leaned laughing over the overfull plastic garbage bag that I was trying to twist-tie so that I could drag it outside. "Well, I never should have sat there, Francis Taylor. Should have just kept walking," I declared for the millionth time. I turned to look up at his rig.

"Sat where, Susanna?"

"I never should have, Francis Taylor. Knew better than to talk to a stranger."

"Sat where, Susanna? *Here*?" He pointed downward towards his still-glorious marital tackle, his blue eyes aglow. Oh, how he loved our little joke.

"Could have spared myself these jerry-builds; they defy description, Francis Taylor." A goofy smile pulled across my face as I glanced up again at his latest and tried to suppress my mirth. I shook my head, "Could have spared myself, Francis Taylor!" What always made these attempts funny was that he genuinely thought he'd fixed the problem.

The garbage bag was too heavy. Somebody had thrown last Sunday's *Times* in it. I began to drag the bag out by both hands. I was going to need his help, but I refrained from asking, knowing that he'd do something idiotic like hoist it on top of his head and walk out heroically, only to find himself wedged in the doorway. Still, by dragging it, I knew the bag would probably break before I could make it to the door; the kitchen floor was bricked, uneven. "Can you help me?" I asked, despite myself, standing up straight and rubbing my hands along my hips.

"Never should have sat where, Susanna?" He moved forward to help me. "Where?" His lips tightened; he was trying to fight a smile. "*Here*?" Oh, he loved it. Every time the joke came up, he milked it for all it had left in it, always with eyes, moonstruck. As I leaned over the bag, he gave me a little spank—we had met by complete happenstance over forty-five years ago as a pair of strangers sitting on a park bench in Central Park.

Now, today, from way up in the attic where I rummaged, I could hear the sounds of Francis Taylor home. Suddenly and unexpectedly. The familiar sounds of him: jars opening, their sides being clinked by a spoon, plates moving, cabinet doors squeaking open and banging shut. As he made his snack, he hummed some music that I guessed was Strauss. Hearing him, I drew back. Wasn't like him to come home from Manhattan at three o'clock in the afternoon. No more than it was like me to be way up here in the attic for no specific reason. But there he was, I imagined, cutting fruit, opening various *Bries* and *Camemberts,* peeling carrots, pouring Heineken into a chilled mug. And here I was, Susanna, hiding with the guilt of a little girl who'd been told that her mother's out-of-season clothes were off-limits but had gone to try them on anyway. As if Francis Taylor from three stories below could hear the quiet creak of the smooth, worn floor planks, I moved on tiptoe toward an old, forgotten armchair and sat down in it and listened toward the stairs.

I'm sixty-three now, bird-sized, Southern, I've never lost my accent. I'd climbed up to our hot attic on a whim and had put on not my mother's clothes, but my own daughter's bathing suit. It was the last suit Jenny had worn. Twenty-five years have passed, but it seems more like a thousand slow decades. Today, for no reason at all, the memories came up, clean and sharp as arms thrashing in water.

I could hear one of our dogs. The collar chinked in a kind of syncopation to the racket of four paws chasing themselves upstairs. I knew it wasn't the Irish Setters, Bansen & Evers as we came to call them. The pair acted like they were an exclusive law firm. They were so sloppily and lackadaisically into each other—OK, so totally in love with each other (they could not keep their paws off of each other)—that it is doubtful they would break away to come all the way up to our attic where I was, even if they heard the thump! of me dropping dead.

Naw. The sound had to be the chink of Mops coming up the stairs. Four paws, off-rhythm, determined to gain purchase. She was, like, one-million-years old. It had to be her, all right. She had entered the Age of Worry. My age. Your age. Anyway, she was my age in dog years. Jenny's age in reality.

Francis Taylor, surely, would be following close behind, perhaps to get his reading glasses.

Nobody reads *The New York Times* as hungrily as he does. Everything important, everything to die for but us. Everyone was always attracted to his lively mind and eyes, bright buttons! Through his eyes, you could catch glimpses of his thoughts every now and again; they appeared like the tail end of a bright yellow piece of yarn, a tease that you had a delightful urge to pick up and follow all the way to its end. But that was all right. Nobody ever did get very far. He didn't mind telling you that no one would get what he had on his mind; him with his whole secret garden inside, blooming. His. Belonged to nobody but him.

Francis Taylor was an investment banker from Wall Street, but for many years his true love has been his work towards protecting our natural earth, especially its water and air. He's survived controversy, and flak, and the envy of people and large corporations lobbying in the other direction. He never told me or complained when someone crushed his vision, save through small domestic incidents: one of the kids spilling a Coca-Cola in the car, the dogs getting into the trash.

Once after a tantrum taken out on me, for having introduced myself with no bra on to one of his Clean Air Committee colleagues, I noticed a hand-written envelope in his briefcase. In it was a letter that read, "The best thing you could do for the environment would be to get rid of yourself."

Why he carried letters like that I just couldn't understand.

"Dog of a day?" I'd asked him later on.

"No, Susanna. Now leave me alone. I'm reading."

"Nobody mean?"

And taking his glasses off, "No, Susanna. Nobody's been mean to me. You're so sentimental. Now grow up."

No. None of your business. Grow up. I knew by now those words meant too painful to talk about.

Still, that man raised my feathers.

Then, as now, Francis Taylor wore gold-rimmed glasses, loose khaki pants, clean-smelling cotton shirts, and suspenders as you would imagine on a senior blue-blooded Wall Streeter, save that his were the very same ones I'd pulled against to get his attention when he'd been a young man—he'd always snapped them at me (and all those others, I'd reasoned, but mostly me). He'd been green and hot-blooded as a young colt then, thinking the whole wide world was in his hands, lean and long-legged, eyes darting everywhere, and pulling with everything he had against the bit.

"Delicious hands," I'd whisper to him after the lights went out, kissing them gently. "Better to belong to a musician, these hands. But slipping down everybody else's panties, Francis Taylor. For a long time I knew it."

"That's because you don't wear any, Susanna," he'd say back to me.

"Might not necessarily mean the other side of the tracks, boy. I like the wind running between my legs. I like it."

"No subtlety, Susanna, none."

"No less'n you."

He had been lucky enough to have been born with lips like strawberries, and I could never get enough of them. Sometimes he'd kiss me passionately, other times like he had more important things on his mind.

"Here, darling, hang your hat." Kissing him. "Here darling, darling, hang your hat, hat, hat." More kisses for him, and he wanting me out of his face. I have to admit that I'd emphasized hat like that because long before we'd married, he had begun to rue his patchy, prematurely graying hair as a sign that he had already used up his chips. He took balding terribly seriously, almost like a robbery! I'd always thought that thinning was the key to his having negotiated down to marrying me—seems years I'd waited.

Once his hat and seersucker jacket got hung up, he'd stretch out half-naked on the bed taking a catnap with a pair of keys in his hand like Einstein used to do.

"Do me," I'd say, kicking the sheets back.

Claiming exhaustion, he'd roll over flat on his back, both arms open to the ceiling. "Come on, Susanna. There were no seats left on the New Haven line, and in this heat. Come on, Susanna, I haven't even been home ten minutes."

Before the keys ever fell out of his hand, I'd have already climbed on top of him. He'd get mad about my books toppling over the side of the bed, then I'd cup him as though holding a basket of fruits, "Lemme at that little varmint."

In five minutes flat he'd of come and gone. The taste of his sweetness, I loved.

I crouched lower now, and as I did so, the popping of my knees made me laugh at myself. I rubbed the swollen but faint purple veins that now rayed out around the side of my kneecap and studied absent-mindedly the light from the far window that filtered across me and exposed years of lint piled beside the legs of a chair. The floor, too, was covered with a film of dust.

"Oh, I know him," I muttered out loud, "Tucking that *New York Times* under his arm. Straight to his favorite chair! One arm holding the plate, the other his beverage. Doesn't even know I'm up here." And holding my breath, as if I needed to, I slowly placed one knee on the floor, then the other, and on all fours, I leaned hard on my right side knowing, even after all these years, that my left knee's too fragile to take the pressure of my weight. I bent an elbow, cocked an ear toward the ground. My daughter's bathing suit rode up my behind, and its shoulder strap fell down my arm. I could see my shadow: my thick, short-cropped hair topped it like a mohawk. If it wasn't confidence I could thank Mamma for passing on to me, I could appreciate having been raised in the kind of good country living that preserves thick hair and good teeth. Even my skin, despite the wrinkles Francis Taylor helped carve, has survived my teenage and married years of mixing so intensely with city life. I'm guessing it's because of the twelve young years in which my pores were blessed with the moist, fresh air of Mississippi.

Except for Mop's thick tail—thump, thump, thump!—the world was silent. I stayed with an ear against the floor like that for the longest while, wondering what on earth my husband was doing home. It crossed my mind that something must have happened at work; maybe he'd over-stepped his bounds and had gotten fired. I could just see it now, the chest puffed superciliously, words too big for his own good, and a tone of voice that would get anybody thrown out.

I hooked a finger underneath the elastic and pulled Jenny's suit down. Now water was turned on in the kitchen, and I heard it running through the attic pipes right over my head. Then I heard the water turned off, and then I heard the succinct noise of our kitchen door slamming.

I got up, hobbled across the attic floor, and made my way back to the dormer window. I never knew when my knee would buckle on me. My beat-up old leg has helped me anyway. For years I've moved as though pushing a box awkwardly with my knees, and as people watch me, they pay attention. Like their own legs feel something mine don't!

When I reached the window, I leaned with bent elbows against the sill and took a deep breath, watching. He walked into the sunlight, his white cotton shirt, untucked, flapped behind him like a little boy's, and his old garden pants may as well have never been washed; green grass stains held stubbornly to his backside. Stepping into his garden, he looked no bigger than a gnome from way up here in the attic. The sun caught coarse, slate tufts of his hair that he *now* bore like a family crest.

"Oh, no!" I said aloud through the windowpane. He'd stepped across four browning rows of squash and bent towards my arugula. "No, don't you dare pick those, they'll wilt before sundown. They're for the dinner tonight." He knows good and well that I love to show off my fresh arugula.

"And after all these years," I muttered bitterly to myself, "he still has the nerve, despite his own gall, to keep an eye on my table manners. Telling me to sit like a good little wallflower and behave myself. Always talking about war with the others. Men. Staking the territory, proving themselves." They uniformly complimented my cooking and fine wines, but to me, my table had always been best in the kitchen, with just us: Francis Taylor, Taylor, Parish, Jenny, and me.

I rapped sharply on the windowpane and he looked up.

"Don't pick my Buff Beauty roses! My Blackberry lily! I grew them for *you*."

He shook his head and clipped off one, two, three, looked like he'd taken at least a half dozen, as though they were common and weedy as Queen Anne's lace. Then he walked quietly down the old back drive, not looking back or up at me again. From the position of the back of his head, I reckoned his eyes were fixed as though going somewhere important. He held the flowers under his arm as a boy on a paper route holds his newspapers. "As if the heads won't break off any minute," I muttered to myself and again knocked a knuckle to the window. "What, are, you, doing, home, anyhow, Francis Taylor? Thought you were a workaholic."

As though sensing my jabber, he found a way to irk me by taking the fork leading to his relatives, his back straight, the flowers still bobbing under his arm. His family always did live so nearby. Like a jury.

I held back, watching where he was going. Not even my shadow came across the window. My breath clouded the pane, and when I moved, the bathing suit's black strap fell over my shoulder. I didn't care, preferring to be naked. "What are you doing?" I whispered. I could see him through the bright phlox.

And when I saw him glance back at the house, pivot gracefully on the ball of a foot, and suddenly walk back up towards our garden, I supposed he was trying to trick me. Then he did something that really threw me. He took a left onto the path leading to the duck ponds. This path he walked in fast, long strides; the flowers he suddenly cradled like a baby. It was the path leading to St. James', his family's private cemetery. We'd buried Jenny there, right beside other members of the Vanheusen and Dewitt families.

"Old lady," I murmured, and all that I had welled inside of me. "Don't cry now, old girl, not after all this and all these years." But the very effort to hold back snapped open the memories, and tears streamed down the parched surface of my cheeks. "Don't." I reached my tongue to the warm salt washing over the corner of my lip, "Don't start now. Just because he never did let you in." Still, I leaned my head to the window and shut my eyes against the sight of him, against all that had happened between us.

Why now? Why now after so many years? Him and me, thinking the same thing and on this same day.

Because we were linked all along, I had always defended to the relatives. *We were linked! Me and him.*

You can't do that, Susanna! he'd say. *You can't use bad grammar and sassy language and that drawl around them and you know it. Showing off, Susanna, bragging, like you've got something over them.*

I do, I'd answered, smiling. *Oh, I do.*

You go on, Susanna.

You. (I liked to stick my tongue out at him, mash my thumbs into my ears and wag the fingers at him. The trick was he'd encourage me. He'd try to act mad and upset, but a look of sheepish amusement would bleed through, like maybe he'd wanted to wink or give a little clap, and right then I would see my moment. I'd go overboard—pull his pants down and run laughing down the pavement.)

You live for upping the ante, he'd say. His voice could cut me in two.

With two fingers, I wiped dust from the window ledge.

"It's too late now," I thought. "We're both too old, and all these years, he never has cared much anyhow." My hand opened slowly like a warm, wet cloth for my face, and, sighing lonesomely, I ambled my way back through the dark attic.

How long now had our bitterness poisoned us? On the morning Jenny drowned in Kingfisher Pond, I hit him hard with a rowing paddle and called him a feckless, yellow-backed little man, as I screamed, *Get her! Rescue her!* while he braced himself in the rowboat sitting with hands gripped to the gunwales in mute and frozen panic.

And afterwards: *Susanna, you who never respected the laws of physics, knew nothing of joists, levels, rivets.*

Damn it, I made it the best I could.

I told you not to build that wooden tower, and when you did it anyway, I warned you. It was unsafe, Susanna. The tower was unsafe.

But she needed to practice her diving and you weren't home, I'd screamed, watching him pull his hat down to cover his ears.

But I was behind her all the while, Susanna, and she knew it. His voice. Not breathing hard enough to blow out a candle.

Behind her! You were right there on the pond and she drowned! When the wooden diving board broke off and came down fast behind her, he froze. Too late, too late to save her.

Susanna! Go away from here. You have been bad for us.

No more than you, Francis. I assure you.

You couldn't be trusted anyway, Susanna, he had said, walking out of the room.

The harsh words I never did get over.

But our love and cruelty, which he came to call our dance of methane and oil, had begun long before this even. He had always said we would never make it because we were so opposite, destined to move forever against dialectics of hatred and love.

I drew a long breath and suddenly saw the old Victrola phonograph that had once belonged to his parents. I went over to it and blew dust off the record it held. Now scalloped along the edges from warping, and scratched in a tic-tac-toe pattern, the record was one Coleman Hawkins. I took my chances, plugging it into a dusty, never-used socket. Through speakers that flanked the Victrola like a pair of elephant's ears, the Bean's—the Hawk's—tenor sax blared out. Triumphantly! Years ago, when he was at the peak of his powers, I once heard his music played in Central Park by a pick-up band—Big Mose and His Brothers. Through his bright saxophone, Big Mose had belted out the famous ballad, *Body and Soul*, and it had rushed suddenly into bebop and then into reprises of strong mumbo jumbo. Big Mose had breathed like he was about to have a heart attack, then it came flying out of him, as though a weight had been lifted off of a tight coil of soul that had needed deep, buried privacy. *Whaaa, da da, wee da, wop shoo da woo!*

Out of the blue, he'd pointed right at me, laughing with his gold-rimmed teeth, and had proclaimed, "Hey, girl, you can dance! I can tell by that dress you're wearing."

But it had not been because of my dress that I could dance.

Now, I turned the music up to put myself way back there, way back there when I was a sixteen-year-old ballerina with nothing to lose but strong legs and a heart in love. Time with him in those days made my jaws and eyes sore from happiness.

I can't say how long it had been since I'd tried to dance again. But I gave a little nothing of a *fouetté* now and turned the music up still higher; despite dust on the phonograph needle, the beat resounded through the house like a human pulse, and I moved off into the cadences of the Bean's music, a little undulation, a little arm, a little hip. I was singing a little bit now, too. I didn't know I was singing so loudly, but I guess my voice had carried straight over the treetops.

Because Francis Taylor had come back inside and was furious.

"Susanna!" he shouted up the stairs. With a bad back and physical feats never at the top of his list of fortés anyway, I never guessed he'd climb all the way up to the attic.

"Susanna," I heard him say as he rapped on the attic door. He opened it, and the quiet, angry man moved up the last stretch of our attic stairs, one step at a time, chest out in the old habit of showing authority. His whole face hardened like petrified wood. "Susanna!" His voice sounded blocked; a sword caught in his throat.

We just weren't right, him and me.

But touching enough, I thought. Him fighting it now. Everything in his voice was restrained, controlled. "Susanna!"

How did it go? A bohemian street dance fenced in with technique and style. The music floated around me, and memory stirred within our oakrootedness to each other, something inextricable. I recalled the dance and moved to it.

But any minute he would explode. As he walked towards me, steady as an old bull, the dance unfolded, fresh as yesterday. Now I no more believed his presence there than I'd believed his absence back then. For years, I'd yearned for him, for years I'd believed he was by my side all along, as I was by his.

A shaky, tense hand flicked the music down. No matter, I went right on dancing, as though the Bean's sweetness had gone out of the big elephant ears only to enter my own.

"You're crazy, Susanna!" Eyes filled with water, pride lodged right in his throat and held him; he lurched an arm forward and tugged against the strap of the bathing suit. "That was Jenny's! Belonged to her. You take it off, Susanna!"

I snapped my shoulder away from his grasp, made a little swoop with my body.

"You're crazy, Susanna." I mimicked. I raised my arms in the air, gospel-like. His upper body jerked in short lateral swings as though resting on a ball-joint at the midriff. But his feet were stuck solidly to the floor, may as well have been nailed there. He tried to push me.

"A fly could knock him down," I thought. The Bean ascended again, fell into staccato'd bebop. I could feel my shoulders and my neck and my head going with it. Oh, this was music! I could feel life in there. I found the rhythm and moved to it around my husband.

Then the old roots, gnarled and aged, reached from their abyss; in our cellars of memory, not all was vinegar. His hands came up, shaking violently as though wringing the necks of chickens, a language now more of helplessness than rage.

I opened my arms out; I was going to have back the turns, the whooshes. In the dressing mirror near the phonograph, my face mocked, showed torment, but also spoke to him, a language strangely loving. His face went stony cold, his whole head shook, and his eyes cut me clean. They were eyes with a life of their own, like two angry, passionate, trapped mistresses. And he had it in for me now; I saw it coming. I shut my eyes, bobbed my head, snapped my fingers, and hid, best I could, the shortness of my breath.

"Is this Susanna as a teenager with her transistor?" he said gently.

"No more'n you, Captain America."

"Susanna, stop! You are not to dance on my head." His voice quiet, steady, and lonesome.

"Dance on your head. Is that all I ever did for you?"

"So mercurial, Susanna. So volatile. Such a child."

I lifted my hands and made "okey-dokey" signs around my eyes and stared, smiling at him. I squinched my nose a little, the way a rabbit does.

"Don't you try to appease me," he said. A trace of a smile pulled across his face and lips.

"Say what?"

"No decorum, no respect, Susanna."

"I've done my part, Francis Taylor. The kids, all but Jenny, grown now. Doing good in this world."

"Yes, but what did you ever do for *me*?"

"I loved you is all."

He wanted to say something, opened his mouth to speak. Maybe this was it, maybe now the eruption was coming.

But nothing, stuttering. Even now I sucked his words. It was an ancient, unfair, nervous habit. And knowing this, I took his hands, tried to recover his feelings. "Come on, run with me. Good for you."

He stood still, hands resisting my pull against them. I raised my knees high, jogging in place.

"Never could be emotionally independent, Susanna. A true marvel of contradictions."

"Come on, run, little boy, make you feel good." Everything twisted, never trusted anyone. Not even his own wife. I pounded the floor harder, landing only on the balls of my feet, thinking how sore my calves would be tomorrow. The bathing suit again slid high on my buttocks.

"Are you Miss America now, Susanna? Trying to show me some piece of ass? Are you going to Paris?"

I drew up my acrimonious poisons and swallowed them back again. I clenched his hands until the blood drew away from my knuckles and stepped my pace up to high gear, shoulders swaying from side to side; my breath became choppy.

"No real companion, Susanna. No companion for anyone." Again he tried to wrestle his hands loose from me.

"Then why'd you marry me, Francis Taylor?" Pulling him into a bear hug, still jogging.

"You really want to know?"

"Yeah. Really do!"

"Really?"

"Why sure!"

He pulled away. The glow came across his face, but he frowned vaguely, and his tongue rested on his bottom lip like he had to show me whether or not it was time yet for me to be privy to the information. But his eyes, lit and shining, spoiled his show.

I started smiling. Which helped me know I was gaining the lead.

He stepped back one more time. His lips were drawn so tight I thought if he breathed, it'd come out as a whistle. But you could see his struggle to hide his smile. He was so uncoordinated—even with something as simple as trying to smoothly hide an irrepressible smile or a fart—just watching him was going to make me laugh.

"Well, this is my long-awaited moment," I informed him, crossing my arms, smiling. "My long-awaited moment, indeed."

Oh, he knew *that*. I can tell you he knew that.

"Are you sure you want to know, Susanna?" He gave me a look of protective, fatherly concern, as though I'd just fall apart if I ever knew.

"Yes, beautiful, I can not wait to know why it is that you married me." As I talked to him, I leaned over to stretch my hamstrings.

"All right."

"All right!" I pulled back up. I rested my hands on my hips.

"Well." He smiled, took a breath, puffed out his chest.

"Well?"

"Because you gave the best head in Manhattan." Announcing this required singing it in a tune similar to "Shave-and-a-haircut-two-bits!"

So I let go of him abruptly and, mouth agape, walked backwards straight into a wooden king post and stood against it. My eyes went big as 8-balls. For seconds I held myself there in a sharp nervous silence. But I was so tired.

"Good one." I said, as if my glorious old geezer of a husband had a clue.

His eyes flashed. Oh, he was proud! He stood glowing with a face that said "V" is for Victory.

My cheeks started to twitch. Next thing I knew my teeth needed to show themselves, and a wave of humor rushed through me. I laughed, I giggled, I clapped my hands over his precious hope of machismo. "Lord, you senile old coot, that wasn't even me! You've got the wrong girl!" God, he was a buffoon.

"No, it was you, Susanna." He smiled looking at me directly with the big blue eyes that still got me to this day. He stood grinning with the happiness of having so gotten my goat.

I said, "I cannot believe this man, going on seventy-two years old this very fall, would say an immature thing like that. This is just *wild*!" With great exaggeration, I slapped my knees several times waiting for him next to call me melodramatic.

Now he lowered an octave: from grin to smile. He exhaled and relaxed his shoulders. You could almost see the tight bundle of nerves fall loose and happy. "Come on, Susanna, I'll take you to bed."

Dizzy from all the running and jumping jacks and going through a dance of years ago, I fell into the armchair, took up a needlepoint cushion, fanned myself. "Cross my heart," I said knitting my eyebrows, "I do not believe it. Let me go and call the *Kingfisher Gazette*. My God, this will make their day. I can see the headlines: 'She Gave The Best Head in Manhattan.'"

"Come on, Susanna, come on." He felt for my forearm.

I breathed lightly for a minute, like a baby. I turned the volume back up. Coleman Hawkins blared, as if separating two fighting children.

He turned the music back down. "Come on, it was a joke."

I balled myself up. (There. He's gotten me to pipe down. He's got me weak enough that he can take care of me. That's how he'd done all his relatives and all his friends, too. And all those other girls—who were they?) I sat up abruptly. Sweating. Must have been one hundred degrees up there in that attic, heat hanging like dead meat. From the perennial hornets' nests in the corners, a flake of mud dropped off, startling the hornets out of their home. They made slow censorious orbits. "You hid me, Francis Taylor, all these years! I had so many friends, so many friends! And my dancing career!" Then, I tried to get up, but my weak knees failed me. As I got up, I fell, missing the chair.

"Shhhh, not now, Susanna. Seriously." He bent over me and was trying to fix my hair. "No commotion now; you've overexerted yourself," he whispered. "How many times did the doctor tell you? How many times? No activity, the valves are too weak." A hand came softly across my face.

"No. No!" I moved out from underneath him and tried to stand.

"Stay still, Susanna. Rest a minute."

"No, you just move aside this one minute, son! You could have helped me back then! You could have made sure I got a decent doctor for my knee! I loved my ballet, I loved it! "I stood and began to pummel him on the shoulder.

"Shhhh, Susanna, please. I tried, I did *try*. You weren't listening to me. Do we have to bring this up again? Come on, we can talk downstairs." He came down on his knees and was trying to hug me tenderly, burying his head against me. But it was too late now—

"No sonny boy, lemme at it. Now you stay back." I stood, knees wrinkled, and borrowed from his mannerisms to get through to him. Secretly, even his anger I'd learned to admire. Both hands went to my hips and I tried piercing him with *my* eyes. "I was so close! And Jenny, she was so close! She was so close! It wasn't much to ask, your being there!" Water filled my eyes as I tried to go after him.

"Susanna, please!" I'd now struck the rawest nerve. Francis pulled back and tried to shield himself with his arms. He, too, exhausted. All these years of wrestling with me—no peace he'd allowed me to know in this taking, this giving.

"Come on." He groped for me, half pulling me, half carrying me. Weak in his old age, but straining as usual to deny the truth, he pushed mightily, and I trotted a few steps in the air, resisting.

"Your back, Francis," I warned him. "Watch it, that disc. You'll throw it out again!" I'm ashamed to say my voice rose to a little touch of hysteria.

He doubled the energy. He held me the way a bad puppy is held when being escorted outdoors.

"Stop!" This was my darling husband, not strong enough and with a bad back. He'd been laid up nearly the whole month of January, and deep down, ever since I'd known him, his hurting made me hurt, too. The scar across his back and mine across my knee, same thing. My true love for him welled up from its quiet dormancy, and the force of it was too much for my weak armor, dropping now to my feet. I shook free from his arms.

Just in the nick of time, though, he spanked me one on the bottom and I yielded again, falling onto a worn, but beautiful, Persian runner that had belonged to his mother years ago.

Now he picked up the two ends and began to drag it. My arms swung backwards and I fell down, but he dragged us on, the rug and me. Dust filtered to the air.

"Worse! Worse for the back, son, the rug, too, with its rip." My pleas came up as desperate, throaty sounds affected by vocal nodules that had grown back in the days when I'd coached Jenny. "Worse." Raspy, but lacking volume. He'd pulled me halfway across the attic floor.

"Oh you," he said. "Just drag you off and get rid of you." By now, we should have at least been able to stop ourselves from going too far.

"Grand, then. Trashcan for a home. Better than your stinking disposition."

Abruptly, he let go of the tasselled carpet, stomped as determinedly as possible for a man his age with his ailments, and climbed down the attic steps one foot at a time, like someone with rocks in his calves.

So I got up, thinking quickly, and bypassed him, hips shifting from side to side, hands making little circles in the air. My flat black shoes squeaked as I pivoted left to right on the balls of my feet. He gave a tired sigh, lowered his head and muttered private curses.

Then I turned, pulled on the bathing suit's elastic, fixed my hair a little and said boldly, arms akimbo, "Do you love me, Francis Taylor?"

He tried to move on, tried not to look me in the eye. So I said it again, "Do you love me, Francis Taylor?"

He had to think a minute, apparently. He put a hand to his chin and looked down, in concentration. When he got ready to answer my question, he looked over at me, fixing his eyes on me, like I might have been a billboard whose typeface was just entirely too small to see.

"Well?" I asked, raising my eyebrows slightly. My voice was quiet and low.

Now he stayed eye to eye with me and answered, "I, don't, have, to, tell, you, every, little, thing, Susanna. That's none of your business."

I sucked in air with a round and open mouth, eyebrows raised, cheeks burning. "Well, it just surprises me that a man in his seventies would say something this immature!" I shook my head.

He ducked his head, smiling, risible, and I went laughing into our book-cluttered bedroom and fell diagonally across the big canopy bed, both feet out in first position, toes spread like rooster combs. An arm lay stretched open. It was Francis Taylor's long body that had brought this habit of sleeping diagonally; for years we'd slept like a pair of skis edging up-slope.

Minutes went by. I dozed off a little. The French windows were open, and our white cotton curtains flounced, but it was not the breeze to which I woke. It was his soft body beside mine, his arms around me.

"What?" I said, waking from a dream. "I know. Time to get up, boil the potatoes, cut the parsley. Lay out the china." I moved a little, nudging closer to him, and looked out the window.

He didn't answer.

"Was dreaming," I breathed to him. "Dreamed Jenny came back. She was in a parade similar to the one they had for you environmental gurus after the Clean Air Bill was passed. She was waving away."

He turned and pulled with him the pillow over his head, both arms hugging it.

I lay my head on his chest and started to move an arm around him when I felt his shoulder shaking underneath me. He still held the pillow over his face, hugging it tighter, and his sobs came out sounding rusty, as a man's so often do after holding so much in for so many years.

I took him now in my arms, hearing him weep, I think, for the first time in my life, and shut my wet eyes against his.

"After all these years, after all this hanging together," I whispered to him.

He pulled the bathing suit straps off my shoulders and then pushed downward until the whole suit lay tangled around my feet. Our hands groped for one another as we pressed faces, tears blending, shared, but inviolate.

"There, you. You come here," I whispered to him, my lips on his cheek. "Please, you listen to me, Francis Taylor. It wasn't your fault and it wasn't my fault. Jenny drowned all by herself." I felt my heart flutter, then still.

"Susanna," he answered, "Get up and boil the potatoes. The fish is still unscaled and they're coming in two hours."

Forty-five years and I still had not understood how to get around the strength of his defenses, and so I moved, grabbed his shirt hooked on a bedpost, threw off the sheets, then left them folded over his hidden grief, the bathing suit he clutched, the hollow place where I'd been, and his lead ears which received probably nothing at the moment save the sounds now coming from the kitchen: jars opening, water being turned on and off, and an old lady humming the music of hot Coleman Hawkins.

CHAPTER 2

Winter, 1939

Benjamin, Mississippi

I'd have died young if I'd of had to stay in Benjamin, Mississippi all my life. For one, the mosquitoes. Some nights I felt drunk with their bites; flat, silent Benjamin is right on the Pearl River.

For two, the radio. Oh, it played jazz on Friday night, but Mamma wouldn't let me listen to it.

Third and my main problem: having to take care of Mamma and Daddy.

Mamma and Daddy said good afternoon by breathing fire on one another. So white you wouldn't know if it was hot or cold, like the packed frost roofing the mouth of our Frigidaire. Mamma was the one with whom I especially had bones to pick: a large pink woman with real tiny hands, a platitude lifter from straight off the pages of the Old Testament, and a woman clearly suffering from the penis envy. Right underneath everybody's noses, she smoked. I wouldn't be surprised if she used the collection plate to ash on. I'm reminded to tell you that I was supposed to have a baby sister once, but she was born dead. Mamma never seemed to make the connection with her two packs a day. "With your Daddy bringing home no money day after day," she blamed, "and you screaming and getting into everything, it's no wonder we had our tragedy. Anyway I'm too tired and old to try again now." She waddled into her bedroom, "Look here, Daddy. You've gone and left your dirty, smelling underbriefs on my floor." Quietly, my lonely father walked over and picked them up. (She was always so mean to him.)

Now, as we were in the kitchen, her voice followed us around the corner and down the hall, "Hank, come here and take a long look at this stack. Good white folks don't get their bills in red lettering. But you. You." As if we were the only ones in America still feeling the effects of the Great Depression, she stood staring for ten minutes, feeling the flesh on the undersides of her arms.

Under my breath I muttered a few inaudible asides.

"Susanna, I heard that. You watch your mouth, young lady."

Pssssst! Daddy opened a beer. Who could blame him? As he jimmied the bottle cap, I watched, wanting to reach out and touch him. I'd always wanted to be close to him, and sometimes my insides hurt, craving. He used to look at me in the olden days. When I was little he'd let me drive to town with him. On Saturdays we'd listen to Southeastern Conference football games together on the wooden Detrola radio with its big Frey clock. At halftime, the marching band would get inside of me and make me suddenly need to stand up and do a little dance, my small feet lifting in place while I made a slow turn with a face stone-serious. Sometimes Daddy would stand, hold my hands and take a little do-si-do with me. But that was a long time ago. I can't remember the last time we did our dance or walked up to Currie's for 3 Musketeers candy. Even the boughs of the plum tree I once shook to Daddy's laughing head were now choking in kudzu, and I don't know how many years have gone by since the tree stopped bearing sweet September plums.

As he swallowed, he seemed to be kind of making love with the suds. Then he set the empty bottle down on the countertop and reached a dry, weathered hand for his hat that rested atop scarves and coats hooked on the hat rack. The hat, a fedora, fell. Irritated, Daddy used a foot to shove Mamma's new box of Barbara J. cookware out of his way. He leaned down, unwinched his hat, and was out the door. Daddy's jaunts could last anywhere from five minutes to ten days; on the longer ones, nobody ever did know where he actually slept.

Tension, as you can imagine, became our major household emotion. Mamma took charge of its thermostat, sometimes raising the level so high you could actually hear the tension crackle. On this day, Mamma guided it with the pile of late bills. In bedroom slippers, she dragged bare-heeled across our rug, pulled the lamp cord, and sat in the Morris chair normally reserved for Daddy. The firelight cast red over the pages and gave her face a momentary look of peace and serenity. But as I practiced my *pliés* against the dining room table, I distinctly noticed her eyebrow arched on purpose. Out of the corner of her right eye, she cut me sentry-like judgments, licking her fingers as she turned the pages.

"Hey Mamma," I asked, "Isn't that the spaghetti burning?" Ever since I'd turned thirteen, I'd gotten to where I could venture back-talking without a bat of an eyelash. My meanness, I'm certain, was connected to my secret habit of dreaming about another life. "Mamma, don't you smell it?"

I swung through the kitchen door to check. Lifting the pot of boiling spaghetti, I noticed I had a little B.O. (that's what I'd smelled). The noodles twisted and turned in the boiling water. I stirred, thinking, "If only my legs would move and float like spaghetti."

While Mamma insisted on undermining everything we did, Daddy, a man of a different set of war signs, liked to just leave home. Me, I liked to keep my ballet clothes on around the house until after suppertime. This bothered them. Recently, I had acquired pointe shoes, and this set them wild. They understood I was using my baby-sitting money for afternoon classes down at the Mississippi State U., Jackson, but what they had no idea of was that I had talent. People were telling me that my extension was amazing! When the dance teacher would mark a pattern, the other girls crowding the class would automatically spread their hands over to the *barre* and let me go first. On this very afternoon, our dance teacher, Mrs. Potter, had come clicking down the hallway. She stopped me, and put a piece of paper in my hand. Evidently it was something she'd taken right off the bulletin board; there was a rip where the thumbtack had been. "Susanna, I sent this to your home a while ago. You could have enrolled in January at the beginning of the semester. I don't know why you haven't responded. Here, take this one. You must apply, Susanna. If you would work hard enough, you could go professional."

I didn't even know she knew my name!

As soon as I got down the hall, I unfurled the flier. Wide across the top was this headline: "The Manhattan School of Ballet Nationwide Talent Search." Down below it listed the judges: Florrie Corley Duvet and Pasha Pavlovski!! I rolled the paper right back up, looked around to make sure no one was reading over my shoulder, shoved it into my leotard, and walked to the bus stop so fast my feet burned.

Now whistling *Hang Out the Washing on the Siegfried Line,* I pulled out three plates, water glasses, and okra-colored placemats. With three fingers I held the water glasses while jimmying the placemats under my chin and taking the plates in my free hand. One never did know about Daddy, but I always set a place for him.

I pushed the kitchen door open and noticed that Mamma, with the bills spread belly-down across her thighs, had pushed against the arms of the Morris chair until it reclined. She lay dozing while I set the table and brought out the food. My stomach growled as I spooned up a bay leaf full of Mamma's delicious meat sauce. The steam rose to my face. "Mamma," I said quietly from the table, "It's time we ate. He'll come on."

Poor Mamma. She moved groggily, turned on the radio, made her way to the table, blessed our meal. Perhaps it was the weather, the grey sky that gave Daddy's absence tonight its lonely feel. I missed Daddy, and I imagined Mamma missed him too, I don't know. While she smoked, ashing on the side of a half-finished spaghetti plate, I stirred my dessert into a kind of pink peppermint soup. Conversation was provided by the newscaster's voice from the Detrola behind us. Neil Williams, the radio announcer, had a voice that made you feel like he was right there on the living room sofa. But in my home, we listened to world and local events with the same stone ears we gave to Uncle Marshall, an old senile from Mamma's side.

Presently, Mamma drew on her Lucky Strike, blew out the smoke, and watched it curl away. Smoke simply fascinated her, and she now gave it the same back-and-forth eyes a cat gives to the fish in a goldfish bowl. Then sighing, she said, "I don't know why I married him, Susanna. I guess to get out of the house." Her famous arched eyebrow appeared. "But I'll tell you something. If I'd of only known that my wanting for a better life would have me wind up with such a bundle of meanness...." She flicked against the butt of the cigarette.

She meant me. I pulled the cold spoon from my mouth, held it in the air, and objected with strong, frozen eyes. I'd grown up hearing that I was out of wedlock, and I would thank her not to remind me for the one-hundredth time. Mamma got extra mean when it got cold like this because that's when Daddy was most often out of work. In the summertime he worked the riverboats going from Natchez to Baton Rouge. The rest of the year it was one odd job after another.

"I just hope you don't live to repeat history, Susanna, that's all." She gave her assessment a throaty laugh.

"Mamma!" I cried out. I crossed my arms and felt myself sliding down in my chair.

"Mischief I made, I don't deny that, Susanna." She had to continue, "but if I'd only known that the Lord would give it back to me ..."

"...in the form of Susanna P. Jackson." Well, she'd said it so many times, I couldn't help finishing her sentence. I sat, smoldering. I wanted to get up and leave, but at the same time, I couldn't resist the impulse to hear what might next come out of her mouth.

"Right, Susanna. And a lousy no-good drinking husband."

I thrust an arm out, covering her mouth. "I will thank you, Mamma. You hear him plain as I do."

Behind us, one by one, Daddy's heavy shoes hit the few brick stairs leading from the carport to the kitchen door of our house. You could hear him scraping mud off their soles onto the doormat. No telling how long he'd been listening out in the yard or at the foot of the stairs. He entered carrying Mamma a wild, yellow fence-rose and a *Life* magazine. Mamma loved the back page. In his other hand he carried the rake she'd left out in the yard. He often brought her little somethings, thinking, I guess, that one day she'd turn around and say thank you.

He stood in the doorway, the tongues of his boots wide open. With a pained, taciturn smile on his face, he held out the magazine. Behind it, two leaves of the flower peeked. His jacket was slung off his shoulder, exposing what I always thought were beautiful lyre-like collarbones. My Daddy is so skinny, I thought. With tired red eyes Daddy looked first at Mamma then at me. Only the weatherman spoke: temperature's falling tonight to the low thirties.

Mamma pushed her chair away from the table, and at first it looked like she was getting up to serve him. But instead she stubbed out her cigarette, turned and said, "Well, Hank, nobody invited you to eavesdrop. Somebody around here has got to be big enough to face up to the truth."

He swallowed hard; his Adam's apple gave a little jump. Then he took a few steps forward, walking in slow motion as though trying to find his way through a fog. I leaned to pick up a fallen napkin. A piece of tomato and a few noodles had fallen with it. On all fours, I picked the food up and hastily put it back in my napkin before Mamma noticed. From my view, Mamma's legs looked like a pair of bowling pins. I pressed a hand on the chair seat and started to pull myself up when the strong, fast hits belted down across the side of my face. Quickly I ducked, pulling my hands over myself, not knowing at all at first what had hit me, but then out of the corner of my eye I saw the yellow petals falling, then the stem, then felt the rolled-up magazine swat across my shoulder. He drank but he'd never been this way before, and I crouched terrified underneath the table, pulling the legs of the chair with me. My hands clutched around them as I tried to drive myself as close to the floor as possible. And as I went down, I turned my head, trusting on a chance to let his face see mine. He knew I was always on his side, no matter what.

But instead, the sight of my scared face must have only infuriated him, as if he'd seen his own face mirrored in mine. He threw the magazine on the table, his eyes reddened, watered. He held the ironhead rake with both hands now, blood drawing away from his knuckles until they were white round spots. And he lifted it to beat me, lips drawn, eyes intent, and held it there as if determined to wipe me out the way you beat a spot off a blanket.

But I was not Mamma, I was not Mamma, and I never sided with her.

"Daddy!" I screamed. Then he lashed down with the rake, missing me. Without knowing what I was doing, I drew in the chair. My clutching hands tilted its forelegs, and I started to push up quickly from underneath the table, fully prepared to use it on my father. I looked at him again and saw not my father but someone else, a face of unspeakable terror and pain. "Daddy!" I screamed again.

Mamma shouldn't have gotten up, but she did, and when she laid two fat hands on him, tried to pull him back, that was all he needed. He began to jab me. He pronged me, and I felt the rake's steel teeth breaking the skin on my leg. "Daddy!" Had he gone for Mamma instead of me, she would have broken his bones—she was that big and strong—but me, I let go of the chair and surrendered to his feet, drew my knees to my chest, and cupped a hand over the place that had already begun to swell. He'd made a big hole in my tights and a wide run ran down my thigh to my knee. Just above my kneecap, the place he pronged me was hot and bleeding, but by morning it would be black and cold and swollen as a tree knot.

"Whore," he said, jabbing me once more as I lay right there at his feet, folded up into a ball. "Whore! Go get some clothes on, hear?"

I grabbed Daddy's rake in midair and used it to pull myself up, glaring at him. I could feel my chest billowing, receding. My hand loosened from the rake, and I turned and took up his plate and water glass and pivoted, my cold grey-blue eyes riveting back to his, "Daddy, you take Parmesan? I can't remember."

I didn't wait for an answer. I ladled a pile of spaghetti and a good deal of meat sauce thinking, "After all that beer, my Daddy must be right hungry." Quietly, quite calmly, I laid the plate on his placemat, backing away from the table. The food was no longer steamy, but it was still quite warm.

Then I made a beeline for my room and felt their lost, struggling eyes on me. I felt Mamma wanting to call me back, stammering, furious, for one time speechless. And my father sitting down out of a need to weep and at the same time pulling with all he had against the last thin coat of his pride.

"Y'all have blown it now, y'all have," I said in a half-whisper, a half-voice.

Entering their bedroom my eyes gave a little good-bye to the family pictures, undusted and askew on the white dresser. There were more bills in there, and right on top was the letter my Mississippi State U. teacher had sent to us concerning the Manhattan Ballet School Nationwide Talent Search. It had been opened; the envelope's edge was ragged. Well, I knew it was Daddy who'd opened it. Mamma always opened an envelope with a kitchen knife, and Daddy would just pry a finger underneath its flap and rip it through.

I walked into the clean bathroom and closed the door. In the background I could hear Mamma starting up on Daddy, and I backed away from the full-length mirror, turned the lock on the door behind me, pulled out that furled-up flier I'd stuffed in my leotard, and carefully laid it on the sink. I pulled off my Mississippi State U. t-shirt, dropped my pink leotard over my shoulders and slid it with my tights down to my knees. I leaned to examine myself, first pressing my hands to the faintly bluing part above my kneecap, then ran my hand alongside my knee and pressed its tender places. It hurt when I touched it. I straightened and let my eyes wander over the rest of me: my bony legs, my too-short ballet feet, my too-wide pelvic bone, my too-thick blond hair. My pubic hairs had begun to grow, and I moved my hands up my thighs, examining them, wondering if they'd ever grow thick as the thatch I'd seen on some of the girls in the changing room of the studio at the Mississippi State U.

On the wall inside the Sinclair filling station was a pin-up of Betty Grable. I kind of wanted to be her. She was a showoff but she seemed to have confidence. I turned around and studied my backside. I had a good ballet back and a nice little bottom, I decided.

In the background I could hear Mamma's bickering was low and steady; there was no danger of her coming.

But just as I reached to get my clothes back on, the radio went off and steps came down the hallway. Their very sounds finally made me need to cry. I could hear dishwater running in the kitchen, but I heard no sounds of dishes being rinsed and piled. Quickly, I darted up, grabbed the flier, and ducked into my bedroom, leaving the clothes crumpled on the bathroom floor.

"Here comes Mamma," I thought, "smelling like a rose." Right then I couldn't stand the idea of her coming to comfort me, and I turned the lock on my bedroom door, too.

But, I was wrong; it was Daddy. He gave a small knock, one I hadn't heard since I was a child when he'd come to my door early in the morning to wake me for the opening of duck season. Shave-and-a-haircut-two-bits. He knocked softly as if the door were made of crystal.

"Susi, come out here," he said, "I want to speak to you."

But it was too late. I'd already unfolded the flier again, and had gone into my desk looking for a pen. I'd pulled out both my journal and my spiral notebook and was there on the bed, one leg clambering up the wall, the other stretched out. I gave my pen a little jerk, the ink loosened.

"Susi, come out here. I want to speak to you."

Benjamin, I wrote. Benjamin, Mississippi, January 9, 1939.

"Susi?"

Wintertime, I scratched. The very last time my own Christian Mamma would call me a mistake.

"Please?" It was so quiet, his knock.

And the day my father hit me and called me a whore.

I shook the pen again. There was something about Daddy's voice that encouraged my neat round cursive letters as I turned away from the journal and began on the notebook paper, "Dear Manhattan School of Ballet."

I heard Daddy's aimless steps head back down the hallway. In a minute I knew my father would be going away again.

"Enclosed is my application for your nationwide talent search. I hear you're starting a school up there. I was wondering if y'all ever took people on scholarship. If so, would you consider taking me for your spring quarter? I am a young dancer from Mississippi."

"Hank! That's a fine way to act."

Now Mamma was shouting. I could feel the draft of the cold winter air coming in from the front door. I reached for the envelope, reread the short letter and application for spelling and punctuation. "I need to put some clothes on," I thought. The draft slipped in under the door, and the wind outside began to whip around the corners of our house. "Better get some clothes on." I started to ball up the letter and throw it away.

I moved up to the window. Cold air slid through the window's cracks in little pieces. Through the windowpanes, I watched. Brown leaves turned underneath him as Daddy ran down our driveway, towards the road. He'd forgotten to button his coat. Both hands covered his face.

I reached for the bedspread, used it to wrap around my body. I tried to open the window to ask him where he was going this time. He was running. I wondered how he could see with the darkness, with his face hidden.

I couldn't get the window open. Mamma always griped that our foundation wasn't right. Daddy was on the blacktop now, becoming smaller and smaller. He'd slowed to a walk. I rushed over to my desk drawer to look for something that could pry the window open. I found a shoehorn and started to wedge it underneath the window but it snapped in pieces. I leaned to pick the pieces up when there on the floor, fallen like petals, I happened to notice a pair of periwinkle three-cent stamps. The stamps bore modern art that I guessed was a ride. New York World's Fair, 1939.

CHAPTER 3

Spring, 1939
Upper West Side, Manhattan

The Manhattan School of Ballet had wanted a lady to come down to supervise me on the train to New York. I said, "Are y'all crazy? I'm thirteen years old!"

So the School booked me on my first big train ride, the Crescent Number 9, a Pullman. Can you believe that? On April 2, 1939, I boarded the train and discovered my own little sleeping compartment. I felt a surge of power, prestige, and respect that I never dreamed of feeling in my whole life. But, as soon as I sat down, I also felt a terrible pang of guilt. I hadn't said good-bye to either Mamma or Daddy. This dream-come-true was all going to my big britches.

Sometime around midnight, though, I fell solidly asleep to the rhythm of the train wheels against the track. In my private sleeping compartment, I slept soundly until we got to Washington, DC. Then I fell back asleep again until the conductor entered my cabin and shook me awake asking for the ticket that was wedged in the rack overhead. "Penn Station, Penn Station," the announcer roared over the PA. The Crescent Number 9 sounded its powerful, confident horn. Bleary-eyed, I got out on the platform and followed the other passengers into the station. The place was beautiful, huge with people hustling in all different directions. I will never forget the tall colored woman who sat down on a bench, spread her knees, and made a little cavity out of her own dress. She poured Corn Flakes into the cavity, then pulled a milk carton from a dirty brown bag and poured. She ate quickly from right out of her lap, the milk leaking through her dress in slow little drops.

Seeing her desperation, I double-realized my own blessed life. I realized that my dance chance had wormed me out of a life as a Woolworth's girl. Ballet was already starting to put me under a bubble of safety. Later on, we children in the Manhattan School of Ballet would be protected for years from even learning about the sick evil that drove the War. No, our worldly struggle was about whether or not our school could keep its lights on. Because of my ticket on a Pullman, I had thought that the Manhattan School of Ballet must be rich. As it turns out, the little ballet school was struggling as hard as Daddy and Mamma.

Strangers helped me get to a payphone in the lobby of Penn Station where I had to open up my suitcase to fish out Pasha's number. The area smelled of urine. A cool draft whipped through the station with its glorious, gawk-worthy, vaulted ceiling. Two discoveries already: 1) I had never been in a place this beautiful or this crowded. 2) I didn't know it would be cold in April. I was suddenly overwhelmingly inhibited, but, when I called Pasha, she picked up on the second ring. In a beautiful, lean-your-ear-into-the-phone Russian accent, she patiently told me exactly where I needed to go to hail a cab and how to do it. I next took my first cab ride ever, a Checker. I was scared to death because all I had was the travel stipend the Manhattan School of Ballet had sent me and my one vinyl suitcase, mainly filled with leotards that I'd ordered on the sly from a *Sears Catalogue*. I had also packed a dress, a coat, a hairbrush, toothbrush, and a picture of Daddy. I had no idea how much a cab would cost. One thing for sure: the cab driver, a man of few words, didn't seem the type who would take leotards for pay. The ride was fun, bumpy, full of lane-changing cuss words, and a craned neck that could have gotten stuck from awe.

The wind whipped as I thanked the cab driver and shut the door. I gripped my suitcase that held everything I owned on earth and took in the people walking their dogs, grey and navy and black scarves flying in this wind. I was in New York!

Pasha's home was in a four-story walk-up between Columbus Avenue and Central Park West. Pasha, the ballet's doyenne, was waiting for me at the brownstone's front door. I do believe she was the most beautiful woman I had ever seen. Her long dark hair was held back from her face with a red ribbon, her skin was milk white, and her dark eyes shone. Delicate crow's feet rayed around her eyes as she smiled. Fabric was already being rationed; Pasha's casual blue-grey rayon dress with a grey wool belt fell just below her knees. In these times, longer hems had become a thing of the past.

As I approached her, still overcome with shyness, my suitcase got heavier and heavier. "Pasha? Pasha Pavlovski?" I asked, inaudibly. I still could not believe I was standing beside *the* Pasha Pavlovski, much less that I was going to be living at her house.

As she leaned over, you could feel her possession of years of ballet training just by the elegant, measured way she moved. She kissed me on both cheeks. Nobody had hardly ever even kissed me before and I blushed. She wore a small touch of lipstick, but her face did not need any make-up at all. Her neck carried the faintest tinge of perfume that mingled with the earthiness of her body.

"You made it!" she exclaimed, "Come in, Susanna, tired one."

I felt my face burn red with embarrassment. I was embarrassed about having no money. I was embarrassed about wearing a dress that looked like it came from the Goodwill because it had. I was embarrassed about my suitcase. I was embarrassed that I was only thirteen. For the life of me, I could not stop wrapping a finger around a strand of hair, over and over again, while I smiled this one frozen smile. Everything, from craning my neck to see buildings like the Chrysler and the Empire State Building to the fascinating number of taxis, to the smells of a big city, had started to blow my mind.

Pasha tried to carry my suitcase, but I stopped her because she was so delicate, and, as I have said, the most beautiful lady I had ever seen. Still, she insisted on helping. So together we teamed up the stairs, sharing the weight of the suitcase. At the top of the fourth floor she turned the key twice and opened the door to an apartment that had three small rooms, each with high ceilings and arched doorways. The floor was wooden, covered with an old Kilim rug, and the walls were peppered with photographs of her dancers, plates from various European countries, and a single painting of a yellow-bellied flycatcher building her nest. Over the old pegged dining room table hung a picture of a handsome man. A smaller one of the couple holding hands stood on her bedside table. Pasha's husband had died—and I never knew how—soon after their defection. But about him, I soon learned, she never spoke.

She showed me how she'd cleared a closet for me in the miniature foyer leading to her room, then she showed me my room, a tiny Russian dollhouse. She said I'd be free to come and go as I pleased.

With shiny eyes she went about helping me unpack my bag, talking with zest about young Nikolai Krimskaya and the Manhattan School of Ballet. Her accent was pretty thick, and I had trouble catching everything she said, but I could have listened to her voice forever.

We folded the sparse set of clothes on a shelf, hung up my two dresses, and lined the leotards on a hook. Shyness continued to overtake me, but I could tell that Pasha understood I was happy because she was already giving me a small list of house chores the way you'd do for a member of your own family. "The orchid doesn't take too much water; you'll find the mop wedged between the stove and kitchen wall." And when we'd folded the last pair of socks in a drawer, she turned down the eiderdown for me, told me to wash up and crawl in. Then she brought me tea in a painted bowl that I loved. She said that from having traveled so much during The Controversy of 1938—when her boss, Nikolai Krimskaya, basically had gotten thrown out of Broadway while she was out performing at military bases and touring for the war bond effort—she knew the tiredness I was feeling better than she knew the sore feet and blisters that came from having danced so many pieces in so many places around the country.

As it would turn out, ballet would not be foremost on people's minds during the World War II years. The Manhattan School of Ballet had just gotten started by Nikolai Ilitch Krimskaya, a young choreographer who'd defected from Russia via Europe. He'd gotten lucky with a backer, Mr. Leonard Stanford, who'd lured him away from Europe to start the Manhattan School of Ballet. But the initial investment wasn't enough. From the get-go, Mr. Krimskaya suffered cash flow problems that would eventually force him to have to stoop so low as to teach elephants how to dance, I'm serious. For a while he worked a deal where the MSB piggybacked like a troupe of strumpets to the Metropolitan Opera, dancing behind gauze in the background of tenor voices. But the Met, too, was holding on for dear life. To pay the rent for the Manhattan School of Ballet, Krimskaya finally had to take a ninety-mile-an-hour tap dance detour on Broadway. Several Broadway flops didn't help matters financially. During those years, WATCH OUT for his mood, as I would learn all too many times in the coming years as I struggled to keep my hurt knee a secret, "Susanna! What kind of *plié* is *that*?" Rap, rap, rap would go his stick against the floor. "And what kind of height is *that* on that leap?? Maybe you should just go home."

"Sally G.! Pay attention! Christ!" Bang, bang, bang, the stick would go.

It wasn't unusual for any one of us to be found dancing the pattern, tears streaming down our cheeks.

Sometimes at practice you could hear parents talking. "There is no way he's going to be able to keep it open." There were thirty of us in all. And I was the only scholarship kid. Instead of pride, I felt both guilt and shame about that.

Krimskaya somehow kept the MSB going, but, to do so, he had to freelance his brains out, here, there and yon. And that's when Pasha would take over. For years, Pasha and Krimskaya did a kind of Virginia Reel together. If Krimskaya got hired to choreograph in Hollywood or abroad, Pasha would take over the teaching. If Pasha got hired to choreograph out West, Krimskaya would take over the teaching. And even though Krimskaya's dream of forming a real ballet company imploded three times during those years, Mr. Leonard Stanford never lost his interest in seeing us become a reality one day.

Right around the time Krimskaya was thinking of freelancing for a European ballet company that would eventually come to set up shop in New York, Pasha Pavlovsky took it all on her own by daring to go out and tour for the fund-raising effort for the Allies. Fame came to her then, stretching from Fayetteville, North Carolina, to Hollywood. As American people, especially young soldiers, fell in love with her, the government became more convinced that she was a spy who was also guilty of identity theft. She was later arrested and put through the ordeal of a trial. Her name appeared all over the newspaper, including headlines in the *New York Times*. It was during that terrible time that I got to stay at Sally G.'s three weeks straight. This was also when Sally G. got it in her head that I needed to have pierced ears. Authoritatively, she froze my earlobes, then stuck boiled needles through them. She claimed they had to "set." I had to go to both academic school and ballet practice with the needles pronged through my lobes. People talked. I'm still not over that.

On Day 1, the church pews along the wall of the studio corridor held neat, primped little ballet girls. They looked like they were blood sisters who'd all been born at the Manhattan School of Ballet, and, as I passed them, they turned heads in tandem, then simply stared at the New Girl. Rudy Rodriguez, Rob LeVine, and Q. were there, too. Staring. I kept my cool, walking straight ahead as if I knew where I was going and what on earth I was doing.

I was literally saved by the bell; Maddie, an older girl, rang it in the hallway. With the others, I entered the studio and found a place in the back by the piano where I could be half hidden by a large Schefflera plant. Mrs. Kaye, the piano player, blue-haired and getting on in her years, situated herself, scooting the piano bench up underneath her. Pasha came in, soft-stepping and holding a timing stick, and ballet class began as business as usual.

Through the leaves of the Schefflera, I eyed the frizzy-black-haired girl who was up front by the mirrors. She eyed me, too. I grew more and more certain that she had a personal vendetta out for the New Girl. She had an attitude. She wore the kind of ballet face strictly reserved for the stage and had the autograph of a mother's careful hand on a meticulous hair bun. And her chosen place at the very front of the mirror next to Pasha brought with it her clear sense of superiority over every other girl in the room.

When the warm-ups moved from *pliés* to *developés*, this little bitty girl seemed unable to resist lifting her sword to me. She turned her Roman head, fixed her large brown eyes directly on me, and however high I was managing to lift my leg, she resolutely managed to up the ante. I pushed, stretched, felt the hot blood on my face. Her leg hit eleven o'clock. Mine went to eleven thirty. Hers to twelve! Her clear, olive-complexioned face gave no hint of struggle. I purpled to the extent that I thought my leg might snap off, and I had no choice but to let her win. The girl offered me a smile the size of a new baby moon.

I should have known that the girl would turn out to be Sally G. Sally G.! You know her!! All her life she has moved to the rhythm of the dance, subtle as seasons, wild as their various storms. And for all the fifty years I've now known her, we've held together in the kind of bond you can't ever find again once you're grown. When she phones me out of the blue, I suddenly have all my years back; I have my Manhattan Ballet back, close as my own breathing. Between us there have never been any absences though sometimes our separate worlds have kept us from actually seeing each other for two and even four-year stretches at a time.

People will tell you that from the outset we had an understanding of one another. People will say that we were aggressive dancers, often taking the front of the mirror, and they'll tell you that people resented us. As Sally G. and I got better over the next few years under the training of the strict, unpredictable Krimskaya, I could feel the narrowing of eyes upon me, and I plain knew they talked ugly behind Sally G.'s and my backs.

So we did what we could to appease the other girls. Sometimes we used our darling Pasha for this. Though beautiful, she was not rich, and she wore the same black dress every day, regardless of how many times she'd wrung it out with hands pressing against warm dyed water and Ivory soap. Pasha had a very unique odor. You had to love her a great deal to tolerate it. So, giggling and pinching our noses, we'd turn pirouettes in the changing room, and though the girls laughed, our behavior left us with a culprit's aftertaste, and when we'd return to the floor, each of us knew how to apologize. Our guilt and our love for Pasha came through in the dance effort, and sometimes Pasha would rise up from a chair at the middle of the mirrors and say, "Oh, Susanna, now dat is energy!"

Years later in nothing more than a camisole and a pair of Francis Taylor's shorts, I'd work in the hot sun until it formed dark blots across my back. I'd prong my pitchfork in the dirt, smell myself, then go inside the kitchen for ice water. I realized my smell invaded the whole square area, so on purpose I'd parade around downstairs until I got the trouble I asked for. "Jesus, Susanna," he'd say pulling the phone away and cupping his hand over it, "Who raised you, wolves?"

"Oh, now dat is energy," I'd tell him.

Two or three minutes later he'd be out in the garden, bent over pulling the weeds.

CHAPTER 4

Summer, 1942
Central Park, Manhattan
And
Benjamin, Mississippi

By the time the War took over in 1941, Pasha had become my mother, my father, my teacher, my choreographer, my world. And Sally G. had become the big sister I'd yearned for my whole life.

But, even by 1942, we still weren't a ballet company; Krimskaya was keeping our tiny ballet school together by preparing us for chances with his choreography commissions on Broadway and on the silver screen. At that time, we thought we were a few weeks away from finding out who would be selected for the auditions for a Broadway piece he was putting together called *Over the Transom.* Sally G. had turned sixteen in January. I had just turned sixteen in late May. Now that we were this old, for the first time ever, Sally G. and I were serious contenders for one of Krimskaya's Broadway pieces. At least, we believed we'd be invited to audition.

It was a beautiful June day, and I was outside in front of our academic school, The Manhattan School for Theater Students, aimlessly toe-tapping bottle caps pressed to the sidewalk. The bell had just rung for second period, math. How could I have stayed in there working Algebra II problems on such a beautiful day when all I had in my head anyway was this chance? Sally G., who was so bossy that sometimes I opted to ignore her for three days straight, had this morning made it known to me that, yes indeed, we were both going to be selected to audition for *Over the Transom*. She bounded up to me just after morning assembly.

"Where have you been?"

"I've got news!" She went. Her clavicles rose and fell as she spoke, catching her breath.

Semi-ignoring her, I hustled for my locker.

"Stop!" she'd said, grabbing my hands. Then she whispered, "I left my book satchel at the studio last night. And when I went to get it this morning?"

My fingers were purpling under her grip. I raised my eyebrows to signal that she should continue to give me her news, but I wasn't ready yet to totally surrender.

"I overheard them."

"Overheard who?"

"Krimskaya and Florrie Duvet and Pasha." She whispered, her eyes widening.

"What did they say?"

Sally G. pointed at me, then pointed at herself, then nodded her head. Eyes shining.

"Do you swear to God?" I whispered. For over two years now, Sally G. and I had been eating, drinking, and sleeping the dream of making it to any stage that would finally trigger the respect needed to turn us into a real ballet company

"I'm telling you, I heard them." Now she covered her mouth, nodded her head, eyes getting still brighter and brighter.

To these antics, I had just simply put my feet together as closely as possible and rolled my eyes heavenward. Her theatrics finally worked up to the genuine in the heartbreaking expression on her face.

"Yes." She whispered again. She held her fingers up in the Winston Churchill position. Alas, my insides at once caved and bloomed.

Now, it was all I could think about. I couldn't help myself. I couldn't make myself go back into math. I stayed out on the sidewalk, the flattened bottle caps in the pavement shining up at me like fisheyes. It was June 11th. We only had three more days of school to go before summer vacation. Who would even notice if I skipped one little math class? I did a couple of *balancés*. Who would notice?

Everybody. The school was tiny.

Sure enough, Sally G. leaned out of the window of class and made a big gesture with her arm, "Come on. What the hell?" She mouthed.

Too bad. I needed to take Sally G.'s too-good-to-be-true news and go sit somewhere privately with it. I crossed the strap of my book satchel over a shoulder and decided instead to amble over to Central Park where I would rest up before afternoon ballet class and think a minute. I was daydreaming about the auditions, confident that *Over the Transom* was going to be *it*, the clincher. How if we became real, I might even make up with Mamma and Daddy. Maybe I'd be paid enough to buy them train tickets to come up for our opening performance. Besides pleasing Pasha and having a hoot like Sally G. in my life, that's really all I cared about. After I'd ignored Mamma's telegram of three years ago—COME HOME WHERE YOUR HANDS ARE NEEDED. COME HOME, MEAN THING—we'd stayed on such bad terms that we never called each other—it was too expensive. And we never sent letters. She hated to write them and so did I. It was like I temporarily didn't even have a Mamma and Daddy, and they temporarily didn't even have a child.

But, I had Pasha. And I had Sally G. And Sally G., who usually controlled the daylights out of me, was having zero success getting me to pay attention today. I walked up W. 79th by the Museum of Natural History where I crossed Central Park West and entered the park.

Inside Central Park, the air was pristine, washed of the mauve-colored grime that sometimes cast a thin pall over it. Everything around me seemed so quiet. The sky was cobalt.

Through the cool leaves, I ambled down a sidewalk where a drink peddler stood. I asked for a Coke, but my mind was elsewhere.

As I waited, I had a vision of Mamma and Daddy: Mamma in her best and trying to suck in her stomach, Daddy in his suit that no longer really fit him after he lost so much weight. I visualized his sweet hands rubbing the pages of the glossy Shubert playbill. I imagined them taking in the warm atmosphere of an audience coming in under the houselights, the perfume, the murmurs, the palpable excitement.

Oh, I know. Mamma and Daddy would sit there not knowing at all or ever what the ballet was all about. But they'd see it wasn't tabletops.

The drink man snapped his fingers towards my face and I came to. From the side pocket of my navy gymslip uniform that we juniors and seniors hated, I pulled out a change purse and gave him the two nickels. He gave one of them back to me. Then he reached into the icebox for a Coca-Cola, proudly showing me that he'd picked one that was so cold the drink had frozen in the bottom part of the bottle. Code for Southerner. He pried open the cap and nodded his head as he handed the fizzing bottle to me.

I held the bottle up and tipped it his way. "Thanks!" It was so cold, I had to drum my fingers against it just be able to hold onto it.

I headed through the trees towards the Westside Boat Pond. Through the leaves came hollow, rhythmic sounds of conga drums. I heard bongos, maracas.

I followed the sounds until I came to a small copper-roofed gazebo bordering the water. Inside were Machitos, five Afro-Cuban musicians with *café au lait* skin and beautiful to look at. They were smiling, singing in high cheerful pitches. They wore white embroidered Cuban shirts and cream linen pants, silver bracelets that caught the sun. Their feet and hands were coffee-colored and shiny, able to move about a hundred miles an hour. One of them played a marimbula. They sang in a mellifluous flow of primal words, "*Obaha Dzeon Zian Ame Na Bahla Nzoon Dzoe, Emene, emene, Na Ding Yoa Abuhi*." And they smiled right at me, harmonizing, "*Alixxah, ha ha,ha ha ah ha Edee, Edee, Nardone Na Ding, Yoa Abuhi*," their teeth jumping like piano keys, their backs rolling in undulations, and their feet keeping time to a picked-up rhythm. I smiled and asked what the words meant.

"Guapa," said the one on the outside, a hand beating the drum precisely on the downbeat. His Cuban accent was heavy, his voice was lyrical and tenor in tone. He said, "*Guapa*, they're singing, '*Tienes el mio et yo tienera el tia*. You Hold My Thing, and I'll Hold Yours.'" And he laughed with a mouth so affable and wide and open I could see chewed peanuts on his palate. "It's a West African spiritual." The Cubans joked. There were so many West Africans in Cuba that stealing from their traditions had become a rite of passage as Cubans defected away from their own country and emigrated to Harlem.

The nerve. I shot away from his hand, cut eyes at him as I bolted down the hill, reaching another sidewalk that led to the edge of the Westside Boat Pond. Behind me a single voice ventured a little improvised aria: "*Honey You Asked, I Answered/ Honey You Was Dying to Know*."

What an asshole, I thought. Then I said it out loud. "What an asshole." This was the first time I'd ever said a cuss word, and I loved it. What a butthole!

I reached the edge of the water, some distance from the musicians but still within range of the music. The cool wind rippled the surface. Mothers and nannies strolling carriages stopped, cooed to their babies, tucked blankets around them. Still, it was warm enough that people, lovers I reckoned, rowed pleasantly out across the water. They had their sweaters tied around their waists, and the women wore the soft straw hats, the new in-thing that followed the hard straw boaters the men still wore.

Near me were some soldiers. They were just about everywhere in those days. One or two from the group whistled at me.

"My, my," I thought, "I'm barely sixteen years old, have never even kissed a boy, and all this in one morning." I will never forget the Sunday in December, only six short months ago, when Sally G. and her parents and her brother, Hansell, and I heard the radio announcer say, "We interrupt this program to announce that the United States naval base at Pearl Harbor has been bombed by the imperial Japanese Navy." Suddenly disoriented, all I could think was, "Where is Pasha? Where is Pasha?"

Ignoring the soldiers as best I could, I took a seat on a park bench. I lifted my face to the sun, pulling down the luff of my gymslip uniform. We had to wear short puffy white sleeves, and they made us wear a striped tie that we tucked in underneath the jumper. I wore a white sweater over my shoulders that I thought was darling.

Even if I hated the gymslip, I knew that it made me look rich and educated. The fact that I was a scholarship apprentice was Pasha and Sally G.'s and my dark, dark secret that we kept to ourselves so that no one would discriminate. The gymslip uniform helped.

Behind me the hollow but happy sounds played on. As I sat, the bench rungs creaked and green paint from its underbelly fell in chips beside my feet. At the far end of the water, looming Manhattan rose up like a great bear over the treetops. I yawned, stretched my arms across the back of the bench, leaned my head back. I thought about Daddy. How I'd turn right around and kind of wink into the mass of dark little round heads, and from somewhere not too far from the orchestra, I'd feel my Daddy winking back; I'd loosen and dance for him, soft as a quiet cool Mississippi rain.

It was right then and there, amidst my peaceful thoughts, that fresh trouble came my way. At first I hadn't noticed him. The *New York Times* was spread in front of him, wide as a drive-in movie. All you had were two legs clad in a pair of khaki Brooks Brothers pants, a pair of matching socks, and a pair of soft, too-worn leather loafers. Befittingly, you had a pair of attractive arms as well, both with sleeves rolled, giving to tanned forearms, magnificent, soft hands whose vein pattern resembled, in my mind, the Mississippi. Judging from the youthfulness of his skin, I guessed he was about twenty-five, twenty-six. Oddly, his hand bore no wedding ring.

I flicked my thumb against the Coca-Cola cap, and it sprung into the air and accidentally landed rolling by the fellow's feet.

At the split second it hit his toes, his head popped up from behind the newspaper. He snapped down the paper, shot me an accusatory glare, suggestive of my having shot a hole right through his grandmother's head.

"Good night." I sat up and, best I could, returned the look.

As though to remind me that everything was under control, he took his sweet time folding his newspaper and then arranged it neatly in his leather brief bag. Next he leaned over, picked up the bottle cap, carried it with two fingers held lightly to the air, the way you'd carry a cockroach.

I admired his walk. I shouldn't admit it, but I did. His left foot was ever so slightly pigeon-toed, giving quite an athletic aura to a rather slender, bookish-looking guy. Naturally he walked a little sideways so he could keep an eye on the objects on the bench, the valuables of which must have included *me*, judging the first-rate performance he put on in throwing that bottle cap away.

Reaching the trash basket that was only about fifteen feet from our bench, he gave a hole-and-corner glance in my direction, rubbed his hands, and waved them a little over the basket, as though he was asking it to bring forth a live rabbit, then held the bottle cap over it a few seconds, apparently giving it a final benediction, flicked his wrist in a slam-dunk motion, dropped it with significant aplomb. Bull's-eye!

He billowed his chest, wiped his hands, shot me a final look before returning to the park bench. I moved back a strand of hair that had blown across my face, tried not to look at him.

Now he was quite calm, had a faint glow of satisfaction across his cheeks and eyes. An elbow rested open across the back of the bench. He turned to the Dow Jones Industrial Averages and took a real stern, grown-up approach to the columns of numbers. He'd quarter-folded the newspaper. Showing off his efficiency, I guess. His forehead furrowed and had a little stress line running down the front of it. That I liked. That I really found attractive and admirable. He had fine cheekbones, a real nice chiseled face. His skin was perfect, and he had the longest black eyelashes I'd ever seen. To match his khakis, he wore a nice clean blue cotton shirt, worn a little at the nape of the neck. His faded finely ribbed navy blue tie bore a small pair of mallard ducks flying across it. A real go-to-hell look. The wind rippled his shirt, and a top button came open. I noticed beautiful, prominent collarbones, something the ballet would have appreciated.

I sighed and he seemed to enjoy this. Again, I pulled my flouncing gymslip uniform over my knees, smoothed its pleats.

"Oh, it was no trouble," I decided to say.

He cocked an ear in a gesture, I suppose, of letting me know he'd registered, but would opt to ignore me.

"You're welcome," I repeated.

"Welcome?"

"Yes, welcome."

"*Welcome*?"

"Yes, for looking after your possessions while you went and threw that bottle cap away."

"Littering is something you ought to know about, young lady." Through a pair of horn-rimmed glasses he gave me a reprimanding look of someone who might as well have been my grandfather. A look that melted my heart.

I offered him a square, embarrassed smile, the kind you sometimes see on a camel.

He wrinkled his nose a little, and you could see he was doing his level best not to smile back. But you knew there was a smile in there, maybe stuck in his trachea. I decided here was a man hadn't had much practice grinning through life.

He licked an index finger, turned the page. I blew into the Coca-Cola bottle until it made a little whistling sound. To that he perked, then inched his way clean to the far end of the bench!

As soon as he'd gotten the distance he seemed to need from me, he turned to the *Amusements* section, a section that is now the *Arts and Leisure* section. On the front page was a picture of three of the MSB dancers, blurred but blown up. I could tell by the spot they always occupied in the studio that the dancers were Paisley and Dottie and Melinda S. This was hardly the first time we'd been in the paper. But this was just the other end, just the first time I'd ever experienced it reaching someone. Friendly-like, I leaned the gentleman's way, shared the reading with him.

But with hot, passionate, and, I must say, tormented eyes, he snatched the paper from my gaze, glared at me until I thought my hair would go up in flames.

What in the world?

I decided to stare right straight at him without blinking. He was still looking amazed that I had encroached upon his territory. I decided to tell him just precisely who we were.

"Excuse me," I cleared my throat. "I'm sorry. But I couldn't help noticing Dottie Oatman, Paisley Pettine, and Melinda Schultz in the newspaper. If you haven't heard of them yet, just wait. Dottie practically *invented* the tango. Our Director, Nicolai Ilitch Krimskaya, has asked her to include the tango in her upcoming audition for a Broadway piece, *Over the Transom*. So that right there tells me that Krimskaya may include the tango in the piece. And he's expecting her to make the cut. If I, too, make the cut, we kids from the Manhattan School of Ballet will be on Broadway! Oh! That's Melinda, the tall one! She has gorgeous auburn hair; no wonder she got in the paper. They call Melinda 'Nate.' That's short for Nakajima, the Japanese fighter plane. She holds back, marks her spot, then hits the leap every time. Like she's flying!"

"Pais, the one on the left, is doing Krimskaya's avant-garde stuff. Have you ever heard of the word avant-garde?"

I blinked a few times, and cleared my throat again. "It's so taxing on the body that, to keep herself from getting injured, Paisley gets to go to Joseph Pilates' studio for rehabilitation. Have you ever heard of Joseph and Clara Pilates? Probably not. They only work with dancers. Krimskaya and Pasha are devoted to him. Mr. Pilates even cured Andrew Hemming when he had that hip problem."

He was nose-deep in the newspaper, ignoring me in a most obvious fashion.

"This is why I came out here this morning. So I could think. You know, so I could think about my career. We've got a lot on our minds these days."

Totally and completely ignoring me, he rolled his eyes and began to work on the crossword puzzle at the bottom corner of the page.

"Luckily," I continued, trying not to act peeved, "I might have a little income soon."

I could not believe it. As if deaf, he sat there and wrote in the answer for Across-4: Craig Hall, co-ed law school in Toronto, founded 1872.

"Hi, I'm a runaway." I went ahead and announced. "I'm as out-of-wedlock and unwanted as a yard dog."

All right. He was listening; he faked Down-18 by filling in the squares with chicken-scratch.

"Well say, my father, drunk one night, beat me with a rake. I almost died."

Not a word. Not so much as a raised eyebrow.

"I've partly come here today to think, to think about my parents. I'm thinking about making up with them now that I might have the chance to audition for *Over the Transom*."

Zip. He had to be partly deaf.

"And get this," I now decided to say. "Hear the Afro-Cuban musicians over there? Well, all four of them pulled their pants down and flashed their gobble-gobbles as I was innocently walking by."

More chicken-scratch. It was absolutely unbelievable.

"Well anyhow, I came over here to this park bench to get some peace and quiet and found a man who acts like he owns not just the bench, but also the whole park and all the people in it." Now I crossed my arms, feeling their undersides the way Mamma did. Gosh, he was strange.

He zipped his leather bag, folded the newspaper under his arm, leaving Dottie, Pais, and Melinda pretzeled over in a backbend.

He glanced around for a better place to sit. He started to stand, but I reached a hand out and pulled him back. I touched his shoulder lightly as a baby would have.

"Wait," I said in the quiet strained politeness of someone asking a stranger on the street what time it is. "Wait," I tried again, touching him, validating him, myself. "Like some?" Carefully, I lifted the Coca-Cola bottle to him.

Now he cooled, smiled vaguely for the first time, then raised a hand to indicate the smudging of black newsprint on his fingertips.

"Won't hurt this old bottle," I smiled. "Have some." I gave the bottle a little nudge, and he took it tacitly, cradled it in such a way that you understood maybe it was too cold for him.

Our eyes fell on each other.

The primal congas in the background broke in a free little moment of rhapsody, then the beat collected, rose to a crescendo, giving rise to a feeling of storm in the air, of a sense that in a moment everything would scatter. He held the Coca-Cola bottle, nodded his head slightly, toasted it to me. Watching him, the amulet quality of his eyes, I began to feel something cave in inside; it was the exact feeling of going down a rollercoaster with "no hands."

Why won't he drink? I thought to myself. And then it occurred to me that maybe he thought I had germs. As though it was made of eggshell, I carefully took the bottle again, used the hem of my gymslip to wipe the lip clean.

"Now," I said, smiling. "Have some."

He spoke, casting a spell over me in a voice that was lyrical, irresistible.

"Pleasant music, isn't it?"

"Very pleasant."

"Very nice, isn't it?"

The way he said it!

"Very nice."

"A fine rhythmic cadence."

"Yes, fine, rhythmic, yes."

"Smooth, practiced voices. The lyrics are probably from Cameroon originally."

"Smooth, practiced, yes."

"I think so too. Too bad they are illegal."

"Illegal?"

"Yes, Mayor LaGuardia banned street music seven years ago. A couple of years before the World's Fair. You couldn't have been a day older than seven or eight. What's your name?"

What's my name!

"What's yours?"

"I asked you first."

"No, I asked you."

"No, no. You go ahead."

"Susanna Parish Jackson."

"Francis Taylor Dewitt."

"Nice to meet you, Francis."

"Taylor. You can call me Taylor."

"Nice to meet you, Francis Taylor."

"Nice to meet you too, Miss Jackson. What part of the South do you come from?"

Fly me to the damn moon.

This time there wasn't anything impolite about his turning back to the newspaper. And he was still reading about us, our struggling School of Ballet! This was the first I'd seen of a man being interested in the cultural arts. I slid a foot out, flexed-and-pointed my black-and-white saddle oxford. Brushed my foot out again, my leg flew a little. Then I held it pointed to the air for a little minute, stretching the turnout. I opened my arm across the back of the bench, then pulled it back. Self-consciously, I pulled my sweater over my shoulders, curled my toes against the ground. I lifted the bottle, threw my head back to drink.

"Miss Jackson, did all four of those men expose themselves to you? Are you completely certain about that?" is the way he ventured the question, I think. Out of the blue.

I held the fizzing liquid in my mouth as my eyes protruded. He *would* need to know. Quickly, I gulped, and the sweet carbonated juice went directly down the wrong alley. I coughed, sneezed, gasped. The Coca-Cola spewed out everywhere. I choked, spit, for a moment forgot where I was. Damn near lost my life.

Then the handkerchief. Smoother than silk, softer than washed cotton was the handkerchief wiping my mouth, patting my cheeks and chin. It touched featherlike against my jaw, then sponged up the Coca-Cola that had spewed into my hair. He spoke with the kind of gentleness people give to you after you've just taken a bad spill on a bicycle. "There," he said kindly, cleaning me up. "There, take it easy. You all right?"

I felt him take my hand. With the handkerchief, he softly rubbed the wet stain over my chest. I let him. But as I did so, all of a sudden something again rushed through me. The park gave way; the trees, people, boat pond, skyline drew back like stage murals, and I felt a sudden flow of something wet between my legs, something I feared would stain me.

And in all that flailing about, I'd unintentionally shoved the Coke bottle back to him without noticing. Now as he took it, the shook-up drink exploded out of the bottle. His tongue licked the mousse that fell evenly down his hand. Then he turned it over, sucked the pool of sweet juice out of his palm. "Delicious," he told me and gave a real charming smile.

The wetness flowed, had no conscience at all. How such an embarrassing thing could have happened to a sixteen-year-old girl, I just didn't know, but when our eyes again tumbled on each other, I looked away quickly and awkwardly said, "You can have the rest of it."

Then zipping my bag, I saw how the drink had wet the side of his bag, how it'd stained some of his right important-looking documents. Something held me from having the decency to apologize, like maybe I'd choke on that, too.

I stood, picking up my book satchel. He gave a disappointed look and asked me where I was going.

"Class," I lied, pulling my gymslip down and walking backwards one step at a time with my knees held as closely together as humanly possible. One hand tried to wave good-bye. A barrette fell out of my hair. I put the satchel down and bent, pretending like I had a dollar bill between my knees, scooped up the barrette, and at the same time surreptitiously put a hand to my backside just to check.

Standing again, I looked up. I could feel my face burning red. And, for better or for worse, I saw that he watched me with rapt attention. My cheeks burned on, and he just stared with bright eyes and a bemused partial smile as I walked backwards a few more steps. But I stopped trying to wave good-bye. I watched his bemused, delighted face, pulled the satchel strap over my shoulder, wheeled around and just started running. I ran fast as I could, thinking, "Now I know what boys are. Now, I, know, exactly, what, boys, are."

It was during that escape that I felt the first of what would become an endless series of sharp electric pangs shooting down my leg. They came from somewhere underneath my kneecap and radiated down to the ends of my toes. The faster I ran the more I anticipated the sharp shoots of electricity down a leg that suddenly felt as fragile as a china plate. But instead of slowing down I ran faster.

I had a sudden, unreal urgency to make a phone call.

After two and a half years of near silence, the need to make that phone call was startlingly clear, irrefutable. I remember actually bursting into tears as I dug frantically through my satchel looking for my other nickel.

But I didn't know real weeping until I heard the dial tone come on, and one slow turn at a time, dialed my Mamma collect, then listening hard to the operator ask her if my mother would take the call:

"He's real sick." Mamma said, "Getting thinner by the day. He's delirious and he calls for you. They say his liver is completely shot. Why didn't you listen, why? It's full-time looking after him, trying to keep his spirits up, and with me working part-time now for the both of us."

I held the phone. Taxis honked in the background.

"Susanna, speak up." She said.

"Mamma," I choked at last, "Do I take the bus today or the train tonight?"

"He's so sick, Susanna. Eyes yellow and his stomach's bloated out as though carrying twins. They say he's just filled with water. You should see his ankles."

"I'm coming, Mamma. I'm coming now."

"This all started with your running away from home."

"Hush, Mamma. Useless to start now."

The train ride took two nights. Coal and gas were by now being rationed and the train was delayed all night in Norfolk, Virginia, waiting for fuel. But we finally made it via the rural transfer to Haverty then to Jackson. Even that little jerkwater train had the gall to say, Whites Only.

Mamma met me in the Buick 2-door, her own tank hovering around Empty. At first she was real nice but then gradually got onto me like July at high noon, saying they didn't feed me right and hadn't prepared me well enough for college or a technical skill. Which was true. The Manhattan School for Theater Children was about the easiest and slackest school in town. But it was a lot harder than any school in Benjamin, Mississippi.

While she talked, I looked around to see what all they'd changed in Benjamin. I rolled the window down. I'd forgotten how hot and green it was back home. As if charmed by the clouds above, the heat, even at that mid-morning hour, rose up and created a mirage on the pavement ahead. Through it colored people were leaned smoking against the Piggly Wiggly on the right side of the street; whites were sitting smoking on park benches down on the other side of the street. I watched while Mamma asked questions. I tried to answer. Neither one of us spoke about Daddy.

Presently, Mamma parked against the curb, and I opened the car door, waded through the white heat towards the front door.

The ceiling fan was on, and the only thing that moved was his hair. He was lying outstretched on the Morris chair with Mamma's summer quilt pulled up to his knees, eyes catatonically fixed towards a faded fishing picture on the wall. Like an old dog hit by a car, he lay listless, eyes glazed. Mamma was right; he was yellow.

Underneath the thin, nearly transparent skin of his belly lay a watermelon.

"Daddy," I said holding his hand. "Daddy, hey. It's me, Susanna."

At first he acted like he didn't recognize me, or that it hadn't occurred to him that I'd been away for three and a half years. Mamma was in the kitchen fixing a lunch of ribs and spinach for the three of us. "He wouldn't eat in the hospital. He won't eat here at home," she said. "But, I still fix it for him." The big living room radio was on, tuned to one of the two motley music stations picked up by Benjamin. Daddy said not a word. You should have seen Daddy's stomach.

"Let me see if I can get him to take a bite or two." I took a plate of the ribs and spinach from Mamma and sat on the big arm of Daddy's chair.

"Daddy, just try a little bite. It's really good." The radio crackled and spit.

Daddy did start to open his mouth as I pulled a rib close to his nose. His tummy probably couldn't take it, but at least he was making a gesture.

Interrupting us, Mamma suddenly barked, "What you could do for us, Susanna, is get back to New York and make us some money with those prima donna legs your Daddy and I been hearing so much about. Daddy agrees."

"Mamma, that's a very old way of expressing yourself. Stop talking to the walls." I had been free of her for so long, I'd forgotten what she was like.

Mamma hotfooted back to the kitchen where she made herself a big plate of ribs. In a pan, she had hot barbeque sauce that she poured over them. My own stomach growled and I wound up diving into the ribs on Daddy's plate.

"Daddy agrees," she'd said again as she lumbered out to the living room and sat on the blue sofa next to the radio stand.

I knelt helplessly beside Daddy. He seemed to be in a complete trance.

"Listen, Daddy." He lay still. I held him. He felt like wood, his hand was dry as parchment paper. I tried whispering in his ear, "Daddy, listen, I'm right here." Daddy's eyes were like clouds. He didn't move. The lonesome music in the background was no help. "Daddy, when you get better I'll take you to New York with me." With a big lump in my throat I looked at him hard. "You'll have a Pullman on the Crescent Number 9 train straight to Manhattan!" I wished Daddy would say something.

"No, she ain't." Mamma said. "She's dreaming. Some people never change."

From the arm of the chair, I leaned close to him. I looked deep in his eyes. All these months had gone by with my dreaming about Daddy and Mamma coming to New York, and here, all of a sudden, I barely even remembered where I'd been.

With glazed eyes, he just looked ahead, and it occurred to me that a spent liver might have brought on deafness, too. I held his hand and looked at him a long time, and then all of a sudden, he glanced over at my vinyl suitcase still parked by the door, and slowly, the faintest trace of smile and memory appeared on his face.

At first I supposed he was trying to tell me, yes, find a way to make some money, how badly they needed it. Then all of a sudden he turned and looked directly at my face, eyes so sick but lambent, as though in love. A top button of my shirt had come undone, revealing the little pink rose decorating the middle of my slip. What difference did it make?

Suddenly he began to move. It was his hands. It took him forever to lift them, the tips and thumbs touching, like someone pulling real heavy taffy. He was weak as a baby bird.

I stayed kneeling, waiting, one hand lightly resting against his billowed stomach. His hands finally reached that button, and as he fastened it, he smiled again with lambent eyes. He held my face, and I leaned forward slowly, without knowing what I was doing, and Daddy kissed me on the cheek. I felt light as crepe myrtle.

Daddy passed away that afternoon. Cirrhosis takes them *like that*.

At the miserable, paltry funeral service two days later Mamma went around showing everybody the obituary from the *Benjamin Daily*. By that evening I was already on the Crescent Number 9 back to New York. Not even death had brought Mamma and me any closer.

On this ride I didn't feel like I was going anywhere. I didn't talk to anyone. I just looked out the window trying to put everything together. What would it be like without Daddy? And what *had* it been like without him? Or had he been with us more than we'd ever been with him?

Someone in the next compartment was whistling. It was most irritating. I stood thinking I might go tell him to be quiet, that there'd been a death. I stood quite nebulously, allowing the train's momentum to jostle me where it willed.

And when I got thrown with all my weight into my left leg, kilowatts of electricity fired from my knee. I fell backwards into my seat, as if pushed.

From that minute onward, I focused steadfastly on my knee, the pains shooting from it, though I didn't then understand why.

But I did come to understand this: guilt collects, forms abscesses. Love pours. Love fills and empties deep vaults that the lover himself has had nothing to do with. I didn't know then that I had fallen in love. But that morning after I got back to the City, it should be no wonder that I gravitated back to Central Park, limping with my abscessing pool of guilt.

Limping as I searched in vain for the stranger who had touched me not just with his hand, or handkerchief, or interested eyes, but with some kindred flame from deep within, lit from cinders strong as death.

CHAPTER 5

Mid-July, 1942

Central Park, Manhattan

Only one person knew about my knee: My father, Hank Jackson. It was in my bed long after Pasha had turned the lights out that Hank Jackson would come to visit me. I could hear his voice. "Honey, I think I should carry you to the doctor. Maybe they'll put it in a cast for a while. Won't take long to get well. We can play cards. We might even get tickets for the Mississippi State VS Louisiana game. Car is running real fine now. You ought to listen to it purr."

My skin would get cold and I'd draw up my knees and rock myself. Oh sure, I knew that my belief in Hank's presence was just part of what you do when death comes down on you too fast to take in.

You ought to listen to it purr. I swear. So clear.

On good days, I could get the momentum to tell him to go away. Sometimes I'd tell him with annoyance, the way you'd tell a dog to get his paws off your lap; other times with a rush of compassion—only Daddy could fall out of heaven and not be able to find his way back. Hearing him also brought on whimpering, strangest little sounds. Whimpering like a baby. Blindly, I'd reach for him in a wish to feel him in the flesh, then order him away. "Go on, Daddy. Please don't come around here." I'd lie on my stomach, my head buried under the blanket.

"What was that darlink?" Sometimes Pasha would hear me and think I was talking to her.

"Do you hear someone, too? Must be the neighbors," I'd answer quietly.

I hoped Daddy wouldn't find his way to my ballet class or report to any authorities about the condition of my knee. Movement was getting harder, and I worried about limping. My hand often went to my knee, and there I'd feel a small bump that did seem to be growing. I'd lose whole nights of needed sleep worrying that someone would see it and make me have it cut on. No operations for me, I vowed. Never.

I found out one chance day that if I stayed on pointe even during the warm-ups, the pain wouldn't be so bad. People got mad. They thought I was putting on airs.

Krimskaya was out of money again, so *Over the Transom* had been put off. Now, it looked like we wouldn't even have dates for the auditions for another month or so. So walking around on pointe looked, I guess, mighty pretentious and presumptuous. Elizabeth McClatchey walked by and said, "Show off." Then she shook her head like I was a nut.

I could handle people thinking the wrong thing, but what got to me was Sally G.'s sudden new way of acting towards me. I was so surprised when one hot July afternoon, she went right over to Susan Gordon who leaned against the big upside-down glass water cooler, gulping down water from a white cone-shaped cup. Sally G. tapped her on the shoulder and said, "Will you please get a load of Susanna now?" I looked down and realized I was walking straight down the hall on pointe. The habit had set in that fast and strong.

I felt like telling her right then and there, but when I turned around I saw Sally G. spiraling a finger around an ear in fast circles. Then I heard her say, "She'll ruin her feet."

The next thing I knew, she started buddying up with Elizabeth McClatchey, Rudy, and Q., leaving me with no one but my locker and Hank to talk to.

Then one day I heard somebody whisper that my father's death had "traumatized me to a loss of reality." Which hurt. Which was stepping over the limit. This lowered me all the way down to where I couldn't even get the energy for a decent leap or turn.

I was so down, I thought I'd ruined my chances of being selected to audition for *Over the Transom*. But, one Thursday morning in mid-July, I reached inside my message box and found a note saying, "Please be in studio 1 at noon sharp for a meeting with Mr. Krimskaya."

All twenty of us who'd received the same note got there early, each acting like she'd never laid eyes on the other before. We were too proud to admit excitement and were instead putting on airs of nonchalant cool. Every girl spaced herself on her own island of linoleum checkered square. Rachel Ellison sat on her legs with her feet outturned, staring at the clock. Vik O. Knoggle pulled a rubber band between her fingers and let it fly to no special place. Sally G. lay prone, aimlessly pulling on the string of a sneaker. Amy Addison seesawed a pencil against the floor until I thought I'd go straight out of my mind. I started my old habit of winding a strand of hair around a finger, over and over and over again.

At length the long hand slowly pushed, then shook a little, and in stiff little hops it joined the short hand at high noon. (The studio had the oldest, most decrepit clocks known to mankind.) Everyone gathered her poise and watched Mr. Krimskaya enter the room as if she had a front row seat to Benny Goodman. He wore a daze suggestive of grander things on his mind, then snapped into real life as soon as he reached the little podium that had been set up for him. He began in his heavy Russian accent with these words: "You've been selected to audition for *Over the Transom*. We hope that the performance will now take place in the fall. If your audition gives rise to selection for a part in *Over the Transom*, you will find that the pressure of the Broadway performance will give you an idea of the difficulties intrinsic to the life of a professional dancer...."

End of speech. Everyone went into spontaneous applause, and before I could even know it was she, Sally G., the stranger, had jumped to my side, grabbed both of my arms. Then she threw her arms around me and started hugging me and saying oh she loved me, she loved me so much. I suddenly saw how touchy we had been anyway on our diet of Coca-Cola and bananas. Mainly I saw how much I adored her, too. But, so far, Hank was still the only one who knew about my knee, that it was getting worse and worse.

Krimskaya calmed us with a few sharp warning claps then started to pass out the mimeographed copies of the rehearsal schedule. He asked Rachel Ellison, whom he knew no one could stand, to help. (Rachel was hardly a scholarship child. One side of her family owned J.C. Penney's and the other side had large bi-coastal real estate interests.) She treated the scholarship child like she had dirt under her nails. I think she thought Sally G. was a scholarship student, too. I once watched her *chainé* dangerously close to Sally G. Then *retiré devant*. Right between Sally G.'s legs. As Sally G. sprawled to the floor, Rachel excused herself of any responsibility by simply moving back a step and continuing her *pas de chats*. Now while Rachel pranced around, obviously overwhelmed with herself, Mr. Krimskaya moved around the room shaking everyone's hand in a cold way that, I must say, made us feel less than loved.

Pasha saved the moment. She entered brimming, releasing pure-D joy in all of us. Krimskaya, who, as the story goes, never could stand the high-pitched racket of young girls, darted quickly out of the room. Every one of us, including Rachel, went wild. Amy, Melinda, Susan Gordon and I banged on mirrors. Helen Gordon, Vik O. Knoggle, and Dottie monkeyed up-side-down on the *barre* with their hands going out like wide baseball mitts. Elizabeth McClatchey and Sally G. skipped around the room tossing leg warmers to the air, going, "Pasha! Paaaaah Sha! Paaaah Sha!" Heavy emphasis on the Sha! Pasha was smiling with her lips closed and her eyes brimming, welling up. Rob LeVine, Q., Rudy Rodriquez, and I made a chair with our arms locked at the elbow and marched Pasha around the room to the tune of *Coming In On A Wing And A Prayer*. And Pasha, using clumps of our hair as handles, likely shocked, maintained her composure but nonetheless swayed and kicked until we nearly lost her.

Through the singing, banging, and noise, someone else had come up with an entirely original way of showing victory: short intermittent screams, the announcements of which were entirely unpredictable. Each time the shrill pitches hit the air, most of us clapped our hands to our ears and looked around for the fool. (Fingers, I am nearly certain, could be pointed to Rachel Ellison.)

Pasha, I guess to do something about that screaming, suggested we head for the out-of-doors. All of us twined arms and promenaded down Broadway prouder and with more to say than a troupe of Marines just out of boot camp and headed for battle.

After lemonades at the Place Pharmacy Drugstore, Pasha assigned everyone an organizational job for the weeks ahead: communicating with the parents. Snacks after the practices. My job was to go put the deposit on new pointe shoes at Courtney's Ballet Store on the Eastside. We weren't going to perform in the shoes that showed blood stains at the toe end. No matter how much it cost, everything we were going to wear was going to be brand new.

There had been so many afternoons when I'd wandered the park, hoping on a chance to see the man who'd crept into my mind and stayed there, always to come home with the sun setting in front of me, the clouds gathering in cumulus shapes, purpling for want of rain. But on this day, I was walking across Sheep's Meadow, hurrying to get to the ballet store. From where I walked I could see the Alice in Wonderland statues and Conservancy Pond where the Eastsiders brought their children for miniature sailboat races. It was hot, and the haze above made the sun look dull as a plate. I looked up, wiped my brow and followed the pathway leading towards the gate at East Seventy-Second when I literally saw him. Chances were one in a million. I tried so hard to duck, but it was too late. He was coming directly towards me, walking with a girl. Each had hands to pockets and they walked in the slow pace of deep familiarity and, at the same time, with distance between them of about two feet, the measure one might expect between two strangers. They were not talking.

I recognized him first by his slightly turned-in walk, and, as I got closer, by his generous lips, rosy cheeks, and large blue eyes which seemed, as we drew closer, to belong to me. Or I to them. The girl was tall, pale, plain, and had strawberry blond hair that roped down her back in a braid.

This was my first experience of stage fright. I tried to compensate by telling myself that he would not recognize me, and pulled the straw brim of my hat over my brow. My ears suddenly warmed up like a pair of radiators.

"Susanna! How are you? I've wondered where you got off to!" He had quite a blush himself.

"Fine!"

"How is your dancing coming along?"

How is my dancing coming along!

"Fine, thank you! And how are your business affairs, Francis Taylor?" I slid my hands into the deep pocket of my red sundress, drumming them against the cloth.

"Very well, thank you. I wondered if I'd ever see you again. I've thought about you on numerous occasions." He was still and correct as an oak tree.

The girl shot him a look, pregnant with history, and began to tug on his arm. I plucked a mulberry leaf and began tearing it up in little bitty bits as I told him about being selected to audition for *Over the Transom,* a performance that is supposed to save Mr. Krimskaya and the Manhattan School of Ballet.

"*Over the Transom*? That's going to be performed at the Met, right?"

"No. On Broadway. In the fall, maybe. Depending on the finances. The auditions are in August."

Seeming to overlook what I'd just said, he put one leg out towards me, both hands still in his pockets. The girl still had her hand on him, though he had shrugged her off once, mildly. He wanted to know the date of the auditions, and here he stammered a little. Over the years I grew so familiar with the stuttering I could anticipate it before he opened his mouth, and sometimes I'd venture talking for him, protecting him. But right then, I was surprised to find him unsure of himself.

"August 25th," I told him. "Those of us auditioning better be ready to wake up early. The auditions will be from 7:30 AM to 10:30 AM. The ones who get picked will get to go to the races. That's right. Mr. Leonard Stanford is taking the lucky ones to the Travers Celebration Horse Races up in Saratoga Springs. Post time is 3:30 PM."

Post time. Who was I to go around using words like *post time*. But, that's what Mr. Stanford called it. And aping him felt pretty good. Pretty powerful.

"Leonard Stanford?" His face darkened. "*He's* your backer? I mean the backer for your ballet school?"

"Why? You know him?"

"I know of him. By sheer coincidence, I have an acquaintance who has a thoroughbred horse farm in Aiken, South Carolina. Stanford bought a horse from them."

The girl started to walk away. He caught her by her short sleeve.

"Susanna, this is my cousin, Christie." The girl put her hands in her pocket and rolled her eyes. But she stopped walking away.

"Hi, Christie."

"Hi."

"How involved is he? How involved is Stanford in your Manhattan Ballet School?"

"Oh, he's involved! He's the reason we're still standin'!"

His face grew somber again. Christie tapped a foot. From his shirt pocket, he pulled out a little note pad and began jotting down something. Then, with the so-called cousin right there, he told me that his other set of cousins have a country home near Saratoga Springs and that he might be joining them for the Travers.

Might be joining them for the Travers! My heart was going thump, thump, thump.

"If they're not going to be at the Met, where will the auditions be?"

"I'm leaving," Christie said. "I'll meet you back at the apartment."

I hated when she said that. I just hated it. "Back at the apartment." Her words totally distracted me.

With exasperation, he shut his eyes. I hoped the exasperation was for her.

"Susanna," he said again, "are you listening? Where will the auditions be held?"

"At the Shubert."

He wrote it down. He wrote it down!

I popped a stick of Juicy Fruit into my mouth. Chewing had always calmed me. Christie, at least fifty feet away now, turned around and cut eyes at me. I readjusted my sunbonnet, then closed my arms real close to my sides in case I was sweating. And I stepped back a little bit. I tried to keep my gum under my tongue. Because I didn't want to look tacky.

He looked up from his writing pad.

"Susanna," he stepped forward towards me, his face darkened.

"Yes."

"Susanna, as you walked towards us, I noticed that you were limping."

"No, I wasn't. No, I'm not!" I was mortified.

"Yes. Yes, you are. I just saw you."

"No. No, I'm not. I stepped on a pebble and it caused me to wobble," I lied. My face felt flushed and hot the way a face always will when someone looks straight through your eyes and sees all you have.

"Well, bye-bye!" I decided to say, "Be nice if I could see you both there at the Travers!" I wholly exaggerated. "I intend to make the cut and then go to the horse races. I'm not auditioning for nothing! I've never been to a horse race in my life! I intend to make the cut!" Then I walked away quite stiffly, quite mannered. I rose up a little on my toes and kept my weight forward knowing this would take the pressure off my knee. My face, still red and mortified, a face he could not see, of course, was at the same time overwhelmed by another emotion: a smile from ear to ear that almost hurt. It was stuck there as a part of the spell under which he put me. I retied the bow of my bonnet, tried to see how I looked in the shine of a metal lamppost, and walked in the general direction of the Courtney's

Ballet Store. The grin upon my face was so big it must have looked slapped on, and I wondered if any minute my head might detach from my neck like a helium balloon.

At Conservancy Pond, a little boy pushed off a small sailboat that promptly fell over on its side in the absence of wind. He looked up as I did to the sudden sounds of music. Far from the rhythm of the African conga band, this music was jazzy, almost Big Band, dominated by the clear, powerful sounds of a saxophone.

Big Mose and the Band, all the way up from a Louisiana bayou, so said the homemade sign, and all looking wise as alligators! The saxophonist, Big Mose himself, spidered his fingers up and down the keys softly. The three others, a drummer, a bassist, a trombonist, followed his cue in a kind of quiet medley.

The little boy took hold of a knot in a dogwood and used it to pull himself up, then shinnied with some effort to the bough of the tree.

"Page, come down from there!" His mom, who'd now joined us, looked up at Page. He swung his legs back and forth, refusing to mind.

Maybe my red dress had something to do with what came next. It had two spaghetti straps, white buttons down the back, large pockets. I laced my hands behind my back, bent them palms outward to cracking knuckles as I moved up towards the band.

Big Mose kept his eyes down turned to the saxophone and signaled. Everything about him shone: teeth, eyes, black sweating skin, as if all had been dipped in a magic oil.

"Yow bro: business." His voice was deep, authoritative.

Big Yow, the trombone man, jerked straight, stood, looked at me. All the eyes followed, clicking bright. Simultaneously, their pink tongues pulled across lips ripe as exotic fruits, and their fingers jumped instinctively to their musical instruments, striking like matches, and lit their faces in the promise of something to come. You might have bristled back into a corner with your hands held in surrender over your head, until you saw them handling their instruments: all instruments clearly Shes, held like a newborn baby girl, each with a name.

"Step it, brothers." Big Mose's eyes made quick rounds to the brothers, then riveted on me.

"You can dance, girl, I can tell by that dress you wearing." His mouth opened wide, playing with me. Gold-rimmed around the teeth, his mouth may as well have been the orifice of the saxophone itself. Timidly, I stepped back. He flashed a gold and white smile, made, I could see, to both provoke and befriend me.

The little boy, Page, found a cradle in the limb of the dogwood and sat in it comfortably, one hand holding the limb, the other hugged around the trunk of the tree.

It was ninety-four degrees Fahrenheit, so hot the green leaves themselves looked like they'd begun to melt. To cool off I lifted both arms.

"Look at her, I told you so. She got gulls' wings. Yow Junior, quick, which one is it?"

"Which one, you say?" Trying to play with the boss' mood. Yow Junior was Skin Man.

"Yes, Lord, which number." Communicating impatience, Big Mose struck a long winsome note on the sax, dropped it clean to the bottom, then flung it way high in F sharp.

"*Do, wa, da, eeee day, wha da, boo, wap, do*." Beebopping, warming up.

"Big Mose?" Big Yow's eyes clicked, then he went into a grimace, teeth and eyes clenched shut; if you couldn't see he was a man, you'd say he was getting ready to give birth, "Oh, I know what it'll be. *You* know what it'll be."

Big Mose pulled the saxophone from his mouth, opened his eyes and mouth, let everybody see him like that with his tongue showing so they'd know he was listening, pretend guessing.

The little boy's mother moved close to me as if things had gotten so crowded she'd had no choice.

Big Mose backed under an oak tree. "Shade baby," he said to me. "Can't take this heat." Giving me a face promising Glory, he zipped down the keys. "Shhhh! It's coming. Take it with me Big

Yow, Yow Junior." His large foot slapped down. "Girl, jump, the water ain't cold."

Skin Man jerked up, coming to like a man who knew he'd been living with a god all his life but had never gotten used to the marvel of it all.

"Come on, Harper, take it now." Harper played the guitar.

"Whaaaa!" Big Mose belted, scooping up the beat, pitching it to the air; the beat of the drum and plea of the sax came together and then invited conversation with the other instruments. Guitar Man's, Trombone Man's, all came alive now, and they brought me with them into their smooth faraway cosmos.

Big Mose's face lit up the park and all of them began ascending the notes, higher, and higher. Then ripped down with equal force, like cascades crashing after one another.

They were playing Coleman Hawkins. The Bean! Their rapturous faces wrapped me into them still more, and I could not help it; my legs began to move, quite willing to go wherever Big Mose and the Band's fury pulled them.

"Never stop moving." This was Sauban, Bass Man, improvising. "Never stop moving girl, never!"

"Go, girl," said Skin Man. One of his feet clapped the ground so fast it looked like the shoe itself was laughing.

Nothing hurt.

"That's right, sister. That is right, ain't she?"

Because, drugged by the music, I'd lifted one arm and presently the other, set them at angles meant to balance me against legs which had no turning back now. The music got inside me, got under my skin, and began to explode back out of me. My legs, in love with the beat, made moves I'd never seen or heard of before: bends, turns, swoops, swings that didn't exist at all in ballet.

"Ha ha!" Big Mose roared the Hawk's notes.

The little boy's careful mother gave her hands to us, first clapping slowly and timidly. And then letting go. We all caught fire.

"The Bean!...smack!....Give it up now!" Bass Man got in between the lines.

"Dance, girl, now dance!" Big Mose coaxed lovingly, his big hands commanding the notes to mesmerize me. Gone the pain, gone the knee, gone! I made hip rolls, whooshes, pin turns. I felt like I was down South. People have no problem dancing in public in the South.

Big Mose, otherwise solid and unrelenting as a black diamond, suddenly transformed into a liquid state. His shoulders began to sway first, then his whole body began to sway in an S-shape, and he danced with the saxophone, holding it now not the way you'd cradle a baby, but the way you'd hold a woman. His eyes were squeezed dry, his tongue came away from the mouthpiece and licked moisture back into his lips.

"Go on, girl, bring it up, bring it up."

I am seduced.

I lifted my face to the sky and began to turn and turn and turn.

"Jump in, girl, the water ain't that cold."

I spun and spun in the insane power of the moment, not caring if I flew straight off the earth. Everybody was clapping, whistling, and others had gathered.

The music came down, and the last voice I heard was Big Mose's. "Girl, it is love making you dance."

The song ended, and while the crowd clapped for us, I slapped hands with each member of the band. Our faces gleamed with sweat and joy, and as I floated away, I raised my hand to Big Mose and the Band. Then I began running. My face turned over my shoulder and I shouted, "You right, brother, the water ain't that cold."

In the evening, Sally G. and Rudy Rodriquez came over to celebrate the news of our having been selected for the auditions. Pasha and Sally G. and I were sitting around her little bistro table. When I got up to get the rolls out of the oven, they saw the bulging place around my knee where I'd stuffed the ice cubes, the water running all down my leg, and I thought to tell them the truth right then.

Instead I lied, "Well, it doesn't hurt, it doesn't hurt. I can't even feel it."

CHAPTER 6

August, 1942
Shubert Theater, Manhattan

Had I known that privacy that deep meant loneliness deeper, I might have saved myself a good many years of the blues. Had I only known what it took for him to get there, or what he was really trying to say behind what he didn't say, a right good bit of heartache could have been spared.

The hot lights of the Shubert stage drew beads on my forehead. I used the back of my hand to wipe the sweat and saw the chalky costume powder come off with it. I drew a breath, inhaling a theater that smelled like dust and old school desks. Parts of the ceiling were black as the inside of an old vacuum cleaner—there had been a fire, once. The stage floor was scratched and worn, and the forest green velvet seats dipped at their centers from years of visits. No telling exactly when the theater was built. But Mr. Stanford had recently been made a hero by buying the landmark building with his own pocket money, preventing a Standard Oil filling station from going up in its place. At the time, we all enjoyed having a genuine hero in our midst, every one of us too young then to have understood the word tax, much less shelter.

Why he took such a keen interest in ballet dancers was something nobody thought to wonder. Much later, all the pieces fell into place and pierced a whole bubble of naiveté, shattering what I then had left to go on, but at the same time driving me across a border that I'd always thought was as far away as my Daddy's grave.

Now I peered through the curtain, roving my eyes along the front rows until I spotted Mr. Krimskaya, Mr. Leonard Stanford, and Florrie Duvet. The rest of the audience, out of the main houselights, looked like the little round heads you see in the comics; some had piled hairdos, others hats, others went natural. Most of them were parents and grandparents of us Manhattan School of Ballet students. An audition was practically like a real performance, or at least a dress rehearsal, and no parent was going to miss it. Except for my own Mamma who knew nothing about it.

The theater had about one hundred and fifty rows. My eyes stretched, strained, but the dimmed houselights made it too hard for me to see the faces, and I began to sweat. All the girls were still in the make-up room talking fast and high-pitched. I wished someone would shut the dressing room door so I could concentrate. I covered my ears, shut one eye, scanning with the other. I remember Mamma mentioning carrot juice as the only hope of sight in the dark outside of direct contact with the Lord and wished for both at that very moment. In the event that he'd forgotten the time or place of the auditions, I said a quick prayer to Saint Anthony, the one who helps the lost find their way back home.

I was on my way to giving up when the front doors of the theater opened and a lone figure emerged. I gasped. He walked slowly down the aisle a few rows, then stepped across two women sitting towards the back, leaned and seemed to be saying something to them, then tipped his hat, a fedora, and found a seat for himself.

I pivoted and ran at breakneck speed to the dressing room.

My heart was going boom, boom, boom. I couldn't pay attention to anything going on around me, especially the time. I sat there going to myself, "Do you think it's him? No, I do not think it's him." I was sitting on the sofa in the corner. The girls around me were going right to my central nervous system.

Suddenly somebody grabbed me by the shoulders and jerked me back and forth. To my surprise, there was Pasha, her face about one inch from mine. Her eyes were full of storm and two lines scored the middle of her forehead, sharp and forked as little pinches of lightning.

"You Miss-Nothing-to-Do-In-The-World and three minutes to curtain! Why are you not ready? Look at your hair!"

She took me by the back of the neck and waited just long enough for me to acknowledge a feeling of being pinned to a clothes-line, then guided me to the mirror, using a tone of voice that scared me to death.

The dressing room was soon empty. Everybody had gone over to stage left to wait for the cue. Sindy Schneider, the make-up artist from Greenwich Village, sympathized with Pasha by clucking her tongue and looking at me despondently. She whisked out a black brush, fluttered it in the rose-colored powder, tested it to the air, and before I could blink my eyes shut, she'd already gotten in these words, "Shut those eyes, Susanna. Before I spit up."

Automatically I sucked in my cheeks. She rosied just under my jawbones, then put the brush down and whispered, "pat, pat, pat, pat, pat," while patting my forehead with a special no-shine powder. Next she dipped an eyeliner brush into a small fingerbowl and teal-blued my eyes.

Pasha stood behind her holding her frown determinedly until the last coat of lipstick had been reapplied. It is my belief that she was holding her breath about that long as well.

"Bite down on this tissue for me, hon." Sindy Schneider bit down with me. Then she tilted my chin, had me stare at the leaf molding on the tin ceiling for what seemed like a pure eternity while she mascara'd me. "Now make me an O, hon." (The rewards of her good work seemed to have brought her temperature back down. I ventured smiling at Pasha as a way of encouraging her to exhale, but she was not ready yet.) I made an O and let Sindy finish lipsticking me, then tried to appease Pasha a second time, this time with a slight bunch to my brow so as to look pitiful and without. No response, even so.

Now came the pomade. I shut my eyes again. Sindy toured me with aqua-blue-glopped fingers, crimping my hair, and all but pomading it until I felt sure my head was beginning to look more like a blueberry pie than anything else. Trusting her, nonetheless, I began humming, quite unconsciously, "Here Comes The Bride."

"Susanna! These are the auditions." Pasha bent over me pleading. "Three years of concentration and work..." She sighed heavily. In the wing, Mrs. Moog, the impresario, began frantically flapping her arms in oblique circling motions. "Curtain call, Susanna, and you are number twelve!" Pasha implored.

Bless her. I looked at the ceiling and multiplied twelve people times three minutes in my head. Why everyone was squawking and losing their feathers was beyond me since I was number twelve, last. But for Pasha's sake I darted up and ran at breakneck speed to join the others before curtain call. As I passed her, Mrs. Moog seemed to be desperately looking for help. Like, how did this kid, Susanna, get in on this gig?

The group was furious! Sally G. made a big X in the air, shook her head. I was crowded around the other eleven girls, feeling like bad weather, but realizing at the same time that had any one of those girls been in love as I was, they might have had some trouble keeping everything together themselves. I leaned over to stretch my hamstrings and calves and tried to acknowledge everyone with exceptional politeness.

To my surprise Mr. Krimskaya called my number (he never remembered names) first. Reverse order. I felt the quick impulse of rage. But, before I knew it, Aaron Copland's *Billy the Kid* came oozing through the pipes. Pasha had been so excited about this piece for me that she'd taken me down to the studio one night after everyone had gone home and had played it for me on a piecemealed reel-to-reel tape. This piece seemed full of nerve, beautiful, soulful but all wrong. It was very hard to follow the beat; the music was skewed. Pasha said that's why she picked it. Because it's a piece that isn't easy and that I'd have to be ready to catch the surprises. She'd sat in her chair, her eyes like foxfire waiting for me. I felt like I was in trouble as soon as I heard its first chords. But, that very night Pasha and I had stayed there past midnight, choreographing, and I started to feel it. But, I fell twice dancing it. My knee buckled and Pasha, rather than coming with great worry on her face, gasped and said, "Susanna! You cannot avord to vall any more!"

Now the sad, sonorous music filled the whole of the theater, and I forgot my own troubles and went into the music. Through the rain of the stage lights, I took my first steps.

I'll never be able to completely cobble together what happened next. Somewhere within the playful part where Pasha had choreographed a cheeky little Mexican dance, I felt the ribbons around my left ankle come undone. Rationally, I understood that the bad luck trailing me would nearly guarantee a bad fall, a ruined career, and worst of all, making a fool out of myself in front of somebody who may have come through on a maybe that followed a chance encounter in the park.

I had seen a ribbon dance once before. Call me crazy but I'd seen one with Daddy at Saturday football. I believe it was Mississippi State versus the Clemson Tigers. At halftime, about six Clemson Tigerettes ran onto the field with their hands up in the air, each gripping orange ribbons about ten feet long. They made a circle, and the brass band struck up the notes of "*Somewhere Over the Rainbow*" while the cheerleaders smiled, evidently hoping for a chance in the Kodak Brownie cameras. They formed a wide circle, then marched backwards doing things with their arms that made the ribbons dance magically, as if they had lives of their own. The ribbon gymnastics were much more beautiful than I'm capable of describing: ampersands, figure eights, swirls, waves, lassos, all to a box step that, at the time, looked completely out of reach to the mere mortal. (I hadn't started ballet yet, but looking back, I give all credit to the Tigerettes' Marching Band; my own first *plié* was executed several weeks thereafter.)

As soon as my own ribbons came undone, out of the corner of my eye, I caught the gesture of someone's hands flown to her mouth. I think it was Sally G. I felt the pointe shoe loosening, the satin laces trailing and I knew I was doomed. Derailing from the choreography we had practiced for so many months, on my good leg, I stood on pointe, listened with all concentration to the notes and cadence of *Billy the Kid*. Leaning into the music with the singular goal of finding a way to retie the ribbons, I executed four *ronds de jambe.* That gave me the momentum for the *developé* of my bad leg while I used the good one as the supporting leg. I *developé'd* to the twelve noon position, held it and began a *frappé* that caused the ribbons to buoy and swirl, catching the stage light, floating outwards as if needing to say something. Moving to the *attitude derrière* all the while with the bad leg to the air, the good one supporting me on pointe, and the ribbons turning in the light as I made the second *tour developé.*

I was starting to manage it, to hit my stride when someone from the audience suddenly stood, virtually where I'd believed Francis Taylor to be sitting, and shouted, "FOR CHRISSAKES, DON'T RUIN IT FOR ME, SUSANNA! I'M DEAD!"

How did Hank get in? I was quite certain he wore his white Atlanta Crackers baseball cap he saved for special occasions such as opening game of the season. Ignoring him, I meant to hold to my notion that the ribbon show brought out the soulful hues of *Billy the Kid,* and that nothing except angelfish swimming could look so beautiful. Plus, here was my ability to demonstrate coolness in a crisis.

Then it hit me. For the first time in I don't know how long, I thought about that evening when Daddy's frightened face shook out the last vestiges of love on me, his own sweat beating me down with no mercy and the rose petal falling in halftime with him, as if begging pardon. He was trying to bring Mamma those presents. Daddy had needed me to know how much pain Mamma had put him in, all those years of having been silenced. Death, I saw, had at last freed him to speak out for what he really wanted. Now it was my turn, else Daddy wouldn't be haunting this theater. I understood now how linked we were; how our boldest actions remained our high displays of sincerity and trust.

I found my quiet spot. Listening. The music gave a sense of the world gone wrong. Why did Pasha pick it for me? She told me in our many practices that, if I relaxed, I would understand it. But I did not understand this broken cowboy piece. She said she picked it "Vecause you could do it, Suvannah! Vecause you have the athletic intuition." Whatever that meant.

Still, I found its plaintive spiritual guts, and I picked up right where the off-kilter music, my father, Pasha, Sally G., and my fantasy of a boyfriend wanted me. I heard Big Mose say, "Go on, girl, the water ain't that cold" and I slid into an *écart à terre*, leaned forward in sync with the disharmonic piece; the accompaniment always seemed one beat late. Why did she do this?. The rhythm is set wrong. But, in the *écart*, I used my upper torso to follow the quirky off-beat, lonely phrase. Isolating left, right, left, right, I got down over the extended leg and wrapped the satin laces in X's above my ankle. Then I tied them in a bow, and I hoped people wouldn't laugh when I did a little choreography with my arms. Then I rotated to the Chinese *écart* position. And that gave me the chance to transition into the yoga balasana, the child's position. On the diagonal I rose to my knees, stretched backwards in an arch, and depended on the flat toes of my pointe shoes to push against. Staying arched backwards, I lifted myself as an arched bridge. It all happened so fast. Big Mose came in again, just on cue, "Ha ha, girl, you can." His voice entered my head sounding like someone speaking through a wide aluminum pipe. Now, flexed backwards, I lifted my front leg and thrust it, straight and eagerly, towards the ceiling. With all the force I had, I stretched the leg further and further still, the muscles in my back and abdomen coiled tight as springs. I shot the leg out into space and it lifted me, pulled me like a rag doll. My arms obediently lifted in first, and then, miraculously, I hit the folk part of the piece, the *allegro* steps that prepared the *coupés* series that would give me the momentum I needed. And from there I danced the piece. I danced and danced, buoyed as if held in the palms of invisible hands.

I don't know how it happened except that the music and the people I loved, took me, saved me. They put a peace inside of me that took over, which took on the dance; I had no choice save to take the long-rehearsed steps. For the first time in my life I understood that people were responsible for me, wanted the responsibility. And it was their wanting to be responsible for me that impelled me to be responsible for myself. As I danced now, I began to think technically—my turnout, the lightness of my hands, the angle of my head, my use of space, my neckline, my hip line. As they pulled me around the stage, taking on the responsibility, I could stop rebelling. I could listen.

And when I got through, Pasha and Sally G. were waiting in the wings. Sally G. came beaming forward, practically tackling me and breaking my neck. Pasha's eyes were bright candles. It was only then that I understood why Pasha picked Copland's "*Billy the Kid*." It was because Krimskaya loved the piece, loved it for how hard it was to dance.

I waited stunned through three more auditions until Sally G., stuck with a strange Stravinsky piece, alighted on stage and floated through her elements: water and air. My eyes brimmed.

And then I ran to the dressing room where I hid my joy.

After all twenty of us had performed our three minutes, the judges, the foremost, of course, being Mr. Krimskaya, took their time. They leaned forward with heads huddled over their notes and thoughts, moving and pointing every now and again, as if we were a display of cantaloupes that needed thumping and whiffing and mashing for ripeness. You could hear someone blowing her nose.

But Sally G., Melinda, Rachel Ellison, Rudy, Q., and I made the Company. Rob LeVine didn't make it. He just never could learn to sit in his plié. I felt terrible for him.

I was too stunned to react, except that when Mrs. Moog came out of the dressing room, holding a dozen roses, I scrambled towards her, fighting to get the flowers in my arms. She gave them to me and I ran to the center of the stage where Pasha stood. Smiling, she fixed her hair a little first, then reached her arms towards me. I laid the dozen roses across them, and she gathered them in one arm and took my arm with the other. We both crossed the right foot behind the left, and curtseyed in exact tandem. Then Sally G. came out, took my other hand, and then came the four others.

I was still in complete shock as we held each other's hands and veered off the stage like walking lamp posts connected by thick, holiday garlands.

CHAPTER 7

August, 1942

Travers Stakes, Saratoga Springs, New York

The sight of the eight who didn't make the cut for *Over the Transom* was beyond heartbreaking. No telling how they would have gotten through it if it hadn't been for Mr. Stanford's offer to take us all to the races. No wonder he planned the three-hour bus ride.

The minute he said "races," I, for example, went into my smooth irresponsible oblivion. The dressing room was stone silent save for the sounds of zipper bags opening, people walking barefoot, and water coming out of the faucet. The winners understood this was no time to whoop and holler and had the good sense and respect not to hog the mirror or tell anyone how sorry they were right then. The unfortunates were at the sink, drooped over each other like willow trees, some hugging this way while randomly hedging an eye up over a shoulder and offering the winners a look of outright war, others washing tears in a bentover warning that winners should hurry up and leave them to themselves. They ran time to its very edge, fixing themselves. I was hoping that their looking in the mirror would help. But how could it have? They lingered, as I say, for some time.

I lingered, too, taking off what Sindy had put on my face, putting on fresh lipstick by Elizabeth Arden. I lingered over the few wrinkles in my dress, smoothing them with drops of hot water. I shined my legs with baby oil, and then I took advantage of my pierced ears: two pretend pearl earrings. The last thing I had on my mind was the actual horse race itself or that I'd just now been initiated officially as a professional ballerina. I had my straw cloche that had been handed down to me by Pasha. It matched my dress well enough, so I put it on and went out to join the others, the new *corps de ballet.*

At the front of the Bluebird were twelve individual picnic baskets, a peace offering to beat all. Beside them, Mr. Stanford stood, holding up fresh dollar bills, one for each one of us. He was dignified from the word Go, and many of the girls had a crush on him. As he spoke, some leaned forward, others literally fanned. (Back then fans were still in vogue and considered a vital part of the love language.) Mr. Stanford smiled, square and long, and told us who to bet on and what the odds were. Naturally, our bet was on his horse, Nefertiti. Satisfied, I guess, Mr. Stanford readjusted his cufflinks and went to sit with the wounded. Mr. Stanford's presence seemed to cheer the girls better than anything.

When we got to the races, there were many dressed-up ladies and there were soldiers everywhere. The air smelled of bleach, and sherry wine, perfume, and pipe tobacco. Once seated in the owners' box, I asked Mr. Stanford if I might borrow his binoculars. I can't tell you how bent I was on keeping them in my possession, looped around my neck, hands gripped to their barreled lenses. Because I was sure that my so-called boyfriend had come to our auditions and I was sure that I was going to see him at this horse race. Such is the nature of the grave mental illness that is so-called love.

Sally G. was in high spirits for good reason. Her performance had been stunning. She'd brought to the performance her blue cotton dress with shoulder pads in honor of the War, cinched at the waist, matching socks, black patent leather shoes, charm bracelets, and a wide-brim straw hat with black knitting. Because she *knew*. She knew she was going to make it and that she deserved to look good at the Travers Celebration races and the exciting "Midsummer Derby."

Amy, Melinda, Susan, Paisley, and Dottie all looked adorable, too. I can't say I looked like much. But, I'd grown to be the kind who would assume that others understood why I had safety pins ringing my hemline.

When the horses broke out of the gate, Sally G. stood on tiptoe, slapping her rolled-up program against her thigh, and posting.

To their blurred flash of color, everyone stood and went wild. Sally G. took up invisible reins. Well, we all did. Amy, Melinda, Susan, Pais, and Dottie, we all took up invisible reins; we were on top of the world.

The horses presently began to fan out around the far bend when a little man no heavier looking than a twelve-year-old boy took a fall. Everyone gasped. Sally G. dropped her invisible reins, and Mr. Krimskaya took off his driving cap and began scratching the back of his head. The horse galloped on, leaving fresh hoof marks in rich, black, clean dirt.

"Christ!" Mr. Stanford cried and wanted the binoculars back before I even got the chance to put them to the use I had in mind. The riderless horse, Nefertiti, took it upon herself to win anyway, galloping freely with the polished stirrups flapping across the barrel of her body, and field hands chasing her ridiculously. With the help of binoculars, you could also see the ironic smile that horse carried on her face, all the way to the finish line.

Mr. Stanford cursed under his breath as he roved columns of numbers in his program.

Then he got stern and quiet. He tapped a pipe against his palm, blushed vaguely, swallowed and said, "All right girls, let's go place another bet. Here's five dollars each."

The girls jumped up and down; that's normal. Rachel Ellison, of course, took the opportunity to stand on a chair and kiss him on the cheek. Right then you'd have never known we'd executed a *plié,* much less been selected to debut a performance that would hook our destinies. Least of all me. All I cared about was getting my hands on the binoculars.

"Mr. Stanford," I said, as he was trying to turn my shoulders. "Might I stay here and watch over everyone's things? If you'll hand me those binoculars, I'll guard them, too."

"You don't want to bet?"

"No, sir, I've bet on enough in my day."

"You sure?"

"No, merci, Monsieur."

"Suit yourself, Susanna." He handed me the binoculars, lined the girls in a row and they skipped off, each with her five dollars tucked away in a secret place. Mr. Stanford and Mr. Krimskaya followed, chatting quite spiritedly.

I was thinking how glad I was to have a minute. But as it turned out, things might have been easier if what came next hadn't happened to me while I was all alone.

The minute I began scanning the rest of the owners' boxes, Francis Taylor's flushed face came directly in the middle of the lenses. He was with yet another girl, far from my kind. She had neat beauty-parlored hair that made mine look hand-me-down. She wore a big floppy hat and pink jersey dress that looked stunning on her. Her lips were valentine red and she had a real pretty color to her cheeks. Then I accidentally panned the binoculars down to her young, full breasts, approximately three sizes larger than my own. Strawberry juice or something dribbled down her chin and he tripped it with a finger.

Next it looked like they were holding hands.

I refocused the binoculars, stepped over a chair, and made my way through the back aisle of the owners' boxes towards those roofed with striped canvas tenting that they called pavilion. These boxes were evidently reserved for the supremely rich, richer, if you'll believe it, than Mr. Stanford. I ducked through the crowd. My arms were getting a little tired, but I remained with my elbows bent close to my waist, and the binoculars held to my eye sockets, moving in what would become my lifelong posture: outside looking in.

Then Francis Taylor and the girl suddenly blurred on me. Abruptly, I dropped the binoculars. They swung between my small breasts and almost hurt me. But there I was in breathing distance. Oh, I was miserable!

Instead of facing Francis Taylor, my eyes stared fixedly at his private table: a spread of some kind of brown liver-looking stuff, close kin to bologna except for the wrong color. Cheeses of all sorts that I could smell from where I stood, and wondered how on earth anyone would get a bite down without overtly holding his or her nose. Pink salmon with its head still on and a little cherry tomato in his mouth, as if he'd earned it.

The desserts, however, watered the mouth, and might be described as works of art: strawberries and whipped cream, cakes of alternating layers of dark and light chocolate, and little cream puffs, all sizes. There was Champagne cooling in a silver bucket. He and she, and their one or two friends around the table, held up their flutes in two or three toasts, one right after the other. Looked to me like everybody was having a real good time, with the exception, perhaps, of Francis Taylor, whose smile seemed stiff and wooden and whose expression remained ice-frozen as he listened to someone's story. Which vaguely gave me the impression that he was simply somewhere else after all.

I inched closer, gripping the binoculars for dear life.

"Freeze!" someone suddenly called. I jerked my head up, and three fingers from each hand sprung up from the bino's hands like little feathers.

The large brass clock across the tracks struck the hour of four. Francis Taylor, a man who never strayed too far from the time, looked up, and, of course, saw me.

As if a bee had stung him, he broke loose of the girl's arm. He stared at me as though I had three eyes and hairs coming out of my chest. Then he averted his eyes, and eschewed me by way of a strong, entirely unnecessary clearing of the throat.

Straightaway, he surprised me by drawing his eyes back onto me, and this time I noticed a glimmer of encouragement or at least recovery in his eyes.

I have never ever felt my cheeks burning so intensely in my life. "Did you like the performance?" I mouthed. What was I doing?

On top of the girl's gaining back his attention by seductively rubbing his arm, Francis Taylor himself turned his back on me—page one of the six saddest years of my life.

I took off my straw cloche, laid it quickly over the binoculars, backed away. I never felt the pavilion's little entrance steps behind me. The instant I missed the step, my knee buckled, and I fell with my hands pawing the air. About halfway down, I hit the rail pole and blacked out.

I woke up to someone putting ice on the back of my head. As the ice-packed cocktail napkin pressed to the base of my skull, I tried to adjust my eyes. A man was speaking to me. Strong hands lifted me. And instead of crying in his arms, I sat back down and started to laugh. I was in pain; my head hurt. But I laughed. I sat laughing in my dress and my cloche hat that someone must have put back on my head. I held the hand held to the napkin at the back of my head.

I'd seen this kind of behavior before—in the New York subway: old shabby men, sitting there by themselves, laughing their heads off. I was laughing from embarrassment.

Later, years later, Francis Taylor told me he thought I'd gone a little crazy that day at the races. About two or three times a day for forty-five years he called me crazy, but once on a walk hand-in-hand through the woods, he spoke about my fall that day, his tone protective, almost pained. As he spoke about the wild laughing, he squeezed my hand and then said, "A little fatuous, I think"—a term from the North that obviously means loony. We walked quietly for some time, and when it got cold he wrapped his arms around me. I was thinking about the children, wondering if they were going to be all right, and he answered for me, "Baby, all three of them are going to grow up fine and strong." He kissed my forehead, all over.

But that day at the races he said something entirely different. As quickly as the man's face appeared, it disappeared. Francis Taylor's replaced it. He knew I was hurt. Still, he bent over me, shook my shoulders quite violently and in one sentence promptly tore down all that I'd struggled to build since I was twelve years old: "Susanna," he demanded, "you *must* do something about that leg." I could feel his breath on me, slightly dry and sour. "Susanna, I order you to get a doctor and tell him about your leg. I'll call you about this next week. Do you hear me?" He seemed to be shouting, punishing me.

All of a sudden I seemed to have my powers back. I used his arm to pull myself up. I didn't care how I looked now. I didn't care about my messy hair, my run stockings, my grease-smeared dress. All I cared about was his seeing my eyes, burning. I opened them wide, held them to his. Behind the glare, I let him see how high was my cryptic anger, higher than any emotion I had.

Then I smiled, triumphantly. I let go of him, adjusted my hat, and limped away with resolve.

What I did next took some strategy and some luck. Below his pavilion, on a direct sight line, stood a group of loud U.S. Marines, rowdier and drunker than all of Singapore on a Saturday night. They wore summer khaki service uniforms: tailored green jackets, pointed pocket flaps, garrison hats, and shiny black shoes. Some had red badges on a left sleeve of the jacket.

Since the horses had hardly broken from the gates for the second race, everyone else in the stands was sitting down, appearing to mind their own business. But these boys, each one of them drinking shots of bourbon in tiny little glasses, seemed to be lonely even in a crowd.

Without stopping to think about what I was doing, I went towards them. My knee was a little numb, but its habit of buckling now seemed no more threatening than hiccups. As I say, I had my powers back.

As if I'd known them casually all my life, I reached and tapped one on the shoulder, "Say! Hey!" I exaggerated. "Might I keep you company for a while?"

Big Lank (as I came to call him) instantly slapped an arm around me. He had to of been from Texas. He exclaimed, "Why sure, gal! Pretty gal like you, we'd be honored! Here, take a drink!"

I moved under his wing.

In a drawl that could pull brilliants out of a Mississippi mud bank, he asked my name, then passed it around almost as quickly as I was able to say it. Two big hands gathered around my hips, hoisted me to the sky, then let me down so I could stand on the chair. The rest of them smiled, looked back and forth at each other, winked. But Big Lank had already claimed me, grabbing me to his chest as if I was his own purple heart. I consciously leaned slightly forward, bracing with a hand held to the shoulder of the Marine standing on my left (who I hadn't named yet) and the other to the shoulder of Big Lank who stood on my right.

I was having fun. The fun and thrill of it had to do with when and how to turn around to verify that Francis Taylor was looking. I took several hole-and-corner glances in his general direction. Then I put my arm around Big Lank and waved my cloche in the air. I took a sip of the bourbon he'd handed me in a jigger. Gads!

Confetti got thrown on us by the people behind us, giving me my best excuse to turn around. I looked straight up to the pavilion boxes. The horses were coming around the homestretch, and evidently Francis Taylor relished the event. He victoriously held the girl's hand to the air.

So I started fondling the back of Big Lank's head, like I'd been doing that kind of thing all my life. Then I let them help me off the seat, and I'll tell you what I did: I leaned up and kissed him.

It felt pretty good to kiss a boy. I kissed and kissed, keeping my eyes wide open. With my head angled that way, I had a superb view, straight up the rows to Francis Taylor's pavilion. The tingling, deep down, I'm pretty sure, came not from Big Lank's sloppy tongue in my mouth, but from the fixed sight I had on my strange friend.

Big Lank must have kissed me for several minutes before Francis Taylor saw me. I shut my eyes tight as shutters and put in another five with the Marine. Big Lank gave me that smitten look of someone who has fallen in love. I slipped from his grip, pretended to be off to buy a Coca-Cola, and took by twos the steps towards Mr. Stanford and the girls.

I reached them panting, smoothing my hair. Each one was just to the last bite of her hot dog. Nobody smiled. I looked around for my basket, acting like nothing had happened. But, Rachel Ellison announced, her tone bordering on the cruel, "The picnic baskets got stolen while you were out touring the tracks. Mr. Krimskaya saw you down there with the Marines. Where does this side of you come from, Susanna? Mr. Stanford tried to talk him out of putting you on probation, but you know how Mr. Krimskaya is when he gets something in his head. He's absolutely furious." She lowered her head, then put on a pair of pink-rimmed eyeglasses.

Horrors.

I desperately needed Sally G., but I couldn't find her. I couldn't concentrate, couldn't see well. I sure wasn't going to try to look at *him* again.

To my relief, she finally surfaced, poking her way over everybody's feet in the aisle. She leaned into my ear and whispered the word to me, bless her heart, after it was entirely too late. Evidently she'd tried to sneak away and rescue me in time, but Mr. Krimskaya himself had come after her. Now as she explained herself to my ear, he came right up and separated us, taking the seat that had been Sally G.'s and making everybody else, including Mr. Stanford, move down one.

So I never got to explain anything at all to her.

Plus, due to my having put a damper on the afternoon, we stayed for only one more race after that, then filed to the Bluebird. I sat way in the back, all alone, and when anybody tried to approach me, I shrugged and looked real hard out the window as if telephone poles were poetry. Sally G. was made to sit way up front, next to Mr. Krimskaya. I had no way of passing a secret note to her, but a few times I caught her eyes in the rearview mirror. They were sad, puzzled, and eager, all at once.

Three hours later, the bus rolled into Port Authority. It was suppertime and I was hungry. Nonetheless, I couldn't get up the will power to subway home and face Pasha. Instead I walked to a phone booth at the far end of Port Authority's giant lobby, found the finger-pawed yellow pages swinging from a chain underneath the phone, and opened them.

By almost nine-thirty, I'd copied down the name and address of every single orthopedic surgeon in Manhattan. My hand was cramped from writing and my eyes were sore. My whole body ached from having held my extension so long during my ribbon show. I was a sorry case bending to pick up my suitcase; it felt heavy as something sleeping.

Pasha had made homemade blueberry muffins, which she had wrapped in waxed paper and put in the freezer for another time. Holding one in my hand, I tiptoed to her door, peeked through the keyhole. Her lamp was on and she was up reading. I slipped my free hand in my dress pocket, pressing the list of doctors deep in the seam. "Pasha?" I used Daddy's knock.

She said, "Come in, Susanna." With her hair down, she looked thinner and paler than usual. I broke the partially frozen muffin and offered her half. She passed, sighing, then giving me a look of deep study. I palmed the pieces of cake in my hands to warm them a little (I always loved the kind of muffins that weren't all the way cooked so that you could mash them into an entirely different taste). For a minute, I had a fleeting hope that word about what I'd done had not yet traveled. "Pasha?" I said again, calling her as if calling *on* her. I always believed she had a special ability to feel exactly what others were feeling.

She raised her gentle eyebrows and seemed to be waiting for an explanation.

I raised my eyebrows, preparing to tell her why I had gone off the deep end.

She closed her book, looked at me and said, "I think you're hungry. I think there's still some dinner left in the icebox." She said this tenderly, a little off-handedly.

In so many words, I told her I was starved, just starved, and asked if I could put dinner on a tray and have it right beside her while she read in bed. She said that would be all right, and I turned away from Pasha's door, started to go towards the kitchen, turned back, thinking, I'll confess now.

"Pasha?" I couldn't do it. I hit the brakes by saying instead, "Have you had supper already? May I bring you some?"

Pasha only smiled and answered frankly and politely. "Yes, thank you. I've had a little bite. You go ahead and get yourself a plate and bring it in here." (I thought so. It was almost ten-thirty.)

I went to the icebox and saw how everything on the plate had little decorations, little garnishes of parsley and paprika, even a real sweet decoration of marshmallow on Pasha's yams. The napkin covering the dish bore a small figure of a ballerina that Pasha had drawn herself.

I sat down on the small cushioned chair in her room, forked some of Pasha's sweet potatoes, and started to thank her when Pasha suddenly sat up in bed, laced her fingers around the mound of blanket covering her bent knees. She looked at me the way you look out over the sea from its shoreline. She sighed and then she said, "Susanna, not all feelings that you think are love turn out to be feelings which mean real love. There are others. There is desire, not at all the same thing as love. And this can only end in pain and sorrow."

I gulped down my glass of milk and reached quickly for another semi-frozen muffin, as if its belonging to a recipe from back home could help. My eyes began to cloud. I put a hand to my forehead and made a little visor bill. Pasha's words, though spoken softly, hit me strong as the sun. I forked a large amount of sweet potatoes and let them go smoothly down my throat.

"Listen to me," she said, throwing the covers back. "For now you must pour your love into the ballet. The real one will come with time, Susanna."

I looked straight down.

I never knew whether she was referring only to the Marines or if somehow she'd found out about Francis Taylor. Suddenly, I wasn't so hungry anymore. I went to the kitchen, washed my plate, then rearranged our bulletin board until I was sure Pasha had drifted off to sleep. I waited a little longer, a little frightened by my own thoughts.

I think my strange childhood gave me my need for deep secrecy about the wishes I treasured most. Somehow Pasha had always trusted even what I withheld from her. I bent over the white pages looking up his address, my finger running down a small column of Dewitt's.

I waited until around 11 P.M.

Then I just did it. I put on a fresh dress and the same pumps I'd worn to the races. I found Pasha's shampoo in the cabinet and with it I coated the door hinges. The door opened without a squeak, and I crept out. The sky was like ink. No one was on the streets. The crosstown bus rolled up, and I made it over to his place on 69th and Park, the little tear of paper bearing his address stuck to the palm of my hand like a small wet leaf.

He was surprised, and I can't quite say, happy. I think maybe he had outgrown surprises, or had never had any. He opened the door and stood leaning against its frame. He wore a pair of shorts, a blue striped pajama shirt, bedroom slippers, and was doing everything he could to wake up.

"Why hey, Francis Taylor. It's me. Susanna, the girl from the park."

"I see it is," he yawned.

"Don't you want to know how I found out where you live?" Just the sight of him produced my goofiest, most awkward grin, and I stood there with it taking up most of my face.

"I knew you'd find it, I don't need to know how."

You knew I'd find it? You don't need to know how?

"Well say, I just dropped by to see if you might know the name of a good orthopedic surgeon." Then making believe that he'd only been kidding about the doctor, I moved forward to kiss him, now that I knew how.

For that he opened the door and let me in without further complaint or yawn.

Kissing him didn't feel one bit like kissing the Marine.

With the Marine, it was a question of endurance, a little like kissing cold artillery, though as I say, fun.

Kissing Francis Taylor was like being lifted on a cloud. His lips were rosy and sensuous, soft, his breath was clean as snow, as if he'd had time to go to the sink and rinse with oral antiseptic before even coming to the door.

He reached around my back, down my dress, and skillfully unsnapped my bra. In unsnapping my bra by myself, something I'd been doing every day for four years now, I had never before felt the remotest sensation. I had also touched my breasts in my day, had needed to know what they felt like, growing. But I had never gotten more out of it than, say, rubbing my nose or scratching my head. Yet, as he unsnapped, coming very quietly around to my breasts, something came alive in me. Alive, soft, quite magical; a feeling to which only he could have had the keys, and I stayed sure about that. I tilted my head back and felt for him as if any minute he might disappear.

He caressed me, and I shut my eyes into his face and let him kiss me. He was taking my breath away, and I tugged my dress upwards, trying to get free of it. He kissed my ear and then my neck and shoulders, taking my hair down as he did so. It swept across my back. His arms were around me, carefully, and his fingers began unworking the buttons on the back of my dress.

I was gone. I needed his clothes off. I tried to unbutton his shirt. He had undone the buttons almost to the small of my back and had drawn the bra straps off my shoulders. He helped me with his shirt, and it fell lightly to the floor. I'd taken my shoes off, and I rested my feet on top of his as he drew me to his body. Then he gently pushed the straps down my arms and the top part of the dress bloomed open and dropped over the pleats. And so I had no clothes on from the waist up. Which was heaven. Pure heaven.

We kissed and petted for the longest time, and I thought this would be as far as we would go. But then he slipped a hand underneath my dress and began caressing my thigh, working towards my ruffled under frills. With his other hand he undid the last three buttons, and then he untied the bowknot in my sash, and my dress fell to the floor.

He began to pull his own shorts off and, at the same time, reached to take my under frills off, and that's when I went berserk. Don't ask me why, but it's not stretching it to say Mamma had something to do with this. Deep inside me, a little messenger with a policeman's voice ran at bullet speed all through my body: DON'T DO IT, SUSANNA! YOU'LL HAVE REGRETS THE REST OF YOUR LIFE!

I took his hand, closed it tightly in mine, and held it from pulling down my under frills.

He looked straight at me, searching with eager, innocent eyes, as if he, too, was discovering something for the first time. He gave me a little smile, quite shy, and I think I returned it. I felt shy, too, quite shy.

I arched back just a little bit, hoping he'd touch my breasts again. He touched them, kissed them, and kept trying to work my under frills off despite the way I held his hand. I was no longer afraid of the wetness. I rather enjoyed it.

I said, "We'd better wait."

"Wait?"

"Yes," I whispered, "it's not time yet."

"You don't want me, Susanna?"

Oh, it is not that, Francis Taylor, I wanted to tell him. *I want you*, is what I wanted to tell him. He stood so still. *If you just knew*, I wanted to whisper. How vulnerable he looked. Who could blame him? *I, too, am on fire.*

I kissed him again passionately. But instead of saying what I really wanted, I said the direct opposite, "No. No lovemaking. Not now, Francis Taylor." My legs were like noodles, and my breasts felt cloaked in velvet and I had chills, and my heart was racing, but I said, "Not now—not yet."

He pulled back, giving me those blue eyes. With the night all around us, they looked navy. He looked good with no clothes on. He looked really nice, and I kind of wished he'd pull the shades because I truly did not want any strangers out there in other buildings to see how good he looked with no clothes on. Down below, something inside me seemed to be drawing in. I very desperately wanted to reach my arms out and pull him to my body. But he'd let go of my under frills by now, and so I was straightening out the part that had gotten wrinkled from being all twisted in our hands. You should have seen what he looked like without his shirt on.

"You're being coy, Susanna," he said. His face darkened.

That hurt my feelings.

I stepped back just a little bit. I needed to get my dress back on. In just my under frills, I looked around for it, crouching slightly with my arms crossed in front of me. There was a slight wind in his living room, a slight draft. Next to the upholstered sofa, evidently made of fine embroidered Italian fabric, was a polished table holding a Chinese porcelain lamp. On it, too, was a frame holding a woman's lovely dark face, which I took to be his mother's face. I picked it up and started to ask him.

"Susanna, that doesn't belong to you."

My word.

I started walking in a little flamingo prance. I was just trying to humor him. Which, as I promptly found out, only heightened his conviction that I was deliberately teasing.

I took a quiet breath. The last thing I wanted him to know was that I was afraid. I had come there scared. Scared from taking the bus at that hour. Scared from what Pasha had said. Scared from all that I'd done wrong today, beginning with the ribbon show and ending with the Marine. And now this frightening look of his. I scooped my dress up and threw it over my head.

Then I mumbled, "Coy? Me?" I had a lump in my throat as I said it. The dress was still over my head, and my voice was muffled by a little piece of the pocket caught in my mouth.

"Yes, coy!" Then he took me by the arm, and I thought for a minute that he might hurt me. He was scaring me, and I wanted to go home. Still, I was too proud to back down, and peering an eye over my dress' pear-shaped collar, I repeated, "Coy, me?"

"Susanna!" He practically choked on this word, and it looked like he was going to cry. I realized then that he really thought that it was *I* who didn't want *him,* that I was trying to make fun of him. As he spoke he seemed to be getting smaller and smaller. Suddenly.

I moved forward to try to hold his face in my hands. He had his hand rested on the corner of an oil painting. There were four oils hung on the wall, and I guessed they were portraits of his grandparents and great-grandparents. With the tips of his fingers, he touched the painting, tenderly, just barely.

As I slowly reached a hand to his cheek, he jerked his face away. I tried reaching him instead through his grandfather, giving the painting a look of sympathy. But Francis Taylor blocked me with eyes flickering; I don't know if he was on the verge of breaking with humility or exploding with anger. He moved in front of the painting and wouldn't even let me see.

"Have I hurt you?" I asked, almost inaudibly. I was still barefooted. With a foot, I surreptitiously groped for my high heels, while trying to hold him with my eyes.

"Oh, don't be such a child," he said. Quite bitterly.

Over the pear-shaped collar, I narrowed my eyes, then snapped the dress down over the rest of my face and reached back hurriedly to tie my sash. I tried to tie the sash fairly tightly and then tried to grapple with the buttons all by myself. He'd pushed me pretty much to my limits calling me a child, and I didn't want him touching me at all anymore. At all.

"A child," I said finally.

"A child, yes. A mere child. Now I don't know what you're doing over here at this hour, Susanna. And I don't know why I let you in." He started to take hold of my arm and push me, and that's when I wheeled around and pointed my finger.

"Well! At least I don't lie and say I'll be somewhere when I'm really having hors d'oeuvres and kissing the nips of some dolled-up girl." I was a little ashamed of myself. I hotfooted over to the shoe that I finally saw beside the wall, turned over with the spiked heel sticking straight up towards the chandelier.

Well! He started smiling real big. And glowing. As if he'd gotten a big kick out of watching me stand up for myself.

I straightened my back, squared my shoulders. And then I said, just loud enough so she could hear, in case she happened to be in the house. "And how is that precious girl, by the way, Francis Taylor? (Here I butterflied my eyelashes.) How is the precious, big-bosomed girl?"

He said, "I don't know what you're talking about, Susanna."

This he managed without that smirk and in his real voice.

I threw my arms open, and then put one finger to my lips. "You better whisper, son. She might hear you."

"My cousin?"

Not again with this cousin malarkey.

He reached for his shorts. I thought the least I could do would be to help him pick them up, so I did, right as he said that.

His cousin. "Oh, sure I'll believe that!" I flung the shorts at him.

"I'm tired, Susanna. It's the middle of the night. Why did you come here? What do you want from me?"

What a jerk. I was now convinced that she was indeed his girl, and that she was indeed resting her feet somewhere in this giant apartment, and that for all I knew they were man and wife. I shut my eyes and tried to think what that ribbon show must have looked like, and what I must have looked like, sitting under the pole of that pavilion, with my knees outspread, and my hair all disheveled. And so with arms akimbo, I took one more step backwards, and said, "I came over to ask you what kind of hat you wear."

"What?" he said. All of a sudden his voice became very gentle, dulcet, "What?"

"I said I, I came over to ask you what kind of hat you wear."

If he could have just said, "A fedora, Susanna. A dark grey felt fedora," I might not have gone all to pieces.

But instead he said, "How's your leg?" And in a soft voice he wanted to know if I could think seriously about getting it fixed.

My throat pulled in a hard knot, and I tried to swallow back its little pulses of grief. I looked down so that he could see no more than the top of my head, and that's when I saw that I had put my dress on backwards and inside out. I quickly laid a hand over the tag, real flat, and looked up, and asked, "Where is your girl, how long have you known her?"

"At my uncle's, Susanna," he said out loud. My eyes were filling. Humiliation does that. Again I bent my head, a hand to my forehead, the other over the tag.

"Well," I said, "That's all I wanted to know. I better get on home. I'm expecting a long distance call from my Marine boyfriend. He'll be worried about me. Marines always did worry about their girls, I don't know if anyone ever told you."

I put the other hand to the tag and must have looked a little bit like I was in prayer or about to choke myself, one.

I took one step for the door and that's when the darkness came over him again. All my concentration, at that moment, was centered on just getting around his noticing that I had my dress on inside out, and I gave him a sideways glance and a vague, stiff smile as I took a step.

Before I knew it, he'd grabbed my wrist, pulling my hand off the tag and jerking it downwards. "Go on, then," he said, angrily, "and don't come back, Susanna." He picked me up from behind and was about to throw me out, lock, stock, and barrel.

I saw that I was going to have to face the elevator man, the bus driver, and any passengers riding at that hour, not just with a splotched face, but with a dress on backwards and inside out.

So I practically raised the roof. "Wait a minute!" I tried. "I can't go like this! You can't make me go like this!"

"What, Susanna," he said, glaring right at me. "Why can't you go? What's wrong?" He was holding me lifted with one arm and trying to work the door latches with the other. His voice was bitter and angry, and I think I was too heavy for him.

"I can't go with my dress on backwards, Francis Taylor."

Well, if he hadn't seen it before, he saw it now. He started smiling. I asked, politely as possible, given the circumstances, if he minded putting me down so I could turn it right side out. He put me down, and I started to pull the dress over my head when it suddenly occurred to me that the so-called cousin would never be caught making such a fool out of herself. Which brought out insecurities.

I was standing practically naked with a living room mirror view of both myself and the hallway's reflection when I suddenly wondered if the woman would finally wake up and come on out all cold-creamed, catching us both.

Don't ever ask my why, but there I was in my under frills, just about to turn the dress right side out, when I suddenly held it by the collar with the tips of my fingers and started up a little Hawaiian dance. I shook the dress one way, then shook it the other, with my hips waving and swinging back and forth. And to the flow, I hummed "*If you can't sing it, you'll have to swing it.*"

Well. That was the end of that. Again he wrapped one arm around me and picked me up, pinching my side, and again used the free arm to work open the door latches. Then he hurled me out into the hall, and I think I looked a little like a torpedo. He next threw the dress out, and it floated down like a small parachute. The door slammed behind me. Then came the sound of the latches working again, then the click of the double lock.

I was shaking. I rushed to get the dress turned around before the elevator man arrived. I wanted to cry and needed to cry, but it occurred to me that he might be able to see me through the keyhole, so I just leaned my head against the wall and tried to swallow, tried to think about everything, just tried to think. My feelings balled in my throat. What I had done, coming over there like that, had been beyond inappropriate.

I heard the rumble of the elevator starting to move from the ground floor and the rustle of the elevator's dust-cloaked cables. I lifted my head real slowly and turned my face even slower towards his door. It was as if my joints had turned to wood. And I said to Francis Taylor's door, "Well, if you ever need a real friend one day, I'm her. My name is Susanna."

The latches unclicked again and then the door opened, just barely. All I had was one little eye, just one. I couldn't see anything else.

But I heard him. He said in a voice so barely audible, "I'm sorry, Susanna."

I went up to the crack in the door and through it, though afraid to rise over a whisper, I said, "You will know. In due time you will know." No one ever said love, or whatever this was, runs a smooth course. At least not where I come from.

I was prepared to do anything for him now, anything.

"Too late?" he whispered, evidently echoing what he thought I'd said. Now he widened the crack about six inches, and I could see his face. He looked vulnerable, discouraged, a little ashamed. He was a beautiful man, beautiful.

I went towards the door again and was close enough for him to feel the whisper from my lips. "You will know," I repeated.

"Too late?" He asked again. He seemed to be stuttering.

"You'll know," I said a third time, whispering.

His eyes pleaded.

Then elevator doors opened with their old jingling sound, and I stepped in and the elevator man asked me if I was going down. His eyebrows went up. They looked like plumes. Then he turned to the buttons and riveted his eyes on them as if they were lights on a control panel.

I had to worry about his reaction to the sight of me. Had to wonder. I was tempted to ask him what all he knew about Francis Taylor from 11-E, but instead I said, "Yes, going down," and tried to laugh, using the back of my hand to get the tears off of my cheek.

Once outside, I craned my neck and counted eleven stories up. There were no longer any lights on in his apartment.

I turned and walked four blocks down Fifth to 79th where the cross town always seems to be there when you need it. I stepped on the bus, dropped my token in the slot. There were only one or two others on the bus, the air was tainted with a faint aroma of liquor.

I sat up in the first row, opposite the driver. I reached in my pocket, dug up the list of orthopedic surgeons. I'd creased the sheet of paper four times, and I opened it now and began to slowly run a finger down a list of well over one hundred names, front and back. Then to the bus driver I said, "Say stop."

And he said, "Stop."

And so I looked down and saw the name of the doctor beside my finger, and I asked the bus driver if I might borrow the pen I saw propped behind his ear. And he said, "Surely," and gave it to me, and then I very carefully circled that doctor's name, creased the sheet of paper again in four, pushed it back in my pocket, flat and flush against my leg.

CHAPTER 8

Late September, 1942

Upper West Side, Manhattan

When the two orderlies rolled me out of the ambulance, Pasha was waiting for me beside the railing of our brownstone's steps. She was shifting weight from one foot to the next. An unloading vegetable truck had partially blocked our views of each other. Pasha's hands flailed in small signs of impatience, then rested calmly again, one folded against the other. The ambulance, that needed no siren (nothing was wrong with me except that I had on a cast to the hip, white as cotton), moved around the truck, almost grazing it. Pasha smiled, and from the stretcher I craned my neck and smiled back. The orderly on the passenger's side cracked his window, and I stretched an arm, getting just the tips of my fingers through it and fluttered. The joy of seeing Pasha's kind face tickled my nose and I thought I might cry. I tapped the window and cried out her name.

She smiled in a way that was a little strange and forced.

"Pasha?"

She waved, then turned abruptly and started walking up and down the brownstone's steps. She'd drawn out her husband's handkerchief and it now covered her face. I felt my eyebrows bunching.

Calling her once more, I started to sit up, but the orderlies stilled me. They'd wheeled the stretcher about halfway out of the back of the ambulance. Trying to move against hands anchoring me in exactly the right places, I jerked forward but the lip of the cast sunk into the top of my thigh.

Pasha abruptly stopped moving up and down the steps, and instead turned her back to us, and leaned her head into the brownstone's doorjamb. She was drooped in the forlorn posture of someone who's been locked out. Then she began to speak in a fast, unbroken Russian, as if the handkerchief bearing her husband's initials also bore her ears and heart.

She was making me feel terrible. Absent-mindedly, I felt a hand over the Band-Aids lined in a row at my elbow joint. They'd hooked me up to wires and taken a lot of blood and given me pills and forced me to exercise with a lead beanbag over my shin. And for the four nights they kept me there, coming in at all hours of the night to check me for fever or give me a pill or pull a blanket over me, they never answered one of my questions or gave me an inkling about my progress.

As I watched Pasha there leaned against the doorjamb, talking in Russian and so far away from me, it all came to me about what I'd done—finding a doctor without telling her about it, and checking into the hospital before the closest person I'd ever have to a real mother even knew I had trouble, and calling her from the hospital cafeteria pay phone and telling her she couldn't come visit because the quarantined veteran population in the hospital had forced a ban on visitation hours. All this because I wanted to win a stranger's trust. And now I saw what it brought: Bills. Loads of them. Thousands worth.

My head suddenly felt feverish, and I tried hard to swallow. "Pasha, I know what it is. We've gone broke."

Pasha still wouldn't look at me. I drew away from the orderlies, balanced myself on crutches, moved towards her, and whispered, "This has bankrupted us. I can feel it."

I tried to push away an image of the two of us working at Woolworth's. Pasha gathered the handkerchief into her palm. Her lips were drawn in a grimace, and her cheeks, partly hidden by the fleshy part of her hand, seemed to have lost their color.

I took a step forward. I hoped what I wanted to say would help. But nothing came out of my mouth. What I wanted to tell her was that I was a professional now, in a position to slowly pay back debts, and I wanted to take her by the shoulders and assure her. I pulled up on the handrail, meaning to get to her side, but Pasha ducked her head in her arms and kind of folded up.

It occurred to me that something worse yet had happened; that something had happened to Mr. Krimskaya or that the studios had caught fire.

The orderlies began to look uncomfortable. Each now placed a firm hand under my arm.

We moved slowly, as if stopped by head winds. Every time I took a step, I imagined the price of the operation, then I'd look at Pasha. Then I'd just become paralyzed with one foot dangling midway between one step and the next.

Pasha finally came forward, and she threw her arms around me and burst into tears. Without having the remotest idea of how hard it is to make thousands and thousands, I spoke now. I tried to console her by reminding her that I had become professional. Which most unfortunately did not help.

Holding each other, we got inside the front door and moved like a cluster of grapes up the stairs. Pasha cried so hard that an elderly couple with look-alike noses opened their door and gawked with their heads turning at a reduced speed. Responding by drawing even closer to each other, we ambled around the bends of the stairway.

Not knowing what else to do with Pasha in this state of mind, I suggested we invite Sally G. over for an evening of Chinese home delivery and radio. Pasha smiled, finally, and I was able to tickle her slightly under her arms.

Then, we got inside, and I saw that my room had tenderly been transformed into something for convalescents only: a pitcher of water by my bed, the white sheets with embroidered borders which Pasha used only for a rare houseguest, and three different bouquets of flowers: lilies from Sally G., yellow roses from the Manhattan Ballet, and red roses from both Mr. Krimskaya and Mr. Leonard Stanford.

I eyed the flowers skeptically. When I tried to ask Pasha if there was anything she needed to tell me, she, having collected herself, and seeming considerably better in the comfort of her own surroundings, laughed a little and then began straightening out my hair. She told me "of course not," except how much she'd missed me, and then asked me if I preferred iced Russian tea or lemonade.

That evening Sally G. brought me little presents and spoke a pitch above her real voice, the way most people talk to little bitty babies. She commented on just about everything belonging to me: the flowers, my long hair, my smooth clean cast, the one picture I had of Mamma and Daddy, and my red dress which I then had on. Which was entirely out of line for the Sally G. I knew and loved.

Outside it had begun to rain. Delivering by bicycle, the Chinese boy from the Peking take-out arrived wet with a rolled bag over his head. He handed Sally G. two large brown bags of hot-spiced food, but stepped backward instead of forward when I offered him an umbrella to borrow. He smiled exactly like a jack-o'-lantern, then found himself in a sudden, terrible hurry and excused himself. The whole world was acting peculiar.

But then over my friendly Southern way, I heard Pasha laughing quietly to herself as she riffled through the kitchen drawer for three pairs of chopsticks. Sally G. laughed, too, the charming way she laughs, as she spread the cushions on Pasha's Kilim rug. We all sat down, and I got picked to say a blessing. I said a prayer giving thanks to the Lord for the Manhattan Ballet, then I prayed silently that we would recover from the debts I'd caused. Sally G. heaped rice and Chinese food into each of our bowls.

Still, right through to the last snow pea, we talked about things we'd never talked about before: A pound cake recipe Sally G.'s aunt had passed her, a linen and lingerie sale down at Macy's, and did I think the Yankees would win Friday's ball game against the Tigers. Everybody had their back turned to my room, and each time I tried to bring up my operation, one of them would twist a pile of sesame noodles around her fork, and suck in a stray like it almost hurt. Or else talk, if they had to, about how pretty my cast looked and could one of them sign it.

By the end of the evening, I had a sudden well of sadness in my throat. Each time Sally G. complimented me, I felt a little bit worse.

I had no clear way to respond when Pasha, quite subtly, switched my fortune cookie for hers: YOU ARE DESTINED TO HAVE A LONG AND HAPPY LIFE. And washing the dishes, I found the one originally meant for me, stuck under a little wad of rice in the bottom of her bowl: YOUR CHILDHOOD DREAM IS ABOUT TO COME TRUE.

I turned the dish water off, dipped my hands into a casserole pan full of suds, reached for the kitchen towel on the Frigidaire door, looked at them both, and said, "I wish y'all would just come forward with it." Then I couldn't help it; whatever was inside me began to leak out through my eyes. Trying to catch myself, I ducked between Sally G. and Pasha, who stood in the doorway, staring at each other while I lumbered quickly to my room, both crutches pressed under my arms.

I made uncalled-for noise unsnapping my vinyl suitcase and digging around for my hospital nightgown; I was mainly mad. I slipped the gown on without even tying the two pairs of strings in the back, then snapped the lamp off, and crawled into bed, dragging my leg, heavy as chain. I lay on my back, the sheets pulled up to my chin, and from underneath them, I blurted, "Don't anybody dare come in here and try to take care of me!" Pasha and Sally G. started whispering, and I heard one of them saying, "I'll call tomorrow." And then I heard them kiss each other's cheeks, and I heard the door squeaking open and Sally G. leaving, evidently obeying my orders.

I was so mad I couldn't sleep at first, and when I finally drifted off I was awoken at three a.m. with the stitches and pangs. Without painkillers, my leg was a long crush of raw pain. I got it over the side of the bed thinking that if I could get blood into it, the cramp might go away. I wish I knew what could have made it go away, but that just was not it.

I sank back down in the sheets. And where was he now anyway? What was I thinking? Why did I try to obey him, try to go to extremes to win this guy's love, a total stranger who didn't even hardly know my name? I stayed awake, drinking water from my pitcher and thinking about everything. Maybe I was just hopelessly nuts from my terrible childhood. Hours went by. I stared at the ceiling. Once, I got up just to smell the flowers.

CHAPTER 9
Late September, 1942
Upper West Side, Manhattan

From my bed, I reached to my desk, opened the drawer, took a ruler, drove it into my cast, and found the itch at the back of my knee. My skin, thigh to toe, felt damp, and at the same time curiously dry.

The sun poured in through our south side window and rayed across my bed. There was a breeze, too. I had begun to sweat and had thrown the sheets off. Evidently, I'd overslept; our apartment was still. I shifted a little, sighed, let the ruler drop to the floor. I laced my hands behind my head, stared at the ceiling and listened to the stillness of our apartment. Slowly, I flexed the thigh muscles underneath my cast. Again, I let out a long slow breath of air. All that time had passed with only Francis Taylor having noticed my limp. Francis Taylor: *Susanna, please take care of that knee. Please have it checked.*

Even in bed, my knee hurt like a broken bone. With the glass of water Pasha had left for me, I took three of the Emperin on my bedside table. I flexed my calf now, watched my foot make a little tent of the sheets. What difference could it have made to him anyway? I asked my foot. Then I lifted myself out of bed and used crutches to hobble my way across the living room floor, moving as rapidly as possible on the outside chance that the ringing phone might be him. Something was wrong with my whole life.

I reached it by the fifth ring. I was out of breath. It was Sally G. She'd regained a normal voice pitch and asked soberly but cheerfully how I was doing. "Well, how is my best friend feeling?"

"I feel awful." I told her I would aim to do right, to rest, and follow doctors' orders until healed. On the word "heal," I listened for signs of doom, pressing the earpiece close to my ear.

Sally G. said that if I needed anything, I should just call on her, that she was just right there.

Without going so far as to tell Sally G. that I craved not her voice, but one two octaves down from hers, I put her off anyway by telling her that I didn't need a thing, thank you. "Except knowledge that I can dance again, Sally G. Just that," I told her.

"Dancing isn't everything," she told me. I slammed the phone, surprising the daylights out of myself.

After she called, the knee hurt worse. I was hungry. Using the crutches to make my way to our little kitchen, I had to take a break after every step I took. But, I made it.

On the kitchen counter, I saw the little painted bowl Pasha had left for me, its spoon placed inside it, bearing not one, but two lumps of sugar. Before now, she always gave me just one.

I saw how the coffee was still warm, its pot wrapped in a blue flowered kitchen towel. The strawberry jam I'd once bought for Pasha was out on the table. The toast was also wrapped in a blue flowered kitchen towel. The butter on the plate beside it had gotten quite soft.

"None for me, thanks," I whispered to myself. "I'm not hungry."

I tried the idea of taking a bath, a cat bath, as the doctor called it. That was so hard. Negotiating my way to the bathroom. That knee hurt so much. Leaning on a wobbly crutch as I tried to bend to turn the water on.

"You can do anything for thirty seconds," I said out loud, as I bent the good knee and reached for the water faucet. I got it. The warm water itself, running over my hands, down my arm, brought the first sense of nurture and renewal. But, my knee hurt so bad. By the time I negotiated my way into the tub, I was taking deep breaths to compensate for the pain.

I wasn't allowed to get my cast wet. I had it propped up at an angle against the sill of the tub. I began to worry about how in the world I would ever get out of the tub.

I soaked. A feeling of hopelessness overcame me. The scant suds gave in under their own weight, leaving the water cloudy. I was crying.

Eventually, I tried to get up the strength to start the process of getting out of the tub. As I reached for the towel on the rack behind me, my leg with the cast slipped from the sill of the tub, and I couldn't find the right muscles to stop it in time. It slid, and then crashed like a tree into the water.

With my arms, I tried to push myself up out of the tub, plank-style. I was able to swing the casted leg out in one fell swoop, like an arch. I thank ballet for that. But, already the plaster had begun to dissolve, and when I tried to dry it off, whole chunks of it came off on the towel. I reached a pair of fingers inside the cast and blew out my breath. The water had gone only surface deep. The inside wall was still cool and dry.

Suddenly, a light feeling, a fleeting little feeling of hope spread through my body. I am not sure if this was relief coming with my knowledge that the cast could be salvaged, or because of the three-star idea that came to my head, simultaneously with the inspection.

I crutched my way from the bathroom and across the living room floor. Chunks of the wet plaster fell off on the rug. Saying it out loud again, "You can stand anything for 30 seconds," I went into the kitchen where I found our best knife, the one Florrie Duvet gave us one Christmas. I tested my finger lightly over its saw-teeth. I felt the thrill of taboo. Knife in hand, I lumbered towards the sofa. Stop-go-stop-go. Inhale, exhale. Stop-go-stop-go.

But, I made it. The *Times* was on the coffee table, and I now spread it out on the floor beneath me.

It was some job. As I zigzagged across the cast, fully intending to cut on it in such a way as to be able to put it back together, my biceps burned so badly I had to give myself two separate coffee and snack breaks. My appetite had come back. I lifted the painted bowl and drank the coffee, "Fine coffee, Pasha, fine!" (I spoke to her as if she were there.) "Delicious, my love." (For the moment, I'd forgiven him, too.) I brought a second bowl full of coffee back to the sofa and got back to work, the newspaper all spread out underneath me. It was getting me in a better mood by the minute.

I'd sawed down to about mid-calf when the phone rang a second time. Which startled the fool out of me. My fingers had become so cramped from the sawing that I could barely prise them open enough to cradle the phone.

Pasha said she was on break between classes and was just calling to say hello.

"Hey!" I said self-consciously.

In a slightly quizzical tone of voice she said, well, she was just calling to say hello. So I told her hello again in the same slightly delirious tone, and she asked, a little more quizzically, if I was all right.

"Me?" I covered. "Just great!" I tucked my chin down and wedged the receiver between my shoulder and cheek so that I could work the fingers of the cramped hand.

"Well, Susanna, what are you doing?"

I took up the painted bowl and took a big swallow of my creamy, sugary coffee, and started to think up an answer when Pasha said, "Stop right there, young lady! What is it you're drinking?"

"Ma'am?"

"What have you gotten into, young lady?"

"Your coffee, Pasha. The coffee you left right here for me on the table."

"Do I need to come home and check on you?"

"Me?" I remembered Pasha's Courvoisier, Russian Vodka, and Brandy kept in a top cabinet, which nobody ever touched. So I said to Pasha, "I'm bombed."

Through the receiver, I felt Pasha's smile coming on.

"Just because tragedy has struck," I announced, "doesn't mean I've gone to the dogs, Mother." This was the first time I'd ever called her Mother. Pasha was clearly smiling quite broadly on the other end of the phone, I could feel it. Then I could feel her trying to get real serious and matronly.

"Well," she said, "I certainly hope not."

"No, Mother," I said, and then I told her I'd have supper for her when she got home, and she said, "Tell Sally G. to come." She said she was glad I was feeling so well and called me her little darling. Then she hung up, saying good-bye in a tone that was, nevertheless, one part quizzical, one part all broken up.

Between the somewhat dissolved outside wall of my cast and the brick-hard inside wall of my cast was a gauze-and-white-powder arrangement that, as I sawed, produced whole strata clouds of white powder; a powder that seemed to hover in the air, then fall with terrific slowness, almost imperceptibly, leaving a thin film on the floor and rug. It was pretty. Graceful like the start and finish of a real light snow flurry. The powder had gotten all over my body, naked except for towels: one wrapped around my still damp hair, the other, bearing little wet clumps of plaster, wrapped around my torso. The plaster powder had gotten in my ears, mouth, and nostrils as well. But the cast was sawed now to the Achilles. I leaned forward, reached both hands to split it open when the doorbell rang.

My heart jumped. What would anybody be doing coming to our door at this time of day? I glanced quickly at my cast and told myself that nobody would notice the sawed line since it was not parting in a real obvious gap. The doorbell rang again, twice, with urgency. I shoved the knife under the sofa cushion.

"Who is it?" I asked. But nothing. "Just a minute!" I'd have to go through the whole rigmarole with the crutches, the shoots of pain, and now a messed up cast.

"Just a minute," I said again. And somehow I got there in due time. But, I was out of breath again.

As I turned the doorknob, I eyed through the small round glass in our door, recognizing him instantly, despite the spyglass giving a fishbowl look to his head. My knee hurt so bad.

As quickly as I opened the door, I shut it. I shut it pretty much right in his face. Then I leaned against the door, trying to catch my breath. My heart was going crazy. I was kind of scared. What was he doing here?

Without thinking, I re-wrapped the towel around my body, and opened the door again, just a little bit. I was going to say something to him, tell him to wait until I could get dressed.

But he didn't wait for me. He just came in, and I clutched the doorknob, pulling the door open real slowly, crouching behind it at the same time.

"We should shut the door," he whispered.

"How'd you find me?" I whispered, but he had already pulled me up from behind the door and begun to kiss me, and we both leaned into the door, shut it, slowly, his hand over mine on the knob.

The towel wrapping my hair came off all by itself. It fell wet to the floor, and I stood on it. We kissed, as if drinking each other. No conversation, no questions.

I wanted him to take the other towel, the one wrapped around my body. Through it, he presently reached a hand to my skin, and felt my breasts like he'd done before, and I thought, *Now I won't stop him*. We were safe. My eyes were shut, I can't tell you where his were. I tried to calm down. But my hands went all over his face, and into his hair, into his mouth. He wrapped me in his arms, our eyes closed. His hands moved damp, tangled hair from my face; my hands hunted for the buttons on his shirt. I opened my eyes, watched the motion of his hand underneath the towel, working in a circle over my breast. At length the tucked corner fastening the towel loosened, and it opened, and dropped off my body. I was not ashamed.

He kissed my neck, slowly moved his face to my breasts, kissing them all over. He went down to his knees, wrapped his arms around me, kissed my tummy, then caressed his hands up and down my back, and I held his head as close to my body as possible, my own head tilting back, my eyes shut, and my breathing quickening, shortening. The wetness rushed out of me, and I was afraid it would drip down to my stitches. I reached a hand between my legs, and then Francis Taylor removed it so tenderly, I had to trust that even my accidents, he loved.

"Take off your clothes," I whispered.

Instead, he blew on my little curls of blond hair, keeping his hand between my legs. I leaned all my weight on the good leg and opened the bad leg. He kept his hand on me, his fingers on me as I collapsed into his chest. He had to hold me up. Gently, he lifted my face, brought his lips to mine.

"Take off your clothes," I whispered again. For a minute, I forgot my knee. My head wasn't thinking about it, and, with surprising control, it hurt less. I groped for the buttons, and he helped me by unzipping his pants, both of us then helping, using our hands to work them off his hips. One at a time he used the toe of his shoe against the heel of the other to get his feet free, then repeated this gesture to pull one leg out of the pants and then the other. He moved the way a baby moves from underneath a blanket. He, too, losing his breath, taking my hand to him.

This was the first time I had touched a man, and I was surprised by its strength. I wanted to taste him.

But instead, he lowered me softly to the floor until I was lying down. My legs stayed separated, and he used his fingers to open me like a small tulip, and kissed: face, lips, tongue washing over me like a warm, sweet milk.

Something was happening to me. A feeling rose through me, seemed to be hollowing me and at the same time filling me.

Hold me," I murmured.

His lips found mine.

"Come home. Come inside." I whispered.

He kissed me passionately, and I made light, purring noises, and quickly, before I understood what was happening, he buried his face in my cheek, moaning softly, and a sweet liquid shot out of him, rested as a thick pool on my stomach. He had not gone inside me.

I lifted his face to show my eyes. But he wouldn't let me. He kept his face in my shoulder. I rubbed my fingers through tendrils of hair which had gathered in wet bunches at the nape of his neck.

Catching his breath, he didn't say a word, didn't kiss me anymore. Instead, he put a hand to the pool of wetness on my stomach, placed it to himself, as if trying to pack it back inside, and then used the floor to wipe his hand. The other hand fumbled along my cast, along its smooth wall, and then to the gashed place down the center. He pulled away, abruptly.

His eyes caught mine, briefly, and I saw that they were trying to tell me something, trying to talk to me.

"What is it?" I asked, my eyebrows bunching.

His eyes darted. He was trying to find his pants. I saw them crumpled by our feet and reached for them, but they were too far away. He was still on top of me.

"Is it my leg?" I asked, wanting to tell him, wanting to tell him why I had to know, not in six, eight weeks: now.

He moved more pointedly from my body and looking away from me said, "Susanna, I am not the man you're looking for, and I know that you are not the woman I am looking for."

Pasha's soft warning voice and kind eyes cloaked me. *Susanna, There is a difference in love and desire*. I bent the good leg to my chest. My bad leg hurt. It hurt in a new way, sharper, more pinpointed. My hair had begun to dry in the ringlet curls that I'd never liked, which I'd sometimes tried to iron out. I now gathered the whole bunch in my hands, pushed it behind my head. I turned my face towards him. Confused and disappointed, I watched him lift a foot into a pant leg.

He dressed, then turned towards the door and made a step towards it. He would not be saying good-bye, I guessed. *This can only end in pain and sorrow.*

I reached for the towel, covered myself with it, and then I said, "What did I do?" I began to feel ashamed, and I wasn't able to speak regular.

Instead of moving for the door, he looked at me, and I pretended to be looking for something under the sofa, to hide the pain. Then he came back to me, lifted me from the floor, and I saw how his hands were gloved on the palm side with the powder from my cast.

I tried to make my weight light by pressing my good leg against the floor. I bowed my head, eyes looking straight down, but held his hands with the fervor of an old woman holding to a church pew.

He put my feet on top of his and waltzed me in very slow motion. My bad leg couldn't support the turns, but I couldn't tell him. I was dizzy, but not from his quiet waltz. I was thirsty, too, so thirsty. I licked my lips of their moisture.

As we went around, I had my eyes fixed on the framed picture of Pasha's husband. Her framed birds appeared, too, seeming to settle for the first time on the boughs of their trees. I held him tightly, but I was afraid to look at him. He smoothed my hair down.

Then he stopped. With no warning, he said, "Susanna."

"Yes." I didn't even want to swallow or shift weight for fear the floor's creaks would drown out his voice.

He drew a long pause, as if waiting for clouds to break storm. He said, "It won't work, Susanna. You're too careless for me. I can't find a way to trust you."

In a whisper I said, "Yes, sir." Crippling towards the door, I held my head high and my back rigid. As I hobbled, I could feel the tension of shoulder and neck muscles gathering. I pressed my shoulders down. It must have taken me quite a long time to reach the door. Quite some time. In slow motion, I opened it wide as it would go and motioned his way out. And then I lamely maneuvered to the sofa, dug a hand underneath the pillow, pulled the knife out, and I made my way, stiff as a violin, to Pasha's room and shut the door, softly. I was crying as I sawed to the last web of gauze, and with bare hands I pulled and pulled against the tough material, but I couldn't get it to rip. Anger rose up in me violently, and I bit my teeth to the gauze and tore it apart.

My skin was dry and ugly. But that is not what shocked me. What shocked me was how crooked it looked. And how bruised I was around the area where they'd put the stitches. The purple-black bruise spread like a stain over the side of my knee, down to my calf, and was yellow and puffy in the center. The black railroad track stitches, covered by a butterfly of gossamer, held together the long, thick, swollen gash. My knee appeared completely disjointed, as if they had broken it to see what was inside, and then carelessly set it back, ball to joint, the way you might hurriedly screw a lid on a jar.

I stood on it to test it for strength. The quadriceps cramped up, and the electricity fired. I looked down and saw how my lower leg had been physically set at a cockeyed angle to my knee joint, such that I could only walk pronated, with all the weight falling to the inside of my foot. I began to feel faint. I stood and clutched for air. I took a step. My leg had no buckling problem anymore. Now, it was the opposite. My knee was locked. I tried to move the kneecap back and forth. It was fixed as solid as an iron lid over a drainpipe. I swooned and tried to get back out to the living room where the windows were open. I dragged, then hopped, dragged, hopped again.

To my surprise, Francis Taylor was still there. The front door remained wide open. He was sitting on the sofa with one leg crossed over the other, and when I entered he stood like a gentleman, and I lurched towards him, pacing my breathing.

I looked at him, but felt my eyes going through him like a pair of stones, and I said to myself, "Now I know what love is." Then I raised an arm and with the flat side of my hand I swung at him. He ducked, and my hand slammed into the stand-up lamp. My leg shook as I stepped backwards on it and when electricity again shot down it, I swung hard at him again, missed him. His head began to shake, and his hands trembled vaguely. And as I raised a hand again, closing it into a fist, preparing to lurch towards him, my eyes caught the terror in his. My hand loosened, then dropped by my side. *I can't even hurt him*. My eyes watered.

And suddenly I said, "Why don't you hit me, Francis Taylor? Why don't you just take a hit, full blow, right behind my knee. Kick it. Come on, kick it." Then I broke down. My face grew distorted, and my weak leg quivered though I couldn't feel it. "Nothing I try pleases him." I covered my face.

"Your towel is falling off," he said.

I'll always think he wanted my towel to fall off so that he could have me naked again. I wrapped the towel tightly around my body, crossed my arms in front of me. Balancing on the good leg, I lifted the crooked leg barely off the ground. "Won't be long until opening night," I told him, bitterly. My eyes flooded.

"Susanna," he said, gravely. "It had to be done."

And I said to him, "Francis Taylor, why don't you be real quiet." Then I grabbed a clump of the plaster that had stuck to my towel and hurled it at him. He drew back as if hit by foul spit. I watched him squeeze his eyes shut.

My leg throbbed, then went into a violent spasm, and I stepped back, bracing my hands to it. I looked up and saw his quivering face, his terrified, clouding eyes. His hand held the clump of plaster, and he extended it to me. And I'll tell you I thought that gesture meant, "Here, girl, put your cast back together."

Now I know how Daddy felt, how he could lash out at me when the pent-up anger from Mamma's cruel never-ending chiding would finally explode out of him. I took the clump of plaster and hurled it much harder and it slapped the side of his face. My leg felt skinless with the naked and frayed nerves shooting haywire, and I bit a lip as I stepped forward meaning to push him off balance. He sidestepped me, and all I managed was to grab his shirt.

But he went down to the floor all by himself, like a man praying for his last rights.

And from somewhere down on that floor, he cried, "Susanna, it had to be done. I can't help what doctor you picked!"

I covered my face and gasped through sudden tears that cracked and crumbled my strongest walls of defense. I stood weak, choking sobs, and my ugly deformed leg mirrored me in terrible fits and paroxysms. I was so thirsty. I licked the salt off my wet lips.

He rose and came over to where I stood and again lifted me in his arms. The towel was wedged between us but no longer on my body. He held me close and kissed my ear, and whispered very, very, very quietly.

He whispered, "I'm trying, Susanna."

And then I calmed down some.

After a long while, I breathed, "Then let's stay together." My voice was so small.

"Susanna!" And after he said this, I heard a long, exasperated sigh, his breath bitter to my cheek.

His message rose above my swelling hurt and confusion, and I wriggled quickly out of his arms. As I twisted, my soldered knee came up and accidentally caught him right between the legs.

The blow sent piercing nerve shoots, and they ripped all the way down through the ends of my toes, and afterwards the leg again went into wild spasms which kept me from seeing at first that Francis Taylor was hurt. But when I looked up I saw his hands flown to his head, and then he was crimped over, cupping himself. Blood rushed to his face, leaving a swollen vein along his temple. Bent over, he hobbled towards Pasha's room.

I put an arm around his shoulder and, barely touching him, tried to guide him. My leg made me move so slowly, so jerkily.

We got to the bed, and he lurched for it, falling right on top of Pasha's pillows beside the headboard. He was lying on his stomach, rocking back and forth. His shirttail was out, but his shoes were still on his feet, neatly tied.

"Love?" I said.

And here I knew he wouldn't let me touch him, not even with my fingertips.

"Love?" I whispered. I started to touch his hair, but pulled away.

I pivoted, knowing it best to leave him alone. But I couldn't get up the heart to leave yet. He lay on his stomach, hands underneath himself. I leaned forward to spread the eiderdown quilt over him. A corner of it was underneath him, and I pulled gently, lightly as possible. I wanted to tell him how sorry I was, wanted to get close enough to kiss him on a cheek or shoulder. I took a breath like I was going to say something.

"Get out," he said.

I misunderstood him; instead of stepping back, my hands went to his hair, tried to massage his head a little.

"Get out!" he repeated.

I had the eiderdown in my hands, tips of my fingers pinching the corners of it. I wished right then that I could have given him everything I had. "Baby?" I whispered, "Love, are you all right?"

"Get out, Susanna! Leave me alone!"

I was shaking. I reached for the headboard, braced myself against it.

"Go on, Susanna. Get out." He propped on an elbow and turned around, and that's when I saw the pain on his face, how far back it went. I moved away quickly, hobbling towards my room and tried to find something to put on. It wasn't raining on this day; skies had cleared. But over the small chair in my room, I saw my yellow slicker, and underneath the slip of the chair were the little red heels of my rain galoshes. Because it was the first thing I saw, I unfolded it, put it on, and snapped its oversized buckles. I squirmed my feet in the boots, using a foot against the wall and tugging with two hands. The throbs were coming now in shoots I can't speak about.

I went back to Pasha's room, partly for myself, in the private hope that I might be given another chance. I opened the door and saw that he was no longer there. I looked in the closet, the bathroom, behind the curtains.

Then I realized that he'd gone under the covers, buried himself under the eiderdown.

"Babe, is that you under there?" I whispered to the puff of feathers.

"I'm not your babe," his muffled voice answered with confidence.

"Well."

"Well what, Susanna? I asked you to get out, and I expect you to obey me."

I rested my hands on my good knee and bent it with the other extended out to my side. With my face close to the puff of feathers, I said, "Well, Mr. Dewitt. Nice to hear from you. Nice to see that you're still with us."

"Susanna, get away from me. You bug me. You're a little stupid."

I crouched lower, leaned closer to him. "Well! Shall I call the firemen?" I could not believe this supposedly mature man had crawled into Pasha's bed like a napping Goldilocks and refused with the stubbornness of a treed cat to come out.

"Susanna, you don't need to fret over me. Now leave me alone. I asked you to take care of your leg." Here he pounded the mattress, and the puff of feathers gamboled about his hand.

"Thanks. Thanks quite a bit, Francis Taylor." Words. Just wrong words.

The slicker made a crinkling sound, and I was relieved he couldn't see me. I sighed, long and disappointed, used the bedpost to straighten up. Reluctantly, I crippled back to my room and looked for the longest time for something right to put on. I was unable to think straight. I found my blue dress that I'd worn to the hospital and put it on. I felt like I was trespassing in my own house, and so, leaving the galoshes on, I limped on tiptoe to the kitchen where I found a Coca-Cola. I put it in the icebox so it'd freeze up at the bottom like the one we'd shared in the park. Then I gulped down a large glass of water. I didn't tell him good-bye. I took up my crutches, muttered something about a surprise being in the icebox door for him, and waved in the general direction of Pasha's room. Then at our front door I pressed the safety lock, closed the apartment behind me, and awkwardly negotiated my way down the stairs. Leaning on my crutches, I proceeded at the pace of an old woman, edging one step at a time, all the way up to W. 84th and Broadway. People on the sidewalk parted for me, and children stared unabashedly at my hurt leg.

Pasha was just beginning to set the pattern for the new batch of young scholarship children. I leaned in the door and waited; she was right in between the count of seven and eight. As I let myself in, she turned and saw me. She held her breath, wrinkling deeply in the brow. The counting stick dropped out of her hand and rolled off on the uneven part of the floor towards the mirror. The piano teacher held her hands right over middle C, as if letting her fingernails dry. The little girls began glancing at Pasha, then at each other, then shifting their weight, and fixing things: hair, shoelaces, sleeves. One little girl started pruning the Schefflera. With a numbed, shocked expression on her face, Pasha stood and stared at my two thin bare legs sticking out from underneath my dress. I, too, held my breath.

Our eyes met briefly, and my lips parted just barely, but nothing came out.

I closed the door so that class could be resumed, and then a few seconds later I cracked it open again. I looked at Pasha, then shut the door again.

I was choking just a little bit here, and that old Rachel Ellison passed me in the hallway. She looked down intensely, as people do when they don't know what to say, and I cleared my throat in a wish of urging her onward, down the hall, down the stairs. I waited for a minute with my head leaned forward lightly against the door. I put a hand flat against the brass plate that read, PUSH, but held back. Still, with my hand resting there, my lips moved against the closed side of the door, anxious to tell Pasha. "Pasha, I've had contact with life," my lips working the shapes of the words, each disappearing into the grain of the wood. My fingers drumming, my lips reaching, "For all I know I've killed him, too. Don't be surprised when you go home and find a man in the bed. It's him." Mouthing this, I began to feel bruised, way inside my skin.

I turned and limped down the hall, tracing my hand along the wall, my fingertips sensitive to each dip, each little rise. I can't remember if I walked fast or slowly, but I felt a little like a seahorse. Every time I took a step, the bad leg automatically kicked behind me, and my hips stayed square, all on their own.

By the time I heard Pasha's steps behind me, her little takes of air as she hurried to catch up with me, I had almost reached the office end of the hallway. I let my hand drag on, along the wall.

"Susanna!" I turned and saw that she was running, her arms wide.

I turned, reached into the pocket of my dress and pulled out the application for secretary/file clerk that I'd picked up from the ballet office on my way to the studio. With it clutched in my hand, I raised an arm and waved it in wide, sweeping gestures, as if the application was a large fan, rescuing her from the heat. And then I smiled, pointing with the other arm to the office door. "Well, Pasha, that's what it says. Big as trees: Help Wanted."

Pasha stopped dead in her tracks, wrinkled up her nose, and squinted her eyes until I couldn't even see them, and I never knew if this was from being upset or gladdened.

I brought the application down, held it with two hands right in front of my chest and asked her if she had a #2 pencil, and she said that of course she didn't have a #2 pencil, and then I went into the administrative offices and sat down in a red vinyl armchair and started to fill out the application in ink.

Pasha came in a short minute later, out of breath, carrying that number #2 pencil, sharpened.

I thanked her and then told her that they did, as a matter of fact, accept applications written in ink, and held the pen up so she could see.

PART II

1942 – 1943

Manhattan

CHAPTER 10

November, 1942
Upper East Side, Manhattan

I was not a great secretary/PR intern. But Mr. Leonard Stanford was the one who'd ponied up the money to make my internship a paying job. I was very grateful for this kindness, though I will say that it was very little money to try to live on.

One freezing evening Mr. Leonard Stanford invited me out to dinner, and I was happy to accept because I had wanted to be able to look him in the eye and thank him for all he'd done for the Ballet and for me. Plus: it was a free meal.

We went to Au Bon Boucher over on the East Side. It was a wonderful, cozy place with its art deco murals and *bon vivant* atmosphere that took the edge off of winter coming. Mr. Stanford told me that the waiters' look was taken from the Paris cafés. They were older gentlemen who walked adroitly carrying silver trays holding a bottle of wine and wine glasses, bubbly water, or white demitasse cups of cappuccino. They wore bow ties and white shirts with black jackets and trousers with white linen aprons that made them look like they were wearing skirts.

Mr. Stanford ordered a Manhattan, asking me if I'd like one also, and when I said, "No, thanks," he helped me order unpronounceable food that took some time to learn to love. *Huitres au cilantre avec caviar. Saumon au grains de coqlicot avec pommes de terre au citron vert.*

"Yes, sir, that sounds sublime." Shifting uncomfortably, I put my napkin in my lap and took a sip of water.

"Susanna, have you seen Krimskaya's new piece, *Fusion?*"

"No, sir, but I've heard it's very strange."

"Oh, but it's marvelous! It's based on the myth of Isis." Gulp, gulp, gulp. He could down that Manhattan. I noticed that the waiter took it from him before he finished it.

"It's hard to dance those asymmetrical pieces because of the music—"

"Waiter? While I've got you. The 1929 Yquem Sauterne for the oysters.

"I bet they are, Susanna."

In a minute the waiter brought the wine with the oysters, and I was poured a glass and Mr. Stanford was poured a glass that he held up to the light. He asked me to lift my glass and take in the bouquet and to study the *jambes de ballet*, little rivulets that ran down the side of the glass. He didn't tell me that the *jambes* indicate the alcohol content. He chinked his glass against mine and said, "Susanna, I am so sorry about what happened to you. You have been very brave."

"Thank you." I took the obligatory sip, and he took another gulp and kept talking about Krimskaya's brilliant work.

As he talked, I watched how he used the little oyster fork to fish his oyster out of its shell, and I did the same, finding, to my surprise, the taste of what I'd put in my mouth to be out of this world. However, as I ate this first course, I began to worry about Charlie-horse cramps that almost always happened to my hurt leg when I sat for too long. I stretched my hurt leg underneath the table and accidentally brushed up against his leg.

"Susanna, here. Take a sip." He lifted my glass to my lips. "Let it marry with the food. One enhances the other."

Whew. Not really.

"Do you taste the pear, walnut, honey, even the butter and smoky quality to the Yquem, even the faint trace of coffee and apricot in the aftertaste?"

"Yes, sir." I lied.

"The soil was *that* dry and that rooty *that* year. The vineyard roots absorb the tones and flavors in the orchard tree roots."

I thought about Mamma and how wine was a sin. Then my leg went into a minor spasm. It was weird how my leg would either throb or spasm when I'd think of my mother. I excused myself to find cold floor to stand on and found it in the bathroom.

When I came back out, a 1929 Clos de Vougeot had been opened, and the waiter was now pouring it into the large red wine glasses that were placed beside the white wine glasses. I hadn't begun to finish my Yquem, but it looked like Mr. Stanford had finished off his glass and had maybe obliged himself to another. When the waiter pulled the bottle out of its bucket, it was about two-thirds empty.

Mr. Stanford said, "Susanna, a lot of people wouldn't think of pairing a beautiful red Burgundy with salmon, but this is what the three-star French chefs have been doing."

Whatever. Just let me bear up under the strain.

The waiter served the beautiful salmon and said, "*bon appétit!*" Then he left me all alone with Mr. Stanford, who chinked glasses with me one more time, then said to me sternly, "Susanna, I wanted to talk to you about something." He cleared his throat. "I wanted to talk with you about the idea of suing the orthopedic surgeon for malpractice."

I put my glass down. I had pretended to take a sip. Shoots of raw nervy electricity shot down my leg. The operation made me sick, not just because it hexed my knee, but also because it didn't begin to fix the nerve shoots. I was done with my knee and didn't want to talk about it.

"Mr. Stanford, I just can't see it, sir." The idea of living through a lawsuit would put me under.

"Susanna, we need to at least look into this."

It was true that my leg was unbendable now, and this should not have been, no way. And any grace I once had was long gone to my strange sea horse walk that made me look so very handicapped.

"How long would a lawsuit last?"

"Susanna, " he said, now looking at me. "Sometimes they can last eight to ten years."

When he said this, my only reaction was to burst out laughing. There was no way I was going to ruin my life with eight to ten years of a legal battle. "Sorry, " I told him. "That would not be my cup of tea."

He looked at me quizzically and said, "Susanna, it carries the potential of securing your future financially."

"I can't see it, sir. A fight like that going on for so long."

"It may not go on that long, Susanna. It may resolve itself quickly. Maybe a year, two years." Bus boys whisked up our plates; Mr. Stanford didn't even finish his salmon. Out of the corner of my eye, I could see the waiter coming with a beautiful tray of something.

"*Voilà, Monsieur, Madmoiselle*." The waiter presented a beautiful tray of pungent cheeses, not one of which did I think I could stand to taste. But I cut three very tiny slices and put them on my plate. Mr. Stanford took his cheeses and continued talking to me, leaning forward, and urging the lawsuit with increasing seriousness. The waiter went to pour more of the Clos de Vougeot, but when he tried to fill my glass, my hand hovered over it and I said, "No, *merci*." Mr. Stanford continued to talk about the ramifications of a lawsuit. I wished Mr. Stanford would get off this lawsuit subject and back on to Krimskaya's choreography again. As he talked, he reached for the wine for help.

"Susanna?"

"I'm all right! I will dance again one day."

Mr. Stanford looked down at his plate, and took up his big dinner fork for a bite of the salad that came with the cheese.

"Did you try it? It's delicious. Here. Try the *Epoisse*. It's the strongest cheese in the world."

Good God, he didn't have to tell me that. I could smell it from where I was sitting. "No, thank you. Really."

"Susanna, I won't push you," he said, looking over at the waiter who was bringing more French bread and creamy butter, "But the financial side of this could save your future." he said again.

"I can't see it, Mr. Stanford. Thanks." My voice rose on *Thanks*.

Mr. Stanford had the good sense to change the subject. We talked about the strategy for raising money for the Ballet. I knew a little about it because the main thing I was doing as a secretary was working so hard on the gala. As we talked about these plans, the bus boys removed our plates and the waiter brought a glorious tray of desserts. I picked the *poire belle Hélène*, and he picked *crème caramel* and then ordered a Grand Marnier.

Mr. Stanford excused himself to go to the restroom, and when he came back he began to act a little strange. When the waiter brought the Grand Marnier, he said in a voice that bordered on acerbic, "Here, Susanna. Have some."

"No, thanks!" I said. He was obviously getting drunk. I was scared.

"Have some!" he demanded sharply. For all he had drunk, he still did not slur his words.

I took one sip, and the alcohol burned down my throat. I coughed.

"Are you all right?" he said, giving me his napkin.

"I'm all right." I wasn't having any fun. He reached under the table and started to rub my leg. As I collected myself, he looked at me in the eyes, tickling his way aggressively towards my inner thigh. He was taking this seriously, looking at me with eyes he had to know were good-looking, moving his hand up as if by way of entitlement.

I raised my hand to signal the waiter. My eyes met with the waiter's, pleading for help. But the waiter only bunched his brow; he seemed to be thinking that I was asking for the check because he came around in a bit, placing it before Mr. Stanford on a brass tray.

I stood and excused myself and Mr. Stanford said, "Where are you going?"

"To the powder room."

"Again?"

"Yes, sir."

But I only pretended to go to the restroom. I went to the kitchen instead and got the attention of someone peeling shrimp. I said,

"Can you help me? I'm having some problems out here. I think the man I'm with has gotten very drunk."

He put the shrimp down, and he came around in his chef's hat and looked out over the restaurant, I suppose fearing that what I was trying to tell him was that someone had thrown up.

I said, "It's him over there, will you remember that?" He looked towards where I was nodding my head. Mr. Stanford was sitting perfectly calmly, his back erect, his face giving a dignified look to the check.

"I'll remember," he said without finding a way to look me in the eye. Then he walked back towards the kitchen. He was shaking his head like I was some kind of nut.

Right as we were going out, I said to the waiters behind the bar, "Please remember this guy. I think this man has gotten very drunk." They nodded, exchanging glances. This time I got a feeling that they were at least paying attention. It was as if they knew him, knew *this* man or knew his type. A sick feeling now overwhelmed me, and I just wanted to get home.

In the taxi, Mr. Stanford attacked me immediately, pressing his hand up my dress, and slopping his wet lips and tongue on my mouth. God, I tried to jerk my head back, but he gripped the back of my neck. I rapped on the glass that divided the passengers from the taxi driver. "Sir!! Sir!" I tried so hard to control my tone. "Can you just pull over here?" I was scared to death.

The taxi driver looked in the rearview mirror; I could see his confused, intense brown eyes. He did not understand what I was trying to ask him.

"No, now why would you do that?" Mr. Stanford asked again, kissing me, then deftly pulling down his zipper and pulling it out.

"What are you doing?" I said, breathing quickly from fear. "What are you doing?" But he began to press the back of my head down towards his penis, and I jerked my head back again with all the force I had.

"Get away from me!" I reached for the door handle, mistaking the cigarette tray for it and finding my fingertips covered in stale ash. I groped quickly for the handle and found it, but the door wouldn't open, it was locked. Somebody, some awful human being, had pulled the plastic knob off of the door lock, and, even though I tried to pinch it up with my fingers, I couldn't get the stupid thing to come up, couldn't get the damn thing unlocked. "Driver!" I said, "Please! Pull over!"

He looked again in the rear view mirror, his eyes flashing in dark confusion. Mr. Stanford whispered, "Look at you. You are all excited. You like it. You want it. Say you want it, Susanna." Then he began caressing me again with the tips of his fingers along my inner thighs, and, in seemingly one motion, he had maneuvered himself on top of me, diagonally, a knee on the seat, the other leg stretched out across the floorboards, pressing. "Stop!" I said, loudly, "What the hell are you doing?" And I started to ball my fist and pummel it against the side of his face, his wine breath coming at me again and again as he crouched up and onto me.

The driver was now trying to pull over in earnest. But, by now, we were in the cross-town tunnel, and there was no real place to pull over. In that time, that short minute that it takes to drive a taxi through the cross-town tunnel at eleven o'clock at night, Mr. Stanford had moved my underwear to the side and opened me up with two fingers and entered me, penetrating me, and leaving his hell inside me. With wide, terrified eyes, I tried to shove him off of me. In vain I grabbed clumps of his silver hair and pulled as hard as I could. "What a pretty little pussy," he whispered, as he entered me, and then, when it was over, he said, "This is our little secret, Susanna. Do you hear me? Do you understand?"

We emerged from the cross-town tunnel, and the driver immediately pulled up onto the sidewalk of Central Park West at the corner of 81st, right in front of the Museum of Natural History. Putting the taxi's lightbox on as he opened his door, the driver got out, then reached an arm through the window that was halfway rolled down and shook the lock until it pulled up. He opened the door for me. Mr. Stanford was pulling his wallet out, trying to give the taxi driver some money. "Here, cabby, that's all right. I'll take her up," the bastard said. And the taxi driver retorted in a Brooklyn accent, "No fucking way."

The taxi driver lifted me out of the taxi somehow, his face bearing horrendous pain, and I stood with an arm around his shoulders, then stood on my own. He held me by the back of my elbow as he walked me two blocks to my brownstone on W. 77th, shaking his head, then looking up for the doorman, a neighbor, anyone.

I could feel Mr. Stanford watching us through the glass window of the cab.

Eleven silent moribund days later I woke up with the most horrible burning sensation; my vagina was dry and swollen and closed up, and a fluid began to leak out of it. That morning, a Saturday, I told both Pasha and Sally G. what had happened, the two looking back at me with frozen horror, Pasha then bee-lining to the phone, calling the office down at the ballet to say we had a medical emergency and that Krimskaya or Natasha should take over for her today. I think it was Krimskaya himself who had by chance answered the phone in the office that morning because Pasha finished the conversation in forceful Russian. Then she hung up and opened up the white pages and tried to look up New York Hospital where her own gynecologist practiced. Sally G. told her to wait; she said she would find me the best, most highly specialized doctor in New York. It goes without saying that the yellow pages were left completely out of this; that was a hard knock lesson that would shut the mouth of even my very worst enemy.

Pasha nodded to Sally G. Sally G.'s mom would know who was the best. Sally G. stood and kissed me on the cheek, then held me by the shoulders and looked into my eyes and promised me again that she was going to get the very, very best. Then she kissed Pasha. She was crying as she went out the door to go over to her mother's over on the East Side. She left behind her little bag of ballet clothes.

As soon as the door shut, Pasha became beside herself, dialing over and over again, I guessed for Krimskaya. But, the phone was busy. "Please, Pasha get me some help!" I know she was doing everything she could, but I was panicking.

"Oh, my darlink." Pasha put the phone down, and burst into tears, and it's hard to say if she was hugging me or I was hugging her.

"Don't cry, Pasha, not now." I whispered.

Pasha nodded her head with a fist closed up against her mouth.

"Whatever it is, I just hope it doesn't scar me, ruin my chance to have babies." And then I began bawling.

"That's not going to happen, that's not going to happen," she said over and over and then began talking in Russian. "Get up, my darlink. Let's go. We'll go to the drugstore." And, red-eyed, we made it down to the Place Pharmacy where she bought Epsom Salt. Then we climbed the stairs back up to her brownstone where she scrubbed the tub with its iron stains, and drew a hot bath, and dumped the Epsom salt into it.

I got in and the tears started to flow again. Pasha took the white wash rags and made warm compresses and put one on my forehead and she told me to put the others anywhere on my body that hurt. So I piled them and put them between my legs while I lay crying in the water.

Sally G., on the other hand, moved with skillful competence getting up with her mother and quickly finding Dr. Stern, the head of the gynecology/ob-gyn unit at New York-Cornell Hospital over on the East Side.

Dr. Stern had no bedside manner whatsoever. As a matter of fact, he was something of a disconnected brute. But he was an intelligent, very competent New York doctor. I heard Pasha arguing with him out in the hall. "She's eighteen now. She's an adult. She doesn't need her mother's consent."

"Right! We don't ever tell Mamma about this!" I shouted through the door. I could hear Mamma in my head, *Serves her right, we told her not to go to New York. She started shaming us a long time ago.*

Out in the hallway, they lowered their voices and kept talking.

Dr. Stern came back in. I was still lying on my back in stirrups. He pulled the sheet up over my body. He put a hand on my stomach and said, "Susanna. We're going to try something called penicillin, an experimental drug that has been tested with good results on wounded soldiers. We are not sure the treatment will work or how fast the disease is progressing. We need to order the drug from Canada. This will take time, maybe three weeks. Are you willing to try? (He didn't want to tell me that it would have to be smuggled in by somebody's grandmother.) The infection could leave scars if not treated."

"Scars?"

"Yes. Cervical lesions that could cause infertility. If this is the disease I suspect that it is, it goes to work expeditiously and ruthlessly."

Dr. Stern said that I should have contacted him within 24 hours of the incident.

"I didn't even tell Pasha. I didn't even tell Sally G." I whispered back.

During the stagnant and agonizing three weeks that I waited for the medicine, only then did I think of Francis Taylor. And I hated him. Even if I had known where he'd gone, I think I still would have hated him. Because I knew he could never handle this. I had a gut sense that he would be nowhere to be found at a time like this. I hated him for the secret that would be mine alone. I knew I'd now likely never see him again because I would not be able to bring myself to tell him that I'd lost my virginity against my will. And, for that, too, I hated him. It was just high time to hate him and get over him. Francis Taylor. So far, he wasn't much.

CHAPTER 11

December, 1942
Upper West Side, Manhattan

Everything changed.

Every three days for the next two weeks, I had lab tests to monitor the progress of the antibodies. The medicine seemed to be working. Some other diseases showed up in the lab tests, but the doctor said that these were minor and treatable. I was all pumped up with penicillin from a doctor who never smiled, and who was at once gravely concerned and greatly relieved that I wasn't pregnant. But, however inscrutable were his feelings, I leaned hard on his actions and seriousness for my very survival. Every night my prayers were the same. *Dear Lord, My leg is no more. My career is over. You have taken my father. You cursed my heart with a stranger in the park. You made me fall in love with him, and that love is a grave illness. I know that you work in mysterious ways, but I do not understand your mysteries. Please, dear Lord, don't take my babies.*

I was scared of God.

Pasha went to bat for me. She had a number of meetings with Krimskaya. Pasha next went to the Board of the Manhattan School of Ballet in a secret meeting to tell them what had happened to me. Krimskaya backed her, I later learned. But when Mr. Stanford was confronted by the Board, he immediately and adamantly denied the whole thing. He'd looked Pasha extremely pointedly in the eye.

Then Leonard Stanford began a campaign via the telephone. He called each board member, one by one. I could just see him leaning into the phone confidentially, as though trying to protect *me* and my dignity, as he told each one of them that I was crazy. That I'd been crazy since my Daddy died.

Though the medical records were private, Pasha lost it one day; she called everyone on the Board and told them they could go talk to my doctor.

"Not that, Pasha! I've been through enough! Close it, Pasha! Close the story! Bury it! We cannot win against the powerful and the rich. Leave the Board alone! Look at that War wimp, Francis Taylor! An investment manager! What kind of a man was he? Leave them, Pasha. We cannot win against them. Whoever has the money has the credibility. Let him call me crazy. We cannot win! My knee. Unrequited love. Now this!" I screamed.

"Susanna, he could ve serving a tour of duty, you von't know!" Under stress, her accent got worse.

"Be quiet, Pasha! Let's just never, ever think about him again."

"Susanna." She sighed loudly, dropping her hands.

"Get out!"

Everything she did in those weeks was irritating.

Pasha quietly left the room with her hands covered over her face.

Very shortly after the medicine had arrived, I was laid off from my paid intern job as secretary/PR assistant.

Now what, now what, now what?

The arrival of a rare letter from my mother. How is your knee doing? She wanted to know. Mamma, she knew nothing about Mr. Stanford. She had no idea what he'd done to me. After she asked about my cast she wrote, "I have been dating a nice man I met at Mt. Zion, Susanna." At the end, she wrote: "Please thank the Manhattan School of Ballet for paying for the operation."

But, it was not the Manhattan School of Ballet who had paid.

Krimskaya insisted on calling my mother. He got it in his head that she was going to help. He'd come over to Pasha's. I was on the line in Pasha's bedroom. He was on the line by the radio in the living room. If he had planned to tell her what had happened to me, he got no further than starting out by asking if she'd help pay for the knee.

My mother: "Her Daddy didn't want her to go to New York. And I told her not to go. She'd come home in the half-naked clothes and stretch a leg up the wall. It wasn't right!" Mamma had avowed. "I don't have that kind of money!" Mamma defended. "Her Daddy told her not to go to New York, she'd get into trouble." As if Mamma still believed it was dancing on tabletops. "It's the school's fault, ain't it?" I felt Mamma blowing smoke through the phone right in Krimskaya's face. "That her knee got messed up? You think that knee had anything to do with me?"

Mamma, Daddy hit me with that iron rake. Tore open my tights. You don't remember the rake?

Pasha had made a second appeal to the Manhattan Ballet Board on my behalf, God bless her. God bless that dear woman for her efforts to help me. The appeal doubly backfired. Mr. Stanford spoke again to the Board. I could see him drawing a stern, masterful fork in his brow, and I knew that he not only continued to deny the accusation, but he also upped the ante with a whole new angle on the story. He said that, in fact, the opposite had happened: "That flirtatious little orphan girl is smarter than you think. Here she has exploited our cash-strapped operation for a four-year scholarship. Now I'm sorry about her leg, I'm not talking about that. I'm genuinely sorry about her leg" (both hands raised, palms opened). "But, she actually comes from a very well-to-do family, you see. Why, one hundred acres of produce from their farm could take care of two or three Manhattan Ballet performances!" Then drooping his eyebrows, lowering his voice, "She lost her Daddy, you know. As I said before, she hasn't been right since that happened. She's hungry. I think she saw me as a kind of father figure. I think she frankly fell in love with me." Leaning in confidentially, a voice filling with pity and sorrow.

Pasha recounted this on the phone that evening. I didn't know who she was talking to, but I guessed it was Krimskaya. I wasn't sure why she wasn't speaking in Russian. I wondered if she was possibly speaking to a Board member who hadn't been able to attend the last meeting.

"Pasha," I said, as she was trying to talk. "I'll do it now. I'll turn in the medical reports. We'll get Dr. Stern to talk to the Board." Pasha, irritated, waved me away.

But after she got off the phone, I said it again, and this time she heard me. "Susanna," Pasha said, her deep, dark eyes looking straight into mine. "You must always trust your courage. It will take you to places higher than you know." But I didn't then understand that I had what Pasha called courage. I understood that I had killer anger, and that's where I was now coming from.

Before we could even get the medical records to the Board, Pasha was let go. Very gently and quietly, she was told that the Ballet didn't need her any more. They gave her three months salary and made her sign a piece of paper, some kind of confidentiality agreement—a gag order—binding her to silence about what happened. Even with severance, Pasha would be struggling very hard now, financially. Pasha had been one of the founding builders of the Manhattan School of Ballet; it was in her blood, it had been her whole life, and, being removed by her own people spiraled her down under the blues of a death, of unfathomable loss. Pasha could hardly put one foot in front of the other.

Of all the hurts that had accumulated in my life, I don't think anything hurt so much as watching Pasha's hurt. Her way of dealing with it was to try to go about her business; I don't know where she was going other than walking up and down the streets. Up and down the streets in order to avoid the sight of me.

Sometimes when she wasn't out walking, Pasha napped. When she was good and asleep, I'd lie down beside her, my arms around her. She slept during the day quite a bit now.

Sally G. found herself caught directly in a conflict of divided loyalties. To my huge heartbreak, she simply pulled away, acting for a time like she didn't even know either Pasha or me any more. I thought there was nothing that could have hurt more than that, more than Sally G.'s distance, but there was. There was something that hurt more than that: I was never called in to defend myself or to be able to tell them the truth of what had happened.

Pasha was fairly quickly scooped up by the Christopher Street Project, another avant-garde dance company that had already won the respect of its audiences, mainly because of its extraordinary director, a woman named Blair Pound. But after she was turned out by the Manhattan School of Ballet, she was never the same again. Pasha and I had grown so distant. Each in so much pain, neither could help the other.

For my part, I stayed alone in the apartment, frozen with fear.

It was during those weeks that the hang-up calls started. It took me a long while to get up and make it over to the phone with its hollow ring. I'd get the receiver to my ear and say, "Hello?"

Click.

And a few days later: "Hello?"

Click. Then the sound of a dial tone.

I was sure that the calls might be coming from Mr. Leonard Stanford. Back then, there was no such thing as a police report to be written up for what he did. Nor were there harassment laws to chain in hang-up calls.

During those hell weeks, Sally G. eventually came back into our lives. On her off days, she'd come to see me, often bringing Chinese food for the three of us to have around Pasha's coffee table in the living room. I got pretty good at handling chopsticks, learning right then that the tiniest little things could come to feel like accomplishments. We would begin with light conversation, and Sally G. could still get me to laugh. Then the conversation would take a turn, and we'd talk about all the ways, in the coldest blood, that we could murder Mr. Leonard Stanford.

One late afternoon when I was by myself, I looked up what I thought might be Francis Taylor's firm: Dewitt & Dewitt. My heart was pounding as I called. It was after five, so no one would be there, that was my guess.

But, on the second ring, he picked up.

"Maria?"

I froze.
"Maria?"
I hung up. And down, down I sank.

CHAPTER 12

Late February, 1943
Manhattan School of Ballet, Broadway, Manhattan

In due time, Pasha would get better. We would both get better. In an amazing turn of events, Mr. Leonard Stanford was removed from the board in December of 1942, let go completely from anything having to do with the Manhattan School of Ballet. He was replaced by Shawn Colton, a man who had a reputation for being reliable and trustworthy.

Almost immediately, Pasha got her job back. And I got my job back. Pasha and I became normal again. In time, I got my own little studio apartment. And the classes I took after work, the sweaty heat of the room, the repetition of the warm-ups, the relaxing power of the music, slowly but surely coaxed my knee to bend again. From its stubborn rustiness, I heard my knee crack and bend, the rush of blood to my face that registered both shock and sudden self-consciousness. My knee became inflamed afterwards and needed ice, but it was bending sporadically, not like clockwork, but the ball and joint seemed to have reconnected with each other. They seemed to be somehow oiling one another. Some days were better than others, I won't lie.

Even though the secretarial job with the Manhattan School of Ballet was not the real me, it saved me. Besides, I was doing what most women did in New York: get up, have coffee and a bagel, walk to work, answer phones, make sure the bathroom stayed clean and well-stocked, take down messages, line up subs for teachers who didn't show up. At times, the job was quite a lot of headaches peppered between mail runs to the post office over on 84th and Columbus. The lines at the P.O. were interminable. Mothers with packages they were sending to their sons. Soldiers in uniform, sending gear. Soldiers were everywhere, everywhere, and this fascinated me. But, my secret reason for standing in interminable lines at the post office was not the soldiers. My secret reason for standing in interminable lines was that I was sending letters to Francis Taylor. Who knew where he'd gone?

Obviously, I never came across as a rock-solid lighthouse kind of influence, but my letters were meant to let him know that somebody was still his friend if he ever needed her. I mailed about one tenth of them, weeding out about eighty-six percent as entirely too mushy and high-flown, considering the fact that we'd only seen each other those few times.

I never once heard back from him, not one word of thanks. Evidently, he didn't like to be babied.

The remaining four percent of the letters consisted of hate mail. Well, he made me mad. Where I come from, folks thank people.

For all I knew he was a raving playboy.

One time I mailed one of the pieces of hate mail. As soon as I heard it land against the built-up pile of envelopes waiting for the five o'clock pick-up, I realized my error. I opened the mailbox lid, wrenched an arm inside, and felt around in a black hole.

For about a month I was in torture.

Sally G. came to help me at the front desk almost every time she had a break. She was so much more organized than I was. Sometimes it was just better if I let her work while I went down the hall to watch what was going on in the studio where Pasha was teaching.

"Well, at least you got the key ring!" Sally G. joked. (My job was actually meant to be an internship for just-out-of-college girls. They called it the Manhattan Ballet Internship in Press Relations, and college girls took the position for free each summer in exchange for being invited to the Manhattan School of Ballet Benefit Gala at the end of the summer season. All interns got a key ring with a plastic figurine of a ballerina hanging off of it.)

"And she'll be the one who gets the husband!" Sally G. would go. It was a good sign. Using the word "husband" was a signal. It meant that Sally G. recognized that I'd finally let go of Francis Taylor. All the months that had gone by without a peep from him; I finally just started to heal. Many months had gone by. "You watch," Sally G. would say.

I always thought Sally G.'s guilt about my not being part of the emerging *corps de ballet* was more intense than warranted. *Over the Transom* had flopped on Broadway, and Krimskaya went on to have one flop after the next. The War was no help.

For me, the sounds of the pianos in the various studios down the hall from the office gave comfort and security that you could only have if you weren't struggling to pay for the enterprise yourself. But, when I'd hear Krimskaya losing it on young students as he had done with us, his voice would produce exquisite pain that would ignite the hot nerve shoots down my yard sale of a leg. Still, my work pretty much put ground under my feet, and I think that if my loved ones understood that, they wouldn't feel sorry for me. The work educated me; it gave me insight into the complex effort it took to make the Manhattan School of Ballet operate and stay afloat, giving me a whole new perspective on why Krimskaya's temper was so hair-triggered. After all, he'd lost his country. His dream of having a professional ballet company still eluded him. Cash flow problems lived with him like fleas. Even the women in his life weren't working out for him. Who could blame him?

In a move that seemed to be the opposite of common sense, Mr. Krimskaya was moving in an increasingly avant-garde direction. Nikolai Krimskaya was beginning to produce some masterpieces, coupling his work with a bald-headed musician whose avant-garde music I couldn't like if I had to at first, but then learned to love. The two of them plus Mr. Shawn Colton were beginning to draw a lot of people who didn't know much about ballet but who'd come from old money and good church habits.

Krimskaya's choreography was so original that it pushed Sally G. and Rachel and the others into maturing into their art, far beyond any known expectation. Krimskaya had found the composer, Mr. I.S., and his music inspired choreographic moves that had never been done before. Sometimes as I watched, I would feel a sharp pain in my gut. Who was going to buy into these avant-garde creations? All day I would feel enveloped in deep, inarticulate regret.

To me, it did not seem rational that Krimskaya was risking these avant-garde pieces even as his cash flow troubles intensified. To me, this was like fixing car engine trouble by turning up the radio. The financial strain was working on Pasha, too. I was sure that it was my hospital bills still bringing her down, and I would offer her one-half of my paycheck each time I got one. She would say, "Don't ve silly, Susanna. How vill you pay rent?" Sally G. and I would bring Pasha bagels with lox and cream cheese and bananas for dessert and we'd talk about the Broadway shows Krimskaya was choreographing.

Pasha kept saying, "Vut he has Mr. Colton. Mr. Colton is crazy avout the contemvorary!" She hated when it came time to pronounce a B. As she spoke, though, she did seem awfully calm underneath.

Afterwards, Sally G. would walk home to Central Park West where she still lived with her parents. I'd walk to W. 86th where I now had my own little studio apartment, the wind whipping, the temperature surely forecasting snow. But the steam radiators never failed to overheat my studio. I'd throw open the windows and lie on the bed with my shoes off, listening to the taxis. Sometimes I'd hear a Vulltee A-31 Vengeance flying over the Manhattan sky on its way to the British Royal Air Force. Or maybe it was a Flying Clipper. Anyway, it was a warplane.

I'd found my studio on W. 86th in a little brownstone sandwiched between two large pre-war buildings. It was tiny. It had creamy plaster walls, and a nice arch that separated the little kitchen from the living room. You had to step up to get into the bathroom. It was miniature. At the south end of the studio were tall French doors that led to a rooftop terrace. In the mornings, the sun poured in luxuriously.

For furniture, I had nothing but a saggy double bed, a side table, a small kitchen table, a lamp, a chair, some iron skillets and pots, and some dishes, an on-again-off-again radio, all of which Sally G. and Pasha had given me. At night, if you turned a light on in the kitchen, thousands of roaches dispersed in a moving pattern across the plaster wall, skedaddling rapidly towards the nearest dark crack they could find.

Pasha had given me the European eiderdown that I so loved. It was a big puff, about a foot thick. You could throw open the window and sleep soundly with the cold air. Other than the eiderdown, my place wasn't much. But, it was home.

Every day after work, I would take a class. I wasn't ready to dance a pattern yet, but the warm-ups continued to do wonders for my knee. Cold weather bothered it. But, heat was its best friend.

One day in February, Pasha came up to me with bright eyes. She said, "We're going to Krimskaya's office now."

Krimskaya was so excited to tell me the news: "Susanna, we would like to invite you to teach."

I liked to died.

And I did feel like crying. But, my big smile took over.

And it was there when I was teaching in late February of 1943 that it happened.

The big, airy windows along the façade of the Broadway building were all cracked open, and all six ceiling fans were on—the studios got that hot, even in the winter. Outside it was snowing. It was going to be one of those days when the snow gathered relentlessly throughout the day.

In the afternoon when they got out of school, I had my itty-bitties, my pink-potbellied, pink-bowed five-year-olds. We went through the warm-ups. Today, they came in as little bundles: hats and coats and mitts connected by a string that you'd run through the sleeves. My itties moved with perfectly confident sway backs, little hands moving tendrils away from their faces, tiny unaligned extensions, their mothers sitting gossiping on the church pews in the hallway.

A couple of mothers peered through the French doors watching the little ones' wobbly pirouettes. In a minute I'd teach my little ones to dance by playing games, Pirouette Around the Rosy, London Ariels Falling Down. Before we could even turn around to check the clock, that would be that; class would be over, and itties would take a Mamma's hand and go chattering down the stairs. Sometimes I'd feel a little sinking spell.

On this particular day, despite the snow storm, Pasha was in a great mood.

She brought me a Coke. She said, "Susanna, I vought you a Coca Cola for later. I vrought a couple of extras, just in case."

"Thank you, Pasha. How sweet. I think I'll have mine right now. I need the sugar." The little ones never failed to wear me out, and my teenagers would soon be arriving for their two-hour classes. "Enjoy it!" Pasha said with a lilt. "I've got more!"

Gosh.

By mid-afternoon the windows, even though they were still opened, were fogged with the heat of our sweat. The snow was coming down harder now. The ceiling fans hummed. My voice was dimmed by the noise of the fans, but the hot, soggy fan wind was better than no wind at all.

My teenagers, two of whom were boys, had lately become rather serious and technically focused, and I had to work hard to keep them from developing an attitude.

"Please stretch your necks to the right, shoulders down, arm lengthening, lengthening, *penché*." Today my knee was only OK. In the warm-ups I could lead the *demi-pliés*, but not the *grands*. As I directed my teenagers at the *barre* by the big opened windows at the front of the studio, correcting this one's alignment, that one's turn out, this one's back, I could feel the cold air, the dance of the wet snowflakes whisking inside. Down on the street, snow had already covered Broadway by a couple of inches.

"Five, six, seven, and eight." We were working on tempo for the little *coupés* when I caught a shadow out of the corner of my eye and did a double take. A tall man was standing outside the French doors of our class.

Ignoring the gentleman, I continued walking down my row of teenagers, opening out this elbow, stretching this hand, rotating this leg open on the turn out and forcing the extension. Because Mary, our piano player, was out sick, we were using a record player for a piano. A Philco bearing *Suite De Danse*, a choreography inspired by the music of Chopin. The recording was so scant, you had to constantly go back and restart it. Now, as I went to put the needle back at the beginning of the piece for the one-hundredth time, I was thinking to myself that I had to remember to get us some new music.

In the mirror, I noticed the girls glancing over at the figure in the door. Other than having been startled by his presence, I hadn't paid much attention to him because I assumed he was there to meet with Krimskaya. Maybe it was Shawn Colton! The teenagers seemed uncomfortable with the way he was standing there, watching us with such claim. He stood so still.

"I'll go see what he wants. Keep stretching on those warm ups." I fanned my face. My lower spine was a blot of sweat, and I was also aware that my crotch was wet with sweat, its contour probably showing. I looked towards the record player, hoping I'd spot my borrowed-from-Sally G. cover-up tunic so that I could quickly pull it over myself, but it wasn't there. I remembered that it must be out on the church pew in the hallway. The hair at the nape of my neck was sopping wet. Even my bosoms felt wet, and I wondered if my nipples showed through. Where was that tunic? I really needed the tunic. As I got close to the doors, I still couldn't make out a face; he was just a profile of a man, a tall man cast in a rim of dim light. I felt every one of the teenagers stopping, now turning curious faces to see what was happening. What in the sam hill?

"Rudy, put the record back on and make the girls continue to work," I said to Rudy Rodriquez. With annoyance, I rolled my eyes, wiped sweat off my brow, using the back of my hand. As I reached the tall figure, he put his hands in his pockets, and, as he did so, my heart jumped.

"It's you," I whispered. "This can't be." I was dreaming. I crossed my arms to hide my breasts. I felt myself blushing hard. I drew a hand to my mouth, the other arm still held protectively across my chest. "It's you," I whispered again.

"It's me," he said. Our eyes locked.

"Go away." I blurted. I had worked too hard.

"No."

He was in a heavy grey Polish wool overcoat. There was snow on its shoulders. He had taken off his grey wool fedora. There was snow on it, too. His cheeks and ears were red from the cold. How could he stand it? He stood with his hands in his pockets, looking at me with a little soupçon of a smile, a charm of a smile. A small, wry smile familiar to my memory. His eyes were bluer than I'd remembered.

"It's you."

"I see you can bend it, " he said, barely. It was a whisper or a bare, comfortable voice. I could feel my heart beating.

"What are you doing here? You should go. I worked too hard to forget about you."

He pulled his hands out of his pockets and took my hands gently. His posture was so fine. He didn't say anything. Just the little sweet hint of a smile, lips closed. I heard the Chopin. Where was that tunic?

"You should go, you are making my hands sweat."

He pulled me to the exit doors and out to the landing at the top of the steps and kissed me. "Tell me about the knee," he whispered.

"It happened one day in here during a warm up. A pop. A cracking sound actually. And then something fell into place, and it bent. Sometimes it hurts. The nerve shoots still happen. Sometimes it threatens to lock again, but I can't complain," I whispered. I bent it a little for his benefit. "There. You can see that it works. You should go. I have to teach class."

"Susanna," he whispered. He took my hands again. Our whole conversation progressed in a whisper, even despite the noise of the pianos in Studios A and C and the Philco in B. We were in church. We were in a secret meeting. We were stealing something together. I felt like reaching to fix my hair. What could it have looked like?

"I can't believe it," I whispered again. Our eyes locked.

"I have missed you, Susanna, " he whispered, still holding my wet hands.

I squeezed his hands. His hands were starting to sweat, too. "I have suffered, Francis Taylor. I have suffered!" I had missed him until I felt bruised inside.

"I thought I would never see you again, either, Susanna. I was ashamed of myself." He squeezed my hands, and then he said, "I have yearned for you."

Could there be a sweeter thing for one human being to say to another? *I have yearned for you.*

I tried to stay frozen, as if taking instructions.

"What made you come, Francis Taylor?" We were still whispering, he still had my sweaty hands. I looked over to see if my teenagers were working even a little bit, and I could see that they were and they weren't. The girls were still eyeing the situation.

The downy hair at the nape of his neck was wet and charmingly curled. "I couldn't get you out of my mind, Susanna. I couldn't forget you. I tried everything."

"Why don't you take your coat off, aren't you burning up?"

He took it off and folded it across the pew.

"Would you mind reaching for that tunic for me, there underneath?" I finally saw it.

"I wouldn't mind." He bent awkwardly and reached under the church pew, this dignified man. He got it and gave it to me. I threw it over my head. Sitting on the bench, he drew me a little closer. I wanted to kiss him right then and there. All the teenagers, I'm sure, trying *very* hard to focus on the tempo of the music, the stretch of the leg. All you had to do was look in the mirror to see their eyes pulled helplessly this-a-way. I held an index finger up and mouthed, "Just a minute."

"Why didn't you say good-bye to me?" he whispered.

"Good-bye, where was I going? You were the one who came close, then bam! Why didn't you say good-bye to *me*?" As I said this, my voice transitioned from a soft whisper to a loud whisper. I felt skeptical, I felt the old anger already rising.

"I was sure that you went back South. And after the way I behaved, I was sure that you wanted nothing to do with me."

"Why did you act like that? Hot, cold, hot, cold. Are you going to act like that again? There were others, Francis Taylor. I knew it!"

"I had conflicts. It's true. I had things I had to deal with. I-I-I was scared of you, Susanna."

"Scared of *me*? I was scared of *you*! You were acting like a fanatic. Why didn't you say goodbye to me? Why didn't you talk to me? All you had to do was tell me the truth."

"I was a fool. I could have done more, Susanna. It didn't even occur to me that they wouldn't get you to the best doctor."

"It wasn't *their* fault. I found him in the yellow pages. And that was that."

"We'll talk about that, all right? We'll talk about it."

"It has its days. It hurts on days like this when it's snowing. But, it's working." Again I bent it back and forth for him. It felt crampy inside, sore with the cold weather.

"Can you step down the hallway for a second? Can you come here?" He got up and moved towards the exit stairs again, and I followed him. He pulled me through the exit door and got me into the corner of the landing. Then he kissed me again. It was different, this kiss. It was more informed, less riotous, more sensuous, more tender than the wild kisses of before. Afterwards, we both looked around to make sure no one was watching.

"There you were, and then there you weren't." I whispered, pulling back, but at the same time, sliding my hands around his waist. Why was I bringing this up again?

"Can you just come here," he whispered. "Come here." And then we began kissing again. I could hear his heart beat. I could feel mine pounding. I could hear the music being restarted, and I prayed my teenagers were operating on automatic now.

"Why did you—"

Even in love, already, almost imperceptibly, was the kernel of war.

"Susanna, before I even met you, I'd already had to register with the Selective Training and Service Act."

"Sally G. kept telling me that you'd gone off to the War! I didn't believe her, but she was right!"

"Conscription—compulsory enrollment—was a fact of life, even before the War had started. It was supposed to last twelve months, but, because of the War, it was extended, obviously.

"And non-combative training wasn't something you could get out of because you're rich or white or whatever, Susanna. I was commissioned for the Navy where I was a boot at the Samson Naval Training Center. I can't say that I can complain about the location, but draft by lottery is not a fun way to live."

"Let me go see if my student, Al, can take over the class so that we can talk." I was starting to believe him.

I went to the front desk and wrote Al a note, then walked fast down the hall flanking the studios, opened the door, and handed the note to him. He was in the midst, but he nodded, Yes.

When I got back towards the front of the studio, Francis Taylor was waiting for me with his coat in his arms.

He said, "Ready?"

"Ready for what?"

"To go to dinner. There is a special place I want to take you to called Café Des Artistes."

"Like this? I can't go like this. And look at the weather!"

"Don't you have a c-c-coat and some b-b-boots?" He stuttered again a little. Over the years, I grew very familiar with the occasional stuttering. It would happen when he felt taken advantage of, or when he felt his privacy threatened, and sometimes, such as now, when he felt guilty or intimidated.

I had one but it was embarrassing. It was a man's wool Navy overcoat that Sally G. had gotten for me down in the Village.

"But why didn't you just say it?" I moved to take his hand.

"Not now. We will talk about everything. Let's go to dinner. You are here. You are not gone, and I'm not gone."

Pasha came through the exit doors and found us there on the landing. "Oh, you're here!" she said. We pulled away from each other very surprised, and she opened both her arms and hugged him in the auntie way. She was flipping my wig.

"You know *Pasha*?" They looked at each other. Pasha was smiling. He was smiling. And then they both looked like they'd just gotten caught on purpose.

I opened my hands in a quizzical way, palms up.

"Would you like a Coke?" I asked him.

"You still have it?"

I realized what he meant. He meant from when we met on the park bench. He was making a joke.

"Yes, I have been keeping it for you all these years." I smiled.

"Pasha, where is that extra Coke?"

"I'll get it!" Pasha said and practically skipped like a little girl back to the front desk. She came back with it, and I gave it to him realizing that I was the last to know that Francis Taylor, the mystery man, would show up today.

He was taking a sip of the Coke when I said, "You know what, Francis Taylor? You've aged me."

He squinched his nose a little bit.

Then Francis Taylor said, "Put on your coat and boots, Susanna. I'll tell you the whole story."

I looked at Pasha. She was smiling the kind of satisfied smile, the one you wear after your underdog team comes up from behind and wins the game on an Indian sneak play. I felt my eyes getting wider, begging for answers.

But he just said, "Come on, Susanna. Looks like it's getting really bad out there. Here." He put my hat on my head for me.

What in the sam hill.

"Go ahead, Susanna. Enjoy yourself." Pasha insisted.

"And it's getting dark. Come on." In my opinion, he turned and gave Pasha a wink, though I won't swear to that. "And the snow is bad out there. We haven't seen snow pick up like this in a long time."

It was true that the crepuscular light was already coming through the windows, the snowflakes coming down hard and fast and thick now.

CHAPTER 13

Late February, 1943
Upper West Side, Manhattan

By the time we got outside, the poles holding up awnings fronting doorways were already icing up. The pavement underneath the awnings was icing up. We both had on boots, but I was dreadfully afraid that he was going to slip, not that I had any more power over the ice than he did. Doormen were beginning to pour salt on the pavement.

Francis Taylor walked with his arm inside mine, and that made me feel special. With a gloved hand, he held his hat on his head. I, too, held a free hand to my Navy turban-style hat that I loved. It had taken me a long time to save up for it.

The snow had gathered and was dumping hard now. The visibility was poor; you could only see a few feet ahead. People were just part of the blur. The wind was bitter. Beyond bitter.

We walked southward no more than four blocks when we decided to turn around. Café Des Artistes was way down on W. 67th. Taxis with a lightbox on were few and far between; we could be out here all night trying to catch a cab. Broadway already had several inches of snow and you could see curvy lines where cars had careened. Buses, taxis, cars were pulling over, snow was starting to freeze on their rooftops.

After we turned around and made our way back towards the studio, the slush at the curb of 80th had become a wide, icy brown liquid pond, and we couldn't clear it when we jumped. Our feet were wet and freezing by the time we crossed the street. And I was freezing in what I had on: my too-big Navy overcoat, my leotards, a tunic, black crochet leg warmers and my winter boots. The cold air seared through my body.

"In here," he said and pushed me into Zabar's where it was warm with its crowd of patrons.

Francis Taylor took his gloves off, blew on his hands. Then he took my freezing hands inside his for a minute. He pushed a hand into each of his pockets. I had never felt material so soft before. Cashmere.

"Is that better?"

"Can I put them inside your coat lining?"

He opened his coat buttons and I slid my arms inside. The whole lining was the same soft cashmere as were the pockets. I held him in a cozy bear hug right there in public.

The smells of Zabar's were about to kill me: coffee beans, cinnamon, vanilla, garlicky roasted tomato soups.

"Let's get some," he said, anticipating me.

"How cold are your feet?"

"Frostbitten."

"Mine, too. How will my students get home?"

"This is New York, Susanna. We're tough around here."

He gave me a little kiss and I know people were looking.

We stood in a crowded line and got the roasted tomato soup, some smoked turkey, some smoked fish, Zabar's pickles, and some Brie cheese from the cheese department called The Daitch. Zabar's didn't have a dining area. Everything was take-out. There were people behind the counters constantly taking deliveries over the phone.

The fish, turkey, and cheese were wrapped in wax paper, and the food was given to Francis Taylor in a big white paper bag with cord handles. Then we stood in another long line in the bakery section where we heard about a million different languages. The bread was running out, but we were lucky to get a baguette. We stood in another long line to pay with ration stamps. All told, it took about forty-five minutes; it was that packed inside of Zabar's.

"I guess people are preparing for a few days of this storm." I said.

Francis Taylor said, "Are you ready?" Through the doors of Zabar's you could feel the wind whipping.

"We're only three blocks away," I said.

"No, we're five blocks away, Susanna. We can't eat dinner in front of everyone up at the school. That would be rude as hell."

Rude as hell. I'd never heard him cuss before.

"But the wind will be facing us now."

"Come on. We have to brave it. This is New York, Susanna."

I *knew* that. It wasn't like I hadn't been in snow in New York before. But, this was my first New York blizzard.

"What about your hat?"

"Here. Put this glove on. Use it to hold onto your hat."

"I've got my hat and I've got the bag, don't worry."

And the bag won't break, right? I didn't want to ask. My stomach growled.

"Susanna. The Zabars know what they're doing. The bag won't break. The bag was *invented* for snowstorms." He started reading my mind like that pretty much for the rest of his life.

We proceeded through the snowstorm at a pace of about one one-hundredths of a mile an hour.

I have never been so happy about my steamy radiators in my life. We made it. The awnings and cars were covered in snow, our noses were about to fall off, our nostrils were frozen, our boots were soaked through the soles, our coats were damp, the soup was cold. Even the door key around my neck was so cold, it felt like it had burned my skin. But, we made it.

We took off our boots. And I gave him some leg warmers for his feet because I had nothing else that would fit. I punched the light button in the kitchen and, sure enough, there were the crazy roaches, and I knew that he'd seen them. Nonchalantly, I got a couple of iron skillets and a pot. We pulled up the one chair, "Watch it. That radiator will burn you if you try to touch it." I walked to my tiny closet and pulled out my vinyl suitcase, and he went over to the gas stove and heated the soup while I sat on the suitcase by the table and made us some salmon sandwiches and some smoked turkey on the few plates I had.

We ate mainly in silence, the cat having suddenly gotten both of our tongues. Finally I said, "My apologies regarding the roaches. Hope they are not ruining your appetite."

"No offense, but I think the Westside might have more roaches than the Eastside."

"I don't think they discriminate, Francis Taylor. Here, have some cheese."

"You have fabulous heat," he goes.

"Thank you. Don't touch it. I'm telling you, it will burn you."

"I hope not."

"You want some tea?" I stood up to get it, but he grabbed my hand.

"Does the radio work?"

"Not really. Sometimes. Occasionally."

He reached an arm for the radio, banged it twice, and we got the weather report. *For the second time this winter, a massive blizzard in Buffalo has caused power outages throughout the western part of the city. The National Guard has been mobilized to ensure that war supplies continue to be shipped through Buffalo to eastern ports. New York City is also under siege with nearly eight inches of snow already accumulated. Snowdrifts have buried cars parked along the curbs of its main streets, especially Broadway, Madison, and Fifth, and Lexington. Power outages throughout the five boroughs have also been reported.*

Our little brownstone seemed to be spared.

"The electricity never goes out in our building. This little brownstone seems to be protected from weather issues."

Francis Taylor gave me a look of doubt.

"It's like it lives between two big bosoms." The two pre-war buildings flanking it had always seemed motherly to me.

"The important thing is that you've got great heat."

"The best." I did love my radiators when it snowed.

Francis again banged the radio on its side a time or two, forcing the station to burp out some Benny Goodman. He banged it again and this time it jumped to the Duke. My favorite! He was belting out, *Take the A Train.*

Francis Taylor was in his ridiculous leg warmers. And as he reached a hand to pull me up to dance under the happy music, I pointed down at them and started to laugh. He laughed, too.

He turned the music down a notch, looked me in the eye, and pulled me closer, and that's when I began to sink. It happened like *that*. A pall of sadness came over me, a feeling of falling. "What's the matter?" he asked.

"Nothing." But, I could feel myself pulling away almost imperceptibly. "What is it, Susanna?"

The lump in my throat formed before I could even swallow it back. "Nothing."

He turned the music down another little notch. "What is it? What happened?" he whispered.

I took a breath, swallowed hard. Here goes, I said to myself, bracing for the inevitable. "Nothing," I said again."

Now he pulled me closer and danced me a little bit, the two of us in the leg warmers, our clothes dry thanks to the overcoats. Fabric rationing was so strict during the War that even a tunic was shortened from just below the knee to four inches over the knee. I was self-conscious about that. We danced in a slow little turn, the lump in my throat got worse. He put his cheek against mine, moved me slowly, tenderly.

But the lump in my throat persisted.

"Are you all right?" he said, turning the music down.

"Something bad happened to me, Francis Taylor." I whispered in his ear. "Something real bad." And before I knew it, the tears erupted.

"Come here." He pulled me closer in his embrace. Then he reached and turned the music off altogether. He pulled me towards the bed. "Let's sit down a minute," he said. "Here. Let me get you a handkerchief." He stood, walked a few feet to the kitchen table and reached into the inside pocket of his coat that was hanging on the back of the chair.

Being on the bed made it worse. I had yearned for him, too. But, I was ruined.

"Something bad happened to me. Something real, real bad." I whispered again, lowering my head.

"I know about it, Susanna." He whispered. "There were rumblings about it."

"It wasn't my fault, Francis Taylor!" I cried. I couldn't bring myself to tell him that I no longer knew if I could have babies or not. I couldn't do it.

"Susanna, stop! I know! I know it wasn't your fault! I know the guy. I know him. I know Stanford. He and I were associate board members of the Century Club. He has a reputation. A real philanderer. A misogynist who takes advantage of artists. The bastard has a reputation."

"What's a misogynist?"

"A man who hates women."

He was still holding me in his arms. He was using the handkerchief to mop up tears. I wiped my nose with the back of my hand and he now gave me the handkerchief so that I could blow my nose. Already I could feel how red and swollen my eyes had become.

"I'm the guy who got him fired, Susanna."

I unlocked from him, sat up straight, got back my composure. "You got him fired? How?"

"Pasha called me. That's how we became friends. She told me what happened. I felt rage afterwards. I went to the Board to second what Pasha had told them. The Board voted unanimously to get rid of the bastard and to get you two your jobs back."

We were sitting on the puff of eiderdown.

"Like that? Just got rid of him?"

"Like that."

Don't ask me how he had the power.

"Wasn't he important to the School for money reasons?"

"Actually, no. Not really. He wasn't consistent or even reliable. Even though he's deep pocketed, he made promises he couldn't keep."

I heaved a big sigh.

"I'm so sorry, Susanna. I'm so sorry about what happened."

"Thank you," I whispered. "Thank you." I leaned to embrace him. Then the thought occurred to me. "Is that the real reason you disappeared?"

"No. Before I left for Service, there were complications. Complications with other women. I didn't know what I was doing. But, when I left for Service, you were the only one I couldn't forget."

"Why didn't you say good-bye to me?"

"I was intimidated."

I still couldn't believe that he had gotten Stanford fired. That he knew what had happened to me. This was like a fairy tale. I pushed further:

"Are you responsible for Shawn Colton?"

"I am."

"You?"

"Yes, me. We've been on environmental boards for years."

"I like Mr. Colton. I call him Monsieur Colton."

"He's trustworthy, Susanna."

"Let's use the puff as a big pillow behind us. Are you sure you're warm enough?"

He seemed to like that idea because he grabbed it up and pitched it behind us.

"You did this? You got rid of him?"

"It was a team effort, Susanna. Trust me, Stanford is gone for good. He was a sham."

"Who paid the hospital bills?"

"Let's just say that was a team effort, too." He said with a vague smile. "Where is your powder room, Susanna?"

My powder room?? My water closet.

"It's over there in that corner on the other side of the kitchen wall."

He got up and I remembered, but I wasn't quick enough to tell him about the step. "Watch it! There's a step!"

Too late. He crashed into the bathroom. I heard the water glass fall and break.

"Are you all right?"

"Christ! Susanna!" He had banged a shin against the edge of the step. I tried to go close, but he raised a hand. "It's OK. Christ! I'm all right." He was rubbing the shin with both hands.

"I am so sorry!"

"Christ, Susanna! It's all right. Just go get a broom!"

Then came catastrophe #2: The lights went out.

"Oh my God, I can't believe they went out. They never go out! Are you all right?"

"Susanna. Get us some candles. Get real."

Candles? I didn't have candles. Catastrophe #3.

Instinctively, I went to the little table that Sally G. had given me. I opened its small drawer and, sure enough, there were a couple of half-burned candles in there. I grabbed them authoritatively and lit them with the gas stove, and went back to him. "Are you sure you are all right?" He was still sitting on the floor. I handed him the taller one.

"I'm all right. But, I need to use the restroom. Where's the candle holder?"

Candleholder? Catastrophe #4.

Thinking quickly, I grabbed my toothbrush and used the end of it to try to carve out a hole in the soap. But, the soap was too hard, I couldn't dig fast enough. So I went to the refrigerator and found an orange. I cut a hole in the top of it, then cut the bottom flat so that it would stand up.

Candleholder #1.

Then I opened a cabinet and got the Skippy Peanut Butter.

Candleholder # 2.

I grabbed the broom and the peanut butter jar and rushed back to him. He was sitting there on the floor, held hostage by a ring of broken glass.

"Here," I said and gave him the jar and started to sweep around him.

"This is it? *This* is the candle holder?"

"Yes. That's the candleholder. What's wrong with it? Here. Stay still. Shine the candle this way. I want to make sure I got it all. Here. Shine it here. Hold on. Let me get a dust pan."

Without paying any attention at all, I deftly got the dustpan, and by the time I looked up, he'd stuck the candle into the peanut butter and now seemed to be holding it with a measure of satisfaction.

"I'm sorry I forgot to tell you about the step."

"Christ," he said, "What in the hell have I gotten myself into?"

Then all of a sudden we both started cracking up. I was holding a dustpan full of broken glass, and he was sitting on the bathroom floor holding a candle stuck in a jar of peanut butter, crochet leg warmers on his feet. "What the hell?" He repeated. "Good thing you've got that eiderdown, Susanna, the temperature is about to shoot precipitously. Hold the candle a minute so that I can get up."

I wasn't sure if the building had a second generator, but you could already start to feel the sudden damp cold. I went to the kitchen, rummaged through the drawers on the outside chance that I'd find more candles. We would be without heat, the snow would not be letting up any time soon. He stood up. "Run the water in the kitchen, Susanna. Hopefully everybody in the building will run the water so the pipes don't freeze."

I'm from Benjamin, Mississippi. I'd been in lots of New York City snows, but I'd never thought of that.

"Shut the door. I'll be there in a minute."

When he came out, he said, "Where should I sleep?"

"Sleep beside me. Sleep inside my bed with me," I whispered.

We nestled down under the eiderdown, warm enough to keep the big front windows cracked and the French doors cracked, the radiators banging and hissing their last gasps, the temperature falling, one candle on the window sill by our bed, the other on the chair that he'd pulled over to his side. The thick eiderdown nesting us, the clothes sliding off, the heart unbuttoning, coming loose.

CHAPTER 14

Late February, 1943

Upper West Side, Manhattan

In the morning I awoke with my nose tucked under his arm. I loved the smell of him. And like blind, sleepy newborn bunnies, we groped. Lightly, I rubbed my fingertips along his collar bones, tracing their lyre-like shape. I felt under his arms and moved my fingertips along the side of his body.

Francis Taylor moved his hands gently over my face, down my neck, under my arms, down my sides, over my buttocks, and down the backs of my legs and up and down my inner thighs—all the peripheral places except the ones begging most for his hands. But he did not relent. I could see his chiseled face in the light. He looked at me while kissing my hands, taking my fingers in his mouth. When he did that I needed to kiss him. Then he moved his fingertips over my body again. Quietly, knowingly, he built me up in this slow, sensuous manner, touching places on my body that I never even knew I had.

My breathing quickened, and I could feel his heart gathering strength in its beat.

"Sweetheart, " I said. "I need to call the studio. What about you? Don't you have to call someone?" This was the first time I'd ever called him sweetheart.

"Let's wait," he said. And then he said, "No, go on and make the call. I don't want you to get into trouble." He seemed to sense that getting up naked and walking around for a minute would intensify the pleasure, that talking on the phone naked would intensify the pleasure. That going to the kitchen naked to make coffee would intensify the pleasure.

"Hey, Sally G.!" I said, swinging the straight black cord of the phone. My old habit. She was covering the desk for me.

"Sally G., I'm sorry I'm late. I've got to call in sick."

"Sick with what, Susanna?"

"Sick with something important," I told her.

"What kind of important?"

"I'll be there later. I promise."

There was something illicit, too, about skipping work. About my very white legs kicking up around the corner to get the painted bowl for Francis Taylor's coffee. About him under that puff in the cold with the snow daring us to try to come out. About lying in bed in the middle of wartime. Even about the coffee itself, the luxury of it in rationed times, there was something deliciously illicit.

And the illicit quality of our time intensified the pleasure of it all by many, many degrees.

I set the coffee down on the chair he'd pulled on his side and watched him in the dim gold light. We were lying side by side now, facing each other, kissing under the soft pour of the snow outside. His hand moved slowly over my buttocks, then slowly to the soft undersides of my small breasts. I thought I would go crazy with the way he caressed my breasts, with the way he took them in his mouth. My hands were all over him, I could not get enough of him. I needed to taste him. Now. I moved forward and took his sweetness into my mouth, the eiderdown we'd kicked back by now, my bottom in the cold air, the cold draft, and the warm throbbing of him in my mouth.

"Wait, Susanna, slow down." He pulled me up by my hair and put his hand between my legs and then took me in his mouth, built me patiently until he'd built me to the top, and, panting, I said, "Wait, wait something is happening to me." My breathing quickened and I wasn't sure if I could take any more. "I think I might be having a heart attack." He stayed down on me and entered me first with the swat of his fingers hard against the inside of me, against something up high, a secret present that God must have given a woman for all that she'd been put through. "Wait, I said again." Panting harder now. And then he came inside me and made wet love to me, slow, careful love, then hard, out of control love. I became lifted to somewhere out of this world: I was gone and when I came down in dreamy pulses of joy, I was no longer a girl at all.

Afterwards, we were in our own little space, side by side, recovering, there in each other's arms, stealing bliss.

"So did you have a heart attack?'

"I think so."

CHAPTER 15

Late February, 1943
Upper West Side, Manhattan

The world came back; we heard a noise, some kind of racket, and I sat up quickly, hugging Francis Taylor for dear life. "Watch it. Someone's here." But, it was only the snow shovelers outside. Francis Taylor put a finger to his lips. The eiderdown had now fallen off the bed, and I leaned over to pull it back on top of us.

"It's your mother," he said, smiling ironically.

"My *mother*?" I had never mentioned my mother to him in my life.

"Yes, it's your mother."

"She clomps around, but she's not an escaped convict, Francis Taylor." You could hear the metal racket of the shovels outside.

Francis Taylor got up and, as he walked to the window, his buttocks and back were so fine in the light of the morning. His legs. He was no athlete, but he was born with beautiful, sculpted legs.

"Come back from there, I don't want strangers to see you."

He pushed the window open a little higher and came back inside my bed with me.

"Will you give me another kiss?"

"No. What time is it?"

"I don't know. Are you hungry?"

"I'm getting there."

"Me, too."

"Should I try to go out and get us some bagels?"

"No. We'll order Chinese in a bit." They used to just deliver in Chinatown, but ever since the rationing started, the Chinese started delivering all over town, always on bicycles. Eastern European Jews were crazy about Chinese food, so on the Westside, you could dial up for Chinese, and it would be delivered to your door in thirty or forty minutes. But, I myself had never ordered Chinese.

Treat #1. But, gulp. With how many other women had he ordered Chinese? I grew suddenly silent.

"Is something wrong?" he asked. "Are you falling back asleep?"

"No. I'm worrying."

"What are you worrying about?"

"The girls, Francis Taylor. All those girls. How would you feel if every time you ran into me, I was holding hands with a different guy?"

What on earth was I doing? From true heaven to picking a fight, what was wrong with me?

"Christ, Susanna. Yes, I had girlfriends." He closed his eyes dramatically.

I couldn't help it. I continued, "There was the one in the park. The one on your arm at the Auditions that you never even admitted you went to—but I did see you. There were the ones who had already been in your apartment before I was there. I don't know their names. But there were girls. Girlfriends, girlfriends, girlfriends."

"I was and still am, I think, a young bachelor. People brought girls to my door like stray cats. I've had a lot of girlfriends, Susanna."

"You don't have to tell me!" Great. I was starting to feel a horrible wave of unconscionable jealousy. Still, I felt like I needed to air this grievance right here and now.

"You've got to kiss a lot of frogs before you find your princess, Susanna. Haven't you ever heard that expression?" He smiled. He was gloating.

What am I? Maybe that was it. Maybe he just knew how to seduce. Maybe he was a smooth operator who didn't want to spend the night alone. Maybe I was going to get dumped tomorrow or maybe now or right after the Chinese. Maybe I was just getting used. So many girlfriends. Some of them some damn good teachers at that.

Anonymous teachers. Teachers without credit. Was I princess or frog? Frog, I suddenly decided.

"Let me tell you something right here and now, Francis Taylor."

"Yes, Susanna?"

"I don't do doubles and triples."

"No offense, but what in the world does that mean, Susanna? 'I don't do doubles and triples'."

"That means 'if you've got girlfriends, you might as well get up and hit the trail. Because you've got the wrong idea about who I am."

"Susanna, first of all, as I already told you at Pasha's that afternoon, the girl you saw me with in Central Park was my cousin. She's still my cousin. She'll always be my cousin. Now, will you get off it?"

No. I won't.

"What about Maria? That was *me* who called that time at your office. You answered the phone, "*Maria?'* Who is Maria?"

"God, Susanna. Maria is my cleaning lady. I thought she was calling to see where I'd left the money for her. God!"

I warmed up a little bit, and a trace of a smile pulled across my face. I lay there kind of wishing we could hurry up and order the Chinese. My stomach growled. I was always excessively hungry the week after I'd finished my period. But, at least the timing was right, at least it was only a week.

"Susanna, let me tell you something right here and now." Then he started to stutter. He held his hands out. He was stuttering, he was trying to get some words out, and his whole face looked suddenly so very forlorn. He took a sip of the coffee from the bowl, then put it down and propped up the pillows behind us.

"Here. Let me help." I puffed up the pillows behind us.

"Susanna," he said. "Somebody once said 'Memory knows before knowing remembers.' I think it might have been your man, Faulkner, from down South." He put the coffee back down on the chair.

I wasn't sure what he was talking about. But, then he just started talking, like stream-of-consciousness. He sighed, looked up at the ceiling, hands behind his head against the pillow, and I nestled guiltily under the crook of his arm and presently heard the saddest and strangest story I've ever heard in my short good life:

When I was a little boy, up until I was six-years-old, I had a best friend. Her name was Cary. She was my buddy, she was like a sister to me. She had thick blond hair and rosy pommette cheeks, and blue eyes that turned downward. Her parents, Laure and Joseph, were from Scotland, and they worked for us. Cary went to school with me. She was a grade older than I. She was in second grade when I was in first.

One day I was the caboose for the first grade single file lunch line one noon at Sudberry Middle School, our small PTA-run school, when a second grader crept up behind me, mimicking, mocking—

"You've noticed that I walk slightly pigeon-toed, right, Susanna?" Here, he turned towards me and leaned up on an elbow.

"Shhhh. Go on with your story. Yes, I've noticed. Your walk is very sexy."

"It *is*?"

"Yes, your walk is sexy, masculine. Now go on—"

Mark, the second grade bully, mocked my walk to a peal of laughter. I had no defense. At school I was shy and closed and self-contained. I hated the leather block that was my corrective shoe, the shoe that turned my school into a dungeon of teasing, chiding, bullying.

But Cary, my friend who was then also in the second grade, and whose parents, Laure and Joseph, worked for us, saw what had happened. In her grey gymslip she came blowing out of the second grade line, and walked right up to the bully, Mark, and spat on him. Her temper had no care for the consequences. She threw him a punch and was made to stay after school, writing 'I am sorry for what I did' over and over again.

I was still at school, too, because Mother had forgotten to pick me up. Mother always was a busy lady. It was nothing for my brothers, Henry and Michael, and me to be forgotten and left on the school playground until sometimes as late as dinnertime. Growing up, Mother had to go see the mayor quite a bit. She had to go into New York quite a bit. She had this board and that board meeting: The Nature Conservancy, the Museum of Natural History, the Met. My mother was the sun.

So that afternoon after she spat on the bully, I walked home with Cary. We walked through the woods of our property and around our mile long, half-mile wide Kingfisher Pond, where we lived in Pope's Crossing, Connecticut, near Greenwich. Cary's Dad, Joseph, always met us halfway. That day he told us that Mother was having a dinner party at our house that night. I remember thinking how glad I was because later that day at school, something else had happened for which we hadn't yet been punished. With the distraction of a dinner party, if the teacher, Mrs. Cunningham, called, Mother wouldn't answer.

At the dinner parties at our house, a big rambling New England farmhouse, they—my parents and their guests—always had cognac after dinner in the living room where the ceilings were high, and where the tall fan windows were flanked with thick drapes that were like plump acoustical clouds. Either Cary's mother, Laure, or else Joseph, would pour the aged cognac. As it would roll honey-colored in the snifters coddled by the guests, I'd listen from the stairwell; I was about five-years-old when I first began eavesdropping from behind the banister of the stairs. I'd listen because, who were these people? Everyone visited us, everyone, bringing little presents, bringing, too, their lively minds and smart conversation, though not necessarily any conversation of the heart. They spoke with caution and precision, as if solely empowered by the fear of making a mistake. When my mother would enter, all eyes would become fixed importantly on her because she was beautiful and compelling and powerful. My mother always held her snifter with two hands, as if seizing with special importance the cognac's power to bring forth feelings in her. One day, from behind the banister, I was going to hear their secrets.

'Come darling,' my mother called that night, as she always did at these dinner parties, seemingly to no one in particular. It would now be time for us brothers to play our instruments. Her old friend, Gabriel Roux, an accomplished French painter from Paris, was there. They'd tagged eyes to each other throughout the night. 'Come, darling,' she said again, seemingly to a shoe, a leg of a chair.

But each of us, each of her children—my brother Henry, my brother Michael, and I—had never been able to conceal our natural conceit of belonging to her. When called, we all fought to get to her lap first. Each of us carried our instrument held out like a gift; we were the princes of her dinner parties.

'Come, darling.' The competition was never so much over who would play best as it was over who would be called upon first.

On this night she called on me *first. I had never before had the honor of being picked to play first, so, for a flash, I felt bigger than anything. I trotted toward Mother with my diffident smile. Her eyes seemed glazed as she watched my fingers open the case, and take up the violin and bow stick. With a cheek leaned to the violin, I stood looking at her, suddenly stage-frightened, pigeon-toed feet held together as closely as possible.—Don't get me wrong. I did hate playing for the grown-ups at Mother and Father's parties.*

When I got picked, my brothers, Henry and Michael, backed away with protesting eyes, maybe hoping for something to go wrong with my playing. They looked directly at Father, but to no avail. (Father had been having a terrible time during this period, something about the bank and many deals falling through.) Everyone was pindrop polite, listening. All eyes on me, the taciturn, uncoordinated youngest son. I struck some familiar chord of beginner's Vivaldi, the instrument was bigger than I. I had always been too shy for an audience—

"Shy?" I said out loud.

"Susanna, be quiet so I can tell my story."

I promised him I wouldn't interrupt again, and I almost didn't.—

When the guests clapped before the piece was over, I became flustered, worried I was in trouble. The few minutes I took to get reorganized seemed a few hours. Mother remained with her intimidating eyes bolted on me, causing me to lose my place on the music sheet. And then I forgot what key to play—

"Well, you were only six!"

"You don't know my mother, yet, Susanna."

Yet? Whew. He said, *yet*. As I cuddled there beside him, I put my arms around him. I no longer cared if I went to work at all that day.

Well, I made it. I made it to the end of the piece, if only to show Henry and Michael a thing or two. And at the end, I bowed dutifully, one hand on my chest, the other turned palm outward in the small of my back, bending a little at the waist, keeping my eyes the whole time on Mother.

She clapped, opened her arms, and asked me to come to her. My face lit up. In my awkward, loathed, leather block of a shoe, I lumbered over to her and climbed into her lap, my heart beating so. Then I remember reaching for her head and closing my little hands over her ears. I thought that my wanting muffs for the chastising and teasing words I heard and suffered in school, meant her wanting. Each time the school kids teased me, surely Mother could overhear the teasing with some kind of maternal radar from wherever she was, even if she was in New York. I had expected that her guests were going to tease her and me for messing up the piece I'd tried to play. Instinctively, I reached for her ears and covered them with my hands.

Instead: 'Don't mess up my hair, Francis! I've told you a hundred times.' Mother flicked my hands off her ears as if they were pests, insects with long, annoying appendages and sounds.

Then, in front of her guests who approved of everything their leader did, Mother said, 'Francis Taylor, that was supposed to be Concerto in C. You played it in B flat. That was appalling. What concerns me is—

I didn't interrupt him. I was too stunned to speak. The woman sounded much more cruel and cold than my obtuse Mamma had ever been, and I was seized with a wave of pure compassion, not just for Francis Taylor but for Mamma, too, for the hard ride I'd given her.

I never forgot it. The moment remained indelible. It revealed everything there was to know about her priorities, but it didn't fix the chase. It was all about the chase. The chase for her love.

Quiet as still water, I slipped from her arms and disappeared from the living room. My brothers crossed their arms and laughed ha, ha, ha, ha as I clunked away, muffling out Mother's words, the ha, ha, ha, ha of my sorry brothers whom I adored, drowning the notes coming from Henry's flute. I pressed my hands over my ears and climbed the stairs on my twig-like legs. I hated, hated, hated my shoes.

Cary's mother, Laure, was watching me; I saw her come around from the kitchen and watch me as I went up the stairs. She was Scottish with ruddy cheeks and thick blond hair and blue eyes and a melting laugh, and she was my sentry. She was the only one who knew of my hiding place, Mother's big closet. In the corner behind a full-length mink that had fox collars hanging clipped to one of its sleeves, I had my secret hiding place. I had named the biggest mink 'Bear,' and behind him I kept a gray striped tub of a hatbox that was my ship, carrying my treasures. I collected things of Mother's that I guiltily knew she needed: a favorite fountain pen (she once looked for it for three days, asking and asking if anyone had seen it), various keys, garters, paper clips, the spiked heel of a shoe that had been left on the kitchen counter with a note ordering its repair. And the tiny bottles of her perfumes. And because the closet belonged to her, it was more secretive, more dangerous than climbing into the hollow of a tree.

I knew that Laure knew about my hiding place because one day when she was cleaning in Mother's room, she opened the closet door to vacuum, and she saw me. For a long time, she respected my secret, my secret place, but I learned that evening that she had been vigilant all along, vigilant about what might be happening to me, vigilant about Mother, under whose reign she knew I might be trying only to survive. She should have seen that it was this way for all of us, each day the same tiptoeing on eggshells. She should have been vigilant, especially, for the sake of Father.

'Yoo hoo,' she called softly that evening from the shut closet door. I didn't want Laure coming in. I didn't want to talk to Laure or anyone.

I didn't want her. But I did. She opened the closet door, and I hid behind Bear. 'You hoo,' she said again, and I poked out a little bit of my big shoe. 'Anyone home?' I poked out a little more of the leather block.

'Let's read,' she said. And holding The Box Car Children *in her hand, she came in and turned the closet light on and shut the closet door and came and sat down beside me behind Bear. She opened to the third chapter, and I sat leaning against her with wide trusting eyes, then skipped a finger along each word as I read, safe with her if I got stuck—*

"You were six, and you could read *The Box Car Children*?"

"Laure had taught me to read when I was four. By kindergarten I was reading chapter books. It had been Laure's idea to keep the gift of reading a secret from Mother and Father and my brothers, though I didn't then understand why."

"Did your mother ever read to you?"

"I have no memory of her ever reading to me, no."

"So you read in her closet?"

"Yes."

'Let's read,' she said again. Laure and I read all of Chapter 3 together, then she had to go back downstairs to pour the coffee for the guests.

When the guests finally went home, I heard Father having an argument with Mother.

'Helena, it's a question of millions in losses. The suit alone is a question of millions. The banks won't... the banks are not in position to...' I could just see him looking at her, helplessly.

'Vincent, we'll talk later.'

'Goddamnit, Helena.' A fist crashing against the table, Father's voice rising. It was Father who was mostly accused of shaking up the family. Out of a deep but frustrated wanting of her attention, grew his swings between tyranny and helplessness. All week, he'd been in a bad mood, and that evening he'd hardly even looked at any of us, much less talked to us. He was way off somewhere, mired in riddles of his own. His face looked discouraged and drawn. He looked lost, orphaned. By then, just about everybody knew he was in trouble. Even my brothers, Henry and Michael, and I knew for sure that something was wrong. Father wasn't suited for business. He was raised for business but not suited for it. I could hear Henry and Michael bickering downstairs in the breakfast room. I guessed Father was too down to bother with them.

I drew back tighter behind Bear and listened to the sounds of Mother coming up the stairs. She shut the door of her bedroom succinctly and turned its lock. She went to her parlor room. I could hear the water running as she brushed her teeth, and it was then I wanted to try to sneak out, but I was too small to reach the lock that was set three quarters of the way up on her bedroom door.

She came back out to the bedroom, and I could hear her taking her clothes off. Once, she opened the closet door and even turned on its light and hung something up. But she didn't see me. Afterwards, she didn't shut the closet door all the way.

Then I heard her sounds, and I wasn't sure what was going on. I was scared. Breathing, moaning, then Mother saying, 'Hold me, Sweetie. Hold me, Baby. Kiss me, pump me.'

I thought my mother was crying, I didn't know what was the matter. I came up from the cramped place where I had been sitting behind the mink, and moved as quietly as I could to the closet door, and tried to peek through the crack where the door was ajar. Mother had taken off all her clothes except her high heels, and she'd thrown her stockings and under garments over the back of a chair. She was on top of the sheets, her hand working quickly along the black hairs, to her arch, her quick pants of air.

She moaned a bereft kind of moan and it scared me. By accident I leaned too hard against the closet door, and it opened a little more. The hinges squeaked, and Mother quickly turned her head towards the closet. I tried to pull back into my hiding place, but I lost my balance stepping backwards in the corrective shoes. With a crashing noise I fell into riding hats, crops, jodhpurs, hunt jackets; they fell pell-mell from their coat hangers as I tried to shrink back between them.

Mother gave a little scream, then bolted out of bed, rushed to the closet where she snapped on her silk kimono, then parted the clothes hanging and found me down on the floor with the riding clothes. She pulled me out by my underarms and dragged me out of her room. I remember feeling like a puppet or a rag doll; my arms were limp, my feet dangling, heels raking the rug into two long squiggling lines of upraised hairs. Mother dragged me to the sleeping porch where Henry and Michael and I slept, and she jerked me into my bed. Mother's eyes were clear but wild and full of storm. She leaned over me and spanked me and said, 'You'll be punished, Francis Taylor. You'll be punished for this! You know better than to be in my closet, do you hear me?'

'Yes, Mummy' I answered. My voice was so small. I was so scared.

Mother stalked back to her room, tall in her rightness, and punched the light out on her way out. In the dark, I pulled Lou Lou, my stuffed rabbit, close to my face, and waited for the punishment to come.

The wait for punishment was short, then long. The first part of it came right away. Storming from her room, she came neurotically back to the sleeping porch, punching the light on again, and whispering over me where I clutched my rabbit, 'I'd wanted a girl. I'd hoped you'd have been a girl, but I'm glad you're not a girl.'

I peeked one eye around the rabbit's face, but it failed to appease. She leaned her face to me with entreating lips, luring me to her side, as if a six-year-old enemy could conquer. 'But that's all right (sugary kisses all over my cheeks), you'll be the man when things go badly between Father and me.'

When I was well enough drugged up with guilt, you could see how Mother gathered perverse pride from her power over me. When I'd shrink, frightened of her, shirking back from the punishment she'd promised, she'd blackmail, 'Don't stay away from me, Francis Taylor. It makes my stomach hurt.' Reluctantly, I would receive her kiss on the cheek, then I would go to wash it off, scrub it off. 'Don't hide, don't hide from me, little Francis Taylor, it gives me a headache.'

For so many days, so many days, I lived in a shell. Coming out only to fight with my brothers—always the rivalry kept me alive, but the fights now were more in the act of soliciting their protection than of getting their attention. Only Cary knew that something was wrong. I hadn't told her anything, but during the weeks afterwards, she shadowed me. At school, it was like she had become my bodyguard.

But, suddenly, she wasn't allowed to come over to play with me at home anymore, and I didn't know why until it was almost too late. But, I thought that this was the longer of the two punishments. And I was very wrong about that. The punishment was to come.

One evening Laure and I were rolling dough for dinner rolls, and I said to her, 'I've made Mummy very, very unhappy.'

'No, darling, you haven't made your Mum unhappy. Your Mum was born unhappy.'

Then a sudden red herring, as if Mother had overheard the conversation. For a couple of weeks Mother became a mother: taking me places (to see the horses, to pet their soft muzzles; to see Grandfather's expansive greenhouse; to row out on Kingfisher Pond; to collect leaves for identifying; buying me things like children's books fresh off the review pages, biology sets, binoculars for seeing the birds).

Before I knew it, I no longer believed the sudden caring was a trick, a marinating before the next punishment to come; I instead started to feel close to my mother. They say I began to change, to talk. They say the muscles in my body relaxed, and that my walk was better. Laure said that sometimes she heard me singing.

Mother kept it up for another week or so. 'Gifted child, my gifted child, see all this?' lifting me in her arms, parading me outside, freeing one arm and making a wide swoosh. 'Don't tell anyone what you saw me do, and all this will be yours....'

Soon I no longer needed her relics to secretly hoard in a hatbox. Buying into her act, I instead began collecting from her: her posture, her hand gestures, her facial expressions.

I went too far with my newfound surge of confidence: jumping rope, boasting to Henry and Michael, parading Mother's gifts underneath my brother's noses, strutting around using the arrogant language and strident attitude that I had learned by aping her, inviting trouble everywhere, as if even the shoes had become ineffectual in rendering me vulnerable. 'You'll have all this,' she bribed, 'Do as I say and you'll be rich like a king.'

I didn't then know that Cary wasn't ever going to be able to come back. I also had no idea that Laure and Joseph had been fired. She and Joseph had been told to leave at the end of the month. I didn't know that my mother had gotten a call from Mrs. Cunningham: 'Francis misbehaved at field day, and his friend Cary Mcbride bit me around the ankle.'

I remember very well when Cary bit her around the ankle. I remember the conversation that provoked her:

'No fair, Miss Cunningham, we're not having him on our side. The blue team can take him.'

And Bill Mercer, the captain of the blue team said, 'Neither are we; they drew the short straw, they have to take him. We're not having a retard on our team. He's a girl, anyway. With a girl's name. We don't want Francis. We don't want Francis!' Larry Sturgis got the whole team to sing-song it.

Though I hated it, I was getting used to it, the teasing. That afternoon when I heard this in PE, I slipped away to the bleachers over on the far side of the field and hid underneath them.

Cary soon slipped away, too. She ran through the woods along the track. When she got to the bleachers, she crawled underneath them to where I was hiding.

'I'm scared, Cary.'

'Don't be scared. They won't get you. We'll stay here.'

We huddled together and she said, 'Don't move. We're safe.'

Then came Mrs. Cunningham. She walked like she had hooves. Coming towards us, she got bigger and bigger, like a dragon. She blew her whistle twice, then took it off from around her neck, held it in her hand, swinging it by its cord.

She walked straight up the bleachers and stopped where we were. She stared down at us.

Then the old witch leaned down and grabbed Cary by the pigtail. And when she did that, I reached up and grabbed Mrs. Cunningham's fleshy arm, digging my hands into her flesh to get her to let go of Cary's hair. Cary was screaming.

'Let go!' I screamed, holding my grasp on Mrs. Cunningham's arm.

'Shut up! You spoiled brat!' And that's when Cary bit her hard enough to draw blood.

Mother hadn't wasted a minute. She got the phone call from Mrs. Cunningham, then hung up and walked directly to Laure and fired the whole family. They had until the end of the month. The mother act, the taking me rowing on Kingfisher Pond, the biology set, the binoculars, all was to cover her guilt before I would find out the news. Nothing ever scared Mother so much as having her reputation on the line—

My arm had fallen asleep, and it tingled like crazy. But the story was too creepy and horrifying for words, and I'd listened to every word of it.

"What time is it? Who *is* this mother of yours. Here I thought mine was something else."

"Susanna, that's not the whole story. That's just the first part of the story. Yes, Mother is very, very screwed up, and she screwed me up. It took a long time to get unscrewed, Susanna." I would learn after we'd married that he had gone into Jungian analysis to get it all straightened out.

"Do I have to meet her? I'm scared."

"I'm scared for you to meet her, too, Susanna. Let's order."

"Let's do."

"No offense, Francis Taylor, but compared to your mother, mine was all sugar."

"Do you want beef with snow peas or chicken with cashews?"

"I'll take the chicken. Do I have to meet her?"

"I'm afraid so," he said, as he got up to use the phone in New York City, a long, long way from Benjamin, Mississippi, a stone's-throw from this Pope's Crossing place where his hell-mamma lived.

CHAPTER 16

Late February, 1943

Upper West Side, Manhattan

I thought things would change. I thought that after Mother fired Laure and Joseph, she would realize the magnitude of the loss. (They did everything from gardening to cooking to cleaning.) And I thought Mother would retract her orders. I thought she would just tell them that Cary couldn't come over and play anymore. I thought that would be all right because I would get to see Cary at school every day, and, if I knew Laure, she would hide me under her skirt if she had to, but she'd find a way to have me over to her house to play.

But Mother held to her word. Laure and Joseph had decided to move the family back to Scotland. During those last weeks, Laure cleaned and cleaned. It was the outlet into which she would channel the energy of her anger. But, at the time, I thought that this was how she was trying to win her job back. She didn't want the job back.

One afternoon Henry came in and said,'Mummy said she fired you.' Then he opened the icebox and dug two fingers in the mousse she'd prepared. Laure spanked him good. Maybe she was fired, but she could still spank.

On Friday of the last week, Cary snuck over to see me when Mother and Father were in New York working on what I now know was the first leg of the merger bail-out plan. That morning Joseph came around in the old black Ford to pick them up and drove them over to the train station in Greenwich where they'd catch the New Haven Line. There was something exciting about this trip; it almost looked like my parents were getting along. (In the end Mother saved the huge business he'd inherited and could not run, having him, her own husband fired, and hiring the investment banking firm, Morgan Stanley, to arrange a buyout through a merger with another company.)

I hadn't seen Cary sneak over; it was the end of the first week of summer vacation, and Cary had ridden over first thing in the morning on her bicycle. She must have come over partly through the woods, because the shins of her athletic little legs were just scratched all to hell.

When I saw her, I sent her a note from my bedroom window. I was scared to go down. I was scared Mother would come back for something she had forgotten and then find me, and that would be that.

I pulled a chair up to my window and dropped the note down by taping the envelope to the end of Michael's camping rope. As I lowered the rope, the envelope fell off and flew down on its own, Cary chasing it with her hands in the air.

My handwriting was tenuous and the letters were askew, but all these years, I have remembered exactly what the note said:

Dear Cary,
You are my dear friend.
And you are my best friend.
And I think you are smart.

Your friend,
Francis Taylor Dewitt.

In the note, I also included two 1928 silver dollars called Peace Dollars that Father had given me. All these years, I see Cary in my imagination, her eager arms reaching for the note as if chasing a butterfly.

Cary rode her bicycle around and around in our turnaround. Henry and Michael came out with their bikes and joined her. I was sure my brothers would tell Mother that Cary had come over, and

I was sure that I couldn't afford to go out to see her because there was no predicting Mother's punishments.

But Laure came up to my room and said, 'Lovey, you go and see her. Your Mum is on the train to New York, and we'll be leaving tomorrow, so this is your chance.'

She took my hand, and I went downstairs with her, and stayed beside her in the kitchen as she made croque monsieurs *and French fries for lunch. I listened to her peel an apple, the sounds of the peeling lightly hitting the cutting board. The window was cranked open, and it was quiet outside; any little rustle of pinecone or leap of a squirrel fairly pierced the air. The birds were napping. Even the weather felt languid, lazy for early June in Connecticut.*

Cary came around and poked her head through the window, a leaded glass window that had been cranked open, and said, 'Come play.' She said it as if we'd never even been forbidden to see each other.

Whatever punishment would be coming my way, Cary would be worth it. Because I went to get my bike with its training wheels, and we all rode along together in the paths in the garden. We were having fun. We were having a good time. We started a game of bicycle tag.

Eventually Michael said he was getting bored, but I don't think he was bored. I think he was sick of being tagged 'It.' He went up to Cary and said, 'I quit. Besides, we're not supposed to be playing with you.'

Cary responded by bending her knees up and resting her feet on the handlebar. Then she went to 'No Hands.'

'Mummy says we're not allowed to be friends with you anymore.'

Henry, listening to the conversation, was taking the flagstone bend of the garden path, and said without looking at anyone in particular, 'Because you come from poor people.'

I was tagging very close to Michael, riding a foot or two behind him. I was trying to navigate the rocks on the path when, impossibly, I came around agreeing, 'Yes, Mummy said poor people spend much of their lives getting rich people in trouble.'

I remember speaking in the high patrician accent of my Mother's—

"Oh, I know that accent. You do that one all the time."

"Well, you can't talk about accents, Susanna."

"What happened next?"

Well, that was that. Cary steamed forward, dead through the center of the garden. When she got to me, she slammed on the pedal brakes, causing the bike to fishtail a little in the pebbles. Then she shot off it and flung it to the ground. It slammed down on its side, the wheels still spinning. She hotfooted over to where I leaned against the larger of the two oak trees. Though I was still on the bicycle, I crossed my arms and puffed my chest arrogantly, trying to win over my brothers. I meant it about the poor people. As she prissed towards me, I watched with a look of calm insolence, almost delight. By then she had already opened the sash of her little percale blue play dress and had dug two fingers into the pocket of the sash; you could see them working like pincers underneath the cloth. Then she hurled the silver dollars at me. Her arm thrust was sharp and clean, and one of the silver dollars ripped through the air at bullet speed, hitting me right on the cheekbone and cutting deep enough to draw blood. Afterwards it became a swollen egg-sized bruise, puffy and purple, then yellowing as it slowly healed.

Then she hit me with the other coin at the base of the skull and took off on her bicycle, pedaling so fast you couldn't see her feet.

One hand flew to the back of my neck, and the other was cupped over my cheek, and by the time I looked up, Laure was coming out the kitchen door, a colander of spud peelings still in her arms, the croque monsieurs *left to burn in the oven as she screamed, 'Cary!,' dropping the colander and running towards the back drive, a private driveway linking all the relatives of the four thousand acre tree farm and used mainly for delivery. Cary was taking the long, steep hairpinned part of the driveway that led towards Kingfisher Pond, the sashes flying behind her.*

'Cary!' Laure screamed. 'Cary, Cary! Watch the truck!'

You could see patches of Cary, a white blink—the short sleeves of her pinafore shirt—through the trees of the first hairpin turn. This turn wrapped like a loose belt around Ben's Knoll, the hill separating Grandfather's house from ours.

I got on my bike and pedaled as hard as I could to catch up with Laure. I, too, had seen the ugly white postal truck coming up the steep banked curve, and I'd seen Cary flying down from the other way. This driveway. Mother and Father had always asked people not to use it because you couldn't see around the bends. Too many blind curves. But, for the postman making his deliveries to Grandfather and our uncles and aunts, this was the road connecting us all. Through the woods I, too, screamed, 'Cary!' The postman's truck flashed faster and faster in white patches through the leaves as he came up around the bend and then descended. Cary was flying down the other way, one hairpin turn, two hairpin turns, three hairpin turns; this part of the gravel drive was like flying down a mountain. She would never see the postman, and she would probably not hear his truck until the last second, and the postman, there was no way he would see her. Because so few people traveled those winding private driveways linking the relatives, almost everyone who did fairly sped through.

Laure wheezed out guttural, panicked screams and pointed frantically. She was still running down the driveway when I caught up with her. 'Do something!' she yelled, 'Do something, Francis!'

I passed Laure at the first hairpin turn, the damn training wheels hitting every pock or root in the road, the wheels squeaking from want of oil. 'Go, Francis! Get her!' Laure said, and she tried to push me, as I pedaled like a windmill, the training rollers, stabilizers Father had gotten for me in England, wobbling behind me. Behind me, Laure ran for her life, calling and calling Cary's name. And the then the postman's. 'Marcus! Marcus! Watch my little girl!' Laure's voice was starting to get hoarse, and then I lost her, I couldn't see her anymore.

That fucking leather block, god damnit! *I pressed the pedals with all the juice a human heart and pair of legs could provide; I was soon way out ahead of Laure. But I couldn't see either Cary or the truck. I had never biked the long private driveway; the turns were too steep. Now, as I went around the second turn the bike flipped. Laure must have heard the spill or known this somehow intuitively because she screamed, 'You're all right. Get back on and go! Scream! Scream to Cary, she will hear you.'*

I wasn't all right, but all of a sudden, something broke loose in me. I took off the stupid leather shoes and got back on the stupid bike, let go of the brakes this time, doubling over and screaming with such depth and volume I did not know I had; my words shattered the air. 'Cary! Watch it!' Rocketing down the nearly vertical turn was the last thing I really remember before finding her.

For a minute my mother's voice came in my head, 'What did I tell you? The poor are bad. See how she caused a fire in the oven, the oil and cheese dropping down through the oven grid! Who do you think you are?' Mother's tyrannical voice slowed me a minute, as if her hands had come down from somewhere, pushing against my shoulders.

Though I didn't know it then, Laure too had taken her shoes off, and she was running behind me. But who could run on that gravel?

It was then that I heard the shrill sound of car brakes slamming, screeching as if never oiled, the fishtailing, the sounds of gravel stones rolling like little heads downhill. The noise of a door opening and then shutting quite quietly, and the crunching thuds of someone's strides through the woods.

Again, I choked for breath and way behind me now, Laure called for her little girl, over and over and over again.

And then she started calling for me.

I had expected to see wreckage, the mangled shapes of fenders and bicycle, and Cary's body. I had expected to hear piercing screams, I don't know why. I had expected to see the postman, a man who couldn't harm anyone, with his face wrenching from pain. As I'd sped down the turns, I'd heard myself saying, 'Oh no, oh no, oh no!' I felt, too, that I might throw up.

Instead, there was the postman's truck parked like a belt buckle, right in the pit joining the ribbony drives. Clean and quiet. No tread marks, no signs of any danger or accident. But for the grave silence.

The postman came out of the woods, his face ghostly white, his mouth partially open, and lips working as if trying to utter words. His eyes strained with horror, and his hands repeatedly went to his head.

"Where is she?" I tried to utter. I was hyperventilating.

He turned and ducked back into the woods, and I followed him as fast as I could, half-limping, stopping once to pull a thorn from my foot. He kept looking back at me.

She must have veered off through the woods just in the nick of time. She hadn't crashed into the truck. I could hear myself panting. I heard the snap of twig and rock falling. At my feet was the long line of upturned leaf and mud and the imprint of bicycle tread. Cary. Here and there, branches had broken off.

It was then I remembered and feared the hard gray cliffs that line Shoalman's Creek, their straight drops of twenty and thirty feet. They just twenty feet away.

Shock first, protecting like pillows: A voice in my head to keep me going, assuring me, 'Cary saw the postman coming and veered off through the woods. She'll be down in the feather pile of leaves, skinned no doubt.'

And adrenaline alone fueled me the last thirty feet.

Marcus did all he could to block me from seeing. But I pushed past him, past his blocking me, past his trying to keep me from seeing, feeling, knowing the sight of my unconscious best friend in all the world, there at the bottom of the cliff, her bicycle mangled underneath her.

Marcus tried to keep me from making my way down the cliff. 'I'll go, son. You stay.'

'No, I know how to do it.' Marcus looking on, then taking his shoes off and following me down, my skinny fingers gripped to the crannies, my toes curling to whatever pock hole they could find, my body flush against the rock, flayed and frozen like a small, dark salamander, Marcus later told them.

When Laure arrived, Marcus yelled for her to go to the truck and get the keys and get in and drive up to the house to call the ambulance. 'Don't look,' he said, 'Don't look!'

Afterwards Marcus said how the whites of my eyes showed, and how I held up my hands, cramped like little crooks. Marcus had reached me about ten feet above where Cary lay, and I quietly cooperated as he got me in his arms and then scaled down the rest of the way. At first he put me as far away from the sight of Cary as possible without losing sight of me. But even that, even the importance of protecting a six-year-old from seeing, became trivial as the blue tint bled through Cary's skin, and Marcus had to rely on me to pump the oxygen into Cary's mouth while he pulsed strong arms against her sternum, the ribs cracking. Marcus counting firmly in fours, the measurements of a breath, nudging me on count as I hunched over, holding Cary's nose, prizing her jaws open, breathing into her, then shouting, 'Cary, you come back! You don't go, Cary!'—

"Get under here, sweetie. Come here." I pulled the eiderdown over us. "Come here. God." Tears were pouring down my cheeks. "I'll get you some water."

I got up and got him some water. In perfect silence we stayed under the big puff of down, my arms around him, spooning him, the tears streaming, streaming, streaming down my cheeks.

He was crying, too. I used a sheet to wipe his tears. I lay there holding him until at length we both fell asleep. It was four in the afternoon when I woke up. He was still asleep. The snow was still coming down and twilight was setting in, purplish. The Chinese boxes of half-finished food were there on the chair beside his side of the bed.

I sat up, watching him. In the dimming light I stayed up, watching him, keeping an eye on him. In the dimming light, I watched over him. I laid a hand on his head, touching it just barely. I watched over him, I couldn't get my eyes off of him. It was too late to worry about the doomed nature of any love in which a pair of naïve human beings think they are marrying their missing ghost, their missing spirit. It was too late for that; I was pregnant with our twins.

PART III

1943 – 1948

New York City
And
Pope's Crossing, Connecticut

CHAPTER 17

Summer, 1943
Upper West Side, Manhattan
And
Pope's Crossing, Connecticut

Now he came almost every day at lunchtime. He brought sandwiches, and sometimes we'd go to the park and sometimes we'd go straight to my apartment.

Most of the time, we didn't even get as far as the bed. He'd come to get me, kiss my neck where I had perfumed it, and then he'd lift me up, and I'd wrap my legs around him. He'd hike my dress up, and slide my under frills down to the garter belt, and with both hands, I'd slowly work his zipper down, and take him inside me. Afterwards, I'd stay in his arms, my arms wrapped around his neck, my head, dizzy, resting against his shoulder, heaving for breath. He would catch his breath, too, then take me to bed, and start all over, going slowly now, slowly, until I was finished. And he'd talk, whisper to me when we made love. Sometimes the windows dripped wet with the heat of us. I was pregnant for sure. We weren't even close to married.

I never felt sinful about what we were doing. Things were changing around New York. Katherine Hepburn and Ingrid Bergman had paramours, and Tennessee Williams had a smash Broadway hit about a Southern belle who ruined everybody's lives around her partly because she couldn't get enough. Plus, the thinking of the late Dr. Sigmund Freud had become all the rage. He had been obsessed with sex and had made a business out of it, in his own way. All over New York people were starting to talk about sex. Women were painting their legs, including a seam up the back of them. Beauty patches, midriff shirts, and strange looking hats were in. The most popular of these hats—the "skyscraper hat," the "blown-up derby," and the "barnyard of feathers"—were what Sigmund Freud would have no doubt flatly referred to as phallic. That would have been his way of saying that women were walking around with penises on their heads as an unconscious way of advertising what they wanted.

But it wasn't like that for Francis Taylor and me. Style, fashion, and what famous people were doing had nothing to do with it. I mean I think this would have happened to us, even if I had never left Benjamin. Sometimes, alone in the day, I felt my body cave under the wish for the feel of his hands.

In the spring, he took me to their place in the Vermont woods. There were clear, pristine lakes on the property, nestled down in the valleys. The water was freezing, but we peeled off all our clothes and jumped in one anyway, right at sundown. The water took all our breath, constricted our veins, and made our lips blue and shivering. We shimmied out, whooping and hollering to prove that we were alive. Then we clasped hands, ran up the hill, threw the quilt down in the field up there, wrapped ourselves in it, loving each other down until both hearts pounded like a pair of tom-toms. Sometimes, the way I could tell he trusted me would be by witnessing his balled fists slowly opening up as he'd talk to me.

One day in late May we were walking in the park and he asked me to marry him.

I couldn't imagine ever being away from him, not after all it took to get him in the first place. The answer was Yes. Even though the concept was flipping my wig.

After that, we were never apart. Francis Taylor took me to the Brambles in Central Park and taught me his love of bird watching. He took me to all the museums and to the theater and book readings. I learned a whole new side of New York. I learned why people fall in love with New York.

The only time anything went wrong was that heebie-jeebie July day I finally had to meet his mother, Helena Dewitt. It was a rendezvous meant for discussing our wedding details and walking through the old colonial New England home where we'd be living in Pope's Crossing. And for her to know what I looked like. But I call it my very own D-Day. The businesslike manner in which this meeting occurred had a strange way of calling up all my flaws: her cold but beautiful eyes made my ears and cheeks hot; her large vocabulary more than once caused a nervous shaking of my left leg. Her authoritative air and command of her world raised the hairs on the back of my neck, and underneath my "abbess hat" (another winner for the times) my hair became a drenched ring of sweat.

I wish I hadn't of been so *limited*. I had no idea what she meant by Jasmine or Earl Grey when she lifted the china pots of hot tea and asked me which I took. I'd have given anything to have had Francis Taylor with me. And why Francis Taylor had had a very important meeting right on that given day was something I plainly could not understand.

I guess he found out about the steak *tartare* blunder through his brother Henry, who was of course married by then, but who nevertheless eyed my legs when I leaned over to scratch the dog behind the ears. The way my dress hiked up in the back seemed to make him a little hot under the collar. As if to say it wasn't fair his brother was getting an ex-ballerina when his own wife was a professionally committed, often out-of-town Yale scientist, sweet on the study of hymenoptera behavior in low temperature habitats, who couldn't have cared less about getting her exercise. Marge. She was great, and I later counted on her plenty. But, judging from the flush on his face, and the fact that she'd already given birth to three children, and how they say that certain things between man and wife get put on the back burner during the child raising years, I can tell you where that man's brain was located. Right between his legs, sealing the evidence that he was indeed a Dewitt if I ever saw one. I bent my knees to get my dress to hang down more evenly and continued to scratch the dog behind the ears.

"Do you like steak *tartare*?" Helena asked with her back turned. She was on her way to the kitchen, I supposed to ask the cook, Linda C.S. (whom I met briefly and liked a lot), to start preparing it.

"Oh, yes ma'am, I love it!" I gathered it was a Northern dish similar to New York Strip and relied on the famous unspoken Southern rule of excessive politeness where anyone's cooking was concerned. "Steak *tartare* is one of my favorites."

"How do you like it?" (Meaning, as I later found out, with capers and lemon, or with capers and vinaigrette.)

"Medium rare, thank you." I answered confidently. (I'd always loved my meat well done. That's the way Mamma cooked it, along with the vegetables so mushy you'd have never guessed they once had living cells. We Southerners loved over-boiled vegetables and meat we could trust to be cooked clean of *trichomonads*. Still, my taste buds were the highly adaptable kind, and for Francis Taylor's sake I had learned to love both medium-rare and the idea of parboiled or even *crudité*.)

Henry was the first to start up, a hand muffled over his mouth. She followed. They shuffled together to the kitchen. And then I heard Henry say, "Where, for Chrissake, did Francis Taylor find her and what in God's name is she?"

It was Linda C.S who had the good sense to turn the mixer on, and from where I sat on the sun porch, it sounded like she'd put it way up to "egg whites." Which helped to drown out the laughing considerably. I just sat there biting my nails and trying to resist my old impulse to run away.

Henry and my Mother-in-Law-to-be eventually got a grip and came on back to the sun porch, each looking down in concentration, as if trying to remember what day Marie Antoinette got her head cut off.

Linda C.S. followed, close on their heels, pushing through the kitchen door carrying a silver tray piled with raw hamburger meat, peppered with sprigs of parsley, and garnished underneath with bib lettuce. And a *raw egg* on the top of it, loose and lackadaisical as somebody in a yellow bikini sunning on her stomach.

It was an ordeal if I ever lived through one. When I got back to Francis Taylor's that evening, after having walked all the way up to his place from Grand Central carrying things his mother wanted him to have (clean laundry, some mail, a lamp Michael said he didn't want), I simply lay on his bed with a face frowning like an ugly jug. My lips were pursed. My legs were crossed. Every time he tried to talk to me, I just simply stuck a finger in each ear.

One thing I did like about Francis Taylor was the way he could always read my mind. I lay in bed, ignoring him. I was thinking about what other kind of torture awaited me with this family. Like would I have to have my picture in *The New York Times*, exposing our love to all the world? Would our simple wedding turn out to be stiff and zero fun? Would they like my dress? I had barely saved up enough for my wedding dress, which I was going to be able to pay for lay-away style because of Francis Taylor's good credit. And, most importantly, was I going to show? I was then at the beginning of my fifth month.

He moved closer to my side of the bed. He propped on an elbow, puffed his pillow a little bit and said, "My mother and I think a small wedding would be best. Are you good with that, Susanna?"

Proof that he knew about the steak *tartare* incident is the way I took it.

From the financial point of view, I guess I was relieved, but it struck me that the two of them were going to be more in cahoots about this whole thing than she and I would be. I felt myself losing a place of importance. I was a cow in quicksand.

"Have you ever had *écureuil cru*?" I decided to venture. I had looked it up. Squirrel: *écureuil.* Raw: *cru.*

He put his hand to his chin and thought about it for a minute. "No, I don't believe I've ever had that, Susanna. Is it an entrée? What does it taste like?"

"You don't know what *écureuil cru* is? Gosh, I can't believe that. I don't mean to be rude, but I think you need some culture, Francis Taylor. *Écureuil cru* is a culinary must for the *haute cuisine* lover, Francis."

It was very important that I called him Francis right then, very important. Still, I was afraid this was going to start up an imbroglio, so I quickly lifted my pillow out from underneath me, put it between us as a kind of wall, then stuck my fingers back in my ears and lay there with my eyes closed, listening to my breathing.

"Susanna, you're hurt. You're hurt about what happened today."

I opened my eyes, and they glistened, blurring him, before I could even get a chance to swallow. "I'm not hurt, Francis Taylor. What on earth would I be hurt about?"

He took my hand, which was just perfect; I might have blacked his eye if he'd of tried anything more intimate than that at that particular moment. With wisdom in his voice, he said, "Look, Susanna, Mother can be difficult and intimidating at times."

I turned my head towards the wall and blinked about a hundred times. Last thing I ever wanted him to see at this moment was me on the verge of tears. To the wall but with my hand still in his, I said, "Did I fail, Francis Taylor? Am I just hopeless?"

"No, Susanna, now come here." He tried to turn me around. "She's a good woman underneath it all. I'm sure you two are going to get along just fine."

I hugged him back and thanked him, but my mind was busy reeling out a movie about the future. I started to drift off a little bit in his arms when my private movie made a sudden turn for the worse, including special effects and scary music.

I jumped out of bed, stood with my hands on my hips, and my feet somewhere between first and second positions.

"Francis Taylor? I have an announcement to make." It was urgent.

It looked like he was trying to doze off. He had the eye closest to me shut, but I should have known. The other eye was open as a window, and I saw how it was catching my every gesture in the mirror's reflection. I cleared my throat.

"As mentioned a second ago, I have an announcement: My name's Susanna. I come from Benjamin, Mississippi, in Rankin County. Closest town to Benjamin is Pearl, population 400. I have worked professionally as a receptionist and a secretary. I have no formal higher education."

He responded by wriggling down into a more comfortable sleeping position and fake snoring. And he shut the eye that had been surreptitiously spying on me.

I sighed and looked down on him from where I stood. Looking at him that way without his knowing always made me feel light, like I could float. His gentle hands rested on his chest.

I bent a knee to the bed, crawled slowly towards him, carefully placed my fingertips on his back, and rubbed them up and down on skin that covered him like the velvet on a jewelry box. I could feel his back and shoulder muscles underneath, strong but loose. He began to breathe like a child.

I started to hum quite low, quite softly. I liked old spirituals from back home. I liked the way they kept me so close to home I could practically feel the heat and the humidity as I sang.

Then, when I was pretty sure he had fallen asleep, I crouched close to him, touched my lips all around his little ear, and I whispered so hushed, my words seemed to almost get lost in the air, "How can I help you, how can I be your light when my past is a shadow?"

Carefully I pulled away, slid to the edge of the bed on my side, and got down on my knees. I folded my hands close to my face and bowed my head into them.

"Dear Heavenly Father," I prayed, "Please help me. My words come out wrong. Please tell him for me how anxious I am to do right." Only with God could I let my hair down completely. With Francis Taylor, half the time I said the opposite of what I really meant.

"Amen." I unclasped my hands, pressed them against the bed, and started to crawl back in when there he was. Right there. Beside me, kneeling down. He wasn't much one to say his prayers, and he pretty much thought the whole thing about God and the Baby Jesus, the burning bushes, the walking on water, the old, old women having babies, cripples climbing down from a tree was the biggest racket on the earth. So quite naturally, it occurred to me that he was making fun of me.

But he wasn't. He was looking at me like he practically adored me. Like maybe I was one of those angels or that hussy over whom Jesus commanded people not to throw rocks. With him looking at me like that, I suddenly had the trust to ask the most important question known to man: "Do you like me?"

"Yes, I like you very much. Do you like me?"

"Better than a pair of new white shoes."

"Thank you, Susanna." He moved my hair out of my face.

We crawled into bed and loved each other so much the neighbor rang up and asked if we might let the cats in.

Four short weeks later, with me then showing evermore at six months pregnant now, and bearing the "animal stripe" that stretched over my round belly, we were married on August 12, 1944, in a very small, simple wedding at St. James', the tiny Episcopalian family chapel at Pope's Crossing. Sally G. stepped lightly, according to the directions, and fanned out my—Pasha's—veil behind me. Mamma didn't come. Pasha gave me away. I took his hand and married the man I'd longed for from the time I was barely sixteen years old.

Afterwards at the reception at the Dewitt's house, Francis Taylor came up and said we were supposed to do the opening dance. I dreaded it. He could not dance. I just dreaded it.

He took my hand and we moved off. Everybody was standing around gawking. Was it my belly underneath my empire-waist wedding dress or his pigeon-toed dancing? I don't know. I stayed real close to him, whispering to him the whole time something about how good he was doing. All of a sudden he grabbed me tightly around the shoulders. Like he believed me.

Then I reached a hand out and pulled his mother in before she had time to protest, and the three of us danced for a minute or two. Then I dipped down, pulled back into the ring of onlookers, and let the two of them take the floor all by themselves.

Chapter 18

September – November, 1943
Pope's Crossing, Connecticut

There was a book out by Grantly Dick-Read, MD, called *Childbirth Without Fear.* I hadn't discussed it with my husband yet, but I'd already decided on a home birthing. By then, we lived in Pope's Crossing, the family's compound in Connecticut, and baby doctors were still making house calls. My babies and I would be far safer than the knock 'em out, drag 'em out method that had become the way it was. No baby of mine was going to be delivered by a mother who had been sedated with morphine and ether to the point of unconsciousness. No baby of mine was going to be yanked out by forceps while the mother remained comatose. And no baby of mine was going to be put in a hospital nursery, far away from the Mamma's beating heart. Were they crazy, didn't they think there was a baby in there?

And another thing: at the beginning, neither Francis Taylor nor I nor Dr. Oatman knew that I was having twins. It is nature that tells you these things. Nature told me loudly and clearly one morning when I rode my bicycle down the long driveway to pick up the milk that was delivered to us every morning in cold quart bottles.

It was mid-September. The weather was nippy in the early mornings. Francis Taylor had just finished breakfast. Carrying his worn leather briefcase, he kissed me good-bye, and walked across the garden towards our driveway. As with every morning at seven-thirty, he was off to catch the Pope's Crossing dinky to the New Haven Line. Family, particularly his mother, Grandfather, and a couple of uncles, had raised the money for the Pope's Crossing Depot and had gotten a real good-looking Governor's Award in return. The walk stretched anywhere from twenty to forty minutes depending where you lived around Kingfisher Pond.

I went out to our garden to check on the last of the blueberry crop. The bushes were still yielding little blueberries. The basil was still coming up, and we were still getting a few tomatos. We already had cucumbers, peppers, peas, green beans, and squash. Our garden could supply every one of the relatives, but it wasn't until I was eight months pregnant that I started inviting my in-laws for dinner. I'd spent most of my pregnancy learning to become a master French chef, but I still wasn't that confident. Still, I'd gotten pretty good. One or two stars.

In the kitchen was a basket of old magazines that had piled up beside our brick fireplace. I pulled out an old *Yale Alumni Magazine* and started to use it to drain some string beans when I noticed that I'd coincidentally opened it to an article called *Antenatal and Postnatal Care* that had been reprinted from *The Times of London.* I leaned over it and read, discovering Dr. Grantly Dick-Read, a doctor in London who was consumed with the logic of natural childbirth over the conk-out method. Shooting a mother up with anesthesia that could kill her was, like, Hey, who are you, Doc? Didn't God get it right the first time?

I was sure—100% sure—that Grantly Dick-Read was for me. Since I was rich now and of good family name, I was sure that I'd be able to secure a doctor to make a house call when the time came. Maybe it could even be Dr. Grantly Dick-Read himself. Well, maybe that was an exaggeration. But, as it turns out, asking Dr. Peter Oatman for a home delivery had proven as easy as being able to get into any restaurant in New York just by dropping the name Dewitt or Vanheusen to the maitre d'.

Of course, while my belly bloomed round and eventually began to feel like cement had set in, I figured out that I was having twins through my own accidental pregnancy test: the bicycle ride down our driveway early one mid-September morning.

I'd put on a sweater and ridden my bike out of the garden and onto the driveway, our big clapboard house behind me, motherly and kind.

It was on the second hairpin turn that I *knew*. I loved these turns and pretty much took them full speed ahead. But these days, I was careful. Francis Taylor didn't want me riding a bicycle while I was pregnant, period. But there was a deep basket on the front of my bicycle, and that's how I carried up the milk up from the bottom of the driveway. I loved these bicycle rides, and I felt that I could manage them.

At first I thought I'd been stung by a bee. Then I realized it was too big a coincidence that both breasts stung to about the same intense degree, not that a bee can't be remarkable.

By the time I got down to the cold milk in its crate at the base of the eighteen family-mailboxes lined in a row, my breasts felt like they'd been in the refrigerator overnight. They were numb and swollen, and the nipples stung like they'd been shot. I cupped my hands over them, doubled over, pressing them against my lap. Then I lay face down on the ground, unable to keep my decorum at that moment, should one of the relatives have passed.

A good fifteen minutes later, the pain subsided.

It was during those fifteen minutes of torture that I realized that I'd been double-dipped. Nobody had talked about breasts hurting this much unless they were preparing for two. Or more. My head was as light as a meringue.

I lifted the four-pack crate of milk, snuggled it into the basket and suffered all the way up the hill back to the house, wondering how to break the news to Francis Taylor.

When I got to the top of the steep, windy driveway, I rested the bicycle against a sturdy oak, and lay out-of-breath on the lawn with my arms outstretched. I was watching the clouds float by like little sheep. A little smile spooned up on my face. I couldn't tell if it had to do with pleasure or dread. But, I was now sure of the chance that there were two babies in there instead of one.

I got up, went upstairs to our room, and mumbled one or two things to myself about the number of magazines and newspapers which he didn't mind keeping around forever. (Some of the *National Geographic's, Audubon's*, and *New Yorker*'s dated 1939, I'm serious. He couldn't throw away anything if he had to.)

I called and got an appointment with Dr. Peter Oatman in New Haven. Then I got dressed and drove over there, waiting in the waiting room with other mothers-to-be. We were all bored silly, stuck with reading magazines such as *Good Housekeeping* and *Ladies Home Journal*. I didn't care about lemon zest in a cherry pie; I wanted to know what was going on inside my uterus.

My name finally got called. In the examination room, the nurse asked me to take off all of my clothes, and she handed me a starched linen sheet and asked me to lie on my back on the table. Dr. Oatman put on a rubber glove greased by Vaseline and said, "What brings you here today, Susanna?"

"A bike ride." I put my feet in the stirrups.

"What about it?"

"It was early this morning; you know how nippy it's been. My breasts felt like they had been shot. Something tells me that I'm producing a double amount of hormones. Something tells me that I—I—that I might be having twins."

His face became stern, you could see the deep lines across his brow. The frown line grew deeper as he inserted a hand.

"Susanna," he said. I could feel him opening his hand inside me. It hurt.

"Yes," I said, wincing.

"Sorry. I know it's sensitive. Just a minute." He felt around in there some more. "I do think your uterus is enlarged. This could be a sign of multiples."

Multiples. Whoever heard of calling your babies *multiples*. The term made me laugh, I couldn't help it. Plus, he tickled me to death after he brought out the stethoscope and put the cold silver thing on my tummy to listen for heartbeats.

"I'm sorry. Forgi-i-ve me." I was having a giggling fit. I couldn't stop. He put the stethoscope to my own heart and that just did me in.

He even started laughing. He said, "We used to have to put an ear to a big breast, and we were embarrassed. And that's how the stethoscope got invented." His comment got me fit to be tied. I could not stop giggling. Maybe it was the giggle of denial.

"Just a minute," he said, now moving the stethoscope back to the womb. My babies were then nineteen weeks old. "Do you want to hear their heartbeats?"

I finally got a grip and Dr. Oatman put the things in my ears and it took a minute, but I finally heard the first heartbeat of the two. And then we felt around and I heard the second heartbeat. My eyes watered. I went from giddy to somber.

Dr. Oatman said, "The position is good. Very healthy."

"Thank you," I mouthed. As if I could take personal credit for the good position.

"But, I'm still having them at home, Doctor."

"We'll talk about that."

"Hey, do you sell that heartbeat thing by any chance?"

"What? This? A stethoscope?"

"Yes."

"Well, no, we don't sell them. But I have an extra one that I can lend you. It might be a good idea to monitor the heartbeat of the two of them."

The two of them.

"Great!" I went. Because I could not wait to show Francis Taylor. I felt lucky enough that Francis Taylor had narrowly escaped being drafted by lottery during WWII, though he did do civilian duty. Now that we were going to become a father and mother, I left Dr. Oatman's office on top of the world.

When I got home, I called him down at the Dewitt and Vanheusen office in New York. His secretary passed him over to me and he got on the phone and goes, "Susanna? What is this about? I'm in a very important meeting regarding Series E War Bonds. Whatever it is, it can wait until I get home tonight."

No it can't, asshole.

When he came home that evening, I just pretended like I was deaf.

He said, "Susanna, come here."

I simply shut my eyes and stuck a finger in each ear and started humming.

"Come here, Susanna. Come here for a minute."

I banged around in the kitchen.

He came into the kitchen and pulled out the big Windsor chair at the head of the breakfast table. "Come here." He sat and then patted his lap, motioning me to come sit there.

I checked on my roasting chicken, added more rosemary.

"Please? I'm sorry that I was rude today. Sometimes I act like a jerk."

Duh. I pressed hard on the ear he could see from his vantage point but lifted a finger off of the ear he couldn't see.

"I've been under a lot of pressure with these War Bond decisions for our clients. I got us in too late."

Whatever that meant.

"Please come here, Susanna. What were you trying to tell me?"

OK, it was his problem if he wanted to hear. I turned the rice way down on simmer and walked over to where he sat. But I didn't sit in his lap.

He had on that charming face where his little eyebrows bent down slightly, like pear tree limbs with just enough fruit on their ends. His lips looked like they were going to smile any minute but didn't want to make any false starts. I accidentally touched his sweet arms, and through my fingertips came tingles of goodness, difficult as this is to admit.

"What was it, Susanna?"

I took his hands and put them on my big belly.

"These." I said.

"*These*?"

"Yes. These."

"What are you talking about?" Then the risible look, the ironic smile came across his face. His eyes brightened and he got a little red. "What do you mean 'these'? Are you feeling, uhmmm, any unusual fatigue?"

I just looked the other way. Oh yes, I had been exhausted lately. "Susanna, can you hear me?"

Ignoring my husband, I looked down at my swelling tummy and laced my hands underneath it as if to hold the twins up. I loved them, I did. I could tell we were going to be close.

"Susanna?" he said. He had his gentle voice back, and his blue eyes looked at me full of wonder. "Are you all right?"

"These guys are tough as turtles, Francis Taylor. We're fine."

He stood up and started to bill and coo me on my neck.

"Stop! That tickles. Now let me get back to my cooking."

"Sus?"

Sus. I couldn't believe that.

"Yes. Fran. *Dos*." I held up two fingers.

"Come here. Sit here. Did you say *dos*?"

"Yes, as a matter of fact I did, Francis Taylor."

"Come here." He was literally aglow, like a little kid on Christmas morning before the presents get opened.

"*Dos*," I mouthed and again held up two fingers.

"Has this been confirmed?"

"Yes."

He next let out some kind of wheezing sound of delight. It sounded like this: *eeeeeep*!

"Susanna. Now sit down a minute."

"I'm not sitting there, the chicken will burn." I turned and walked to the oven and checked the chicken roasting. I turned the gas way down. I was trying to hide a smile. What a nut, he was.

"Come, Sus. Come sit with me for a minute."

Sus. He did it again.

The twins and I cut him a break; we went and sat in his lap.

"Now, Susanna, just breathe," he goes. Like he was the expert. "Take in that good air, deep and strong, and let it out slowly."

I just sat there with my hands folded, looking at him like he was a real hard calculus problem.

"What I think about the situation here (I loved this. I kept my face perfectly straight) is that... well... are you trying to tell me... I mean do you think you might be..."

"I'd like to know what you're trying to tell me, Francis." I shouldn't have said it in the tone of voice I chose, I couldn't help it.

"Sus?" There he went again. He was smiling, trying to tickle me. "You're not trying to tell me that we're having twins, are you?"

"Well, why don't you just put an ear against my stomach, if that's what you want to know. Here. Hold on. I've got something." I reached for my big purse on the far side of the table and pulled out the stethoscope. I put the two rubber thong-like things in his ears and watched him lean to my stomach like he was getting a peek inside a crystal ball. I moved the disc slowly over my stomach and asked him to hold up a finger if he heard something.

Chu-chu, chu-chu, chu-chu, chu-chu.... The most beautiful sound in the world!

"Susanna, I hear something. I hear a heart."

I adjusted the two things in his ears and asked him to listen tighter. It would be nearly impossible to hear the hearts of both fetuses, but I let him try anyway.

He gently put his head back to my stomach, laid his hands over its dome shape, moved the disc himself.

"Susanna, damn. I think you're right... I think I hear two hearts. There might be two children in there." I'm sure he didn't really hear both hearts, but I was privately amused.

I had never seen him act like this. He said, "Stand up."

And I stood and he stood and kissed me. Then he literally pranced around like a two-year-old getting to stay up past bedtime. He skipped. Making an idiot out of himself, he skipped all around our room humming *Mary Had A Little Lamb*. He was not a masterful skipper. I could secretly tell that he'd been the last in his class to learn how.

O Lord, I loved him.

After awhile he collected himself, and I was able to set the dinner out for us. I was sitting there waiting for him when he started rubbing his hands through my hair and talking paternal-like about how I better get to Dr. Oatman's for a check-up at least once a week.

"Sit down, Francis Taylor. I think we better talk." It was a vulnerable time to tell him that I had no plans to go to Dr. Oatman's more than necessary, much less that I had no plans to go to any hospital, period. I'm sorry. I wouldn't be going back to any hospital after it'd already taken away the one chance in life I treasured almost more than my chance to raise a family.

To thwart the good chance of a squabble, I said, "Here, try the beans. I used nutmeg for them. They're really good."

But he got back on the hospital subject.

I had to proceed. I took a breath and rubbed him softly on the back of the neck. "I have to show you something," I said.

I went to the kitchen drawer where I kept my Bible that I'd months ago covered with brown paper bearing the red hand-inked title, *The Best Seller*, so he wouldn't bother me about my love of reading it. That was the one thing my Mamma had ever given to me. Underneath the Bible, I drew out the *Yale Alumni Magazine* and opened it to the Grantly Dick-Read article. Quite quietly I gave him the article, then disappeared quickly from the room.

In my mind he would explode in primary colors if he found out that I was not only interested in natural childbirth, but that I had also gotten Dr. Oatman to agree to the home birthing.

To my wildest surprise, he didn't go ape. On the contrary. He embraced it. "It proves, once again, your down-home common sense. Your decisiveness in arranging this matter reminds me all the more of your independence and capacity, Susanna."

He was flipping my wig. I don't recall that kind of sophisticated compliment coming from him. Ever.

"You're a ballet dancer. Your body will know what to do," he said authoritatively. The encouraging words gave me the courage to next tell him I wanted to have a home birthing. *Eeeep!* He took this in, too. Not one time did I have to explain my intense fear of hospitals.

He could be great, my husband, he could.

The next months crept on fairly slowly. Francis Taylor worked hard in New York. He also got in touch with Dr. Grantly Dick-Read who got him in touch with women who had chosen natural childbirth. Most of these women lived in London, so I imagine that he ran up a high phone bill, but he was confident that the key to natural childbirth was to utterly relax. Hence, his signing us up for Dick-Read inspired breathing and visualizing exercises at Yale. Starting from my seventh month on, we would be committed to a forty-five minute commute out to Yale twice a week to learn how to breathe deeply and think beautiful thoughts while going through the most painful experience offered to womankind.

"You'll know what to do, Susanna. You'll find your quiet spot. Remember, you're a ballet dancer," he said, again.

I appreciated that. I appreciated that he called me a ballet dancer..

I mainly concentrated on developing my skills as a master French chef. Nausea, which had come on hard and fast, often prevented me from cooking, but when I felt good, I took great pleasure in cooking, not only because of my born touch, but also for a number of private reasons of my own. Silencing for life the people who'd teased me about the steak *tartare* incident, for one.

I cooked up *Saumon Bearnaise, Pastilles D'Agneau en Sauce Lionel, Crevettes au Cognac*, and I made up plenty of delicacies just from my head. I learned to make homemade croissants, a big hit with Francis Taylor. It felt good to be trying my hand at something creative again. Plus, the chance of injury in a kitchen was mild compared to the same chance on a dance floor.

Gourmet foods ran a high bill, but Francis Taylor never complained about it. Sometimes he'd help me by bringing home foods found only in ethnic markets of New York City. Later on I found out he saw my cooking as an investment that would pay off someday. I just didn't know it would be for politicians and bankers. High-minded politicians and investment bankers.

Meanwhile, Francis Taylor was focusing intensely on the buying and selling of War Surplus Commodities. And he was even more focused than I was on our growing babies. If my belly hadn't gotten so big, you'd have thought *he* was the pregnant one in the family. He'd lie down with me, breathe with me and visualize: Wood Duck Pond in Vermont or the Seychelles Islands, I think he said. He held my hand while we breathed. One day he thought of squeezing tennis balls as a relaxer, so we tried that, too.

One snowy November afternoon close to The Day, I was in an exceptional mood, whistling as I basted my *poulet rôti avec liqueur prunneaux* that I had a confident feeling would turn out to be a hit. By now, we were starting to have dinner parties that would become a part of our life. I had cramps, quite vague. Still, they alarmed me at first, but then I thought, "Well, we still have a week to go and I've been in here sampling every dish to be served on the table."

So I passed it off for mild gas and forgot about it.

That evening Francis Taylor and I stayed up late after the dinner, laughing and talking in bed. We were in one of our moments when stories just rolled out to each other, mainly stories about being young. This was the night he told me about that awful teacher at boarding school, Dag Bruce. I palpated my hands along his soft skin but stayed frozen quiet. Then I made up a tall one about how one of the older girls at the ballet had tried to touch my breasts. Then I told him that I bet my Mamma had wished I'd of turned out to be a boy, so she'd have someone to bring her home some money. He laughed a little and said, "Well, too bad for your mother, Susanna. She got a one hundred percent girl." Then he rubbed me real softly on the cheek.

We rustled in the sheets, kissing and loving each other with comfortable knowledge of what worked best for each other in our love making. I loved the gentle way he touched my breasts, I was appreciating his soft touches over my now quite voluptuous body.

I now had real bosoms, round and full and firm and tender; the big bosoms turned us both on, but then right there, all of a sudden and without a jot of warning, my water broke. It gushed out of me, wetting the mattress. I got out of bed quickly. It gushed. It ran down the sides of both of my legs and left a puddle on the floor. It smelled a little like semen.

My poor husband! He jumped out of bed and ran down to the kitchen and got a mop and started mopping up the nasty mess and, as he did so, he told me to "remain calm" in a voice that was hopelessly playacted. His words trembled. "Remain calm, honey. Just breathe deeply. Go get in the bed in the guest room. Easy does it."

With a towel between my legs, I started to wobble down to the guest room. I could hear him searching frantically, in vain, evidently for the tennis balls.

He came into the guest room with some balled-up clean socks for me to hold. He also brought a pair of socks for my feet. He put them on me. He got the phone book out of the drawer of the bedside table. It was horrible watching him try the telephone book, at first looking like he had forgotten the alphabet, then running a finger up and down the row of Wilson's throughout the county. At length he found Dr. Peter Oatman. He started to dial the number, but seemed to have forgotten it, so he looked it up all over again.

He finally spoke, though, rumbling up Dr. Oatman from what had to be rapid eye movement (it was by then around one in the morning). "No contractions yet," he said, "but her water broke." Then he said, "Uh huh, uh huh, OK, will do."

He got off the phone and told me the doctor wouldn't be coming until the big contractions started. He was considerably calmer. He crawled into bed with me with all his clothes on. We slept for a couple of hours before I was jerked awake with the first of the real deal contractions.

"Baby, call him. Call Dr. Oatman." I shook my husband awake. He called Dr. Oatman. I shut my eyes, partly from fear. I breathed long and steady, squeezing and releasing the socks as I did so.

"It's time, Doctor," he said.

And then there was a long silent minute, after which he hung up and came to the bed and lifted me out by the armpits and made me start walking. We walked to the top of the stairwell, which he took by two's, calling back over his shoulder that he was going to get the water prepared and for me to keep walking. But at the bottom of the stairs he looked up at me for help and stayed frozen that way, one heel lifted.

I went back to the guest room and got in the bed again. Some minutes went by, then bam! The contraction was killing me, like somebody was using a household plunger on me. My teeth ground, and my eyes screwed up, and my face became contorted. I clawed at the sheets, then the pillow, which I wedged between my drawn up knees. Chewing on a corner of it, I pressed two strong hands underneath my swollen belly, and tried to make it go away. Then it passed, leaving no trace save for the thin rivulets of sweat coursing down the sides of my face.

"I'm coming, darling!" he shouted. Now I could hear him ransack the closet, throwing things off the top shelf and letting clothes fall off their hangers. I didn't know what he was doing, but I guessed he was still hunting for tennis balls. He wasn't. He was hunting for the pink rubber hot water bottle. The doctor had said that I would need it.

I got hit again and let out a terrible groan. I really thought I might die. He ran down the hall to the guest room where I was, and he launched into some coaching. "You have to get up and walk, Susanna. Dr. Oatman insists upon it." His voice was cracking and I thought he was going to start crying.

"No! I don't want to walk!" What I wanted was a bathtub. I wanted to be in water. I wanted water to float me against gravity. But, Francis Taylor wouldn't let me. He said the Doctor insisted upon walking until he got there. It was all I could do to get out of bed. I stepped one foot on the wide polished pine and got hit again. I doubled over, leaning like a hinge against the bed, and wailed. No words could comfort me. He got by my side quickly, but no matter how gentle his words were or what he was saying, the pain made them too loud for my ears. After a minute, the contraction again went away, and I motioned to his dresser. Then, preparing for another unpredictable blow, I used him for support on one side, and clutched my free hand to the bedpost, top of a chair, whatever I could find for support on the other. The two of us hitched our way over where I pulled open the top drawer and blindly found yet another pair of socks. I balled them in my hands and gave him a pair to ball in his hands; we worked the socks for a minute, trying to calm our nerves.

Francis Taylor let go of me, went to his desk and reached for the keys in their little china bowl. Weakly, I staggered towards him, placed both my hands dog-paw-like on his wrists, the balled-up socks underneath my palms, and braced hard against his arm as I said, "No keys, love, no keys. No hospital, remember, no going to the hospital." He nodded respectfully, as if he hadn't quite forgotten my principle, but hoped I would have.

Everything after that became wrenching. I shut my eyes, partly from fear. I breathed long and steady, squeezing and releasing the socks as I did so, and tried to get back into bed.

"You can't, Susanna," he said.

"When is he going to hurry up and get here?"

"He's on his way, Susanna. Dr. Oatman is on his way and said that I have to keep you walking." His face was beyond sincere.

I surrendered; leaning hard on him, I started negotiating my way through all our upstairs rooms. I even picked off the brown under-leaves of the little mandarin orange plant we kept in the corn flower wallpapered room which we'd fixed up with toys, twin changing tables, and twin antique French fruitwood cradles for the little ones.

I made it all the way back to the guest room at the far end of the rambling hallway, but by the time I had gotten over the threshold, a contraction came on again, and I doubled over, again letting out cries. Right then I decided I would never have another baby.

"Come on," he said, "we can make it, Darling." Instead I was able to wriggle out of his grip and go down on the floor, my knees open, my hands wringing my hair. The pains were coming in a pattern now, about seven minutes apart.

He started to hum from Mozart.

"Oh my God, shut up! Do you not know what this feels like?"

"OK, but we have to learn how to relax. That's what Dr. Oatman said. We have to relax, above all, we have to relax."

"Where is that bastard? What time is it?"

"Come on. Inhale deeply. Exhale. I don't know. About three or four. I don't know. Inhale, Susanna. Exhale." He inhaled/exhaled with me. He next made me tense and relax each major muscle group in my body, and he tightened and released with me each time. Then he made me go through the exercises to relax all of the muscles at once, and for a little minute, he made me feel better. He loosened me and I even thought I could sleep for a few minutes. He said later that I dozed a good five minutes before I woke, shaking him with the words, "I've got to push now. I've got telephone poles up me."

He got up, jerked me by the armpits, and made me stand up and start walking, "Walk, damn it, Susanna. The doctor said not to push until he gets here. He said if you tried to push, I'd have to make you walk. You're supposed to pant. So pant. Please!"

I didn't want to walk or pant. I tried to wriggle away from him. He had me in a hammerlock.

"Stop! This is horrible! Let me go!" The push came strong and I groaned, my knees buckling and body yielding to his arms.

"Susanna, pant. Just try." He began to take up short breaths to show me and jerked me hard, forcing me to walk.

I had forgotten how frightened my husband could become.

My unnatural pants happened not for him, but for my twins. I was hating him for making me walk, for the cruel, unnatural pants against my need to *push* rather than gulp air in short bites. The contractions felt like broken bones. Something was wrong. Nobody said it would feel like broken bones.

I clung to him, his arms tightly around my waist as he made me walk and walk and walk; I don't know how many loops we did through the wings of our house, and each time I tried to lie down he spanked me hard on the bottom, jerking me up by the armpit like I was a horse with colic. After so much heat and panting he finally let me take off my nightgown. Then something made him risk going to the window where he cussed the night for the damned doctor. Cussed the night for the snow coming down. That move gave me time to lie down again.

We were in the east room, a cream color that hadn't been painted in years. I lay on my back staring at the oval ceiling, my knees bent and open, my spine pressed to the Oriental rug, and I began to push hard, becoming oblivious to my husband, where I lived, who I was.

He came to his knees, hands under my armpits, and I said, "I'll die. I've got to push or I'll die. You've got to believe me." I flailed my hands and my toes curled.

He shushed me, looked at me with strong eyes, then kneeled down and hoisted me up to sitting. But before he could get me on my swollen feet again, I slapped him hard across the face. My back screamed with pain, low down, like the end of my spine was going to snap. The contractions were stacked, one on top of the other. The shape of my stomach was changing. "Help!" I screamed.

He lowered desperate lips to mine, and said, "Oh, Susanna, I'm sorry, I know it hurts, but try. Try." You could tell that he was desperately looking around for the hot water bottle.

I pushed, using his shoulders to bear down against, exhaling hard and pointedly, my teeth gnashing and my head leaning back for want of air. Hoarsely, I whispered we'd just have to go at this alone, and I braced with straight arms against his shoulders.

I don't remember the doctor coming in, his opening my legs and moving a gloved hand inside me, up to my cervix. I remember Francis Taylor leaving the room, evidently to get the water boiling. Or to get a break.

I was pushing hard, sweat rolled down my armpits, and my hands shook as I groped for the socks. When my husband came back with the pot of boiling water, he said something to the doctor about my being an athlete, how that had justified his decision to let me give birth at home. Briefly, I tried to concentrate on how strong my ballet body had once been, how I'd trusted abdomen muscles to tighten like little cobblestones, helping me sustain my leaps in the air. I leaned hard against memories of my youth and gained momentary strength.

"She's completely dilated," the doctor said. "It's time, all right."

Francis Taylor started encouraging me, taking a hand, and squeezing the sock with me. In unison they asked me to push again.

Pushing, I groaned long and guttural, and, as I did so, I hissed out the word, "Elephants" hissing the "s" between my teeth.

They both looked at each other.

"I may as well be giving birth to a couple of mature elephants."

"Push," they said again sternly, commanding me.

I was exhausted. The lassitude was intense. I wanted somebody to move my hair out of my face, but right then I couldn't stand either one of them, and couldn't stand the idea of asking them to do me a favor.

"Push!" they demanded again. What nerve.

Underneath the pillow I flipped my husband a bird. I wanted to cuss, but couldn't get myself to do it in front of my babies.

Again, for *them*, not for this doctor, this husband, I pushed. My hand twisted underneath his, and I dug fingernails into the fleshy part of his palm.

"A good push." It was the doctor now. "You'll be home free soon, the first one's head is in the canal."

It must have been the words "home free" or the idea that there really was at least one real human baby in there that brought Francis Taylor to believing he could take over here, like he'd been delivering babies for his whole life. He rolled his sleeves, came around to my head, spread wide fingers over my crown, while the doctor used his hands to bear down on the tops of my feet. My bent knees opened out all on their own, and I pushed on while Francis Taylor launched into what I thought was going to be one of his famous "visualize" fantasies. He rubbed my temples and said, "Now, Susanna, I want you to think about galloping along the seashore on a real pretty palomino horse with a long blond mane, your naked body, your hair blowing in the wind behind you...."

He wasn't lying. It had actually been a fantasy of *mine*. At the time I'd suggested it, he'd complained of my not having enough sophistication to pick a thoroughbred over a palomino. He'd called my palomino "tacky" and my fantasy of galloping my palomino along the surf, "pure corn." But now that I was giving birth to twins, he gave me my palomino back. Wind, beach, wild hair flowing, and all.

"Now just gallop, Susanna. Just ease on that horse, bareback and free. Let the wind blow! Let the sun set in rosy hues! Let the frothy waves roll in!"

For a man who'd name a black dog "Blackie" and a spotted dog "Spot," this was pretty good prose, I thought.

"That's it. Let him rear and buck a little... let him neigh and frolic in the waves."

All right, this was enough. I had been as patient as possible, but his trying to get me to bump up and down on the withers of a galloping palomino at this very moment was too much. So I opened my eyes for a second, pierced him with them, meaning business. Between pants, a face pouring sweat, a face so distorted with pain, I'm sure he wouldn't know it was me anyway, I said dictatorially, "Francis Taylor, say one more thing about riding a horse while I'm trying to give birth to twins, and I'll divorce you, I will."

Then I started crying a little, and my husband started kissing my wet hair, squeezing my hands while Dr. Oatman was yelling "PUSH," and I was pushing and screaming and grunting and finally cussing, realizing they couldn't hear me anyway.

All of a sudden I gave one final push and reached a hand between my legs when I saw the head come out. I reached. Francis Taylor moved my hand and told me the doctor had to do it, which he did: out came a crying mess, covered with blood and white stuff. Three minutes and a strong push later, out came the other one in the exact same condition; both had curled miniature fists and toothless, half-opened mouths and shut eyes.

Dr. Oatman had already spanked one, cut his cord, and now held up the other, wedged strong fingers between a pair of baby's ankles, and gave him his spanking. Francis Taylor used rubber gloves to dip scissors into the pan of hot boiled water, and then cut the other's cord, which he said was tough as towrope. Then Dr. Oatman let my husband wash off the blood and white stuff while he waited for me to deliver the placenta, a mess I can't talk about out loud.

Between the spanking and the umbilical cord and the washing, I felt a huge release of thanks and pride and appreciation and love rising uncontrollably in all of us. And so, as my husband jubilantly held up the cutest little more-or-less cleaned up, but damp and jelly-covered little boys you ever saw, we all started crying at once: the doctor, my husband, my babies, and me.

It was most memorable.

CHAPTER 19

December, 1943 – November, 1947
Pope's Crossing, Connecticut

I could not stop looking at them. Francis Taylor could not stop looking at them. Sally G. and Pasha, who both came up to Pope's Crossing a week after they were born, could not stop looking at them. Linda C.S., who came over from my mother-in-law's, could not stop looking at them. It was not that they were identical because they weren't. It was not because they were good looking—all babies look like angels. It was because we understood, for the first time in our lives, what the word miracle means.

We realized for the first time that no dance, or choreography, or environmental effort, or cuisine, or investment, or building, or house, or land and lake, or any invention period could ever come close to the pair of miracles we held in our arms.

Within a minute of their being born, my little babies, Taylor and Parish, rooted blindly for my breasts. The second my babies took hold of my nipples, sucking the daylights out of them, I pretty much knew what they were going to be like the rest of their lives—strong, life-loving tigers. They turned out to be babies of the night, sometimes waking me every two hours for feeding. Dark circles grew under my eyes. After about a week, I couldn't take the rocking chair feedings any more, so I began to bring our babies into our big bed. I'd pile pillows on the floor on my side and when Taylor or Parish would wake up snuggled between Francis Taylor and me, I'd grope for the pillows, deftly pile them behind me, and sit up. Then I'd wake up whoever was still sleeping and hold my babies like footballs and let them nurse together. This method kept up the milk supply and allowed me to get some sleep. But, the warm security of our family bed didn't last long because Francis Taylor complained of getting no sleep. So, I eventually booted him out, and he slept in the guest room for all ten months that I nursed, except for our honeymoon time on Sunday mornings.

During those months, I found I had little time to comb my hair in the morning or worry about what I put on. The milk would come out as little fountains from my nipples when I would shower. At the first sound of my babies crying, the milk would let down. It would seep through my bra and leak down the sides of my body. And here Dr. Oatman had been worried that I might not have enough milk. He had encouraged the canned milk formula that most Moms gave their babies; the babies would sleep more soundly through the night, he said. But, how could canned milk ever be as healthy as the mother's milk? Nearly a year pressed on before I could get up the heart to wean the twins. I was hardly prepared for the bond, and I just thanked God that the milk lasted.

Every day as Taylor and Parish grew, they provided me with unending challenge and joy—a kind of unpredictable choreography that made all my years of ballet pale weakly by comparison. And I just loved those child-raising years, I just loved them.

On Sundays, Francis Taylor and I hung out in bed together, saying hello. After we reacquainted ourselves with each other, we read *The New York Times* in bed and drank Yuban coffee while Linda C.S. took the twins on a stroll around Kingfisher Pond.

And almost every weekend or day off, Pasha came up. Sally G. was really running the Manhattan Ballet School while Shawn Colton served in the Navy, and Krimskaya, in another cash flow jam, had gone abroad to work with a ballet down on the Mediterranean. Sally G., who I think was lonely and who became the godmother of our children along with Pasha, would come up almost every time she could find a day off. My mother-in-law, Helena, also sent Linda over often during the weekdays, too, so that I could try to get a little rest. I think that was her best way of welcoming our babies into the world. Even though she had three children of her own, Michael,

Henry, and Francis Taylor, you never got the feeling that she'd been around babies much. Or even liked them very much.

The opposite was true with both Pasha and Linda C.S. And they saved me. It was as if Pasha had already had a million children. She was extremely at ease with the twins and they loved her. Linda C.S. was as instinctive as anyone I'd ever known. Sally G. was more into visiting us than helping with the twins. On more than one of Sally G.'s visits while my husband was still exiled to the guest room, I could swear they exchanged flirtatious eyes with each other. More than once. Even with the nursing burning up calories, I had a long way to go before I could ever come close to looking like Sally G.

Sally G. wouldn't do that to me, I reasoned. Still, the trust was just slightly off-kilter, slightly strained, and I was privately relieved when Shawn Colton returned from WWII and came up with the idea of subscription-only audiences for the Ballet for the next two years. The performances were so successful that, a few years down, City Center offered the Ballet a permanent home. Krimskaya was on fire. Sally G. was on fire, too. Her chances to come up and visit us became fewer and more far between. I felt guilty that I had suspected anything.

I will always remember the day WWII staccatoed to an end. It was spring through summer of 1945. First Europe. Then Japan. My babies were six months old, sitting in high chairs at the breakfast table. With their tiny hands, they were able to pick up a new cereal, Cheerios. The cherry trees were in early blossom and the pear trees would bear fruit in about a month. Every morning at the breakfast table, my husband was engrossed in *The New York Times*, following the War:

Monday, April 30, 1945: ***NAZIS IN BERLIN COMPRESSED INTO 18-SQUARE-MILE POCKET.***
TODAY THE TWINS ATE CEREAL.

May 2, 1945: ***HITLER DEAD IN CHANCELLERY, NAZIS SAY; DOENITZ SUCCESSOR ORDERS WAR TO GO ON; BERLIN ALMOST WON; U.S. ARMIES ADVANCE.***
PARISH SAT UP!

May 2, 1945, Evening Edition: ***BERLIN FALLS TO RUSSIANS, 70,000 GIVE UP; 1,000,000 SURENDER IN ITALY AND AUSTRIA; DENMARK IS CUT OFF; HAMBURG GIVES UP.***
TAYLOR AND PARISH BOTH CRACKED UP LAUGHING WHEN I FELL DOWN REPEATEDLY ON PURPOSE.

May 8, 1945: ***THE WAR IN EUROPE IS ENDED! SURRENDER IS UNCONDITIONAL. V-E WILL BE PROCLAIMED TODAY; OUR TROOPS ON OKINAWA GAIN.***
TAYLOR BIT MY NIPPLE. BOTH TEETHING. AFTER HE BIT IT, TAYLOR CRACKED UP LAUGHING!

May 8, 1945, Times Square: ***CROWDS TAKE TO THE STREETS ON V-E DAY, CELEBRATING GERMANY'S SURRENDER IN WORLD WAR II.***
BOTH TWINS FASCINATED WITH DROPPING LEAVES IN THE STORM DRAIN.

The War wasn't really totally over; Japan forged on for another few months and was preparing for an urgent and desperate defense in the event of an American invasion of the home islands. Atomic bombs were dropped on Hiroshima and Nagasaki on August 6 and 9 respectively:

Tuesday, August 5, 1945: ***FIRST ATOMIC BOMB DROPPED ON JAPAN; MISSILE IS EQUAL TO 20,000 TONS OF TNT; TRUMAN WARNS FOE OF A 'RAIN OF RUIN.'***
PARISH IS CRAWLING WITH ONE FOOT THAT HE'S USING TO TRY TO PRESS HIM TO STANDING! TAYLOR STILL CRAWLING BUT STANDING AND HOLDING ONTO CHAIRS.

August 14, 1945: *JAPAN SURRENDERS, END OF WAR! EMPEROR ACCEPTS ALLIED RULE; MACARTHUR SUPREME COMMANDER; OUR MANPOWER CURBS VOIDED.*
IN TIMES SQUARE A SAILOR KISSES A NURSE HE DOESN'T EVEN KNOW.

August 15, 1945: *RESTRAINT THROWN TO THE FOUR WINDS.*
SO HAPPY THE SAILOR WAS NOT FRANCIS TAYLOR.

September 3, 1945: *THE SURRENDER WAS SIGNED ON SEPT. 2, 1945 ABOARD THE BATTLESHIP A.S.S. MISSOURI IN TOKYO BAY. PRESIDENT TRUMAN OFFICIALLY DECLARED AN END TO HOSTILITIES BY PRESIDENTIAL PROCLAMATION.*
SLEPT THROUGH THE NIGHT!

1947

By the time Taylor and Parish turned four, I was eight months pregnant with Jenny. Taylor and Parish were inseparable, talking all the time, getting into everything. When they would take all the pots and pans out of the kitchen cabinets, this was a discovery, an adventure. Bang, bang, bang; it didn't matter, they were having a learning experience. They were checking out their world.

"Bye, Linda C.S.!" Taylor said, as she went out the door, wrapping a scarf around her head and facing the first few snow flurries of the late afternoon.

"Bye, Sugar Lumps!"

"Bye, Linda C.S.!" I said.

"Bye, Linda!" said Parish.

We were in the kitchen working up a Chocolate Charlotte cake. We were trying to hurry because it was late in the afternoon and we wanted it finished by the time their Daddy came home. The twins had each tasted a spatula's worth of rich batter and had offered the rest of it to Mop, our beloved sheep dog (the first of a series).

I filled cake pans with the rest of the batter, put cake pans in the oven, and turned my back for just two minutes to try to clean up. I turned the water on, let it get hot, and had just barely gotten the wooden utensils and mixer bowl clean when I heard Taylor and Parish's small feet dancing around in our bathroom upstairs. I flicked the suds from my hands and raced awkwardly upstairs, holding my hard swollen belly with one hand, the other hand holding the handrail. I was completely out of breath by the time I got to the twins.

"Mom, look, candies!" Taylor was standing on the bathroom chair. He was in his green shorts that his grandmother, Helena, had given him. He'd pulled the chair up to the medicine cabinet and was raised up on tiptoe, one arm outstretched towards me, holding an uncapped pill bottle of baby aspirin. "Decorations!" His blue eyes aglow, and little Parish marching his feet with glee.

I grabbed one twin under each arm, sat them on the edge of the tub, threw Taylor's head back, wedging my fingers inside his mouth, and wiped the orange residue off his tongue. When I checked Parish, he choked a little, and both twins' eyes watered, but neither cried. I had no idea how many baby aspirin had been in the bottle, but I was losing it. I turned them over and slapped their backs. Then I gave them water and a long lecture about the difference between medicine and candy. They sat close to each other on the edge of the bathtub, each sitting on their hands, cheeks quivering. The rest of the afternoon, they stayed distant from me and silent.

I emptied the bottle and tried to figure out how many they'd eaten. I couldn't really tell. I called the doctor. The doctor said to watch them for drowsiness and to come in if they vomited or broke out in a rash.

When I put the twins down for their nap, I did not leave the room. I listened to their breathing. I sat reading *The Common Sense Book of Baby and Child Care*, a best seller by a new pediatrician, Dr. Spock, who'd come on the horizon. *You know more than you think you do*. I read that line over and over again. My gut sense had been to take the twins to the doctor anyway; the doctor's gut sense had been to wait and see if there was any reaction to the baby aspirin. There was no reaction. I, too, was distant and silent with worry for the rest of the afternoon.

I decided not to tell my husband. Don't ask me why.

We had dinner around the kitchen table as usual. Afterwards, in our great room Francis Taylor went down on his knees and played horsey with Taylor and Parish. Both twins were laughing their brains out, and so was Francis Taylor. Francis Taylor then did the dishes while I took the children upstairs, bathed them, and then crawled into bed with them. (They slept in twin beds by now; we'd cuddle up together in one or the other on alternating nights). I read *Madeline* and *Curious George*, a favorite book of theirs. Then my husband crowded in with us and read the twins *The Story of Ferdinand*, using some of his dramatic acting skills that we only got to see during reading time. When Ferdinand the bull sat in the middle of the bullfighting ring and refused to cooperate, Francis Taylor made all sorts of mooo sounds. *I refuse to mooooooove*.

"Shhh. We're trying to get them settled."

But it was too late. They laughed and made Francis Taylor mooooo again and again.

After at least three more books, they started to wind down and Francis Taylor sang *Taps* in a fairly pitched baritone. I kissed my children goodnight, turned on their night light, and their Daddy, staying in, went through a whole medley of nursery songs. (I loved to listen in at the door.)

After the children were asleep, we both stayed up reading for quite awhile. Reading had become something of a passion for me. Having children had brought that about: I could go worlds away without even having to leave my rocking chair. Francis Taylor got up and had a piece of Chocolate Charlotte cake and we went on to bed.

In the middle of the night Parish started crying and that got Taylor crying.

No vomiting.

No rash.

I held them and rocked them, and they finally fell back to sleep in my arms. Then I tucked them in and crept guiltily back to our room. Francis Taylor woke up.

"What's wrong?"

"I can't sleep."

I tossed and turned not because of the baby aspirin incident but because our little girl, Jenny—anyway, I thought she was a little girl and I *knew* she was a night owl—was very active in my womb.

"You want some water?"

"No. It's Jenny. I do believe we've got an athlete on our hands. Good night, darling. I think I will go try to sleep in the guest room." As if listening, Jenny threw another back flip.

I started to leave, but the guilt got to me. I had to tell him about the baby aspirin incident. I worked up the nerve, "Francis Taylor, there's something I have to tell you."

Drowsy and grouchy, he got upset first because I hadn't reported in right away, and secondly because the children should have known better (don't ask me how), and thirdly because I'd failed to spank them. I'd flipped their wigs enough. I wasn't going to spank them. I stayed on my side, facing the wall, and rubbed my swollen belly to calm the baby kicking inside me. Trying to assure my husband that the twins were all right only sent him into a tirade. I tried to close my ears, but I could hear him get up and go down the hall to check on them. Then he went over to his chest of drawers. He pulled his rolled up alligator belt out of the top drawer and laid it across the doorknob.

"Don't. Dr. Spock says 'No spanking'."

But that wasn't the way Francis Taylor was raised.

When he got home around six the next day, Taylor and Parish ran to his open arms. Francis Taylor became stern and said that he needed to talk to them. He went upstairs and got the alligator belt. Outside, it was already dark.

"Don't," I said again. "Don't. It will humiliate them. They didn't know."

Francis Taylor wouldn't look at me.

"Don't," I avowed. "They learned their lesson. It was my fault that I didn't have the baby aspirin higher up in the cabinet. Spank me instead."

Francis Taylor quickly put the belt in a pocket. In a stern voice, he asked the twins to come over. He was standing by the fireplace in our great room. The twins looked at each other, then walked forward reluctantly. Taylor was gently cupping the back of Parish's neck.

"Hey, Dad."

"You are never to go into the medicine cabinet again." Only then did Francis Taylor turn around and look at me for help, and I merely looked back at him, shaking my head No, feeling the underside of my uppers with my tongue. I laced my hands underneath my big, pregnant belly and lifted it to displace the weight.

Sitting in his big leather chair, he laid Taylor and Parish across a knee, one at a time, and gave each one a spank, none harder than an over-zealous love pat. Parish started laughing.

Later on, in the middle of the night, both twins woke crying hard. Second night in a row. I wasn't sure what was going on. I went out of our bedroom, shutting our thick oak door tightly from the sounds of Francis Taylor sleeping, went to the twins' room, lifted each into my arms, and sat in the rocking chair whispering to them, kissing them on the tops of their heads until they calmed down.

"Does your tummy hurt?" I asked.

"Yes," cried Taylor, and he started crying again.

"Does it hurt really bad?"

"Yes," he said now holding his tummy.

"What does it hurt for?"

"It hurts for some chocolate cake."

"Mine, too," said Parish. And he started to fake cry.

"Well, let's go."

"Let's go where?"

"Down to the kitchen."

Call me a bad mother, but I couldn't help it. Holding their hands, we crept down the stairs and into the kitchen. I let each one help me cut a piece of Chocolate Charlotte cake. I poured Taylor and

Parish each a tall glass of milk. Then I let them stand on a chair in their footie pajamas and drop the Chocolate Charlotte cake into their glasses of milk. I handed each an iced-tea spoon so that they could stir their concoctions until they were gooey, yucky looking, and just the way they liked them.

CHAPTER 20

January, 1948 – May, 1952
Pope's Crossing, Connecticut

The twins loved Jenny from the moment of her first bleat to the air.

Dr. Oatman delivered her at home, too. Linda C.S. stayed in the guest room. She brought the twins to our room shortly after Jenny was born at 9:46 AM. Francis Taylor hardly got a chance to hold her before the twins did. Sitting double in the armchair, they held Jenny for at least ten minutes, staring down at her face beatifically.

"Look at her yawn."

"Look at her fist."

"Look at the way her mouth is moving."

"That's called rooting, darling. She needs to nurse. Francis Taylor, do you mind bringing her? Dr. Oatman, you did a great job. Twins, tell Dr. Oatman he did a great job."

"You did a great job."

"No, you did, Susanna."

"Do you think I can have my little muffin now?"

"Here she is."

"I love you so much, Jenny. I love you so much."

"Here is some water."

"Thank you. Come here, Taylor and Parish. Come sit beside me. Do you think Jenny will grow up following you around all day, wanting to be just like you?"

"Uhmmm hmmm."

"Watch her soft spot." The twins were petting her like she was a dog.

It was Parish who that afternoon made the sign with the help of his Dad:

We have a new baby sister. And she kisses us. And she hugs us. And she just cracks up laughing at our jokes!

He taped it, cock-eyed, to our kitchen door, the only door that anyone ever used.

Everybody from Kingfisher Pond came to her christening. Pasha and Sally G. came up again and became the godparents for the second go-round. Francis Taylor's favorite brother, Henry, became the godfather. Everybody ogled over Jenny, who seemed at once laid back and terribly, terribly *on it* at the same time. Focused and observant, especially when it came to black and white colors.

People said she looked like me, but I couldn't see it. She had my blue eyes and thick blond hair, true, but she mainly had my husband's inquisitive expressions, his turned down eyebrows, and his sense of obedience from the word Go. During her early months, the twins would lay small hands on the back of her soft head while she breast fed, and when she grew old enough to crawl, they'd try to pick her up, and I'd have to quickly stop them. "No, no, Sweeties, you can't carry her yet. She can sit in your lap in the big armchair." She was easygoing with her brothers; we could all count on her for big open-mouth kisses. But when she got mad, her screams were ear piercers.

The tenderness between her father and her put me all to pieces. When she was just born, he took three weeks off from work just to have her in his arms. He'd carry her off in a little homemade canvas sling strapped over his shoulders and take her on long walks through the woods, showing her trees and telling stories about them, picking laurel leaves for her, tickling her with its round balls of petals. During those weeks, the bond between them grew so strong, his very holding, breathing, carrying, and heartbeat changed the rhythm of her feeding times, and sometimes my swollen waiting breasts leaked milk all down the sides of my rib cage.

I raised no eyebrows when by age four, she had already become the effortless miniature of my husband, aping his every gesture. She walked like him, tried to talk like him, gestured like him, carried a briefcase like his, slept in pajamas like his. Sometimes she'd sleep between us at night, sometimes with the twins, and sometimes she'd have her Daddy all by herself—when the twins would extend an invitation to me. For their sixth Christmas, the twins had gotten a pair of Alexander Graham Bell play telephones, and from their post in the breakfast room, they'd ring to mine in the kitchen near my chopping block. From my post, I'd plainly hear their live voices, of course, as well as the ones coming through the wires. "Just a minute," I'd say, and set the receiver down, and pretend to ask my mother's permission. "My mother says I can come spend the night after I help her with the dishes."

"Okay!"

"Okay! Goodbye! See you guys soon!" Then I'd arrive that evening carrying my little overnight bag, filled with singing music, books they loved, an extra pillow.

As we grew, one of the things we all loved to do best as a family would be to go camping on the weekends. Sometimes we'd stay around Kingfisher Pond so Francis Taylor could be close to work calls or family commitments. Other times up in the Vermont woods, sometimes staying in our cabin, sometimes in open air.

We did all that you do when you have the privilege of time alone in the woods with the family you treasure, and it was here Francis Taylor would give back to the twins the attention he had almost habitually reserved for Jenny: playing, wrestling, running with them, and letting them win. We took bird censuses, hiked with Jenny piggybacked to one of us until we dropped, swang on wisteria vines, and fished for trout, secretly using our bare hands for their figure eight shadows hidden behind wet mossy rocks.

Later, the children would gather kindling while Francis Taylor would be off cutting the first branches for the fire, and I'd set large rocks up in a circle and brush the pine needles away. Then I'd help him gather the large dry pieces of wood we'd find on the ground up around the hemlock hills and along the riverbanks.

He'd get the fire going, and I'd let the children climb what we called a Black Bottom slide, which mainly meant a fairly steep bank, guaranteed to ruin the backsides of clothes. They'd slide laughing with their hands up, then after their backsides were black as coffee, I'd make them quit. I'd peel my children down, then I'd peel down and we'd all go in the river for a cold skinny dip and a few minutes later Francis Taylor would join us, the campfire kindling behind us, set up like a tepee.

We'd stay in for as long as we could stand it, then he'd towel them off, and I'd tend the fire and get our supper going, usually saving the trout in the stream until morning since we rarely had time to cut, clean, and scale before sundown. Sometimes we brought Campbell's can victuals, but most of the time we brought T-bone steaks and potatoes, which we'd cook on a small grill placed over four heated rocks. I'd of already made the salad at home.

The best part of the trip for my children, by far, seemed to be s'more roasting—marshmallow sandwiches with Hershey's chocolate between graham crackers, roasted on the end of a good green hickory stick. They'd eat until their faces were smeared in chocolate and until their full tummies drugged them to sleep.

Once their teeth were brushed and faces cleaned of melted chocolate, marshmallow, and graham cracker crumbs, we'd all crawl in our sleeping bags and somebody would be elected to say the prayers, *Now I Lay Me Down to Sleep*, which Taylor knew how to say in French, and which Parish knew how to say in Spanish, or Jenny's solo of *He's Got the Whole Wide World in His Hands* that she'd sing with extreme seriousness while the twins did their best not to giggle but failed.

The twins would sleep in one sleeping bag, and Jenny would sleep curled close in the crook of her father's arm, his free arm outstretched towards mine, and mine outstretched towards his. In about thirty seconds, I would hear the steady, pure breathing of four people I loved better than all mankind, each yielding to the cool, safe, quiet blanket of God's kind sky.

I'd shift, sighing, looking up at the multitude of lambent stars bolted to the night. I'd open and shut my fingers, sore from the vine swinging, the carrying of logs. Then I'd lift my hands to the back of my head, with cocked elbows winging out against the leaves, and take in the smell of the earth. My eyes would stay fixed and open to the pour of stars across the sky. I'd find the Big and Little Dippers. I'd try to find Orion and The Great Bear. I'd let the air out, inhale it back in again, listening to the peace-filled sleeping of my children and my husband all cuddled together. Then all of a sudden, I'd feel a little apart.

PART IV

1957 – 1965

Pope's Crossing, Connecticut

CHAPTER 21

Summer, 1957
Pope's Crossing, Connecticut

They grew up like *that.* We started a Little League team in Pope's Crossing, but we had to train down to Pennsylvania for the games. Except for the team we started, there weren't any other Little League teams in Connecticut at the time. Taylor and Parish were both crazy about baseball, and so were we. The team travel drew us close to the parents. We made it to the play-offs, but in a heartbreaking third game, we made an error in the bottom of the 7th, and, after that, we never recovered our confidence. Josh Minor from the Pennsylvania Bucks hit a line drive that brought a run in at the top of the ninth. We lost the game 4 to 3. The boys were twelve-years-old: this was their last game with the Little League. When the game was over, the team cried, the coaches cried, the parents cried, even the dogs cried.

Jenny, eight, became an entrepreneur.

One day towards the closing of the school year, my twelve-year-old boys came huffing up the hill. Their shirttails were pulled out from the fuss, and their faces were flushed.

"Mom, Jenny's going into business!"

I put down my garden shears.

"She said she's going to help Daddy make money so he can come home." Both forced a laugh. It wasn't funny to me. Francis Taylor was spending more and more time at work and less and less time at home.

"Well I'll be." I brushed my thick hair from my eyes. "What's her business?"

"She won't tell us."

"She's real excited about it."

"I'm sure she'll tell us soon enough."

"I think the phone's ringing."

My knees creaked as I got up from where I bent over the gladiolus. I ran for the phone, mainly escaping having to deal with the fact that I had just now discovered Dutch Elm blight in my favorite elm on this side of the house. Over half its leaves were dead brown.

I didn't catch the phone, but Jenny was inside the kitchen waiting for me.

"I heard you're going into business. Come sit at the table and tell me what you've got."

She ran her tongue over her teeth, then blew the tendrils out of her face, and came and sat by me. She pushed the chair back on two legs.

"No, no. Don't do that. Don't lean back on the legs of the chair."

She put the chair back down on all four. "It's a secret," she said.

I said, "Well look here, I may be interested in investing in this business. I know where to buy the freshest lemons."

"Mom, I'm not selling lemonade."

"Cookies?"

"No," she said smiling.

"Apples?"

"No!".

"Furniture from our house?"

"No!" She clapped her hands and kicked my shin softly with the ball of her foot.

"What is it?"

"O.K., I'll tell you, Mom. But you can't tell anyone." She sat up and whispered in my ear, "Rocks."

Rocks. I put a hand to my chin and looked thoughtfully up at the ceiling for a second. I white lied, "Jenny, I think there's a market for rocks in the area, I really do. I think a lot of people would die to be the proud owners of a nice rock."

"Mom, they're not just rocks. They're memory rocks." She reached up and kissed me sympathetically.

"Memory rocks. Hmmmmmm. How do you make a memory rock?"

"You paint them with memories."

"What a great idea. You know, I think we could enlist the twins' support in the venture."

"No, Mom, no twins in this." She crossed her arms and pouted with a lip out.

"They could help us, Jenny. They could help us gather some of the bigger rocks. They're strong now."

She wouldn't hear of the idea until I reminded her what fun it is to carry sack loads of rocks on your back. "Don't you need some workers?"

"I guess so."

"You decide what to pay them. Course they may not even want to do it."

"Well, then that will be their tough luck."

"Can I ask you something?"

"What?"

"What makes you want to set up shop?"

"Because it will make Dad come home."

I pursed my lips, sighed. It was true. He was gone by 7AM and he didn't come home until at least 9PM. His hours down at Dewitt were becoming ridiculous.

All day Sunday, and despite a back already threatening to hurt him even at the young age of forty-one, Francis Taylor roved the woods with the boys looking for rocks the size of a man's hand. They filled and dragged back to the house three great burlap sacks of them. Later, Jenny negotiated the employment deal with her brothers. They would be paid one buck.

That evening, Jenny wouldn't leave my side while I made my phone calls to each relative's house, eighteen families in all. Almost all of the relatives either smiled or laughed affectionately on the other end. Most said they'd try to come to the rock sale. Some said they already had a previous engagement.

Jenny painted for three weeks straight. As it turns out, she painted a rock for every single cousin, aunt, uncle, godmother, grandmother, grandfather in our family. The best ones she saved for us, her own family. The paintings were really thoughtful. For example, Parish's was a painting about the time he got to go to school with Mop. Taylor's was of his Dad teaching him how to ski, a most unfortunate memory since Taylor was far more coordinated than Dad. So the painting was basically of Taylor going down the slope, speech balloon above his head, cussing out his clueless Dad. Mine was of me doing a leap in the air. "Best Ballerina on Earth," it said. Evidently, she surmised that Sally G. would understand.

The twins made the sign with red and purple letters, ten inches high, on poster board: MEMORY ROCKS FOR SALE. OCCASIONAL RARE QUARTZ, MICA, SHALE, AND GRANITE. PRICE SOMEWHAT NEGOTIABLE.

Dad helped them spell "negotiable," and he was the one who tacked the sign to a two-by-four and then sledge-hammered it into the ground down by the row of mailboxes. Jenny spent the week painting on a different rock the initials, the school logo, the sport of every family member we had. For Linda C.S. she made a green bean casserole with smoke plumes.

Jenny's Rock Shop opened its doors for business at noon that first Saturday in June, just before mail delivery. Her shop consisted of a card table, a red & purple sign with ten inch letters, a cigar box for the cash, and the painted rocks displayed on the table.

What if nobody came?

The painted display—granite, limestone, and quartz—was priced according to its three sizes: jumbo, medium, and petite. Underneath six or seven of the pieces of quartz, Francis Taylor had put labels, written in the scrunched up, reserved handwriting that told his whole story. The labels read: PURE QUARTZ. PRICE ELEVATED.

And they came! Each one picked out his or her own rock and paid a premium for it. All told, including the help, Jenny received thirty-eight patrons.

Jenny hit pay dirt.

Even Bob Eckardt, the postman, came. For him, she had painted the words, "The New York Yankees."

Helena didn't make it. Until evening fell, this was the one sad note of the day. On Saturdays, she often had company, and we were hoping she would bring the company down.

Throughout the day, Jenny treated each customer with stark politeness, and everybody showed superb support and enthusiasm as they walked away holding a memory rock.

By four o'clock, Francis Taylor came striding up to Jenny's booming business, chest billowed with pride. He had a farmer's tan. He was going to pop. He leaned over to Jenny to see how the books were looking, casting an eye one or two times in my direction. He looked at me like I had the I.Q. of a geranium and the attractiveness of its roots. So what if I couldn't count change? I gave him a square, fake smile, then flipped a bird at him through my pocket.

He and the twins and Jenny counted the revenues of the day. Thirteen dollars!

Jenny wriggled out of her chair with the cigar box of cash under her arm and went away. She came back a few minutes later with calling card envelopes stuffed into her pink belt. She must have gotten them out of Francis Taylor's Edwardian desk. One of the drawers of that desk was locked. I always wondered. Wish I knew. But, I had a locked drawer, too. I understood that curiosity might be the worst sin of all.

Jenny came to where we stood around the card table. Authoritatively, she handed each one of us a calling card envelope with our name on it.

"Can we open them?"

"Ummmm hmmmmm."

We all opened, heads down, our fingers gently prizing through the gum of the flap.

To each of her twin brothers, she tipped three dollars (on top of their one buck in wages). To her Daddy she tipped four. I got one dollar fifty. (I was Mom. Moms don't need money.) And Jenny gave herself the remaining profit of one dollar and a shiny Eisenhower half-dollar.

We stood there holding our envelopes, grinning.

It was complete family harmony.

CHAPTER 22

Summer, 1957
Pope's Crossing, Connecticut

The sun was going down, and the air had softened. Jenny, Taylor, and Parish had just started up the driveway and were talking all at once. Francis Taylor came towards me. He stopped, took a deep breath. I stepped back vaguely and waited. I was throwing the last Dixie cup in a two-handled shopping bag.

"Have you been down to Kingfisher lately?"

"No, why?"

"Dead fish. Second time I've seen one down there in the past week."

"Dead fish?"

"Rank and silver; bream with eyes glazed over slapping up against the side of the dock." He rang some change in a pocket, took another breath. "Something's wrong."

I wiped sediment from the card table.

"Susanna?"

"Yes, Love."

"Susanna, what are you doing? Are you listening?"

I looked up and focused my eyes on him. "Yes, Love," I repeated. "I'm listening. But, fish *do* die." He'd been acting a little strange lately.

"Susanna, I'm going to have the water tested. Don't let any of the kids swim in Kingfisher until I give you the word. I'll tell everybody else, too."

Gulp. Was he all right?

"I'm concerned, Susanna." He had on his wire frames, which made him look like a non-outdoorsy-type. He lifted the water thermos and turned to go up the driveway without me, the thermos swinging at his side.

The country was headed towards a recession. It was making him hyper-sensitive to just about everything.

I followed him up the driveway. "Hey!" I barked, "Can't you at least help me carry the card table?"

He kept walking until he got to the mailboxes. I could see his white oxford shirt as he strolled down the syrupy country road.

This was the way he was dealing with me lately. Especially if I didn't agree with his increasingly out-there fears. He'd just take off. The way Daddy did.

I knew he'd be entering the path at the edge of the woods and that he'd take the whole three-mile circle that had been named Rhododendron Loop; it was abloom, and the warm, rich smell of the rhododendron felt like receiving a hug. Something he needed. A hug.

Me, too. I needed a hug. I needed a good word.

The bottom of the big paper bag of Dixie cups bumped against the side of my leg as I headed towards the house to fix dinner. It was twilight, still light enough out. But three miles is a long walk and it would start to get dark before he finished his long, angry meditation. And I didn't want him in the dark. Truth is, we had a black bear population that was becoming a problem.

Even though I moved slowly, cups toppled over the top of the bag and were starting to roll down hill. I ran after them picking them up and nesting them.

"Dead fish," I heard myself say out loud. "Dead fish. I don't see no kind of dead fish."

All around me, I heard the creaky, un-oiled chirp of the crickets, and then came the harsh, greedy call of a jay, the raspy chick-a-dee-dee-dee of the black-capped chickadee perched in the loblolly pine. I heard the barking rattle of a red-bellied woodpecker and the peeta, peeta, peeta of a titmouse somewhere in a red maple.

"See?" I said to myself. I dragged up the driveway pulling the card table with one hand, and holding the shopping bag in the other. "See?"

Francis Taylor awoke that next morning in a horrible mood. "Yeah, I'm getting Kingfisher tested, all right. I'm getting the vegetable garden tested, too. Matter of fact, I'm getting the whole property tested."

What in the hell was he talking about?

"And this morning? Something bright red caught my eye when I went out to get the paper. Dead cardinal right on the lawn."

Weird. I'll admit it.

"Maybe it was old, just shy of becoming the Pope." This was the kind of joke that he couldn't stand.

He responded by snapping. Each word bit equally hard, "Susanna, this is not something that you could be privy to anyway. You're just not remotely a part of the real world."

What was with him?

I personally could not stand him.

I should have known that this would be the beginning of the end. From here he got heavily involved in the environmental movement and his hours down at Dewitt grew longer and longer and longer.

I became convinced that he was having an affair. And inside my conviction were the words, Sally G., my Best Friend.

CHAPTER 23

August, 1958
Pope's Crossing, Connecticut
And
Washington, DC

One morning in late August, Francis Taylor left at the crack of dawn, before I could even clear my cobwebs and at least have a cup of coffee with him. When I got downstairs, I saw that on the kitchen table he'd left a manuscript copy of Rachel Carson's new book *The Edge of the Sea*. He and Rachel had become friends through the pesticide regulation lobbying effort. Over the years, Rachel had given Francis Taylor early drafts of her manuscripts to read and critique. He had become her trusted editor and critic. At first I worried about what was going on. But, in due time, I got to know Rachel. There wasn't anything going on. Anyway, there were some murmurings about Rachel and her nature-lover friend, Olga Huckins.

On top of the manuscript was a little file card bearing Francis Taylor's scrawl in blue fountain pen ink. "Read this," it said.

I was already having a terrible enough time because this was the day I'd be packing the boys for St. Augustus Prep. I was totally unprepared for the enormous wave of sadness that came over me.

Right before lunchtime, impulsively, I picked up the phone and called Francis Taylor down at the office.

"Aren't you even going to miss them? They are leaving in two days, you know."

I could hear him sigh. I could tell he was taking off his glasses. "Susanna, of course I am going to miss them."

"More than the fish? More than the birds?"

"Yes, Susanna. More than the fish. More than the birds."

"Well, then, come home."

He hung up on me.

But, faithfully, he came through. We all drove to the Greenwich station together to put my big boys on the train North. The minute the train doors shut, the tears started to fall. And, he did hold my hand the whole way home. Jenny rubbed me on my neck and shoulders.

Still, Francis Taylor was hooked. In due time, he was a full-fledged lobbyist who was now headed down to Washington DC nearly once a week. And while he was gone, I read. I read the Rachel Carson: *The most alarming of all man's assaults upon the environment is the contamination of air, earth, rivers, and sea with dangerous and even lethal materials.*

While Francis Taylor was gone, I read the book cover-to-cover. Every chapter gave me the willies. The progressive willies, with each chapter snowballing further the book's message of doom and gloom. We were all going to be dead, if we didn't get a grip.

By the end of the book, I came to respect and honor the last paragraph of the jacket, "This book will come as a shock to many readers. To others, *The Edge of the Sea* will be a clarification and a revelation. And to the growing number of informed people who are already deeply disturbed, it will be a godsend. They know that the time has come to speak."

For the first time I saw where the drive and the passion was coming from. For the first time I saw that there would be no turning back. And for the first time since the dead fish, I cried my own little *The Edge of the Sea* of shame and respect.

But, still I couldn't let go of the bone. "Come home," I'd nag. "What about Jenny? What about her diving? Jenny's diving is already brilliant like a swan's, a lark's. She doesn't want you to miss this!"

She'd begun a year ago in the summer of 1957 at age nine, the summer of her rock sale. A ring of us had stood awed, watching her for the first time at the Greenwich Country Club: her lithe hurdle; her clean, sharp arms setting, then parting as if splitting a second; her arched back, straight sinewy legs, and toes pointed like a dancer's of fifteen years training. Throwing the reverse layout, she pierced the water so clean there was no splash. I watched my frustrated dream passed onto my daughter through the airborne dance and found peace I can't explain.

He'd answered, "Susanna, I'm behind her and she knows it. Let me concentrate, Susanna."

My awake eyes and no longer nurtured body would hold up for him, watching where he'd sit silhouetted by the desk lamp until one a.m., reading science journals. Reading and reading and reading. Drinking the pages. I would fall asleep sitting up, then wake up abruptly a few hours later, finding him in bed. Finally. I'd want to tell him not to forget us, but the words would break off, and I'd lose the courage and drift back to sleep.

And, if he woke, he'd squinch his eyes and pull away from me, frowning, "Goddammit, Susanna, I need to sleep." Negotiating diagonally for more space on the bed, pushing me away from the cradle of his body. "I've got to catch the 5AM to Washington tomorrow morning."

By fall, the environmental movement was really gathering in storm and momentum. Outright protests over pesticides, especially DDT, were beginning to happen on the mall in DC, the parks and streets of San Francisco, on the Portland Green, and on the Boston Common.

Francis Taylor wound up opening an office in Washington. He spent six months preparing his case that would go before Congress. He surrounded himself with top academics and lawyers. As a team, they prepared their paper and presentation, the data and analysis to back their claims. As a team, they went to Congress to face the facts. And, as a team, their cries fell on ears that did not understand the language of people who cared about the earth. All the hard work that had gone into the process of winning their case was stopped by glazed-over eyes, congressmen checking their watches, surreptitiously. Their months of preparing for this moment fell away like film burning on a screen. Helena Dewitt had come down to support Francis Taylor. I'd seen her often, driving by with a determined look on her face, as she passed our house; I knew that she'd been going down to DC a lot in those days, likely to raise money for the lobbying effort.

My husband, keeping a brave face, holding it all in, called to say he'd be very late coming home; they were going to work out Plan B. In his voice, I could feel the tenor of his pain. I could feel the disappointment that was going to burst if I said the wrong thing. So, offering neither sympathy nor challenge, I said, "Of course, my darling." Then I was the one who hung up and cried.

That evening, exhausted, discouraged, I made sandwiches for Jenny and myself. I called Taylor and Parish. They cheered me up. Just hearing their voices cheered me up.

While I was on the phone with them, Jenny slipped out with Parish's flashlight and found a bright piece of pink quartz, which she placed on a flat magnolia leaf and put on her father's plate.

By eleven-thirty, when he still hadn't come home, I sent Jenny to bed.

I sat downstairs in the sunk-in old chair near the fireplace and listened to the rain dropping against the chimney stone. How many times did I go to the window to check on him? I can't even admit it. Rain poured through the light of floodlights beaming from the corners of our house.

He got home around 2AM. He was brought home by limousine, all the way from DC. It really wasn't like him to spend that kind of money. The sound of car and the car's headlights careening across the wall woke me out of my light, uncomfortable doze. I stood yawning and poked my way to the kitchen and then out to the veranda. He was coming through the garden. The rain was coming down hard, hitting the tin of the gutters.

"You have no umbrella." I cupped my hands around my mouth to shout this at him. The rain was coming into the veranda, and already I was feeling my nightgown getting soaked at my shoulders and breasts.

He opened his arms slightly, as if to say, So?

"Wait then," I said. "Wait, I'll get your raincoat."

I went quickly to the hall closet and pulled off the first one my hands found, the coat hanger swinging free. I ran with it to the kitchen door and through the garden where he dragged beside the fall mums, their heads bent over towards the ground.

The rain poured against the fence line where he braced. On tiptoe I walked, reaching the raincoat to his head and shoulders. All around him the thick, strong smell of liquor floated. I couldn't imagine how much he'd drunk, but even Hank hadn't smelled this strong.

He was a wild horse and dodged his head. My feet sunk into a puddle, and he laughed. I started to go back to the house without him, but as I stepped out of the puddle, he took the rain slicker out of my hand and put it over both our heads. Together we lumbered back towards the house. He leaned hard on me talking a drunken blue streak.

I guided him upstairs, took off his clothes.

I said, "I'll make you some *tilleul*."

"I'd like that a lot, Susanna." His words were a little slurred.

By the time I'd come back with the bowl of steaming *tilleul*, he was in his PJ's, propped up against a mountain of pillows. Both of our bedroom lamps were on.

My bright little drunk was flushed, and a shy smile pulled across his face as he took the tray.

"Are you all right?" I asked.

"Oh, I'm all right," he answered. "I'm plenty all right."

"In due time, they will listen. You just have to keep going back. Back to the Hill to educate them."

Francis Taylor kind of nodded while he drank his *tilleul*.

"Yep. You have to keep going back. Back and back and back until they listen to you." I went to the bathroom and brushed my teeth, washed my face, then let my hair out of its bun, and leaned over to brush it upside down. As I was bent over brushing, I reached for his wet clothes on the floor, and that's when the opened packet of condoms fell out of a pocket.

I thought so. I'd had that hunch earlier.

When I came out, he was smiling and satisfied looking.

Thinking I'd wait until morning to confront him, I climbed in, turned off the light on my side. For a long time I just lay there. I knew I wouldn't sleep. But, *he* was asleep. I decided to wake him up.

"Francis Taylor?" I turned on the lamp.

"Yes." He squinted awake, disoriented.

"What is *this*?" I held up the packet.

"What is *what*?" I knew that he knew; he became suddenly alert.

"*This*. I found it in your pocket."

"What? *That*?" He forced a laugh, sounding more than a little fake. He got out of bed with those pajamas on, his good healthy bird sticking straight up through the pajama fly. Great.

"Was it Sally G.?"

"Sally G.? Susanna, she's your best friend! God, no, Susanna! It was just some escort girl. I went to dinner with the team, and they got me drunk, and one thing led to another."

"One thing led to another," I repeated, arms crossed in front of me.

"'Now we're going to really introduce you to the town!' they said." Francis Taylor laughed again in a contrived way. He put his hands over his boner.

What a complete child. I couldn't believe how immature he was.

I could not stand him.

I got out of bed, pulled the plaid top blanket off, and dragged it down the hall to Jenny's room, where I slept the rest of the night.

And to my surprise I lay with my hollow cheek against the pillow, my eyes wide and open to the night, and thanked God he'd at least only gone drunk to a whore and not a mistress.

CHAPTER 24

Summer – Christmas, 1961
Pope's Crossing, Connecticut

Francis Taylor's obsession got worse and worse. At the height of the Cold War and shortly before the Cuban missile crisis, Francis Taylor got it in his head that our family needed a fallout shelter. How odd was that? For weeks he was on the phone to the Department of Defense and the National Emergency Bureau, asking about necessary wall thickness, minimum depth for the shelter, the supplies that needed to be stocked. He talked directly to the Secretary of Defense for the inside on probable sites for atomic attack. He called Dr. Avery and Dr. Robert Boxley, distinguished scientists and physicians at Princeton and Yale. He needed the facts about the intrusive ability of radiation and the permeability of various wall compositions. It was truly hard not to listen in. Once I was in the kitchen feeding Bansen when I heard Francis Taylor talking to the National Weather Bureau. Wanted to know about wind patterns in New England. One time when the twins came home from St. Augustus for the weekend, they tiptoed into the kitchen, put a finger over their lips, then pulled me by the shirt sleeve across the creaking living room, through the den, and into the library where my husband was sitting in his leather arm chair looking at the book, *Living in the Atomic Age,* which was full of pictures of a family huddled around in their basement shelter, eating their cans of beans.

It was none of my business. Don't ask me.

At age seventeen, you want your Dad to be *normal*. All I know is that just when we thought we were feeling the first of summer's goodness, we all awoke one early morning to the sounds of the construction workers, out in the side yard, digging that hole in the ground, Francis Taylor out supervising, my sweet alfalfa scored to pieces by the tread of tractor tires.

After the cement was poured, and the hole was left open for a few days for the sun to help dry it, Francis Taylor went down into it one evening and felt his hand along the thick cement wall for results. He came out and called for the twins and, right then and there, he made them unload from the large, parked dump truck the drab, olive, vacuum-sealed drums of dried food and ten gallon water barrels. Making sure the fallout shelter logo (yellow "caution" triangles) faced outwards, he had them proceed in an orderly, military fashion—dried food first, then water barrels, then the empty tin canisters for waste products. There was a box of potassium iodide. My twins shook their arms from soreness, shook their heads from bemusement. Parish looked over at me as he was getting himself a glass of water and said, "Mom, what is with him? He's just *too* weird."

But when Francis Taylor finally came in from the fallout shelter, he wore the kind of renewed face that only happens after finishing and feeling good about a long, taxing, tedious task that's been all your own baby.

"We're sorry, Dad. But we just think this is weird."

"Then you haven't been reading the newspaper."

"Dad, they're not coming to Pope's Crossing."

"You guys need to hit the sack." It was already after midnight. "And then you both need to get yourself a pair of ears."

I went out there first thing in the morning and saw the line of dug-up earth where the construction workers had carefully laid the electrical wires under ground. I found the buried place where they'd carefully hidden the generator. I saw the trap doors to the shelter itself, camouflaged with a painted effort the color of dirt and the shape of fallen leaves. It was locked two or three different ways, like a patchwork of chastity belts.

"Yeah, he's weird all right," I mouthed.

Francis Taylor stayed down in Washington for longer and longer bouts. He and the others were driven to lobby Congress again and again, just as I had unfortunately encouraged him to do. Weekends too, his mind was elsewhere, lost in brown study. He stayed mainly with Jenny. Bike rides. More water sampling down at Kingfisher. With me, he hardly communicated. He looked at me blankly, as if I were a room boarder in this large, rambling house, and what started out as his months of the blues stretched out to over a year of distant, aloof self-containment.

While he lobbied, Vanheusen and Dewitt suffered the recession. The stock market was down and losses for his clients did not help matters. I worked clumsily at trying to rebuild his self-esteem, but he'd just go out in the garden all day long and work it hard till no weeds showed and every vegetable or flower plant had been pruned perfect.

Showing such a lack of trust in me, it was as if I had been the one to cause him to lose his lobbying efforts. A hick from Mississippi. Who had no real education, except through him, his friends, and his relatives. With subtlety, they taught, via osmosis, all about how the rich should behave. In due time, I began to take wealth so for granted that I sometimes fell into the deluded impression that the whole world was loaded like us.

But, of course, deep down, I never forgot.

It was our children, especially Jenny, who finally got Francis Taylor out of his funk. It happened over Christmas break. The twins were home from St. Augustus Prep. The snow was nearly a foot high by that December, and not all of the trains were running. LaGuardia had closed for three hours earlier in the day. But the trains coming from the north were running. These trains knew snow. I picked the boys up from the Greenwich Station on Saturday. At home we had hot tomato soup and sandwiches and caught up. Then we all immediately went out to the forest to cut down our tree, just as we always had. It was not that they were so inclined; they would have much preferred to hang out, watching a NY Giant's game.

The twins cooperated with the tree cutting tradition for *me*. The snow had crunched under our feet as we'd walked, and the sun shone on the little crystals blinking on its white surface. We'd have it up before Francis Taylor got home that evening. He was over at his parents', visiting.

Once we'd found our tree, a Douglas fir, the sticky, delicious sap oozing through the end we'd sawed, all three of us dragged the tree back up the hill. With it roped on top of the station wagon, we slid our way home on the salted, country roads that, even after all these years of trying to become a Yankee, I still couldn't negotiate for the life of me. Ever a blessing that I could make it from here to there without crashing into one of the old stone walls that border these tiny, gorgeous roads.

Linda C.S., who had now been Helena's cook for twenty years, and the twins and I decorated the tree and put up wreaths with red bows and pulled out the Christmas decorations and set them up as we drank hot, spiced cider and listened to Christmas music. After that, I put all my energy into creating the feast.

On Christmas Eve, we all went to the little chapel that belonged to Pope's Crossing. You could smell sherry. By candlelight everybody sang Christmas carols. Except for Francis Taylor who was somewhere else, deep in thought.

Afterwards, everyone went outside under the stars and bantered for a bit. I slipped my hand inside Francis Taylor's; it had been a long time since I'd done that. Still, he was distant.

Linda C.S. had come over to help me with all the preparations for the Christmas feast, and Taylor and Parish had helped me, too. But as soon as they'd snapped off the ends of the string beans, the twins ran down the runny path to the dock house at Kingfisher and smoked pot. When they got back, something smelled. I was thinking that maybe Francis Taylor and I should let down our hair and go down there and learn to smoke pot with them. Maybe that would help Francis Taylor get in a better mood.

When Christmas Eve came, we had the fires going strong in all the rooms downstairs, and the heat was turned up high. But everyone, once seated around our long pine table with its double plates and twinned wine glasses and lit candles and holly and berry for centerpieces, felt nonetheless the presence of a cold Yankee draft slipping through our very old windows. We held hands and said the blessing. From Francis Taylor's side of the family were Francis Taylor's oldest brother, Michael, Michael's wife, Patricia, and their two grown kids, Lehman and Curtis. Francis' brother Henry and Marge were there with their two grown kids, Vincent and Patrick, and Patrick's girlfriend, Sophie Stapinski. Some of the Vanheusen cousins would be coming over later for dessert. The Hartofelises and the LeJune's, from the other side of Kingfisher, were coming. Pasha, who had spent every Christmas with us since Francis Taylor and I had been married, was with us for this Christmas, too. Sally G. was once again dancing *The Nutcracker* with Peter B.—this was her sixth season in a row of starring in *The Nutcracker* with Peter B. Sally G. had given me the sick news that half of the Corps dancers were now fully hooked on drugs and were almost always high when they performed. She never said whether or not she'd tried anything, but I had to trust that she had better sense than that. Still, there is nothing worse than loneliness in New York City.

Our house was suffused with the smell of Douglas fir and cinnamon and spices. And it smelled divine, if I may say so.

We started with *croquis de fois gras avec crème* and Dom Perignon that my usually rather hoarding and frugal husband had brought up from the wine cellar. Each of the four bottles was so covered in stuck dust you couldn't even see the vintage. The *croquis* seemed to explode in your mouth as you relished it. It was blessed. People told me it was blessed, and I believed them. That particular recipe was very good for my self-esteem.

Next we had '49 Chassagne Montrachet served with the second course: nutmeg lobster bisque. Then '49 Pommard Rossignol for the main course: garlic and rosemary venison braised with pecans *au jus de vin rouge*, spinach, wild rice with cranberry, baguettes with hand-churned sweet cream butter from the Lorna Dune Dairy Farm. With the salad that came afterwards—baby mixed greens with arugula and pine nuts and hot goat cheese—I served a '49 Gevrey Chambertin Grand Crus. For dessert there would be Blue Mountain Jamaican coffee with raspberry sorbet and pastries and chocolates that were peppered over the table. Grand Marnier was offered at the end.

Family at Christmas; the fires going in all the fireplaces; candles lit on the table, wonderful food; everyone getting drunk and loosening up to say affectionate things they might not have said otherwise; singing and dancing; weaving into the kitchen in lame, charming, impotent promises to help with the dishes—did it ever, ever get better than that? You think of the old countries, the countries who have lived through their wars, their losses, and who have learned the true meaning of life, the true art of living. Every peasant family from every tiny farm village in France, for instance, has the wisdom to have family feasts like this, not just at Christmas, but also on every Sunday of the year. Even Francis Taylor, who started out at the head of the table, sitting straight with tense shoulders, let go. You could see his body slowly come open, his shoulders relaxing.

The twins had the good sense to over-pour the wine, especially in Francis Taylor's glass. Francis Taylor. It was hard to remember what his laugh had even sounded like. But pretty soon into the dinner, the twins and Jenny were able to get Francis Taylor to crack up again. Through their mining of old stories about him, about what a goofball he really was, they finally got him to laugh at himself again.

It was Parish who got Francis' brother, Michael, to tell us again the story about the time when Francis Taylor was on the phone with Theo Bami, their brilliant colleague at Vanheusen and Dewitt Partners. Michael sat up, cleared his Yankee throat, dabbed the corners of his mouth and said, "Well, folks, my good brother here and our luminous colleague and partner, Theo Bami, were on the phone talking the other day about the deal they were in the midst of with a chain of environmentally friendly grocery stores out west, Good Earth Foods. Since Theo Bami's office is directly across the hallway from Francis Taylor's, Theo could of course hear Francis Taylor perfectly well. No need to be on the phone, right?

"So, Theo Bami says, 'Francis Taylor, since you can hear me perfectly fine, and I can hear you perfectly fine, I'll just put the phone down and saunter on over to your office.'

"'Yes, of course, Theo, you're quite right. Come on over.' Francis Taylor gestured for him to come on over.

"So Theo Bami put the phone down in his office and ambled over to Francis Taylor's office and stood politely in the doorway. But Francis Taylor, who is still on the phone, talking away, glances up at Theo, holds up a finger and says, 'Just a minute. I'm on the phone with Theo Bami.'"

Everybody cracked up. We'd all heard that story a million times, and we all cracked up each and every time we heard it. Francis Taylor, at the head of the table, had squinched up his nose, and he was laughing, too. Blushing and laughing.

Taylor stood and raised his glass and said, "To our Dad of Skull and Bones!"

"Hear, hear!"

"Tell the one about JFK."

"Oh, I'm telling that one!" Jenny raised a hand and frantically waved it, as if she had to have permission. "Right after Kennedy got elected? Dad wanted to meet him soooo badly." Jenny's eyes brightened and she made a gesture with both hands cupped beside her face, like quotation marks.

"When he finally got his chance?

"Dad was so nervous? So nervous that he walked right up to President Kennedy, put his hand out and said, 'Hi! I'm Jack Kennedy!'"

Everybody burst out laughing. Francis Taylor was laughing, too. His face was so red from a surge of joy and embarrassment that a vein bulged in his forehead.

"To Dad! The recipient of the MacArthur Genius Award." Taylor raised a glass and everybody followed. "Hear, hear!"

"Thank you," Francis Taylor lifting his wineglass, then taking a sip. He was just fine. For now.

We were having a good time. How long had it been? We were having a good, good time.

CHAPTER 25

1961 – 1962

Pope's Crossing, Connecticut

It was the summer of 1961. This was a year after the Greenwich Country Club had the devastating fire that destroyed the clubhouse but spared the pool area. This was also the summer that Francis Taylor spent at home researching and writing reports about the devastation going on at Lake Erie. But, it was the summer he'd spent a lot of time watching Jenny dive. She had gotten so good by then, the Country Day School had offered her private coaching. Sometimes we'd both go watch these coaching sessions, and sometimes he'd just go alone. In her red cross-strap Jantzen, she'd spring up the ladder of the high dive, throw a double and a half in pike position, then dart the water clean as a javelin. We'd look at each other, our eyes shining.

She was becoming the talk of Pope's Crossing. The Greenwich Country Club Coach, Ben Frank, had once vaguely mentioned something about her being talented and driven enough to get to the U.S. Nationals.

A year and a half later, Christmas break of 1962, the twins were seniors at St. Augustus. Taylor had gotten into Yale, early decision. (Pull helped.) Parish was waiting to hear from Dartmouth. Taylor came home that Christmas with Coach Claus Vonhelm, the then diving coach from Yale, a former Olympian himself. And this event, as I guess the twins understood all along, shifted the U.S. Nationals suggestion from a distant dream to a plausible reality.

Jenny had become a full-fledged high school teenager with smooth shaven legs, cruel period cramps, lacy bras. But, to the best of my knowledge, there hadn't been any boys she'd fallen in love with yet until the blond Claus, a '48 gold medalist from Sweden, came around. Lord, he was built like the David. I even felt tingles the day he peeled off his T-shirt to show Jenny height techniques on the three meter diving board at the Yale inside pool.

Jenny became a dangerous case of teenage love-at-first-sight. Every time she was around him, she giggled and blushed and generally lost all ability to articulate. It was most annoying.

Both of them had their sights fixed on the '65 U.S. Nationals, and this Christmas as I watched her dive, I watched, too, how she broke out of herself, how practice and commitment had pushed her to a different level of quiet confidence.

Proudly, I pointed this out to my husband, and at first he seemed to take this in—all through the holidays he was in the best mood he'd been in for months, I want to say years. My sons' absence had brought him much closer to them, and all that Christmas he enjoyed them in a way he hadn't before, as little adults with whom he could now discuss politics, history, family history (which had, to this point, been kept a mystery). And, of course, women.

More, he was clearly beside himself that Jenny had committed to the goal of making the U.S. Nationals. Sometimes at the dinner table, he'd look at her with infatuated eyes. As I observed them, I suddenly had a hunch that the two of them shared a secret, a private vow that the rest of us weren't going to be privy to yet, if ever.

Then, the closer I looked, the more I realized how cool and unfriendly he was acting towards Claus. I started watching how uncomfortable he made Claus feel, how he alienated him.

"Francis," I finally said. "She's your daughter. She's not your girlfriend, and she's not betraying you."

"Susanna!" he answered in a kind of singsong. I'd asked for it. "Susannaaaaaah, Susanaaaaah!"

What a brat.

Francis Taylor had become deeply preoccupied with the effort to get the Endangered Species Protection Petition heard on the Floor. He became engrossed in the effort to get the Clean Air and

Water Act passed. He sweated over every single word, doubting and doubting himself over and over again.

"It's not *you* whom you should doubt. It's *them*." I tried to point out who was stonewalling whom.

But, the days stretched on to months in Washington, and I was starting to worry that we were going to wind up having to move.

Which wasn't going to be an option. Because, while he was down in Washington with his worries, and the twins were at Yale and Dartmouth, Jenny became more and more obsessed with making the Nationals, obsessed with filling the void.

"Jenny, at least be home by dinner time." It was just me all by myself in that big house now.

"Mom, talk to Coach Claus. He knows what he's doing. Have you seen the winter schedule for the meets?"

"No, but I have seen that, for the first time ever, all the beds around here are made. I wish you would all come home. I miss the mess."

If only Francis Taylor—engrossed in the horrible news about the growing endangered list, the near disappearance of the bald eagle, the fight to ban the pesticides—had looked up just long enough to have heard me when I cried, *Come home, your hands are needed*.

Come home.

If only he'd have come home when the horn blew for him, before the fog rolled in, and before Jenny grew fragile and lonely as a desert bird.

CHAPTER 26

1963 – March, 1965

Pope's Crossing, Connecticut

Jenny's practices at the Kiphuth Pool at Yale now stretched three hours towards the evening. And sometimes she'd go to school at 5 AM. to dive while the swim team swam their morning laps. By then, Claus had been coaching Jenny at Greenwich Country Club for two years. She was almost sixteen.

I'd occasionally go along, watching the butterfly swimmers make waves down the pool, the wakes fanning out behind them.

But watching, my mind would be way off somewhere else. I was that way all winter. Whether cooking, or sitting down to write the twins, or going off shopping with Jenny, I'd suddenly drop to a daze. I'd go to the grocery store, pay, then leave the filled grocery bags right there on the conveyor belt at the checkout stand.

I missed my husband, and I missed the twins something fierce. Once they got to college, they were just plain gone. Neither had time to write or call anymore, and when I'd call each one's dorm phone, it'd ring and ring as if the campuses were deserted. Even if someone was right there on top of it, a prep school child wouldn't answer because it might be for somebody clean down at the other end of the hall and they would be far too lazy to go get the person.

At first, Jenny didn't act like she missed either Daddy or the twins. At Greenwich High with their narrow, leased window of time at the Yale pool, she had won the state junior trials. With luck, Jenny would be going to the Nationals in the spring of '65. All her time was swallowed up in that Yale pool. That, or in books. Like her father, she remained both driven and right secretive. To her, slowing down or telling anybody what was on her mind was the same thing as yielding to a strong gust of wind that could knock her whole plan down. Jenny couldn't stand the thought of sliding off the dean's list just one small time, nor could she leave practice without the satisfaction of championing a particular dive. Despite the long hours needed for homework at night, she'd hang in for as long as it'd take. Part of her formula, I'd figured out, involved making herself keep going until she'd hit a certain dive at a near ten performance, three times in a row. Only then would she allow herself to quit, never mind if the sun had long set.

As the fall wore on and the trees shed down to nothing, Jenny seemed to shed with them. At first you could say she was simply beginning to look a little on the thin side, the way we'd had to look as ballerinas.

Christmas came, and we all convened at the cabin in the Vermont woods. My husband arrived with the company of Senator Briggs, the Stokeses, all of whom were on the committee working to get the Clean Air and Water Bill passed. They stayed pent-up together, working practically the whole time in the room that we called the hunt lodge (nobody from the present generation hunted) because of its smelly moose head, strong rafter beams, and large stone fireplace.

On Christmas Eve when the men went home to their families, we sat around the long square pine table, at last as a family. I noticed Jenny didn't touch her fruitcake, and it wasn't because she didn't like it. She passed on the eggnog, salmon, roast turkey, potato soufflé, cheeses, fruits, and all other variety of cakes. She had Bibb lettuce. And a little squash.

Her Daddy said, "She's just getting ready for her gold medal." Smiling while he said it with his chest puffed out. Jenny lifted one shoulder, shrugged it, as if to minimize his expectations. But I could see she was scared, scared of failing him.

Then, at the table on Christmas Day, the twins sang,

Jenny, where are you going?
Upstairs to take a bath....

Jenny, with legs like toothpicks,
And a neck like a giraffe!

Jenny steps in the bathtub
Jenny pulls out the plug....
Jenny? Jenny?
Glug, glug, glug.

Jenny tried to laugh along with her brothers, but I could see it hurt her. I could see it, but nobody else seemed to.

On New Year's Day, we put the twins on their separate trains, and we put Washington-bound Daddy on another, and the way Jenny said good-bye said something. Like she was the train fading out of distance, and they were on the platform.

All through January, the coldest Connecticut had known in thirty years, the less we heard from them, the more driven Jenny became. And she ate less and less. She grew bare and gaunt as the birch trees, and through her wet black bathing suit, her ribs were starting to show, stacked like the black velvet swags in theater curtains, stiff and macabre looking as they are when the theater is empty and the lights are out.

"Why, Jenny, why? Why the starvation? For the hungry in Africa?"

"No, Mom," brushing her hair, "Don't worry, Mom. Nothing's wrong... times have changed, women are thinner now, look around you. And for the U.S. Nationals, I must be lean, lean as a child."

I tried making the goodies she'd loved as a child. *You know that orange peel cake? I like it, Mom, can I have some?* begged Jenny during my husband's first campaign.). I made her cookies. *I like them soft in the middle, Mom. Can you always make them that way?* she'd said as a child.

But by the time the snowdrifts rose around our house, and the walkways reappeared only after shovels had cut snow banks a foot deep, Jenny weighed about eighty pounds. The goodies piled in the freezer, waiting for somebody else's stomach to growl.

She went on, small as a flea and on its same curious energy.

"Tell me, Jenny. Tell me what's wrong." I begged for information. Her behavior wasn't like my child's.

"Nothing's wrong, Mom. Why do you always ask me so many questions?"

"We'll go for a check-up. You know, a physical, something routine."

"Mom, you don't believe me."

I wanted to believe her, but couldn't find a way, watching her pick at her food.

"Jenny," I rubbed my hands over my knees, "Please eat."

"No, Mom, no. You eat. I don't have time tonight with all my homework: two tests tomorrow and a paper due." She pushed away from the kitchen counter.

"Come back here, young lady!" My voiced rose sternly, my fingers curled underneath the pine brace of the kitchen table.

"Mom, what's with you? I can't understand what's making you so uptight."

"Jenny, please, something. A half a potato." Using one hand to pull the chair back for the sixteen-year-old in a ten-year-old's body, I watched her pick the tines of the fork along the brown potato skin.

"Please?"

For me, she ate two bites, and I let her go, my back turned and clouded eyes pretending to look for something in the pantry. Soft footsteps went up the stairs.

I walked stiffly back to the table, gathered up the plates, and began rinsing them when I heard the coughing upstairs. She coughed, choked, then stopped. Coughed, choked, then stopped. I raced up to her room, knocked at the bathroom door. Over the coughing, she must not have heard me. I gave a strong kick to its base.

"Jenny, what is it?" I grabbed her, rocked her as I hugged—thinking leukemia, kidney malfunction—and looked for blood splattering the mirror, the floor. But even as she choked out, "I'm fine, Mom. Please leave me alone," her eyes watery from the gagging and coughs, she seemed to evaporate in the circle of my arms.

"Jenny, tomorrow we're going to the doctor. That's final."

"Mom, there's nothing wrong."

"Come on, Love, there may be nothing, you may be right. But we're going to New York Hospital tomorrow to check, to know."

"Mom."

"Yes, Jenny," My voice trailed off as I pulled away.

The internists gave her all the tests they could think of and showed us the clothes-pinned plates of her X-rays. "We can find nothing wrong. No evidence of carcinogenic cells, viruses or other diseases, no gastrointestinal disorders. Probably anxiety (lowering their voices, looking through a pair of bifocals, paternally). She puts herself under an awful lot of pressure with that determination to get to the U.S. Nationals, and the Nationals hanging over her head. She's a little anemic. Here, give her these pills for iron. Take her home, and make sure she gets good rest, red meats, vegetables, her vitamins, plenty of water. Call us if she isn't better in a few weeks."

Jenny, smug, looking at me like I was crazy. "See, Mom, I told you so," she chided. (This chiding: the calcium and salt used for the shell she was making to hide in and be safe from me.)

"Lots of rest, Jenny. That's what they said. You heard them. Plenty of red meat and vegetables." I was chiding her back, for chiding me, for its echoing the way my husband had chided me all these years, and for its echoing the way the doctors chided me now with their patronizing, their charts and X-rays I could not read. Eighty pounds. All five-feet-four of her! Whose fault could it be but mine, the only parent around?

That evening I fixed her a large steak and set the iron pills, blood-red and oblong, on a napkin by her plate.

I waited until I was sure she slept before I called her father. I spoke in a whisper, "Come home, Jenny's not doing well at all."

"What did the doctors say?"

"They didn't find anything, but...."

"Susanna, they're some of the best internists in the country. I didn't call earlier because I'd spoken to them myself this afternoon. Now easy does it, you were lean like that, too, when you danced."

Because of the softness of his tone, I took some comfort in what he said, worrying the same, but nagging her less. For a few weeks, I stopped hearing myself say, "Jenny, eat. Please. You haven't touched your vegetables."

Others, too, believed this was only a phase, and for a while their believing helped me.

Coach said, "The Nationals are a shoo-in; we'll need to fatten her up, but she's diving for ten of us. The energy!"

It was true, all the while she starved, an unnatural hyper-energy nonetheless charged through the fissures of her lean tissue: her arms and legs worked mosquito-like, compact and from some inexhaustible power source I could not understand. Like a bird she dove through the air!

"All right," I conceded, "I promise to let her keep diving if that's what she needs."

For a while, I kept my promise; kept it out of hope, out of the deeper knowledge of my child's love of her family, her honesty outside of this, her wish to please. Through the winter I struggled hard to allow her independence, to treat her in an attitude of love, not mistrust, to feign belief when she'd look at me, eyes unfaltering, "I ate already, Mom. At school. I got so hungry, I ate for five!"

"That's good, darling."

For those short days of February, March and April while I let her be, she grew sweet to me again, but her body was a skeleton: the bones of her hips, knees, ribs, and shoulders showed. Her clavicles were round snakes crawling towards her chest, and you could count all the knots in her spine. The gauntness of her face made her teeth look big and frightening as a skull's.

At last I could not playact any longer. Driving her to practice, I suddenly blurted, "Jenny, are you sure you want to dive?" I slowed the car as I asked.

"Mom, it's all I have. I have no friends anymore. I'm losing them all, and I don't know why."

(Through the grapevine I had heard about this. I had heard that no one would sit with her at lunch. Teachers were beginning to call me, "Her grades are up, but she seems so unhappy.")

I stopped the car. "Jenny, come here." I kissed the top of her head. "Do you know that the twins and Daddy and I love you? Do you know how much?"

"Yes, Mom. I think I know that. It's not you guys, Mom. It's me." She put two hands on my forearm, looked at me with her bony face, blankly, resolutely, as if she did not even have enough salt in her body to pull together a few tears.

"Yes?" I waited. "Do you feel well?"

"Yes, Mom. But I can't catch up with the rest of you." Here, she did look like she was going to cry but didn't.

"Jenny, what on earth? What are you talking about? Where did this come from?"

She jerked away, looked at her watch, and said, "Come on, Mom, you've got to get me to practice on time."

I realized, suddenly, that my look of surprise had bordered on a look of anger, and knew I had rejected her even as I tried to help her. Huge, overwhelming was my resolve to get my husband home.

That evening, from the Bible, I read, "Set these lands in order...."

I reached Francis Taylor at six in the morning, sure to get him before he left for the Hill. I was in a terrible mood. "You won't miss Jenny's spring meets. I know you're not that evil."

"Susanna, no, I won't miss Jenny's spring meets. Of course not, she knows that. Not unless a Congressional session is called. We've got a lot going on the Clean Air and Water proposals. And Jenny understands this. I've discussed this with the boys and Jenny. Plus, it seems highly unlikely that this matter will be brought to session before May 15th or so."

"Well good, you better be here!" I shouted.

"Susanna, ever since I've been here in Washington, you and Jenny have been acting so unhappy. Every time I talk to either one of you, you're complaining and bitching about something. Now, I wish you would go and get yourself involved in some kind of project, I don't like seeing you this way."

Here I simply hung up on his face.

And every time I called the office for the next two weeks, he was either 'out' or 'in a meeting.'

Jenny's biggest regional meet, April 6th, clocked its way to reality. And sure enough, he couldn't come. The Congressional session was indeed posted for April 15th. It was a major event considering how long they'd been working on the Clean Air and Water Bill, and how close they were to getting it passed. He said he and Senator Briggs and Senator Clifford were committed to a last-minute trip to Lake Placid, Lake Erie, and then California for collecting final quarter data concerning the effects of DDT on fish, wildlife, and crops in those areas. He said he'd explained this to Jenny, and that Jenny understood how vital the situation was. He said he couldn't understand why I couldn't see it.

"Oh, yes, I understand," I told him bitterly. "Jenny understands too, all seventy-five pounds of her." For a second time, I hung up on his face.

I arranged to have Jenny's three best friends over for dinner on Friday night. The girls talked of boys, and Jenny laughed and play-acted interest. (She'd never told me that Claus had fallen in love with a Yale professor. I'd found out through the twins. It was true that Claus' letters, which had staggered in fairly frequently, were now quite random and infrequent.)

I served cake, foolishly. She ate her bite, then, like a polecat, slunk away from the table and went outside. I crept quickly to the study, threw open the window. The coughing, spitting, and gagging hacked and spewed in disturbing measures to the clean air.

My eyes chaperoned, stood witness. I hid for a moment when she came back in, listened to her resume her strained laughter and semblance of happiness in the company and conversation of friends. Listening, knowing how she had deceived them, how she had deceived me, I no longer knew, at that moment, whether I hated her or loved her.

After the girlfriends had gone laughing home, Jenny and I were in the kitchen doing the dishes. She was a lamb. She said, "Mom, you're so good to me."

All I needed then was a compliment like that, even if she meant it. The blows to my too-high expectations about the party, the hope I'd had for his coming home, ripped through my worn veil of love and caring. Instead of showing her how good I am, I showed her all that I mistrusted. Knowing her eyes were following me, I scavenged through the debris in a trashcan, hunting out the food she'd chewed and spit out in a napkin. I held it up: breast of chicken, carrot, bites of a roll made into mush by her mouth. "At least to the birds, Jenny! At least some crumbs to the birds!" My hands struggled to hold back from shaking her, from frightening her into throwing up the answers.

Competitive Jenny turned back to the dishes and later that week thanked me by losing two more pounds.

In the extremeness of our isolation, the stubbornness of our wills, war was waged. I couldn't sleep anymore. Here we were, at least the two of us under the same roof, but our chosen distance sent cold chills through the house. All I had left of her was her breathing at night, her little moans as she'd shift in her sleep.

Oh, in those bleak days, I cursed myself, twisting my hands in my hair as I'd stare into the trash can, at its motley assortment: green beans, uneaten duck wasted among spilt yolks of egg, coffee grounds. I cursed my whole family for leaving me all alone with this.

COME HOME FROM THE TRAVELS, I telegraphed to my husband.

(We're getting messages to him as fast as we can, his secretary pleaded, but the delay is sometimes up to four or five days when they're out in the wild.)

She'd become sallow now, the deep in-draw of her cheeks made her lips protrude. Her blue eyes looked empty and dark as sockets. She walked on toothpick legs, picked at her food with bird-like hands, and in time she began to emit a strange smell, pungent, garlic-like.

When presently I noticed large clumps of her blond hair tangled in the drain, and the garlic-like smell grew stronger, immune to showers, or teeth brushing, I lied and said, "Jenny, Dad called today. He's coming home to see you."

For a few days she seemed happier and ate a little more. But the strange smell and her hair falling out like that pushed the small boost of encouragement deep under stronger currents of fear, which persisted despite the doctor's insistence that it was all in my head. I began acting out of fear alone. Out of survival, I hid half sticks of butter under her bird's portion of white rice on her plate. And with a needle, shot honey and sugar water in her oranges.

But somehow I controlled a fierce impulse to make her stop diving. As far as I could tell, her supernatural body now ran only on air. She with her hipbones like brittle shopping bag handles, knees protruding like a pair of doorknobs, and blue veins swelling down her legs, cold as rivers. Running, mosquito-like, on what?

On a cucumber today.

A stalk of celery and a pickle the next.

A teaspoon of cottage cheese, two bites of apple.

Or the oranges that spewed sugar water and honey into her mouth.

"Mom, you didn't. You tried to trick me, Mom."

"When your father gets here, he'll know how to deal with you!" I called after her as she raced up the stairs on spokes for legs, arms like levers moving at sharp right angles behind her.

As the door slammed, she screamed, "Good! Call Dad! He doesn't care! He's no father anymore!"

Inside her room she lay limp on the bed, knees to her chin, arms around her pillow. I walked towards her, the floors thin ice. I spooned up to her and wept against the sharp bones sticking out of her back. "I miss him, too," I whispered, my lips close to my child's neck, a hand lifting her hair to one side. "I miss him too, Jenny. He was this way when I was a young girl—going away to prove things he needed to prove to himself, to others. All that proving is what makes him feel able to get closer to us, if you can believe it. He'll come home soon."

For the first time since the gauntness began to appear, Jenny cried, gripping two fingers of my hand.

The April suns came earlier than usual, like an Indian summer whose languid daylight you wanted to capture in a glass box.

But even the sudden weather change lent only shallow support. Jenny hovered at seventy-five, seventy-three. Even as a skeleton, she had won the regionals. The Nationals she was determined to win were still twelve weeks away.

My telegrams to my husband increased. I used the very words Mom had used on me all those years ago when I was a little girl about Jenny's age: COME HOME WHERE YOUR HANDS ARE NEEDED.

His brief calls back: "Susanna, my God, if you only knew how busy I am, how important is this bill, how close we are to getting the majority vote. You're sounding histrionic, Susanna. I don't know what to make of all this, don't know which end is up with you. Don't call me, Susanna. You're like an insect." Now he was the one, still green under pressure and conflict, who slammed the phone on my nose.

But I had to find a way to make him hear, and remembering how Mom hadn't said enough when she'd tried to get me home, I tried telegramming again, telling everything: COME HOME IMMEDIATELY. JENNY IS LOSING WEIGHT, EVERY DAY SHE IS LOSING ANOTHER POUND. YOU CAN COUNT ALL THE MUSCLES AND BONES, SEE ALL THE VEINS IN HER LEGS AND ARMS. SEVENTY-FIVE, SEVENTY-THREE, SHE WEIGHS.

I tried reaching him through the twins. "Oh Mom, since when has bull-headed Jenny not known what she's doing?" Taylor asked.

Then, hearing my disappointed sigh, Parish promised, "Mom, when we get done with exams, Taylor and I are driving straight to the Nationals. Tell her, Mom."

Finally, my husband called at the end of the week. "Susanna, What is it? I got a message saying there was another urgent telegram."

I wanted to tell him exactly what she was doing, how she was behaving. I wanted to tell him about her purging. But as I tried, the words came out stuttered, and the courage drowned.

"Susanna, I think this is starting to sound a little like the girl who cried wolf...."

"Not crying wolf, unhappy, uncaring husband!"

"Then what is it, Susanna?" His voice lowering, soft. Listening? Perhaps.

"You won't let me say my real feelings, you never let me...."

"Susanna, I'm sorry, I'm meeting with the Senator this afternoon. Unless you're going to say what's on your mind, I'll have to hang up."

"Come see Jenny. Misses you." My voice so low, only the s's studding the words could be heard.

"Susanna, Jesus, I can't hear you. I'll have to call you later."

"Stop!" I tried to say, but only the long S hissed through my teeth.

"California. Hearings! The President will live till tomorrow," I muttered to myself.

Hot rage rose within me and in my sleep, the sheets twisted around my body; my hand groped towards the hollow place beside me.

Often I woke in the middle of the night now, awake as an owl, as a traveler trying to adjust to the clocks of a country on the other side of the earth. On this night I read the Bible first, then furtively pulled out other books from underneath my pillow, *Diagnosing Leukemia, Understanding Muscular Dystrophy, How to Cope with Family Depression.*

After blurring through so many pages of words I could not understand, I dropped to sleep, finally, and dreamed we built a tower on Kingfisher Pond and Jenny dove from it, rising phoenix-like. The water was indigo blue, surreal, and our family and others we didn't know were eating a picnic spread on the shoreline, laughing.

I believed God had something to do with that dream; believed it was His voice high above the blue lake. I awoke to it, sat up thinking for a long time. Just thinking.

Suddenly, I had the urge to get up. I put on blue jeans, a cotton hat, cotton gloves, and walked down to Kingfisher. The lake was black as paint under a sky whose clouds obscured the moon. Lugubrious, stone quiet.

I stood at the water's edge, arms wrapped close to my chest, swayed a little, wondering why I hadn't thought of this before. I imagined a tower built on strong stanchions, rising out of the water. Hers.

I saw it as practical and convenient, a place she could go to anytime for practice, with or without Coach. How our extended family, ringing the lake, could amble down to watch her, how they could replace her absent father with the encouragement she needed. And without moving from their fold-up chairs, Jenny could take them on a trip clean through outer space.

I climbed up the hill, the air cool, but my cheeks warm. My fingers were hot, and I curled them to fists inside my gloves. Surges of energy and hope and sudden happiness pulsed through my body. And tired as I knew I must be, my idea kept me from sleeping for the rest of the night.

CHAPTER 27

Summer, 1966

Pope's Crossing, Connecticut

The promise of summer held in the air through the sweet scent of new baby-sized leaves, wild ginger, trout lily, lady slippers, buttercups, yellow jasmine. Believing that the rains might be delayed for a few weeks, I hired foresters from the maple forest and bought the wood planks and a host of other things the men needed: catches, hinges, brackets, flat tee's, dowels, joint fasteners. They brought their own buzz saws, tools, and sawhorses. None were carpenters by trade, but all of them knew carpentry like women know, say, fashion.

We worked while Jenny was at school. The wood lay hauled and piled in neat rows at the water's edge. One of the men rowed out to the far away quarter-mile buoy in Kingfisher, dropped a line to test the water's depth, then waved his arms overhead, signaling all systems go. It was forty feet deep.

Under a good blue sky, I rolled up my sleeves and mixed the concrete myself while the men unfurled rough blueprints, measured, sawed, and hammered out the first layer of the tower's triple decks. By sundown the maple planks were nailed straight and evenly across its frame. Then me and the four men bent down and spaced ourselves with hands gripped along the long forty-three foot pilings lying there on the bank. I called, "One, two, three" and we all erected them to the sky, then one by one, sunk them into my concrete pods and called it a day. With the large body of water in the background, they looked like tall ship's masts.

In the morning, the pilings had set firm in the concrete, like pintles. The men used pulleys to lay them breadth-ways over the gunwales of four adjacent rowboats. We pushed off from the bank, rowed slowly out to our mooring point, and again using the pulleys, the men hoisted the pilings to the air, grunting as they did so, and one by one, dropped them into the water. They sunk like legs in a water ballet. Little whirlpool patterns swirled around the edges of each as they dropped.

It was quite a feeling of satisfaction. The ends of the posts stood a clean foot out of the water, like strong legs of an overturned table. After some shoving and tugging and a fair amount of grunting, the deck was placed on top of them, flat as a graduation cap. We rowed back ashore and reloaded the boats with our tools, wide flat pieces of plywood, planks, sawhorses, and the whole array of joint fasteners, then rowed back out to the new deck and got to work, nailing up the frame for the second level of decking. I was whistling away.

From the hollow valley in which Kingfisher rested, the blended sounds of voices and hammering echoed all around the hillsides and, little by little, brought the whole crowd of family down to peer through the leaves at what was going on. Some wore walking caps, some had binoculars; some came alone, others in company. All were wordless.

Offering no explanation, I stayed hunched over, nailing together the cross slats of the ladder that would lead to the second level. I told the men, who were becoming my friends, not to give a word about our surprise tower to anyone.

I knew my doings would cause a stir, but I had no idea that the news would reach Washington so soon in the game. Francis Taylor called, irate.

"Susanna, I really... You've just gone hog wild. Nobody can control you. I understand you're building some kind of tower out in the middle of the pond. Well, Kingfisher is not your property. It is not your pond; it belongs to the entire family. I am certain this project is dangerous, and I am warning you to stop building it. It's an irrational pipe dream, Susanna."

I was mad enough to kill him. I glided my tongue across my teeth, then used the tip of it across the roof of my mouth to write every kind of profanity I could think of.

I put the phone down, quiet as could be, and resolved to build the tower as quickly as possible before anybody tried to tear it down.

I said something to Jenny as soon as she came home that evening.

"Jenny?"

"Yes, Mom, I have to get upstairs to study for a math test."

"Jenny, I'd wanted it to be a surprise, but you're bound to know. I'm building you a tower out on Kingfisher so you can dive anytime you like. If anybody tries to say anything controversial, just turn around and look at them funny, then keep right on going."

"Mom," Jenny said. At first I thought she was disappointed. "Mom!" But then I turned and saw how she was hiding a wide smile in her lifted shirt collar.

When it was finished on Friday, a short twenty-one days after we'd begun it, the tower stood ten meters high out of the water. Each deck was framed with crisscross railing, and it had three sets of ladders leading to the decks through trap doors in the floors. I made the platform diving board myself, using strong pliable wood and a stand made of bricks, some of which I'd taken up by hand, most of which we'd hoisted in burlap bags by our pulley system. The board, straight and slightly inclined, rested like a tongue stuck out to the world. But friendly and funning.

A pleasant wind blew across Kingfisher the evening it was finished. Water sloshed against the wood of the first deck level. But the tower itself stood still, solid and tall and naked and proud.

"Joe, Tommy Tuck, Eric! Who wants to go first?" I called from the top. Then I just jumped right off, my arms flapping all the way down. When I bobbed up to the surface, I held two victory fingers to the air. The men clapped, and I let out a sound of joy that would shake up the flyways of a whooping crane. The water was plenty cold, refreshing.

That evening I brought Jenny down to see. I was giggling along the path, and Jenny was giggling, partly because I held her hand too tightly, partly because it'd been a long time since she'd heard me giggling like that. Plus, she was excited.

Both of us peeled down, swam out to it, climbed the ladders to the third level. I did a few ballet moves, then went right off. She followed, nothing fancy. Just a real solid jump from which she came up giggling and claiming she just loved it and wanted to go off again.

"It's exactly ten meters. Do you think you can use it for practicing?"

Here she hesitated before she answered, but went ahead and said yes, I guess for my sake.

I saw immediately that her hesitation might have come from the fact that my pliable wooden board gave off a little spring, whereas a professional platform is generally made of cement and is stone flat and springless. So I promised her we'd have a real cement platform for the tower soon enough, and she laughed, then kind of ducked me under the water, and I kind of ducked her under the water, and the two of us bobbed for a while, one ducking the other and laughing, then together swam back to the tower where we sat with our knees drawn up and teeth chattering every now and again as we watched the orange-pink sun go down slowly. Even though the air was cool and our skin goose-bumped, we felt easy and safe and warm inside, like we'd both just been baptized.

I decided we ought to invite all the relatives down for a show. At first Jenny pooh-poohed the idea, but she later appeared in my room, just as I'd laid my head on the pillow, and said, "Yeah, Mom, let's do. It's a good idea."

I dreamed sugarplums. I dreamed Jenny grew fat and round as a cherub.

She'd written her Daddy that very night. I could tell from the way she pranced around. First prancing I'd seen from that child in months.

Francis Taylor called that Wednesday. He sounded tired and disappointed, but real kind and loving. Everything seemed to be going along so much better, including the way he told me that, once again, he couldn't come home quite yet.

"Susanna, Jenny wrote me," he said, first thing after I picked up the phone. "She sounds happy about the tower, and it's nice to see her feeling so cheerful. Please tell her I'll be in late tomorrow; we're trying to outlast a filibuster. I'll only be able to stay for one evening, at this point. Big noon lunch meeting on Friday. But it won't be much longer. I know it hasn't been easy, Susanna. You've been pretty good, despite everything. Tell Jenny I won't miss the Nationals if my job depends on it."

He kissed me. I mean he kissed me through the phone.

But when he got home, he was so shocked by the way Jenny looked, the happy homecoming turned into a rained-on Dixie parade. He was clearly hurting for her, and he milled around a little bit like he didn't know us and didn't exactly know what to say. Every little conversation he tried to strike up was of a strained cheerfulness that made us all quite uncomfortable.

"Hey, how is school going?"

"Fine, Dad.

"Good, good, that's great!!"

Every time she turned her back, he stared at her with a mortified look on his face. I had to cut eyes at him, warning him in case she turned around.

In the evening he helped Jenny with some real hard "pi equals" algebra problems, and later I heard them in there talking about the significance of the rain in *A Farewell to Arms*. Then. Well. Soon enough, I heard their whispering take on fluency, a closeness they'd known since before he became, as you know... a politician-type. I heard little laughs, a little billing and cooing, and him teasing her. Listening, I lay back in my bed and smiled, long and hard.

I thought we'd at least make love; I'd gotten all dolled up. But he just pulled the covers back, spooned up real close to me and said, "Susanna, you were right. The problem is serious, I should have listened. We're going to have to talk about this. I should have been here."

Vain thing, I thought pretty suddenly, but held my tongue; I was lucky to have him. I turned, looked at him, thinking, "There you are ... in the flesh," but said soberly, "I've been trying to tell you."

He answered, "We may have to resort to some kind of behavioral conditioning, and I think we'll send her up to Mass. General to be checked out by internists up there."

I shook my head hard, wriggled out of his arms, and sat up. "I've tried all that."

"Susanna," he said, sitting up with me. He tried to say something, but I interrupted him.

"It's not a physical problem, Francis Taylor."

The words seemed to rebound off of him, as if his ears were made of metal. I saw how he was collecting his defenses. But before he could speak, I repeated, "It's not." I put my hands underneath my thighs and looked straight down.

"Susanna."

"It's not, I mean it."

"Then what is it?"

"It's what I already told you. It's about homesickness. About missing the main love of her life, her Daddy. About being scared, scared of the future. About feeling like she hasn't pleased us enough. It's about you and me when we can't see eye to eye. It's about controlling us with her pain so we'll listen."

"Susanna," he blinked back, shut his eyes tight, then opened them.

"Yes."

"Did you make sure you set the alarm for five a.m.? Would..."

I nodded my head. My eyes were closed, trying to keep sorrow down.

"Would you mind passing it to me so I can double-check it?"

With my eyes still closed, I felt for the old wind-up clock we'd had since our wedding and handed it to him, dropping it at the last minute. It landed between us on the blankets.

In the morning I woke up abruptly at five-fifteen, and the first thing I did was look around for the clock, too drowsy to remember having given it to him right before falling asleep. As I looked, I saw that the covers on his side were thrown back, and that his bathrobe and pajamas were hanging on the bathroom door.

Then, cracking through my safe wall of sleep, I groped down the hall. Our house was so quiet. There were no sounds at all, save for the floors creaking underneath my feet.

I passed Jenny's room. At first I thought, "Well, her body is so small, I can't even see her underneath the covers." Then I realized Jenny wasn't there.

I rushed first to our window overlooking the forest. The trees bore new foliage, but their color was purple under a gossamer of fog. The air smelled sweet and fresh. The sun cast a vague first wash of light, bluish.

I went down to the kitchen. I saw two emptied glasses of orange juice on the table, and I knew then where the both of them were—he still loved to listen without letting me know he was listening.

I went back upstairs quickly, put on a pair of my husband's khaki pants, one of his shirts, and my old canvas tennis shoes. From our bedroom window, I looked through the trees, down the valley and saw Kingfisher. Like a brew, it looked. Like dry ice. The fog had set close to it, rising about five feet off the lake. I buttoned up and got outside. I walked at a clip, then broke to a run.

The fog obscured trees right in front of my nose, but I knew the path, could take it with my eyes closed. Still, wet leaves sticking underneath the rubber soles of my shoes warned me that I might slip as I ran fast down the poorly banked curve at the lower part of the path. Yet I slowed not from this warning, but from the sounds of their voices down below. Their voices were soft, free as water. As I descended, I smelled the dew, the strong, earthy odor of the lake. I took in deep breaths, slowing to a walk, quiet but clipped. The water was about twenty feet in front of me. I crouched toward it then bent behind a cluster of cattails and watched.

The vapors rose up from Kingfisher and wrapped around the tower like a petticoat. Mosquitoes bit. I had slept through a thunderstorm sometime early this morning.

I pulled the weeds apart and peered, watching them row quietly across the pond, Jenny at the bow, my husband at the stern, his back straight as an Indian's. I watched the feather curl of their oars, listened to them, their lyrical, lifted, at-ease voices.

From the trees overhanging me, I reached a branch, pulled it down and washed my face with its leaves, one eye on them. I felt the old guilt of trespassing into moments he cherished most, but something held my feet strong as roots to the bank, and my eyes periscoped through the rushes. As they rowed, the fog spread out, dissipated down to the ankles of the tower, as if the pitch of their voices held some oracle's authority over it. There were bald patches now on the water; the sun hit them and turned them into silver mirrors.

I walked quietly around the cattails to the ferny bank, bent down, ran a hand in a figure eight through the water, through its thin film of pollen, and drew up debris carried by the night's strong winds. Pine needles, bits of bark, old winter leaves. I listened. Frogs startled me by plopping from the bank, hands out Geronimo to the water. I listened harder. Francis Taylor was talking about the tower. He was saying good things about it. I wanted to stand, to get closer. But this was their moment, their secret. I crouched, and then I sat.

At length they reached it. The tower stood about two hundred yards from the bank; I had good, awake eyes now, and could practically see the expressions on their faces.

My husband moored the boat to the nearby buoy, then Jenny stood, dove into the water, swam underneath, and came up at the tower's deck ladder.

"Got it?" he asked.

"Freezing," she said, "just freezing." I knew she was smiling; I imagined her face as all teeth, radiant.

"Afterwards, I might have to jump in and take a little dip with you."

"Okay!" She took two hands to the ladder and climbed merrily up the rungs, stopping once to tug at the bottom elastic of her black bathing suit. She stood at the top, looking down through the low cloud at her father. "I'm on top of the clouds, Daddy," she said, standing in her starved scarecrow of a body, her two arms stretching for each end of the lake.

Unmooring, and rowing backwards from the tower where the view was better, he said, "I'm watching, honey. I'm right here."

"Which dive, Daddy? Name a dive."

"How about a swan dive, Jenny?"

"Oh Daddy, that's cake!" She rolled her eyes. I couldn't see that, but I knew she had.

"Then let's see a swan dive with a half-twist."

It was like my husband to request the cleanest and purest of the dives. No acrobatics for this one. He was soft that way. Acrobatics pretty much scared him.

"Okay, Daddy," she said, pulling her thick wet hair back, tying it in a ribbon. "Look through the fog and see how clean my legs go in, Daddy. Tell me if I make a splash."

"I won't take my eyes off you."

Her steps were spring-like to the board, and again she gave her little laugh. My heart pounded, at once thrilled, aloft, and terrified, the special blend that only a child can arouse in her mother.

She stood a long time. She was a quarter of the way to the end, her dark pencil-straight body inclined slightly forward. Her arms rested by her sides, barely cocked. I didn't need to see the fierce concentration on her face to know she meant to go in without so much as breaking a bubble on the water's surface. He waited patiently, the two oars crossed over his lap. If I could have seen his face, I'd have seen pride. We were one then. One.

Jenny took four slow, controlled steps to the end of the board. Her stick arms and bone-knee lifted in exact tandem, her rhythm here remained slow and paced. Through this build-up, from the self-containment gained through hours of practice, she was assured of height.

She got about two feet on the hurdle, landed on the board squarely on the balls of both feet (it was soaked from the storm, but she was so sure-footed that you wouldn't have known it), and carried her arms through. Reaching them straight and extended to the sky, she rose up, up, up, then parted her arms at the top of her height, six feet above the tower, and hovered cruciform for brief seconds. Her feet were pointed, clean as half-moons and pressed so closely together they seemed to be one. And turning her right shoulder slightly forward, she eyed down her right arm to signal the twist. Her body followed, twisting, lithe, arched, contained. The dim sky seemed to want to hold her forever. Jenny held her poise all the way through.

But it was as she had landed from the hurdle, before lifting to the air, lark-like with airfoils closed upwards, that the board had snapped. I'd bolted up from the weeds the instant I heard it. It had cracked from the impact of the hurdle. I'd made it too long. I'd wanted it to be long so there would be no chance of her ever hitting the tower. The board cracked right at the edge of the tower's top railing.

At first, it seemed to have only split a little, a warning calling for immediate repair. Then all of a sudden, it snapped open slowly, hung hinge-like at a right angle to the water, the splinters at the crack opened to the sky like thick black teeth.

I gasped, both hands flew to the sides of my face. The board hung that way as if by the invisible sure-fired hands of sinister spirits, cocked and aimed and waiting for Jenny to drop into the line of sight.

I watched. He watched. Nothing came from either of our mouths. We were one now, too, but only in terror.

But Jenny also must have heard the board crack, all on her own. I'll always think she did. I'll also always think she knew I was there, too. Her arms flailed twice as if to signal help, and then retrieved the form of the dive; her swan's presence held as if trumpeting out some last flicker of gratitude that we were still together.

The board loosened, shot after her as she dove clean as a bullet. I believe she heard it whispering behind her, otherwise why would she have folded up at the end? She curled her knees to her chest, wrapped her arms around them, ducked her head and the speed alone caused her to flip; she landed flat on her back and the smack of skin to water was cruel enough to tear her open. And she laid out from the pain, her arms flagged once, vaguely, spasmodically, before the board spiked down, flipped over twice as if in some sardonic mockery of the effort itself, and smacked her so hard in her gaunt and fragile face the bones shattered like glass.

In his stark panic, Francis Taylor dropped the oars and they glided into the water. Then there was no motion at all on the lake, save the brief bob of her body once, perhaps twice before she sank into the misty, mauve water and disappeared.

Buttons flung off as I pulled my shirt over my head. I tore at the zipper, got my pants down, used my toes to wedge the heels out of my shoes. I screamed first. I screamed, "Get her! Get out, get her!" Then crashed into the water and swam out with all that I had. I swam, furiously, destructively, kicking my legs when they no longer wanted to move, breathing hard against crawl strokes. I pulled and pulled against the lake, swallowing water, then choking. I stopped to cough, looked up, and saw that he was still there in the boat. As far as I knew, Jenny had not resurfaced. "My God, what are you doing? Get out! Get out and get Jenny!" I yelled.

Unable to trust him, I kept my head out of the water, breast stroking, and screamed again, "Get her! Get out of the boat! Where is she?" I was panicking, and the panicking broke to sobs, as I thrashed onward, tugging against the thick water with arms seeming to move in place, my legs kicking. My husband frozen, stone-like, paralyzed. His mouth was open and he was trying to utter something, and he looked my way, desperately. It occurred to me that he was having a stroke. My sobs choked into the water. I was panting hard and slowing down, then suddenly kicking harder. Jenny hadn't come up.

"Goddamnit, Jenny hasn't come up!" I screeched to my helpless husband. My teeth chattered, my hands, already bluing and wrinkled, pawed at the water.

Then I reached it, reached the spot where the cracked board floated like flotsam, where Jenny had bobbed, thrashed once. And where my husband still sat in bizarre, frozen, motionless bewilderment. Only a frantic hand pointed, shook towards the spot where she had landed. His mouth was open, and he was still trying to utter something. His head jerked back and forth, stricken eyes first searching me, and then the spot.

Without waiting another moment for instructions, I dove down, down, down, through the brown kidnapping water. I swam deep until my eardrums felt like they would burst from the pressure. But no Jenny. And want of air had me turning before I could go down deeper; I reversed directions, wrestled upwards towards the sunlit patch at the surface, broke through, took a deep gasping breath, and ducked under again.

I dove recklessly again and again and again.

Too late, though, too many minutes had gone by now. Six, they always warned in swimming safety, six minutes and the brain suffers irreversible damage. But I thought, "Even if she's in a coma, she'll live," and the very thought sent me down again. I was disoriented, my eyes were open but I couldn't see. Still, the weight of the dark water seemed to be pushing behind me like a hand. My feet fluttered and frog-kicked behind me as I roped arms, one then the other, plunging down into the cold. Then again I needed air; I'd been down too long, and as I struggled to surface, I thought I might not make it.

I gasped, my legs limp. I shook my head and began to yell for help. If Francis Taylor couldn't move, some relative would have to hear me and get here. My help calls were piercing, wailing.

His face was hidden in his hands, and his head has shaking.

And beside myself with frustration, and pity, and confusion, I swam towards him, uttering, "C-c-can't f-f-find her!" It was all happening so fast. Help.

He put both arms out to me, his eyes darting the water, as if they were suddenly searchlights that she could see by and come home to. His hands shook, as if palsied.

"Oh help us!" my voice was hoarse, raspy. "Help us! Jenny is drowning!" I clung hard to the side of the boat.

"Susanna!" He was trying to stand up. "Get in the boat, we've got to get help, we've got to...." His voice trembled and water filled to the brim of his eyes.

As he pulled me into the stern, I let out more bootless cries for my daughter. "Jenny!" I bellowed, "Jenny!" Then lowered my voice and hung gasping over the gunwale. I couldn't look at him.

"Susanna!" Then I did look at him. I saw his face, white with terror and helplessness, the wanting to help, as he hand-paddled wildly towards the oars that floated on the water.

He reached one and tried to paddle with it. He was rowing us towards the shore.

The water was still now. I looked into it, felt the forward tug of the boat. I couldn't do it. No matter how practical it was to get to shore and get help, I couldn't leave Jenny. I wanted to dive until I found her. And in my impotence and rage, it's all happening so quickly, I looked at my shaking husband and despised him, suddenly, to the core of my heart. For having sat there, trembling, heartstruck and powerless. For abandoning her. "I won't leave!" I suddenly screamed, bitter tears rolled down my face, into my mouth. "I won't."

His head was down, his shoulders convulsed, and in a thin voice, he said, "Susanna, cooperate."

Cooperate.

He could have said almost anything. "Sit down." "Help me row." Anything then would have triggered me; all I could see now was a feckless, yellow-backed little man who'd spent the whole of his life hiding in the shadows of safety, running from the chance of personal injury.

Then I stood, stepping bent over along the keel, my hands gliding along the gunwales. I reached him and, without knowing what I was doing, wrapped my knuckles tightly into the curls of hair around his ears, then pushed his head into the water and held him there. For seconds. For almost a minute. His feet kicked, his body went into spasmodic jerks, and his hands slapped my body over and over and over again.

And in the crazed desperation, I shouted, "I hate you, Francis Taylor. You have no idea how long I have hated you!" I jerked his head further downwards. With one hand I wiped bubbles of spit from the corners of my mouth.

He fought back hard, pounding my back with his fists now.

Finally, I lifted his wet head, groaning raw unhappiness as he hacked and choked for breath, the water pouring out of his nose. "Give me the oar," I said.

He climbed in, panting hard, and as he did so, he said, "You're mad, Susanna. You're completely insane. There's no way we'll be able to continue together now. I think you know that."

I gunned the oar through the water, hardly able to see for the hair stuck wet in my face, and my ugly voice cried, "Our daughter is drowning, and you talk of divorce!" Then I stood, and whacked him across the back with the oar.

He half jerked to his feet, hands protecting his head, and wheeled around, almost capsizing us, and said in a steady but severe voice, "Go on, Susanna, kill me too. Kill me with a wooden oar like you killed her with a wooden jerry-built plank."

His words threw me down, and I deserved worse. I landed against a thwart, grabbed two hands to the sides of the boat to try to still it. Then I was on my feet again, screaming, "Get out! Get out of the boat." By now all the relatives had to have heard me. But no matter. All our years of toil and effort lay fallen down in the water now. "*You* stay here and keep looking for Jenny. Get out, all your life a coward, get out!" Uncommon strength rushed up from deep pockets throughout my body. How long I had stored the liquid rage, from him, from myself, I can't say. A long time, though. A long time. I wrestled him, toppled him, and he splashed to the water. I oared fast and furiously while he tread, tread twenty years of a marriage not fit for a family. "Dive for her, damn it. Dive for her until you find her." But even as my words struck across the water, deep, deep within I knew why he froze.

And as I reached the shore, I turned and saw how he'd swum to the tower and now clung like a small, still gibbon to one of its posts.

We were fortunate, as good fortune goes; we were spared the agony of having to wait for Kingfisher to drain. It was never even a question. Nor was the prospect of not finding her at all. Because of who we were, because of who he worked for, they sent in rescue crews—a Coast Guard man helicoptering above, and Navy and Coast Guard scuba divers swimming below. The scuba men seemed to have been through this kind of thing before, and they gave a certain calm, a certain assurance that if they had to find a way to keep the sun from setting to do it, they would find Jenny.

Taylor and Parish got in that afternoon. Both walked trance-like around and around the pond. I was there, of course. There at the lonely, foolish tower I had built. I was way up top, alone, the scuba people bobbing below like yellow zebra fish. I was up there praying. My praying never came out in real words belonging to the English language. It was praying in moans and hums as if repeating a mantra. People said I rocked; they said the twins couldn't get through to me when they tried. I had heard my twins, their soft, scared voices, but I don't even remember their efforts to bring me down. Parish had come up, wrapped his arms around me, and begged me, but my arms locked around my knees. Taylor was below, crying.

After many hours, Sally G. came. That was the twins' idea. She climbed quietly on her little ballet feet, rung by rung, her hair still thick and black, her face pale and wrinkled from the pressures of the dance. She moved my hair back and whispered in my ear, "Darling, Susanna, come down now." And I rumbled up not knowing where I was for that moment, my hand held inside of hers.

They said my husband had locked himself in our room and wouldn't see anyone.

And that right away the public began seeping in through all the holes in the fences, and that it was my mother-in-law who ordered police in and stood out there herself to keep reporters out. Diplomats and dignitaries had already started to fill up our house.

Some thought the divers should go home and come back to try again tomorrow, but the men said they were not going to quit until they found our little girl. They rigged searchlights and used underwater flashlights for the scuba men, and sometime in the wide emptiness of that black night, they found her. She was face down, they told the coroner later, hands out. Feet spread a little. The lake bottom gunk covered her. Her skin underneath the rivulets of slime was shriveled, blue-white like ice.

Afterwards, I could not bring myself to look either my husband or my mother-in-law in the eye, knowing that my husband had been right, knowing that I had built that tower. And the homemade diving plank that I had insisted on building and putting up, all by myself. *You who knew nothing about joists, levels, rivets. You who never respected the laws of physics.* His words echoed in my head. *Go away, Susanna,* he'd ordered. *You have been bad for us. You couldn't be trusted anyway.*

Grief came beyond all consciousness, beyond all capacity to put into words what the human heart is made to withstand. At the funeral, there were no cameras, no public, no family we didn't know. Just us: Parish and Taylor, Pasha and Sally G., my husband's brothers, his mother and father, my mother, Laure and Joseph who Helena flew in, and my silent and broken husband. The twins gave her a eulogy, and I tried to give her a eulogy, and the minister tried fruitlessly. Grief filled us beyond the strength of sustaining ourselves on our feet. Pain finished the funeral before the funeral finished itself; mid-speech we left the small family chapel where we had been married, walked to her burial in the wooded churchyard family cemetery. Henry, Michael, the twins, my husband, Vincent, and old Joseph were the pallbearers. Behind them walked Sally G., Pasha, Helena Dewitt, Laure, Linda C.S., and I.

With clumps of dirt lifted in my family's hands, we stood over Jenny's grave. We watched the quiet lowering of her coffin, and then each of us, at the same time, extended our arms. The twins, facing opposite, each held one arm out, slightly lifted, like a drawbridge. Francis Taylor knelt. Then I knelt, and the twins knelt, and very slowly through the folds of our curled fingers, the earth poured out of our hands like rice.

The twins and I never even went back to the house. Our bags were already packed and put in the trunk, and Joseph drove us to the Greenwich train station where we climbed aboard the Crescent

Number Nine, meaning to move with its steady pulls all the way to Benjamin.

We got as far as Baltimore. With no warning, I stood and began to pull the heavy trunks off the rack. The twins both stood, unquestioning, and said at the same time, "Mom, let me help."

I sat down, holding parts of them the tail of a cotton jacket, the ribbed texture of a corduroy pant leg. I was bent over at the waist with my forehead pressed to my knees. The twins slumped over me, both holding me. I got my breath and slowly the words loosened. The details seemed jumbled, and the sentences didn't connect. But it all did flow out. I did not know if my sons could understand me, but when the conductor came in and asked to see our tickets, they kept their hands gripped to mine and stared at him sternly with their eyes. The conductor backed away and left the compartment to us.

"Long before us," I began, "before even you and I were born, he loved a girl. She was poor and feisty and built of fearlessness and pride and heart."

I felt the twins lift their heads quickly, glancing at each other. I motioned for Kleenex. My sons offered me all they had, digging down into duffle bags for socks, ties, anything.

"Mom," Taylor said with suddenness. Then his voice cracked as he felt for me. Both sons trying to hold themselves up while they tried to hold me up.

"She fell off a cliff, and it was then life stole his courage, leaving him to the permanent remembrance and a whole life of loneliness and guilt and insecurity and impenetrable secrecy."

"Mom!" Now it was Parish. "Mom!"

I pinched the bridge of my nose and wept about failing my husband. About failing Jenny. About failing the twins. About failing God.

"Mom, no, it was fate," Parish tried.

"I know." I felt the folds in my face deepen as I lowered my head again on the upended trunk. "I-I-I know, I know it was fate."

"Mom."

"And the coroner said, 'Had Jenny lived, she would have been an invalid.' He said he could not measure all of the bruising and damage to other parts of her spine, but her neck was fractured. 'She'd have been paralyzed,' he said."

For a brief moment, I drew some measure of peace from the knowledge that what had happened could have been even worse; then all of it, the whole scene, flashed before my eyes: my begging him to come home, his closed ears, the tower he warned me not to build, the plank. Jenny's thinness, Jenny's silent thinness. And what we did to each other right there on the pond.

"Oh, help," I cried, the tears coming again. "I hurt my husband. Oh, what do I do, I hurt him. I hurt my husband and I didn't mean to. I have known for all these years what he lived!"

The twins stopped me. They interrupted at the same time; I don't remember who spoke first. "Mom," I heard, their hands in mine, each tightening, "Mom, we know about Cary. And we know about you, too. About the ballet, and how good you were. Mom, if you knew how many times Dad has told us about your ballet, how many times he has kicked his foot to the ground blaming himself!" Taylor rushed to my knees and pressed his face to my old numb scar, and the hot salt of love and grief poured right out of our bodies.

At length I sighed long and hard, looked up at each of my sons. Then Parish said, "How do you think Dad is going to get along without Mom now, Taylor?"

I was expecting Taylor to humor me, to say something about guessing he'd soon be dialing up some home delivery geishas or an imported harem of Egyptian beauties.

But he didn't. He looked at Parish. Then at me and said, "Mom, he can't live without you anymore than he can live with you."

I rumbled up to a half stand. My legs tingled and my whole body felt weak and drained. I lost my balance, looked at my sons, each bracing an arm behind my elbow. I tried to smile as I said, "There are going to have to be some changes around Pope's Crossing. I'll have to learn to leave him alone when he wants to be left alone. I'll have to try to stop showing off, thinking I know more about life than he does. Course, these are sacrifices." I looked up, smiled a little hidden one. "We'd better hurry. The train whistle has already blown, and this train will be moving again before we have time to get our things and get off of it."

My two boys towered over me, each carrying a trunk on a shoulder. Each with a firm arm around my waist as if any minute I'd fall down and slip through a crack in the linoleum floor and land somewhere on the tracks.

Taylor almost got his jacket caught in the closing doors as we hobbled off. Slowly, we crossed the ramp, each drained but holding the other up, and waited at Platform C for the train north to carry us home.

It was 1:30 a.m. when we finally reached our drive. In our overwhelming lassitude, the walk up the drive was up Everest, across the Sahara.

It didn't take but about five minutes of steady knocking for us to understand that he had no intention of letting us in. And none of us had thought to bring our own house keys.

So we got some clothes and blankets out of the trunks and spread them out on the wooden porch, lay down and gave way to extreme exhaustion.

And I dreamed of that flat slap as she landed in the water, of the noise of hammers and buzz saws, of the bubbly sounds of scuba tanks.

But it was only he pulling the latches, bars, and bolts. The door opened with a squeaking sound, and I tried to adjust my eyes as I stood up, walked through our door, and watched my husband bolt up the stairs. I stood listening, seeking, for once in my life, no explanation, while he hunted each upstairs room, one by one, for a safe little hiding place.

I guess it was while we were on the train south that my husband had called in Mitch or Helena's Jim or some other handyman. I woke up around four-thirty to the first minutes of the dreadful, unwanted dawn. I'd fallen asleep lying across our bed in my clothes, the bed already rumpled and unmade from where my now hiding husband had been before we got home.

Underneath me, the papers made crinkling sounds. I reached a hand beneath my belly and tugged them out. They were yellow and wrinkled. Telegrams. Mine, sent to me by Mamma so long ago, was there. I looked over at the desk drawer, whose key I had broken off in its lock almost fifty years ago. How did he get in there? I asked myself. What made him think he had my permission? There was the telegram, too, which I'd sent to him in Washington. How alike they were, one more yellow than the other, both bearing the same type: *Come home where your hands are needed.*

I turned the older telegram over and saw my promise—*Never come before your child and a dream that's hers.* My lips quivered, and I wept.

I guess Francis Taylor must have heard me. Because he came out from his hiding place and crept into our room and lifted me in his arms and carried me to the bathroom, using the heel of his foot to wedge the door open. While he ran the bathtub water, he slowly stripped the spent clothes off me, then picked me up and gingerly put me in, and with a soft warm wet cloth, he bathed me like a baby. Just the way Pasha had bathed me, all those years ago.

He was talking to me, too. But I couldn't hear him. I was crying like an old woman who's been left all alone to die.

PART V

Here and Now

CHAPTER 28

1965 – Present

Pope's Crossing, Connecticut

Twenty-five

years

went

by

but, we

survived.

Somehow

we

survived.

CHAPTER 29

Here and Now

Pope's Crossing, Connecticut

Shouldn't have had that fight up there with him in the attic. Lost track of time. Yonder they came. Every one of them wore sunglasses and double-checked his or her looks in the rear-view one quick time before walking across the garden towards our front porch. Many years of golf or tennis revealed fine, deep dignified wrinkles all the way from where I greeted them at the kitchen door. The political colleagues walked in a cluster, all looking in a good mood. They always did enjoy coming over to our house for some of my fancy cooking. There was Senator Norris and his adorable wife, Chris, up from D.C.; there were the Gordons from Manhattan; the Griffiths from Lincoln, Massachusetts; the Adamses, also from D.C.; and Bett and Talbert Williams from Sharon came. The Shapiros and Bryants drove down from Boston. Mag Shapiro. What a hoot. I could hear her voice from clean across the garden. What I liked about them was the way they always stopped in our garden and admired our perennials. Especially the Conlan Camellias.

Their wives carried large canvas pocketbooks, wore cotton sweaters tied around their necks, and shared a reputation for being stable. What I admired about them was how tall they were. How did these dignified, handsome men find all these tall women to match them?

Another thing I liked about them: they stretched between my age, sixty-three, and Francis Taylor's, seventy-three, and were still active. Participating and giving their time to various philanthropic endeavors. Mrs. Edith Adams practically runs the Phillips Art Collection down in D.C., and Helen Gordon has more to do with keeping Central Park alive and happy than practically anyone I know. The whole world knows what a trouper Chris Norris has been throughout Mark's campaign seasons. Claire Griffith has been an unreal contribution to education, especially her work with kids suffering from the dreaded SATs. And what about Nancy Bryant? She is the most generous person I know. It kills me about Bett Williams. She works out three times a week, first thing in the morning, to the *Jane Fonda Aerobic Dance Video*.

Still, even after all these years of dinner parties for my husband, I couldn't help feeling uncomfortable. Their speech, for one thing. It was like they all had a built-in purifier through which every little word automatically ran before leaping out to the public. The words came out wearing white gloves, polite and formal. Something about that purifier put accents and long vowels on certain words such that they came out sounding straight from London, England. Manhahhhtan, for example. So graceful. Think how my unpolished Southern sounded compared.

Also, their intelligence. Well, you've known the feeling of being around people who make you wish that you'd brought along your pocket dictionary. And it wasn't just their being naturally blessed with a big vocabulary that made matters difficult, either. It was what all they knew, where all they'd been, and how on earth did they ever retain all their information? They knew things like how satellites were built and why the Pershing II missiles held a strong chance of deterring the Russians. Things like what galleries represented which chic painters of the moment, and whose book would be published at what publishing house. They knew stuff like what Kashmir, India, looked like in person, and what kinds of birds could be seen down in the tropics of Trinidad. Some knew Charles and Di. Still, I always understood somewhere that time, too much of it, could become the adversary.

All these years, I stayed inspired, but quite uncomfortable, quite inferior. Even though I had gotten my education osmotically through Francis Taylor. Because these dinner parties were about the only occasions in which any of his friends could get a glimpse of me, I earned a reputation for being shy. A real hiccupper of a joke for my family to tease me about.

One lucky break: some of the men turned out to have real dry senses of humor and liked to tell jokes. Mr. Joe Dan Shapiro, for example. Gosh, he's a funny man. At the dinner I got the feeling he had a little crush on me because I'd laugh at his jokes. Well, he did flirt. Here I was sixty-three and he was up to telling me I had legs like Jennifer Beals from *Flashdance*.

All the wives were very polite and talked to me like I was steady, trustworthy, and down-to-earth. But, they spoke to me carefully, with a certain measure of reserve. Still, through all these years, I have never gotten over a feeling that while they conversed with me with white-gloved words, they also probably had little thought balloons over their heads asking, "What do you think he sees in her? She's so *country*... I don't think she comes from family. Maybe it was her cooking."

Well, we know better, don't we? Considering his revelation up there in the attic a few hours ago about my having given the best head in Manhattan. You can imagine the insecurity.

What I'd do to get through would be to sit back and listen. *Listen for what wasn't being said*. The conversations would invariably fall into lively political discussions, most of the informed wives helping out, giving an opinion here and there. A few would sometimes break off from the whole, falling into little *tête-à-têtes*, then come back to catch right up without missing a beat. Me, I'd just sit back, study hand gestures, facial expressions, and little nuances that'd send me way off in my own little world. I found that if I listened hard enough, I could pull up a story from each one, based on reactions, expressions, and any little messages I could pick up from the quieter language under all the shine.

One thing I liked to wonder, for example, was who was still getting orgasms? And which ones had gone all their married years without ever having one at all? I liked to try to guess which ones were married to the achievements and money, completely overlooking the real person on whom these accomplishments had piggybacked all these years. I liked to wonder, did they talk formal like that at home, or did they let their hair down? I liked to guess how many minutes a day they actually had to spend time with each other. I thought about their children. Who had had a discipline problem in school, and who had problems with women, which ones did drugs? And who would grow up afraid of the world, and who would grow up safe and secure?

All in all, I'd say they were batting just about average with the rest of us. Some knew real love, some knew steady convenience, some should never have been married in the first place.

I know that the latter is what's been running through your mind from the moment I started telling you about my husband and me. That we never should have been married in the first place, and that, especially after we lost Jenny, we should have just had the courage to face facts.

Well, believe me. It's crossed my mind, too. He could have been a lot safer and better off with someone from his kind. Maybe someone from the Ivy League who could speak French. I could have been happy and a lot freer with a catfish farmer from Ballyhoo, Mississippi, or a real sweet high-school teacher who talked even more Southern than me and could reel off the score of every single Tarheel NCAA championship since the beginning of Dean Smith's coaching. Shoot, I might could have married a Southern lawyer. But that's probably stretching it.

Thoughts like these often came to me when he'd make me mad or I got lonely, missing him. What I could have had, or what he could have had that would have made the course of life a little smoother going.

But right during that dinner something happened to me. Something that I had waited for almost fifty years.

I was taking the grilled almond bluefish out of the oven. I leaned into the oven's hot face and was suddenly overcome by heat and a strange dizziness. I wove my way to the refrigerator, opened the door, and hoped the cool air would quell the waves inside. But instead, they rose up higher and hotter, and the dizziness grew worse.

I was seeing dots. I put my head in my hands, pressed my feet to the ground, and clung to the refrigerator door, hoping it'd help me get up. But as soon as I stood, I had to sit right back down. My body was helpless, weak as a rag, and I knew right then that my time had come.

I had to tell him. I couldn't go without saying good-bye to him. But my body was overcome, my muscles felt soft, jelly-like, and all I wanted was to just lie down on the floor and go to sleep.

Still, I had to try. I tried panting for air. I took eight short breaths. One long one. Eight more short ones. Like I had learned from aerobics. I used my index fingers to hold open my eyelids so I wouldn't pass out. Slowly, I found the floor, lay belly down on it and began to drag myself across the kitchen to the swinging door. I dragged about a foot, then stopped. Took more breaths. Dragged another foot. Took eight more breaths. I felt like I was in high altitude. As I pulled, my arms fatigued and tightened up, as if I was hanging by a thread on the edge of some unexpected cliff. I kept shaking my head, thinking I could throw the dizziness out of my body, but that only made the dots before my eyes dance harder.

"What in the world was I doing dancing up there in that hot attic?" I muttered to myself. "Am I crazy?"

Then, too, the memories of Jenny coming up. The memories coming up in both of us after all those years, for each of us at the same time. How grieving saps all your energy until you sometimes feel like you're dying right along with the one you're missing. Twenty-five years it had been.

They must wonder where on earth I am, I thought. Why the bluefish is taking so long to broil. I clawed hard towards the door, using the worn edges of the coral-colored bricks that made up our kitchen floor. I kept trying to monitor my breathing. I dragged; at length I reached the door.

I cracked it just barely so that no one could see me and called for my husband. My voice was weak and faint.

I heard him excusing himself, saying he'd be back in a second. I imagined him standing dignified, patting his mouth with a corner of his napkin, and then walking tall and quietly towards me.

I looked hungrily at him as he came in and looked down at me.

I whispered, "I don't feel good, Love."

"Susanna," he said. His brow wrinkled, and his face gave a look of true concern. He went immediately to the sink where he soaked a dishcloth and got me a glass of water, then came over and made me drink.

He knelt down to where I was on the floor. "Your face is grey, Susanna. What is it?"

"I don't know. I don't feel good."

Someone got up from the dining room table, and he blocked the kitchen door with his body and said, "It's all right. We'll be out in a minute."

Why he and his kind needed to go the whole of their lives covering the real truth from each other, I didn't have the strength to ask right then. What's wrong with a little mortality, a little bit of facing our mortality? I looked at him with concentration, asking for answers without so much as moving my lips.

"I'm taking you upstairs, Susanna."

"You can't lift me with your back," I barely whispered. "Let me just lie down here, let me sleep." I tried to move his hand that held the rag to my forehead. My body felt waterlogged, floating.

He lifted me anyway. As if my own body was his, I felt the strain of his old ligaments pulling against the burden of me, causing small painful rips along the fragile lower knobs of his spine.

"No lifting," I said. "No lifting." But I was too weak to try to worm my way out of his arms.

He was concentrating with all he had. The stress mark I loved creased down his forehead, and the vein around his temple bulged blue. His face grew red and his lips were pursed tight.

"Please, Love, I'll be all right," I begged. For one of the few times in my life I couldn't fight him.

In his thin old arms, he carried me as far as the cobwebbed servant's stairs at the other end of the kitchen. Then he took the first step and fell down with me.

He was short of breath. He winced and for a brief moment I thought he might have fractured a hip; he'd landed hard against the edge of a stair. But he got up, eyes struck with worry for me.

From somewhere I can't explain save through my love for him, I found enough strength to make it up about three quarters of the way on my own, my hands pulling against each banister rung, one at a time. I braced my weight against his arm that hugged around my waist. I was panting. "There's no air," I said, "I can't breathe."

"Come on, you can breathe, Susanna. Just do it." Gripping me by my armpits, dragging me up the last five stairs. Then got me in his arms again and carried me to our bed.

He put me down gently, went to the bathroom sink, got more water and made me drink again. Then, bending over me, feeling my forehead for fever, he whispered, "I'll just run downstairs and quickly serve them dinner, and then I'll be right back." It was just like him. He was that way, you know, always trying to make everything appear smooth running. His eyes were still and stern, but watering.

I nodded my head.

As I did so, he said, "Susanna, don't you go anywhere. Do you hear me? I'll be right back in an instant. You stay here, Susanna. I mean it. I'm going to call the doctor."

I clawed at the covers weakly wondering where on earth he thought I'd be moseying off to in this condition. Then I must have passed out.

I woke under attack. Frightened hands were rattling my shoulders. And his voice. The harsh critic's voice of his youth. I opened my eyes. The harsh tenor rang in my ears, and I lifted my hands to cover them. He seemed to be yelling at me, castigating me.

"Cary!" he shouted, his voice rattling through my bones. "Wake up!" Now lifting me, propping me against the pillows, still taking my shoulders.

Cary?

"You wake up, Susanna Dewitt, damn it."

"I think you just called me Cary."

"Susanna, be quiet. You're not going anywhere. Not you too, Susanna, I order you. You're not leaving me, I won't let you abandon me!" Then he started checking my pulse.

Good Lord. I tried to get him to be quiet long enough to tell him that I was just having a little dizzy spell and would be all right. I tried to hold his arms.

I think it was his seeing my open eyes that calmed him down. Or maybe it was the way I was trying to smile at him.

Here he found at least enough trust in me to let go for a minute. But with that granted peace, I was scared I'd fall asleep again. To fight it, I turned over on my side, hummed little jazz tunes, and I watched him go to his closet, riffling hands mysteriously through the top shelf.

Then all of a sudden, I stopped humming. I saw that he'd pulled out his beautiful little English letterbox that he always kept way back in the back of the closet.

He opened it, and I heard him fumbling through his letters, certificates, old coins and stamps, and passports. Presently, he pulled out a lovely old key.

I'd long ago stopped asking myself what was held in the locked desk drawer below that one that held our babies' calling cards.

Now he put the key in, opened it, pulled the whole drawer out. His delicious, full lips were parted, and his eyes were fixed steadily on me as he seemed to weave through some obstacle course to get back to me. In his arms he cradled the drawer.

Then he stood over the bed, bent over at the waist, and let the contents dump out the way you empty a wheelbarrow.

All over my tired body came a cascade of envelopes. Some were opened. Some were sealed. Most were yellowed.

I couldn't imagine. I stayed awake just from the desire to feel one, to look at them.

"It's my handwriting!" I suddenly announced, recognizing it.

He nodded, smiling timidly.

"Why, they're my letters, Francis Taylor! My letters I used to write to you back when I was a young girl." I held one up so he could see, as if he didn't know what they were himself. "You nut! Which one is the hate mail?"

He wrinkled his nose, laughed in it. My favorite.

"Oh, I'm sure it's in there somewhere."

I looked down trying to focus and then suddenly gasped. All over the place, I saw envelopes with his chicken scratch handwriting scrawled across the front. They were all sealed. Some were even postmarked, I guess from his office: Manhattan, New York, 1942. Manhattan, New York, 1943.

Before I could say anything more, he said, "Pick one."

And so I did. I picked one of his, and he let me open it before he could change his mind and take it back.

I couldn't see to read the whole letter. My eyes were blurry and my vision had been fading from me. I blinked, turning the letter over in my hands, and then got enough eyesight to where I could see the last paragraph.

It said something about being in love with me, how he knew it was wrong, but couldn't help it.

It said something about him *needing* me.

I held my breath, praying strange words wouldn't come out of my mouth. Praying I wouldn't say anything that would sound like teasing or upping the ante. I breathed until I knew I'd calmed my words down so that I wouldn't have to cover up my joy, and could say what I really wanted to say.

So I took his hands and said, "I guess they'll be looking for my *tarte aux pommes* à la mode right about now."

With sudden adrenaline pumping, I felt just like I had when I fell in love with him that day on the park bench. He now let me pull on his arms to lift myself out of bed, and the two of us old fogies helped each other down the stairs, and I cut the *tarte aux pommes* into ten pieces and he à-la-moded each one with a scoop of vanilla and he carried them out on a tray.

CHAPTER 30

Here and Now

Pope's Crossing, Connecticut

After everybody had gone home and the dishes were piled lackadaisically in the sink, Francis Taylor and I happened to be both standing in front of the dining room mirror at the same time.

"Look at this, Susanna," Francis Taylor said in a revelatory kind of way.

"What?"

"Look. Just look. We've come to look alike."

"No way. I'm not doing it. I'm not having those mushy lips."

"And I'm not having that wild hair. But look. Our eyes. They look alike."

"That's because they're so damn hooded. We've aged. Christ, we're old, look at that."

"Speak for yourself, Susanna."

"Well, I never should have sat there."

"Sat where? *Here*?"

By now it was an old, old joke. He gloated each time he said it. Each time, he'd stand there with a look of enormous satisfaction, as if he was cracking the old joke for the first time.

And I loved our joke.

"Let me ask you something."

"What?"

"Why didn't you just send the letters? I was so lonely for you. That blue year in Manhattan in my little apartment. That was the loneliest year of my life. If you'd just sent the letters, all that pain could have been spared."

And here Francis Taylor put his arm around me, protectively—the two of us staring into the mirror, into the two faces that had indeed at last come to look alike—and he didn't say a word.

The End.

THIS BOOK BECAME REAL BECAUSE OF YOU

ADAM FREY, Frey Clock
ALIX NARDONE, Afro-Cuban Conga Player
AMY ADDISON, Dancer, Manhattan School of Ballet
COURTNEY ADDISON, Courtney's Ballet Store
ANDREW HEMMING, Dancer, Client of Joseph Pilates
ANDY STAPINSKI, Michael's Girlfriend, Sophie Stapinski
AVERY OATMAN, Professor, Physicist, Princeton University
BARBARA J., Cookware
BETT WILLIAMS, Dinner Party Guest
BOB SAUBAN, Guitar Player, Big Mose's Band
BRENDA EVERS, Irish Setter
CATHY CRAIG, Craig Hall
CHRIS COWAN NORRIS, Dinner Party Guest
CLAIRE GRIFFITH, Dinner Party Guest
DEBRA KAYE, Piano player, Manhattan School of Ballet
DOTTIE OATMAN, Dancer, Manhattan School of Ballet
EDITH ADAMS ALLISON, Dinner Party Guest
ELAINE LECRAW BAKER, Dedication, Major Character
ELIZABETH MCCLATCHEY BROWN, Dancer, Manhattan School of Ballet
FLORRIE CORLEY JOHNSON, Choreographer, Manhattan School of Ballet
FOSTER SOULES, Dedication, Major Character
HELEN MILNER GORDON, Dinner Party Guest
JOHN YOW, Trombone Player, Big Mose's Band
JOSH MINOR, Outfielder for the Pennsylvania Bucks
THEO BAMI, Francis Taylor's Partner at Vanheusen and Dewitt
KIRA POTTER, Dance Teacher, Mississippi State
LAQUAINNE ("Q"), Dancer, Manhattan School of Ballet
LINDA SPEVACEK, Cook for Vanheusen and Dewitt Families
LISA HAVERTY, Haverty, Mississippi
LUCY CURRIE, Currie's Store

MADDIE OATMAN, Dancer, Bell-ringer, Manhattan School of Ballet
MAGNOLIA SHAPIRO (AKA BILL ALBRIGHT), Dinner Party Guest
MATT DODSON, Dedication
MELINDA SCHULTZ, Dancer, Manhattan School of Ballet
MOPPY DIMON BRUMBY, Mop, The Dog
NANCY BRYANT, Dinner Party Guest
NEFERTITI ROBINSON, Thoroughbred Race Horse, Saratoga Springs
PAGE GRIFFIN, Little Boy in Tree
PAISLEY PETTINE, Dancer, Manhattan School of Ballet
PETE BANSEN, Irish Setter
PETER OATMAN, Obstetrician
RICHARD YOW, Drums Player, Big Mose's Band
ROB LEVINE, Dancer, Manhattan School of Ballet
ROBERT BOXLEY, Professor, Yale University
ROBERT ECKARDT, Postman
RUDY RODRIGUEZ, Dancer, Manhattan School of Ballet
SALLY HANSELL, Sally G.'s Brother
SAM HARPER, BAse Guitar, Big Mose's Band
SHACK DODSON, Dedication
SHAWN COLTON, Philanthropist, Executive, Manhattan School of Ballet
SINDY SCHNEIDER, Make-up Artist, *Over the Transom* Auditions
SUSAN CONLAN, Camellia
SUSAN GORDON, Dancer, Manhattan School of Ballet
VIKK O. KNOGGLE, (VICTORIA NAGEL), Dancer, Manhattan School of Ballet
HARRY HARTOFELIS, Christmas Dinner Guest
APRIL LAJUNE, Christmas Dinner Guest
ANONYMOUS, Christmas Dinner Guest

And to the memory of **NEIL WILLIAMS** (Radio Announcer), beloved friend of my Dad's in real life. Beloved friend and torchbearer for my Dad's firm, Alston & Bird. A huge, booming, beautiful, and important voice for the arts in Atlanta. Thank you, Neil and Sue, for all that you mean.

KICKSTARTER